The
Ambassador's Wife

Also by Jennifer Steil

The Woman Who Fell from the Sky

THE

Ambassador's Wife

A Novel

Jennifer Steil

Doubleday

NEW YORK   LONDON   TORONTO   SYDNEY   AUCKLAND

Copyright © 2015 by Jennifer F. Steil

All rights reserved. Published in the United States by Doubleday, a division of Random House LLC, New York, and in Canada by Random House of Canada Limited, Toronto, Penguin Random House companies.

www.doubleday.com

DOUBLEDAY and the portrayal of an anchor with a dolphin are registered trademarks of Random House LLC.

Grateful acknowledgment is made to the following for permission to reprint previously published and unpublished material: Ernest Tubb Music, for permission to reprint lyrics from "Waltz Across Texas."

Book design by Maria Carella
Jacket design by John Fontana
Jacket photographs: woman © Wojciech Zwolinski/Trevillion Images; city © Nadeem Khawar/Moment/Getty Images

Library of Congress Cataloging-in-Publication Data
Steil, Jennifer.
The ambassador's wife : a novel / Jennifer Steil. — First edition.
pages ; cm
ISBN 978-0-385-53902-9 (hardcover) ISBN 978-0-385-53903-6 (eBook)
I. Ambassadors—Fiction. 2. Artists—Fiction. 3. Kidnapping—Fiction. I. Title.
PS3619.T4485A83 2015
813'.6—dc23
2014018579

MANUFACTURED IN THE UNITED STATES OF AMERICA

1 3 5 7 9 10 8 6 4 2

First Edition

FOR TIM AND THEADORA, MY HOME

The
Ambassador's Wife

As she curls herself around the wasted body of a stranger's child, cupping the tiny head in her hand, the remembered glow of a painting emerges unbidden from the gloom of Miranda's mind. A woman sleeps in a boat, reclined in her husband's arms and draped alongside the body of her sleeping child, bathed in a benediction of pale light. Around them are dark water and a darker shore. The woman's body is limp, trusting, abandoned to its fate. Opposite the slumbering family, Fortune plies the oars, with the assistance of a hopeful Cupid. Something about the image—the family's relinquishing of control over their destiny—fills Miranda with terror. They drift, serenely dreaming, into darkness. Wake, she wants to cry to them. Wake up and take an oar. *Fortune and Cupid are unreliable guides. As the baby tugs at her breast, Miranda gazes down at her with dull eyes, trying to remember the name of the painting. What was it?* The child whimpers as the nipple slips away from her mouth; she is too weak to suck for long. The Dream of Happiness. *That was it.* Constance Mayer's Dream of Happiness. *She who had known so little of it in her own life. When Miranda thinks back on her brief life with Cressida and Finn, this is the image that keeps returning to her. A moment of blissful unconsciousness, and then black.*

Part One

AUGUST 9, 2010
Miranda

Miranda watches her left hand move across her sketch pad as if unsure of its destination. Up it swoops, leaving a sooty trail across the thick white paper. Then across to the right, down again, across. A frame. The pencil lifts from the page for a moment, hovering in midair as her eyes turn toward the window. Dawn arrives abruptly in Mazrooq, the sky slipping from black to gold in the few seconds it took Miranda to pour a cup of coffee. Their garden is already gilded, its vast lawn glittering with last night's rain, its neat rows of flowers unclenching and tilting toward the sun. Along the periphery is a procession of crooked trees, leaning against the iron spikes of the gates like tired sentries. Bougainvillea crawls up the walls and thrusts its blooms through the bars, unwilling to be contained. Across the far end of the grass stretches the pool, as yet undisturbed by morning swimmers. The sky, as always at this hour, is a relentless, cloudless blue.

Miranda's view of this paradise, this oasis of theirs in this desert country, is partitioned into eight nearly equal parts by wrought-iron bars. Painted white, they form a lacelike scrim across the window. The ornate metal curlicues strive to disguise their utilitarian nature, but fail.

Her hand has gone back to work. The iron bars unfurl across her page, but as they would be seen from outside. For behind the bars is not a garden but a girl. A woman, vivisected, her head framed here, her heart here. Here her hand and here her mouth. Drawing, Miranda often feels like an adolescent toying with a Ouija board, wondering to what degree she subconsciously controls the movements of its indicator. Simultaneously creator and conduit, she can rarely predict exactly what will emerge.

So absorbed is she in her puzzle pieces that she doesn't hear the alarm at first. How long has it been buzzing? She hasn't yet touched the mug of coffee on the table in front of her, or made Finn's cup of tea. Barefoot, she runs down the hall to their bedroom and lunges for the alarm on Finn's bedside table. Why had they set the alarm? They have a child. They do not need an alarm. Then she remembers: The policemen. The policemen are still here. Which means she has to dress for breakfast.

Pausing by the bed, she listens. Nothing. Cressida still safely asleep. "Sweetheart." Gently, she shakes Finn's shoulder, kisses his eyelids.

"I'm awake," he says.

"Clearly not."

"I am, I'm wide awake." He says this without moving, without opening an eye. Finn is not a morning person. On weekdays he rises at 6:00 a.m. to eat breakfast before heading to the embassy by 7:30. But on weekends he'll sleep all day if she doesn't wake him.

"I'll get your tea." In the little private kitchen between their room and Cressida's, where she habitually spends the first hour of the day with her sketch pad, Miranda brews a mug of Earl Grey. Finn won't drink her coffee; she makes it too strong. After leaving his tea on the side table by his still-motionless head, she returns to the kitchen for her own mug.

At best she gets an hour of blissful solitude, but today she has only twenty minutes before she needs to scramble into a sundress. She rarely has the luxury of solitary mornings once she leaves the relative privacy of their upstairs suite. By the time she slips down the marble staircase, their Ethiopian housekeeper, Negasi, will be busy in the kitchen, slicing mangoes and melons, peeling pomegranates, and brewing coffee. Birdlike Desta will have already begun polishing the downstairs bathrooms. And Yonas and Semere will be pulling up weeds in the flower beds and tending to their vegetable patches. Miranda wouldn't have thought much would take root in the cracked earth of this arid city, but their figs, lettuce, broccoli, tomatoes, and rhubarb thrive. By the time Miranda and Finn have finished their muesli and fruit, swallowed the last of their coffee or tea, and wiped their mouths with the rainbow-striped cloth napkins, Teru will be in the kitchen, slowly turning the pages of their cookbooks as she writes her shopping list.

Though often deprived of solitude, Miranda is awash in other luxuries. She doesn't have to cook. She doesn't do her own laundry. And best of all, she doesn't have to leave the house unless she wants to. She can paint all day. Or play with her daughter. Or stare out the window and daydream.

But there's no more time for dreaming today. Miranda finishes her coffee, then pads to their bathroom to brush her teeth. There are two sinks, two cabinets, two toothbrush holders. His and Hers everything, plus a bath (Hers) and a shower (His). She wakes up every morning and cannot believe this is her life. Sitting on the toilet, she thinks, My god, I *live* here. Even after three years, it still hasn't sunk in. Though it should, when she has a choice of seven or so toilets to use. Still brushing, she wanders down the hall to their daughter's room. Cressida lies on her back in what Miranda refers to as the "surrender position," her arms thrown above her head and her chubby knees splayed open. Insulated from the chill of the desert night by her blue-and-white checked flannel pajamas, she breathes deeply, her round little tummy straining against the buttons at regular intervals. She is a good sleeper, Cressida. Has been from her fourth month, when she began sleeping through the night. Miranda was prepared for years of interrupted nights, but it hasn't happened. She finds herself keeping this information from other mothers, feeling guilty for having such an easy child. And not only does she have an easy child but she has help whenever she wants it. She makes a mental note that she must never allow herself to complain about anything, ever again.

Back in the bathroom she washes her face with frankincense-scented soap and runs wet fingers through her tangled curls before

Finn finally staggers in, spiky-haired and sleepy. "Policemen this morning," she reminds him. "Last day!"

"Romantic dinner for two tonight, then?" He smiles, his arms circling her waist.

"I wish. But you've got the EU ambassadors tonight, remember?"

"Damn ambassadors."

"I don't know. Some of them aren't so bad."

Finn turns her to face him, and she presses her cheek against the soft hairs of his chest. She has never felt so lucky.

CURRENTLY, THERE ARE three policemen—Scotland Yard hostage negotiators—in their guest rooms. Not the kind of company she'd had in her old life. In her old life, in the house she'd once shared with Vicenta in the Old City, she had taken in students, writers, photographers, rock climbers, adventurers, and the occasional tourist. They filled the void Vicenta left in her wake. Her guests came from all over the world, drifting in and out of her house, staying for days, weeks, months. Sometimes one of them would make dinner. Sometimes one would share a bottle of bootleg Scotch. But they were generally self-sufficient souls, content to wander out to the souq for a plate of beans and bread or to pour themselves a bowl of muesli for dinner.

Here at the Residence—a shiny white fortress in a city of gray rock—their company is of a different caliber: ministers, policemen, intelligence officers, politicians, journalists, academics, businesspeople, development workers, and military officers. And they all require three full meals a day plus tea and biscuits, guidance around the city, hours of polite conversation, an open bar, and usually, protection. They occupy the five en suite guest rooms, furnished with an eclectic mix of British and Mazrooqi beds and bureaus, and decorated with mismatched curtains and carpets chosen by a succession of ambassadors' wives with divergent tastes. "It's like a high-end bed-and-breakfast furnished by someone's eccentric but wealthy aunt," Miranda once said to Finn. None of this bothers her; she loves the constant flow of new faces.

Alastair is the most senior of the current three cops (Miranda had to know this sort of information in order to figure out who got the "Minister's Suite," their largest guest room), then Mick, and then Gary (called Gazza). They've been living in the Residence for nearly three weeks now.

Police and military officers are Miranda's favorite guests. Which surprised her, given her lifelong bias against anything to do with the military-industrial complex. But the British officers she has met since moving in with Finn have been kinder, more polite, more interesting, and more articulate than just about anyone she has ever met. The night Alastair, Mick, and Gazza arrived, she entertained them in the front sitting room alone for several hours while they waited for Finn to return from the embassy. As the pistachio shells piled up on the glass coffee table and the gin glasses were refilled for the third time, the men leaned back in the arms of the fat, white sofas and regaled Miranda with stories of hostage situations in Iraq, Nigeria, even back home in Britain. Miranda had forgotten that the West had its share of hostage takers. They avoided discussing why the policemen had come. Miranda knew she shouldn't bring it up without Finn around, and the police didn't broach the subject themselves. Of course, she couldn't help but notice their bulging bags of equipment. Mick had snapped his open while she was in the kitchen preparing tea, and as she came back through Miranda had caught a glimpse of latex gloves and plastic bags stamped with the words FORENSIC EVIDENCE.

"We had a suicide once, a man threatening to drive off a cliff in England. A high cliff. He'd had some sort of domestic dispute with his wife, been arrested the night before, and spent the day in the bar drinking," said Mick. "Had a bottle of wine with him, if I recall correctly." Mick had been talking to the man through the window of the car, trying to convince him to get out and live another day, without making much progress. The man had become sullen and silent, refusing to speak. But one of the car doors was left slightly ajar. With his gloved fingers, Mick quickly pried it open, leapt into the car, pulled the emergency brake, and grabbed the keys. The would-be suicide was apprehended and taken to a psychiatric institute. "I got an award for that intervention," said Mick, "even though it was probably one of the daftest things I've ever done in my career. Who gets into the car of a man about to drive off a cliff?"

"If I were your wife I'd kill you," Miranda said.

"She tried."

The policemen, who travel constantly in and out of the UK, have just come from Uganda. "Tough on a marriage," said Miranda. Gazza said his wife was in the same line of work. "Doubly tough, then."

"Yes and no. . . . At least she understands what I'm doing."

It's not the time away that causes problems, said Mick, but the shift in priorities. When he got to Baghdad in 2003, he had telephoned his wife to let her know he was okay. Shells were exploding all around him as he dialed, standing in a building missing a wall. His wife was crying when she answered the phone. "What is it?" he'd asked, alarmed. "The Hoover!" she'd wept. "It's not working!"

Mick hadn't known what to say. "Do you know where I *am*?" he'd finally asked. "This building is missing a *wall*. People are *dying* all around me. But hey, with the hazard pay I'm getting, you can buy a new Hoover!"

They all laughed at the Hoover story, but Miranda wondered how long a marriage could last between people inhabiting such radically different mental spaces. The story reminded her of a New York firefighter's description of the collapse of his marriage after September 11, 2001. He was no longer able to work up an opinion on what kind of curtains to hang in the living room.

Miranda and Finn found the policemen's stories so engrossing that they all lingered at the dinner table over glasses of port until 11:00 p.m. It wasn't merely that these men had such captivating stories of their own; they took an interest in the people around them, asking endless questions about Mazrooqi culture and politics, Miranda's work, and Cressida's latest milestones. It was amazing how few politicians and diplomats asked them anything at all. Why was it that police were reliably better conversationalists than ministers?

EIGHT DAYS BEFORE the policemen arrived, seven foreigners had disappeared in the northern mountains: a Dutch family of three,

a German, two Brits, and a Frenchwoman. The group had been working for Muslim Mercy, providing food, shelter, health care, and education for those displaced by ongoing tribal conflicts. On a Friday
afternoon, they had set out for a hike up a river valley, or wadi. They
never returned.

The first challenge was that no one had yet claimed responsibility for their disappearance. Hostage negotiators need people with
whom to negotiate. So for their first few days, the policemen found
themselves with time on their hands. They questioned Finn about
the country's culture and history; they headed out for secret meetings with German, French, and Dutch intelligence. And still there
was no word. This was unusual. Kidnappings here were usually the
result of a tribal dispute. Tribes took groups of foreigners hostage in
order to pressure the government to force a rival tribe to release some
of its prisoners. These hostages were treated with warm hospitality.
They were fed large meals of goat and flatbreads, given the best blankets, and returned after several days or weeks unharmed, as a result
of mediation. Only rarely have kidnappings turned violent. But Al
Qaeda has been gaining strength in the region, says Finn. And they
have an entirely different style of kidnapping.

The disappearances have aggravated the mounting tensions between the North and the South, with the government (located in
the wealthier South) blaming the unruly northern tribal leaders, who
deny any knowledge of the captives.

Several weeks have now passed without progress, and the men can
no longer justify their absence from the UK. So until there are further developments in the case, the three policemen are heading home.

DINNER WITH THE most recent visiting minister, in contrast
to dinners with the police, had been a colorless affair. All the Arab
ambassadors were invited, so that the Minister could solicit their
views on local politics, particularly on the increasing friction between
North and South. A civil war would prove disastrous, as civil wars
typically do, and the UK was anxious to support mediations in order
to prevent it. Miranda had plenty to say, having lived in the country

for several years, longer than most of the men at the table (including Finn), but as the Minister hadn't come to get her opinion, she kept quiet. Besides, she could never hope to be as eloquent as Finn, who was doing admirably at articulating the challenges they faced. Still, her legs twitched violently under the table and she sat on her hands to restrain herself from shattering a wineglass just to break the monotony. Everyone was repeating the same tired litany of the country's problems, but failing to suggest solutions or a way forward. She got depressed about this. As the crème caramels were delivered to the table, she could stand it no longer.

"Look," she said. "We all know what the problems are." The corrupt government siphoned off oil money that could be directed to public services, brokered illicit arms deals, and starved its people. Hardly any oil money made its way to the resource-poor North, where unemployment was soaring and anger over state corruption was festering. Rot, dishonesty, and betrayal ran so deep that northern rebels could often purchase weapons directly from government forces. Water was increasingly scarce, and at least two cities could run out of it entirely within two years. More than half of the population was illiterate. The press was censored. Women had few rights. Sure, they were allowed to work, drive cars, and travel unaccompanied by men, unlike in other parts of the Middle East, but they couldn't choose their careers or their husbands. Terrorists were allowed to operate training camps in remote areas (mostly in the North) as long as they didn't blow up any of their fellow countrymen. Conflicts raged off and on between government forces and northern rebels. Foreign companies had to negotiate separate deals with the government and the tribes for permission to operate in certain areas, or risk finding their offices suddenly surrounded by armed men.

The Arab ambassadors looked up in surprise at hearing a female voice, before staring back into their coffee cups, but the Minister's head swiveled toward her attentively as she continued. "We know all of this; we have known all of this for years. But what are we going to *do* about it?" Only then did she allow herself a glance at Finn, who was smiling slightly while also managing to convey that she should stop there.

"Exactly," said the Minister, smiling. "So, *gentlemen*, what shall we *do*?"

Over coffee in the sitting room, the visiting Minister told Miranda that he had had a similar conversation ten or so years ago—about Iraq. Leading Finn to suggest—with a completely straight face—that the British start planning to liberate the country from its ruthless and immoral president. "It worked out so *well* in Iraq," he added. Even if he wanted to, said the Omani ambassador, this president couldn't fix things. While a totalitarian despot, he still fell short of Saddam's absolute domination. When several ambassadors claimed that the country's problems could not be solved with money, the head of the World Food Programme chimed in to say that they certainly couldn't be solved *without* money. The country director of the World Bank added that many reforms just had to wait for the country to become magically secure or for its economy to turn around. But we can't wait for that! cried others. By the end of the night, Miranda noticed that the World Bank director was asleep in his chair. She was relieved when they could finally tuck the jetlagged Minister into bed and stay up for another port with the cops.

WITH THE MORNING light slanting through the bars of her dressing room window, Miranda stands in front of her closets, contemplating her wardrobe. She still cannot get over the fact that she has an entire room in which to dress herself—a room that serves no other purpose. It was particularly ridiculous when she first moved in, with the two suitcases she had been living out of for the past few years. One of the things she had loved about living in this country was that she never had to think about what to wear. She could live in a succession of long black cotton skirts with long black cotton blouses, or jeans and a T-shirt under an *abaya*. It was so simple.

But everything changed when she moved in with Finn and was suddenly hosting dinner parties for high-ranking officials. At first, she had borrowed a few dresses from her friend Marguerite, the French ambassador's wife—the only ambassador's wife even close to her size, corpulence being part of the job description—before going on a shopping expedition to Dubai, the fifth circle of Hell as far as she was concerned. Despite the profusion of clothing stores in the sprawling malls, it was nearly impossible to find a single dress, skirt, or even a pair of jeans not pasted with sequins and spangles. Arab women love glitter, the flashier and gaudier the better. They also favor synthetics, such as rayon and polyester, despite the unsuitability of these materials for sweltering climates. Perhaps they were simply cheaper. Still, Miranda had managed to find enough cotton clothing to keep herself covered until her next trip to London, when Finn had patiently spent an entire day with her choosing outfits.

But she doesn't need to dress up for breakfast with policemen. Her gym clothes will be fine, as long as she isn't leaving the house. She slips on a camisole and shorts. These are British policemen; there is no danger of shocking them with the sight of female skin.

When she arrives in the dining room, Alastair is already at the table, tucking into a bowl of porridge. As she slides into her seat, Negasi bustles in with baskets of toast, her rows of stubby black braids tucked under the Japanese poppies scarf Miranda had brought her from the Metropolitan Museum of Art. (Every morning she asks Miranda and Finn if they want toast and eggs, though they never have anything other than fruit and muesli on weekdays. Miranda gets the feeling she is almost relieved to have guests, so that she can *cook* something.) "Good morning, Madame," says Negasi, smiling. Miranda has been trying to get her to stop calling her Madame ever since she moved in. "Miranda is fine," she said. "Even Mira." She doesn't feel old enough to be a Madame, even at thirty-nine. But though Negasi always smiles and agrees, she can't seem to get her lips to form Miranda's name.

"Good morning, Negasi! Good morning, Ali." Negasi hurries to pour carrot juice into her glass.

"Morning! Looking forward to getting rid of us?" Alastair smiles, bits of oat stuck to his upper lip.

"Of course not. Whom will I be able to bore with my political rants?"

"You'll miss us, then?"

"We'll cry ourselves to sleep every night." Miranda smiles and pulls her napkin into her lap. Finn appears a few moments later, showered and dressed in one of his gray pin-striped suits and a blue tie with tiny sheep on it. It is one of Cressida's favorite ties. "She's awake," he says to Miranda, before greeting Alastair and pouring himself a cup of Negasi's coffee.

"I'll go up." Miranda is still breast-feeding two or three times a day, though Cressida is nearly fifteen months old. She never thought she would nurse for this long, but it had been such a struggle to make the breast-feeding work in the beginning that now that she has it figured out she wants to do it forever. The first few months had been torture. Her nipples had cracked, bled, and succumbed to thrush. Against her affronted flesh, Cressida's lips had been razor-sharp blades. The brush of a soft cotton T-shirt had left her weeping. But she'd persisted, motivated by the health benefits and the threat of having to wash and sterilize bottles every day, until finally, miraculously, the two of them figured it out.

Upstairs, Cressida is standing in her crib, a new trick. She still doesn't have much hair, just a strip of wispy black curls down the middle of her scalp, a milquetoast of a Mohawk. Her eyes have turned from blue to a dark phthalo green, framed by eyelashes so long they brush the tiny bones of her eyebrows when she opens them wide. "Bob bob bobobobob BOB!" she cries as Miranda enters. "BOB BOB!"

"Morning, sunshine!" she says, lifting the little girl into her arms. "And how many times have I told you not to call me Bob?"

Just as Cressida is finishing nursing, Finn calls from downstairs. "Come say good-bye!" She slides the straps of her camisole back up over her shoulders and hefts Cressie onto her hip. Downstairs, Negasi rushes to take the baby, enfolding her in a patchouli- and perspiration-scented embrace. Miranda had initially felt uneasy about asking their housekeeper to look after her daughter—it wasn't part of her job description, after all—but Negasi adores the child, often prying her from her mother's arms to rock her, singing in her lilting Amharic. When Miranda tracks her down in the kitchen to retrieve Cressida, Negasi pleads for a few more minutes.

The men are lined up in the hall with their black cases. "We can't thank you enough for putting up with us, Miranda," says Mick.

"Any longer and Ali here might have gone native," adds Gazza.

"You're welcome anytime." The bland words of diplomacy slip off her tongue so easily now, though this time she means it.

"I hope we won't have reason to come back anytime soon. Though we may not be able to keep Alastair away."

Miranda stays in the doorway as Finn walks the men down the garden path. Bashir and Yusef emerge from either side of the front steps to escort them, their eyes scanning the surrounding rooftops. The rest of the team waits in the armored cars, already humming in the drive. Finn jogs back to kiss her one last time (surprising Yusef, who has to leap out of the front seat and jog back with him). "See you tonight."

"At an undetermined time?"

"As usual."

Finn cannot ever call her from work to say what time he is coming home. They have to assume that all their phones are tapped, and thus it would be dangerous to disclose the ambassador's whereabouts. Sometimes Finn calls to say he will be late, but never exactly *how* late. "Dinner or no dinner?" she asks. "Dinner," he always replies. Though it isn't unusual for Finn to have dinner at 10:00 p.m. This didn't used to bother her, but since the most recent attack on the US embassy she finds herself unable to focus on her work after 6:00 p.m., when the sun plunges behind the minarets. Her ears strain for the roar of his convoy as she prowls the upstairs, peering out of each of their dozens of windows in turn, seeing nothing but the night.

"Have a happy day, sweetheart. And don't forget, the bug men are coming this morning!" he whispers, before jogging back down the path and climbing into his forest-green Toyota Land Cruiser. She had almost forgotten. Two Brits are coming this morning to sweep the house for electronic bugs. "Seriously?" she had said when Finn told her. "How would bugs have gotten in?"

Just about anyone in this country is bribable, Finn had said. Even their own staff members could be persuaded to settle a bug into a potted plant if it meant feeding their family back in Ethiopia for a month. This had startled Miranda. She couldn't imagine anyone more loyal than Negasi. Or Teru. Or even Desta. Could they really so easily be bribed? Then again, she probably also couldn't conceive of the poverty of their families back in Ethiopia. Betraying an employer might feel fairly minor next to keeping a small child alive. "But we've been here three years!" she'd exclaimed. "The Mazrooqis might already know our darkest secrets."

"It's not routine," he said. "But with the increased security concerns, we want to make sure we are crossing all of our T's. Chances are, though, your secrets remain dark."

The bug men arrive at 8:00 a.m., half an hour after Finn's convoy pulls out of the gates. Miranda is in the kitchen discussing the evening's menu with Teru when she hears the growl of their armored car. Cressie sits in the middle of the metal counter waving a wooden spoon, occasionally whacking a cookbook. Miranda leaves her there with Teru to run to greet the men, pulling the door to the kitchen shut behind her; the staff are to be kept away from the rooms being swept.

The bug men strike her as young, possibly not out of their twenties. One is tall and blond with the lean musculature of a surfer, while the other is stout with a shaved head and round belly. He wears a tiny Union Jack stud in his left ear. They lug in a series of heavy black suitcases, dropping each with a thud on the floor of the sitting room. "Do you mind if we start in here?" the blond one says, glancing around. "Start wherever you want," says Miranda, slightly self-conscious in her shorts. "Tea?" The offer has become reflexive. No one enters the Residence without having a mug of English breakfast thrust into his or her hands.

"Yes, please!" The bug men settle into the living room and get to work. Miranda closes the door before the staff becomes inquisitive. When Gabra arrives to play with Cressie outside, Miranda grabs a water bottle and trots to the gym at the end of their garden for her morning run and swim. She doesn't love the treadmill, but running outside is out of the question. No one in this country runs, except at gunpoint. Women least of all. It is one of the things she misses most about life in America. At first the Residence staff were bewildered by her daily workouts, but after three years they have grown accustomed to her peculiar Western habits.

When she returns an hour later, her hair damp from her laps in the pool, the bug men are still at it. She creeps by them, wrapped in Finn's blue-and-white-striped terry-cloth dressing gown. The fat one is waving a wand across the surfaces of furniture while the blond stares at a laptop screen. When they finish with the living room, they move on to the dining room and Finn's office—the rooms where interesting conversations are most likely to take place.

Finn is scrupulous about discussing sensitive information with Miranda only in designated areas. They do not talk about his work in bed or at the dining table. When he wants to share something particularly intriguing, he takes her into the stairwell, and they walk up and down the stairs from floor to floor, whispering. Or they take a walk in the garden or around the top floor, moving quickly from room to room.

Miranda showers and changes into walking trousers and a blue cotton men's shirt, twisting her unruly curls into a knot. She's lacing up her hiking boots when her cell phone rings. Finn. "Hello, sweetheart."

"Is today your hike?"

"This afternoon. Why? Is it still okay?" Her spirits sag at the prospect of another day locked inside. With the new security restrictions in place there is hardly anywhere she is still allowed to go.

"Of course, I just . . . You're not going too far?"

"Not even crossing a checkpoint. Tucker says it's perfectly safe. It's near the president's village."

"Who's with you today?"

"Not sure. Whoever isn't with you, I guess. Mukhtar?"

"Your favorite."

"Well, he's the only one who ever asks me questions. He takes an interest."

"Not too much of one, I hope."

"Finn! You do realize I used to do this every week. *Without* a bodyguard."

"But that was before you were an ambassador's wife."

"When I was just an ordinary mortal."

"A very bewitching ordinary mortal."

Miranda smiles at her phone. "I'll see you tonight, okay? By the time you get home I'll even have all the pistachios in bowls."

"That's what the staff are for, sweetheart. Put your feet up."

By the time she gets downstairs, Gabra and Cressie are outside playing on the front lawn. Dressed in an oversized embroidered Ethiopian shirt (a gift from Gabra) and a floppy flowered sunhat, Cressie is teaching her teddy bear to do high dives from the edge of the dried-up stone fountain at the end of the garden. She is a fortunate child; few other children in this city have lawns—or any outdoor space. Miranda thinks of the children in her old neighborhood, who play their games in the streets, barefoot and unsupervised, dodging cars as they kick small rocks across the cobblestones. When she lived there, they would chase after her as she made her way around the markets, buying tomatoes and tiny greenish raisins, their ranks growing at every intersection. *"Soura, soura!"* they'd cry, making picture-taking motions with their hands. Or *"Qalam, qalam!"* Why these children were permanently fixated on pens was a mystery to her. She understood why they wanted her to take their photographs (and she often obliged). They wanted to see themselves in a way they normally couldn't. Many had never seen a mirror. They would stare in silence at the photo in her camera, wrapping filthy fingers around it to pull it closer. But why the pens? She never saw them using pens, even when she was in their homes.

"Mummy, Mummy!" Seeing her approach, Cressie totters across the lawn, falling on her face every few steps when she catches a foot on the spongy turf. Their grass is inexplicably springy, sinking beneath every footfall, tugging at the heels of shoes. When the embassy staff gathers to play badminton someone always ends up twisting an ankle. Not that that deters anyone. The British must have their bit of lawn, and where else could they find a patch of green? Yonas and Semere spend half their day on the turf, tenderly watering, weeding, and mowing. If Cressie could learn to walk on this, thinks Miranda, she'll be able to walk on anything.

"Hello, my love." Miranda swings her daughter up into her arms. "Have you had a happy morning?" Cressie is heavy and hot. Miranda presses her close, kissing her chubby cheek until the little girl squirms to be let down. To Miranda's dismay, she has never been a cuddly child. She tolerates the occasional embrace, but is impatient for it to end so that she can get on with whatever she is doing—collecting flower petals or pretending to make porridge for the bears (even Miranda says porridge now instead of oatmeal, as well as anorak, chuffed, knickers, biscuit, and dual carriageway. Finn's language has been slowly colonizing hers) or sending her small plastic cows on a Tupperware boat down a pot-holder river. She is a perpetually busy child.

Gabra updates her on the minutiae of Cressida's day thus far as they walk toward the house and wander back to the kitchen to see what Teru has left them. Miranda sets Cressie on the floor to open the refrigerator and peers inside. As requested, Teru has made a Thai salad, strips of tofu, carrot, and cucumber in a peanut sauce. Every morning, Miranda picks something out of a cookbook, and every afternoon it appears in the refrigerator. This never ceases to feel miraculous. Gabra has chicken, rice, and Ethiopian injera bread, her favorite. Miranda invites Gabra to join them in the dining room, though she knows it's pointless. Gabra would rather stay with Negasi and Teru in the kitchen.

It was an awkward adjustment, eating separately from the staff. At first Miranda took her meals in the kitchen, wanting to be egalitarian, wanting to be their friend, feeling lonesome in the empty Siberia of their dining room. She didn't know how she was supposed to relate to staff, having never even had a housecleaner. Servants were people she thought of as existing only in fairy tales and Hollywood. But eventually she realized how uncomfortable her overtures made them. The kitchen was their province. They didn't know what to do with her when she was underfoot, interrupting the flow of their work. She was the Madame, and therefore she belonged in the dining room.

Negasi, Teru, and Desta were a seamless team. Whenever Teru had a particularly large dinner to make, Negasi and Desta would be in the kitchen, juicing limes and slicing carrots. Miranda admired their effortless choreography, the way they never discussed who would do what but sensed what was needed. At night when they had large dinners, all three women worked together serving the drinks and food, not one of them leaving until the kitchen once again looked as though it had never been used.

Now, Miranda has adjusted to her solitary meals. She reads, listens to music, or plays with Cressie. A relatively recent issue of *ART-news* lies open next to her plate. Miranda hasn't managed much more than a glance at the headlines, though she's had the issue for two months now. Today, Cressie sits in Miranda's lap as she eats, pulling strips of cucumber and tofu off her plate. When she's mopped up the last drops of peanut sauce with a tomato slice, Miranda carries her plate to the kitchen and leaves it in the sink. She hasn't washed a dish in three years. *Don't get used to this,* she reminds herself every morning. *This is not real life.*

UPSTAIRS SHE WANDERS through their bedroom—past their canopied, king-sized bed, which Negasi has already made up with clean sheets—to her studio, Cressie in pursuit, babbling a monologue that once again seems focused on her invisible friend Bob. "I'm starting to worry about your relationship with this Bob fellow," Miranda says absently, as she lifts paintings and sets them down again. Unfinished canvases lean against the sides of a large wooden worktable. So fast and furious have the ideas been coming here that she doesn't have time to finish one painting before the idea for the next one propels her onward. She wants to pin down every single inspiration before it floats away, like a helium balloon. There will be plenty of time to finish them, she trusts, when the visions abate. Still, her New Orleans gallerist is expecting at least a dozen new works for her next show, a mere ten months away. She'll have to finish something. It will be her first opening with Finn by her side—and his first trip to New Orleans. She wants to make it spectacular.

They have less than a year left of Finn's four-year posting, and then they could be anywhere. If he's lucky, if he continues to impress London with his work here, he'll get another ambassadorship. If not, he'll have to spend a few years back in London before applying for new posts. Miranda wonders what this will mean for her. A geographic shift always echoes in her work. It takes time for each new environment to settle into her bones, dissolve into her plasma, seep out into her brush, saturate her colors. For how long after they leave in June will Mazrooq's inimitable energies pulse through her veins? How long before London's frigid mists cloud her eyes? She pushes the thought away. They have time. Anything could happen.

On her easel rests a painting. A Mazrooqi man kneels in prayer in the stony *diwan* of an Old City home. Dressed in a long, white *thobe* that floats around him like a Halloween ghost costume, he curls forward, his forehead brushing a thick carpet of Mazrooqi design. At first nothing appears unusual about the image, but after a moment, women begin to emerge. For the carpet is crafted from their limbs, from their thighs and elbows and bellies and necks and breasts. Everything in the room—the man, the cushions strewn about the floor, the lamps—rests upon this foundation of women.

Older paintings lean nearby. A well-dressed man in a *thobe* and dark Western suit jacket (the typical Friday outfit of Mazrooqi men) strides down an Old City street clutching the handle of an unusual umbrella. It's fashioned from a naked woman, whose ankles and feet rest in his palm and whose long hair spreads a protective tent over his head. Her face is devoid of expression. On the ground next to the easel rests a painting of a middle-aged man at work, writing at a large, ornate desk. But it is to his chair that the eye is drawn; it is fashioned from the limbs of another nude woman. At ease in the embrace of her arms, he leans his head back against the softness of her breasts, a satisfied smile on his face. *His own private Atlas*, reads the title. In every corner of the room are more of her women, never clothed, always useful. Women serving as sofas, coffee tables, easels, ovens, even churches. Since she and Vicenta first set up house in the Old City, the women haven't stopped coming.

Still, she is frustrated with the literalness of her work, her inability to free herself from narrative. She is not fully the contemporary surrealist she aspires to be; she is too caught up in directing her compositions. She hungers for liberation, to remove the analytical screen between her unconscious and her easel. Someday, she hopes. Someday soon.

In addition to the women are several simple sketches of Tazkia curled on the end of Miranda's studio sofa in jeans and a T-shirt, her thick black hair pulled back in a loose ponytail. Miranda idly picks up one of these from an armchair by the window. Tazkia is smiling, her mouth slightly open as if she is about to offer the punch line of a joke. It hadn't been easy to get Tazkia to sit still for very long. And impossible to get Tazkia to stop talking. In the end, Miranda had taken a photograph of her and worked from that, though often Tazkia drifted off to sleep while posing, giving Miranda time to work with a live subject. Like centuries of painters before her, Miranda has always preferred to stroke her brush along the lines of a female form. But unlike Rubens and Renoir, Miranda favors the slim-hipped and small-breasted. She would say boyish, if to do so did not imply that a slight form was somehow less female. The male body is capable of arousing her, but she has never found it beautiful.

And then there are the secret paintings, locked away. Their presence in her home makes her uneasy. She will be relieved when they are gone, when they are ashes. It won't be long now.

"Mommy's friend," says Cressie, pointing to the drawing. "Mommy's friend!"

"That's right, sweetheart. That's Mommy's friend Tazkia."

"Tazkee, Tazkee!" Cressie knows Tazkia as well as she knows anyone.

Miranda looks at the disordered sprawl of her work, the tangle of feminine arms and legs, and sighs. She comes here every day, even when she doesn't have time to work. It's a way of checking in with herself, with what is central to her. It's the one room in the house the staff is not permitted to enter, barring emergency. In the beginning, Desta had come in every day to try to scrub the desktops and floors, but she had overturned so many palettes and left brushes in such disarray that Miranda had begged her not to clean. She lived in terror of Desta accidentally splashing a cup of turpentine across a canvas. "I'll do it myself," she'd said. Desta had just looked at her, the dark crease between her eyes deepening. She clearly didn't believe Miranda to be capable of cleaning anything.

Cressie sits on the floor of their bedroom, turning the pages of her books, as Miranda organizes herself for her afternoon hike. Perpetual motion and painting, the two surest ways to maintain her equilibrium in this surreal world. She stuffs a phone, lip salve, and her camera in her pockets. Would she need money? Probably not. But she folds a thousand dinars (worth about five dollars) and slips it into her pocket just in case. In a small backpack she tucks a bottle of water, a sketch-book, a pencil case, two hard-boiled eggs Finn made for her the night before, and plastic bags of raisins and almonds.

She is meeting the other women at the Al-Bustan café, several blocks away. Miranda is never sure who will turn up on their weekly excursions. People are constantly in and out of the country and busy with work. These women knew her long before she became an ambas-sador's wife, when she was simply Miranda the painter. In fact, not until she had actually moved into the Residence did she confess to them her relationship with Finn. "I didn't want anything to change," she'd said to Doortje, the Dutch wife of a Royal Dutch Shell executive.

"But it will," Doortje had said. "For one, we will be hitting you up for your wine cellar."

These are not women awed by diplomats; these are women for whom diplomats are an unexceptional part of their daily landscape. These are women who have walked across continents, for decades. Women who have lived in Nigeria, China, Sierra Leone, Malta, Guy-ana, Laos, and Pitcairn Island. Rangy, athletic women who carry their worlds with them, refashioning their lives every three to five years. Women who gave birth to their first child in Singapore and their second in Krakow. Women who are at ease with strangers and strange landscapes. Women who sleep in the shadow of loneliness and wake looking forward to a simple exchange with a fruit seller. When she is with them, Miranda doesn't feel the need to speak. She is sim-ply happy to be among them, listening to their stories, their differ-ent languages weaving together. She picks up strands of Arabic and French, admires the icy inaccessibility of Norwegian and German. Monday—their hiking day—is her favorite day of the week.

She sits on the bed to zip up her backpack and feels a pudgy hand on her knee. Clinging to Miranda for balance, Cressie waves a book with her other hand. It's a raggedy red paperback with folded-down corners that had been Miranda's when she was young. Her father had sent it over when she told him she was pregnant. Miranda lifts Cressie's small, pudgy body onto the bed, nestles her between her legs, and inhales the dusty jasmine scent of her hair. Gabra often brings her garlands of the flowers, ubiquitous in this city, hanging them around Cressie's neck until she grows restless and tears them off, scattering brown-edged white petals across the marble floors. Miranda opens the book and begins to read. "Corduroy is a bear who once lived in the toy department of a big store. Day after day he waited with all the other animals and dolls for somebody to come along and take him home."

Once Corduroy has found refuge, Miranda carries Cressida down the corridor and through the little kitchen to her room, where she lays her in her cot. Negasi has already drawn the blinds and lined up Cressie's sleuth of bears at the edge of her mattress. With a wail of protest, Cressie stands, reaching for her mother. "Tesas!" she yelps. "Tesas!" Miranda sighs. "Okay, just once though." She heaves her daughter out of the cot and takes one chubby little hand in hers, as if they are ballroom dancing. And swaying in circles around the room, she sings:

When we dance together my world's in disguise
It's a fairyland tale that's come true
And when you look at me with those stars in your eyes
I could waltz across Texas with you

A few choruses later Cressie grows limp in her arms, her head abruptly heavy against Miranda's shoulder. Her voice fading to a hum, Miranda tiptoes over to the cot. When she lays her daughter down on her back, Cressie's eyes fly open for a moment, find her mother's, and apparently comforted by the sight, she falls instantly back to sleep.

MIRANDA IS HALFWAY down the front steps when she remembers the wine. Damn! She drops her backpack, fumbles with the key again, and races back through the house. "Teru!" she calls, skidding around the corner into the kitchen. Teru looks up from a mixing bowl, placid, imperturbable, accustomed to Miranda treating the house as a running track. Miranda has never seen her flustered. You could say to Teru, "We'll be having twenty-seven people to dinner tonight, including five vegetarians, four vegans, three people with celiac disease, two with lactose intolerance, and one on the Atkins diet," and she wouldn't even blink. Of course, she, Negasi, Desta, and the men are all Orthodox Christians who observe seven fasting periods a year, eschewing all meat and dairy, so they are perhaps unfazed by dietary restrictions.

"Wine, I forgot the wine. Remind me what we decided for dinner tonight?"

"Fish," says Teru. "With garlic and chili. And the spinach and mashed potatoes."

"Right! Thanks! Where's Negasi?"

"Here, Madame." Negasi has appeared from nowhere, her hands folded against the white apron she wears over the green-checked uniform.

"Hi! Would you mind helping me with the wine? I almost forgot about it."

Negasi follows her downstairs to the door of the wine cellar, which Miranda unlocks with the key they always leave in the door. She loves the smell of the wine cellar, its dank alcoholic air like that of a pub toward closing time. How this happens when every bottle and can is sealed is a mystery, but it does. The wine cellar is one of their greatest pleasures. Over the past few years Finn and Miranda have slowly filled it with wines from all over the world. They have been experimental, ordering things they'd never heard of, from every price range. They've even ordered the odd liqueur, like Bénédictine and Suze.

Miranda turns toward the wall of whites, running her fingertips over the dusty bottles. Something light and dry, probably something Australian. She chooses a sauvignon blanc and passes several bottles to Negasi. Together they carry them upstairs and load them into the drinks refrigerator. Plenty of time for them to cool before dinner.

"Thank you," says Miranda, already running back toward the door. "I'll pick out the red when I get back!"

AUGUST 9, 2010
Finn

By the time Finn gets to his office 347 e-mails await him, the average number lying in wait after a weekend. Sighing, he turns away from his computer and opens his briefcase to pull out the morning's newspapers. They don't necessarily illuminate what goes on in the country, but at least reading them exercises his Arabic. No surprises today; nothing about the looming threat of civil war, the restless youth of the North, or the increasing scarcity of food. Rather, "Saudi Arabia donates dates for Ramadan," "Minister beautifully unveils new democracy project for children," "UNICEF holds fund-raiser at the Sheraton." Stop the presses! What he wouldn't give to just once read a headline that tells it like it is. "President once more pays off corrupt cronies with country's oil money" perhaps. Or "Women still treated like crap in every single governorate." Miranda would like that one. He smiles. Mira. His stomach still does a delirious flip when he remembers she lives in his house, that she will be there at the end of the day. If only there weren't the EU ambassadors' dinner this evening. It has been more than two weeks since they had the house to themselves, free from guests. At night they had to make love surreptitiously, hands over each other's mouths to keep from waking the police in the bedroom next door, often dissolving into fits of laughter that are equally hard to stifle. It would also be nice to get home early enough to read Cressie her bedtime stories one of these days, before she forgets who he is. Still. He is a lucky man; he doesn't lose sight of that for an instant. He had all but given up by the time Miranda splashed down in his staid world.

He's still glancing through the headlines, struggling to fend off the image of Miranda's tawny limbs tangled in his sheets, when his personal assistant, Lyle, pokes his head in to remind him of his first meeting. It's all-staff first, then a meeting with his defense attaché about the pirate situation. If it weren't for the incessant meetings, he might be able to get some work done. As he heads out, he glances at his computer once more. There are now 368 e-mails, at least a couple dozen marked URGENT.

Most are probably pirate-related. He had worked all weekend on the pirate situation, much to Miranda's dismay. Friday, a British Royal Navy ship picked up a Mazrooqi dhow that had been boarded by Somali pirates and was attacking a Finnish vessel. In the confrontation with the Brits, three Somalis and two Mazrooqis were killed. But even with the pirates all either dead or in captivity, Finn's work was just beginning. It was the embassy's responsibility to figure out what to do with the boat, the crew, and the corpses. First, he wants to repatriate the Mazrooqi corpses, which requires getting diplomatic clearance to send them in a British helicopter over Mazrooqi waters. Then he needs to figure out what to do with the Somali bodies. Both Mazrooq and Somalia refuse to accept the pirates' bodies. Not a lot of countries clamoring for decomposing criminals, actually. So Finn then has to figure out how the navy could give the Somalis a proper Muslim burial at sea. Merely tossing them overboard could trigger a diplomatic crisis with unpredictable consequences.

After the dead are taken care of, Finn needs to decide what to do with the living. The surviving Mazrooqis must be brought home. He has sought assurances from the Mazrooqi Foreign Minister that the surviving Somalis would not be put to death if they were brought to trial here; the UK forbids the death penalty. The Foreign Minister has thus far refused to guarantee this, saying that to do so would undermine the independence of the justice system. So then where are the Somalis to be sent? Maybe Kenya? Finn reminds himself to put in a call to the British High Commissioner in Nairobi later this afternoon, to see if he can sort out a way to get the prisoners tried there.

The Defense Attaché is waiting in his office when Finn gets back from the staff meeting, legs crossed, reading a dog-eared copy of Hisham Matar's *Anatomy of a Disappearance*. "How did you get here so fast? Didn't we just come from the same meeting?"

"Teleported. A new stealth technology we're trying out in the navy." Leo closes his book without marking his place. He memorizes the page numbers, he'd told Finn. A shared love of order was one of the many things that bonded the two men.

"Glad to hear it. Might come in handy with the pirate situation."

"Figured if that kid Harry Potter can do it, why not the world's best military?"

"I think he apparated, actually."

"Same thing, from a technical standpoint. Good to know you're keeping up with contemporary literature though."

"I do my best. So?"

"Well, the good news is that we have permission for the helicopters. They'll bring the Mazrooqi bodies back here later this afternoon."

"And the living?"

"Them too."

"I've got a call in to the president's imam to find out how to bury the Somalis at sea." Finn flips open his pocket-size calendar. Paper. He's endlessly mocked for his old-fashioned tastes, but he's sure that if his entire schedule were on something electronic, he'd accidentally drop it in the toilet. At least paper dries out. "At three p.m. If he actually rings then, and you know how unlikely that is, I'll let you know our instructions."

"Do we need to get ahold of a Quran?"

"Probably. But I don't know. Ever been to a Muslim funeral?"

"Seen them go by my house. With the corpse on a stretcher under a rug. Not sure where they go with it though."

"Find out. Could be useful someday. Not with the Somalis, of course. They're off to make a whole lot of fish happy."

"A pleasing role reversal." Leo is the only military man Finn knows who is also a devout vegetarian. And he isn't a small man. At six foot seven, with glossy flaxen hair, a rosy complexion, and thickly muscled torso, Leo is a poster boy for the vegetarian lifestyle. Must blow the Mazrooqis' minds, a vegetarian DA. "I see enough death at work," he'd said simply. "I don't need to see it on my dinner plate."

When Leo heads off to organize the helicopters, Finn turns to his e-mails, now numbering 379. Lyle brings him a cup of Earl Grey and he opens the first one, an update on a water project down south.

If only he could do his job without e-mails. He is a slow, methodical thinker and he types with two fingers. E-mails that would take Mira ten minutes to write take him two hours. His talents lie elsewhere, in negotiating agreements with the president and his men, arguing politics with tribal sheikhs, and encouraging consensus among disparate groups, which is why the other European ambassadors chose him to lead mediation efforts to head off open hostilities. And while he is typically self-deprecating when speaking of his linguistic abilities, he is secretly proud of his Arabic. When the president meets with Finn, he dismisses his translator in favor of Finn's superior ear for nuance.

When Finn has cleared 170 e-mails (mostly by hitting the ever-handy Delete button), he allows himself to ring Miranda. The sound of her voice, cheery and warm, soothes him. Reassured of her continual presence on the planet, he opens his lunch bag. He never has time for lunch out unless it's official, so Negasi packs him sandwiches. He's halfway through the first one when Dax, First Secretary Political and their resident spook, sticks his head in the door.

"Got a minute? Oh, sorry, you're eating."

"I can listen and chew at the same time. If you don't mind. Come in." Finn waves a hand at his leather sofa.

"It's about the kidnappings up north." Dax comes in, closing the door behind him. "We may need the police back, to do some forensics."

"Oh, Dax, no." Feeling suddenly queasy, Finn drops the remains of his sandwich back into the aluminum foil.

"I'm afraid so."

"All of them?"

"All except one. The Dutch boy is still missing."

"Jesus."

"I know."

The two men sit in silence for a moment.

"Anyone claim responsibility?"

"Not yet. A few hallmarks of AQ, but could be Zajnoon's people. They can be pretty brutal. But we don't know."

"I'll ring the families," says Finn.

"They're still here, at the InterContinental."

"I'll go over then. Brief me."

Dax unfolds the particulars of the horror, the search that led to the row of headless corpses found in a mass grave up north. The heads were buried several feet away.

"The Dutch and the French know? And the Germans?"

"Their guys were with us."

When Dax leaves, Finn rings the other ambassadors to offer his condolences and vow to collaborate further on the search for the killers. And then all four of them head off to strip the frantic families of their last remaining shreds of hope.

IN THE CAR, a new dread leaps onto his shoulders. Miranda is out walking today. She wouldn't have heard of the killings, no one would have. The Foreign and Commonwealth Office had managed to keep the disappearances out of the papers entirely. It had surprised him when he began his career, just how much the FCO managed to withhold from the press, how many missing people. But this was critical; publicity was disastrous for hostage negotiations. Not only did it give violent men the spotlight they craved but it gave them an exaggerated idea of their victims' importance, often resulting in astronomical ransom requests. The media were also all too frequently stupid enough to disclose details about a hostage—that he was Jewish or gay or American—that put his or her life in further danger. Finn was all for freedom of the press, but not at the expense of a life.

Struggling with the seat belt, he extracts his mobile from his pocket and rings her. It goes straight to voice mail. She's probably just out of range. He rings Tucker. "They're nowhere near up north, Finn," he says. "It's a totally safe area. Never been an incident. It's Sharaq, where the president comes from. Just a forty-five-minute drive."

Somewhat more at ease, Finn flips his phone shut. He has got to stop being so paranoid. She'll be fine. She always is.

IT'S NEARLY 5:00 p.m. by the time Finn gets back to his office, having left two disintegrating families in his wake. The father of one of the British women wouldn't even look at him, just sat on the beige leather sofa with his face in his hands, tears running through his fingers and soaking the cuffs of his shirt. His wife had sat rocking beside him. "No," she'd said over and over. "No no no no no." The other couple had raged at him for not throwing their daughter out of the country. "How could you have let her stay in a country like this? Why didn't you warn her?" Finn had explained that the website of the Foreign Office did, in fact, warn against nonessential travel to the region, but that people ultimately had responsibility for their own safety. Muslim Mercy isn't ordinarily targeted, he'd added, so she may have felt she was safe with them. "She was doing good work, important work." He'd paused, searching his memory for something to ameliorate their devastation. "She saved a lot of little children from starving. Where she was, the babies under one were all dying of malnutrition before Muslim Mercy arrived."

The room had been silent save for the creak of the sofa under the rocking woman. The crying man had finally looked up from his sodden fingers. "She should have let them die."

His words had hung in the air for several minutes. The angry couple had wilted, sinking together into a sofa across from the others, their hands falling limply into their laps. The rocking woman had stopped and looked up at her husband. Finn had pulled himself clumsily to his feet. "I am so, so very sorry about your daughters."

The four parents had sat silently staring at the floor. Apologizing several more times for the tragedy he had been powerless to prevent, Finn had left.

He's going to have to hurry to get home in time for dinner. Miranda is remarkably talented at entertaining diplomats over cocktails when he's running late, but it's very poor form to show up after one's guests. He has no time to switch gears. The tentacles of the families' grief still cling to his rib cage. The whole afternoon has hollowed him out, left him enervated and despairing. And now he must get home to discuss how the EU countries can collaborate more effectively on various development projects. Over the years he has had to learn how to seal off parts of his psyche, but it's never easy. Compartmentalization does not come naturally to him. When he cries during a movie he doesn't just cry about the movie, he cries about everything.

As he stuffs a stack of papers into his briefcase, he notices the light flashing on his phone and picks up the receiver. Seven messages. The first three are from various government officials wanting him to personally fast-track UK visas for their children. A downside of working in this tinderbox of a country is the incessant demands for visas. The Mazrooqis simply refuse to understand that there is truly nothing Finn can do to ease their way into his country. Several have offered him money. "Look," Finn often repeats, patience ebbing. "If you really want a visa then I would start by filling out the forms properly." The elite seem to think they can bypass the paperwork, leaving most of it blank or incorrectly marked. This disregard for process drives him mad. He hangs up the phone before the fourth message begins and takes one last look at his computer. Four hundred and one e-mails. He'll have to get back to work after dinner. Again. He'd work from home if he could, but he can access classified work e-mails only from the embassy.

He's locking the door of his office when the phone rings. Cursing under his breath, he turns the key back and lunges toward his desk. It's Miranda, breathless and panicked, not sounding very much like Miranda.

"Sweetheart," she says. "We're in trouble."

AUGUST 9, 2010
Miranda

An hour after leaving the crenellated towers of the Residence behind, Miranda is in the mountains. It's a forty-five-minute drive to a village just outside the city where they turn off the road and rattle over a series of long dirt tracks before leaving their cars in a dusty patch of earth. The others rode together, but Miranda had to come separately with her driver and guard. There are just three of them today—Doortje; Kaia, the Norwegian wife of a French banker; and

Miranda. And of course Mukhtar, who is Miranda's guard for the day. None of the other women have guards. Usually it's just the diplomats who have close protection. *Close protection*. She had never heard the phrase before she became an ambassador's wife. It sounded like a euphemism for birth control. No, Finn had joked. More like death control.

Few of the other ambassadors' wives are keen on hiking. The athletic American ambassador's wife had wanted to get to the mountains but was evacuated after the most recent attack on the embassy. Not that she would have been allowed out anyway. Only the American embassy has stricter security regulations and more bodyguards than the British. The few Americans Miranda meets complain that they hardly ever get to leave the compound. None of them have trekked across the western mountains, swum in the sea off the southern coast, or traveled over the desert heartland to mud-brick cities resembling children's crude sand castles baked in the sun. Presuming that one becomes a diplomat in order to experience other cultures, this posting must be a disappointment to them.

Other diplomats—the Omanis, Egyptians, Qataris, Turks, and Saudis—have no need for such restrictions, having made fewer enemies in the Arab world. Yet the Arab wives, in Miranda's experience, do not hike. A few times Miranda has convinced Marguerite, the French ambassador's wife, to come along, but none of the others.

Miranda feels self-conscious about Mukhtar, as if his presence suggests her life is somehow more important, more valuable than the others'. Still, she has no choice, and the other women know that. She had felt much safer living with Vicenta in the Old City than she does living with Finn, surrounded by gates, guards, and security procedures. For nearly three years she walked the streets alone every day, shopped the markets, met friends at tea stalls, explored the mountains, and chatted with strangers, unmolested. She and Vicenta even freely held hands on the street, as it was not uncommon for people of the same sex to do here. Then she fell in love with Finn and the cage descended around her.

The day has grown uncommonly hot, the sun blazing drily down. Miranda pulls her Mariners baseball cap low on her forehead. As they set off across the parched ground, Mukhtar stays just ahead. Miranda hurries after him, her limbs rejoicing in the freedom. It is wonderful to be outside; the new security restrictions mean that too many days are spent cloistered at home. In the wake of the attack on the US embassy, a series of attacks on oil companies, and the kidnappings up north, embassy employees (and their spouses) are banned from anywhere Westerners might gather: the souqs, coffee shops, hotels, certain restaurants. The British Club, one of the only bars in town, has been closed. And recently even the weekly hiking trips have been canceled. Despite the tragedies, the restrictions feel slightly absurd to Miranda. She has been hiking in this country for three years without incident, and no one she has encountered on her journeys has ever been less than hospitable. In fact, she is treated more royally in this country than she has been anywhere else in the world. The kidnappings up north were unusual; they happened in a rebel-controlled area beset by periodic violence and regularly bombed by the government. It was also an area ruled by Sheikh Zajnoon, perhaps the most formidable sheikh in the country. He terrorized his people, confiscated land and money, and claimed it was all in the interest of the antigovernment cause. More than one of his tribesmen has accused him of beatings and sodomy, after having reached the relative safety of the capital. But none of those complaints ever came to trial. No prosecutor would dare take the case.

Foreigners rarely venture into Zajnoon's lands. It would certainly never have occurred to Miranda to go there. She is perfectly happy to hike within recommended areas. These were the arguments she presented to Finn when she asked if she could resume her hikes after Cressie turned one and she could leave her for a bit longer. "If I don't get out of this house and stretch my legs, I'm going to have to be taken out in a straitjacket."

"There are worse places to be kept prisoner," he'd said wryly.

"I know, I know. But do you honestly, really, truly think I would be in danger?" If he had said yes, she would not have gone. But he did not say yes. Finn hadn't seemed worried last night, though he never does. Finn is constitutionally calm (a helpful quality in his line of work). "If I thought you were going to be attacked I'd lock you in the safe room and never let you out," he'd reassured her. Adjoining their bedroom and the bath was a tiny room with double-reinforced doors, a radio, and a week's supply of water. This was where they were to hide if the house came under attack. And this was where, in the tall, locked mahogany cupboard, the secret paintings lived. Not even Finn had a key.

THE WOMEN TAKE turns in the lead, chatting with each other in French, their one common language. Kaia, in her sixties, is a strong walker. Her close-cropped hair is still blond and her face bears only faint lines. Her slender form is all the more remarkable given that she has four grown daughters. When she married Stéphane, she didn't speak a word of French, she says. But when they moved to France just after the birth of her first daughter, a desperate loneliness made her quickly fluent.

"It was Siri who saved me. When she was born she gave me the excuse to talk to people. I needed other mothers. My best friend was a woman I met at my local crèche, and unsurprisingly she didn't speak any Norwegian. So I learned fast."

Many of the women Miranda meets have more than three children. She wonders if it's because their line of work has allowed them to live in places where child care is cheap. She hadn't thought she would want more than one child, but she and Finn have already started talking about a second. Watching Cressida evolve has been more thrilling than Miranda had ever imagined. From a purely scientific point of view, observing the process by which Cressie discovered her hands, learned how to clap, and put simple words together was riveting. It was like living with the greatest science experiment ever. However, at thirty-nine, Miranda isn't sure she could get pregnant again. Conceiving Cressie had taken sustained and concentrated effort. Pleasurable effort, to be sure, but effort nonetheless. "Could we adopt a Chinese baby?" she'd asked Finn once. "A baby girl?" She'd become obsessed with news reports from China about baby girls murdered at birth, dismissed as less than human because of their sex. It made Miranda want to adopt every girl in the entire country. She cannot imagine anything more wonderful than a baby girl.

"No."

"No?" Miranda had been surprised. Finn was the pied piper of the local children. When they'd had a children's party around Christmastime, Finn had led every game, tumbling on the ground with the children and swinging them onto his shoulders. If there was ever someone who could love a stranger's child, it was Finn.

"I just don't think I would feel the same as I do about a child who is part of me," he'd said.

Miranda couldn't get her mind around this. "Seriously?"

"Seriously," he'd said. "Couldn't we just try again the fun way?"

UNDER THEIR FEET, the ground is dry and cracked, yet large patches of the flat valley are carefully cultivated. Miranda wonders at the source of water until she sees the irrigation pipes emptying into furrowed fields. After an hour or so, they pass a field of tomatoes just coming into ripeness. "Tomatoes are on me!" Doortje declares, waving a five-hundred-dinar note. Two bearded, white-robed farmers lingering by their field happily scamper off between rows to pick them the reddest ones. Crouching beside the irrigation pipe, the women dip the tomatoes in the gush of water and dry them on their trousers before sinking their teeth into the sweet, slightly mealy flesh.

Doortje catches up with Miranda as they finish their last tomatoes, juice running down their forearms and into their shirtsleeves. "I'm thinking of starting a dance class," she says, tipping her blond head to smile at Miranda (who wonders, not for the first time, if Doortje is flirting with her). She'd been studying salsa and ballroom dancing in Amsterdam before she moved here, she says, and she wants to keep it up. "But we're stuck in this stupid company compound, with a tiny living room."

"What about somewhere near us?" says Miranda. "Everyone has these enormous houses they hardly use. Want me to ask around? I'd offer our living room, but there are kind of constant meetings and lunches and pre-dinner drinks and after-dinner coffees going on there. So it's a bit hard to schedule." And bug men, she adds to herself. She isn't sure whether to mention the bug men. When she isn't sure whether something is confidential, she stays silent. In fact, since meeting Finn she has probably grown quieter than she has ever been. Her head is so full of things she isn't supposed to know that she constantly fears letting something slip.

It's another hour and a half before they stop for tea and snacks on a rocky outcrop. Miranda's feet ache as she stretches them out in front of her, nibbling at her almonds and raisins. She isn't terribly hungry. Near the top of the hill behind them, where he can maintain a good view of their surroundings, Mukhtar has stopped to eat his lunch. Miranda gazes before her at the sea of gentle hills and cultivated valleys. A cool breeze brushes the sweat from her brow. Kaia unscrews a thermos of espresso and pours tiny cups, passing them around the circle. She can always be counted on for the extravagant gesture—the flask of gin and tonics, the box of Swedish black licorice, the tiny, handmade chocolate truffles. Doortje passes around a plastic container of pomegranate seeds.

"That's a lot of time in Hades," Miranda says, watching Doortje pour a few hundred into her hand.

"If they've got good pomegranates there, then I don't mind," says Doortje, her eyes crinkling with her smile.

As she lifts the second forkful of pomegranate seeds to her lips, Miranda notices the shouting. Part of her mind had registered it moments earlier but dismissed it as insignificant. Men here were always yelling. They yelled their greetings, they yelled comments on the weather, they yelled in arguments. Miranda sometimes wondered if the entire country was hard of hearing. She had noticed several men approaching Mukhtar, who had wandered up the hill to inspect their surroundings, but again, this was not unusual. Mukhtar and the other guards often befriended the locals where they walked, talking and sharing their food.

But suddenly something sounds wrong. They all notice it at once, a sharpness of tone. As they turn their faces toward the top of the hill, Miranda hears another familiar sound: the slide and click of a rifle being cocked. A small, elderly man dressed in the standard white robe and twisted turban stands training an AK-47 on them. He waves it back and forth, screaming Arabic words that are lost to the wind, and then holds it steady. Behind him, several disciples fan out, raising their own weapons.

Instantaneously the women scramble to their feet, stuffing everything haphazardly back into their packs without speaking. They have all made the same assumption; they are trespassing and the man and his posse want them off of his land. Miranda looks up for Mukhtar. He will know what to do. The others are starting down an incline to the dusty trail, moving as fast as they can. But Mukhtar is frantically waving her back.

"We can't go," Miranda calls, interpreting her bodyguard's gestures. "They want us to go up there." More men have appeared now, spreading across the ridge.

The other women stare at her but quickly realize they have no choice. While it is counterintuitive to walk toward a group of men pointing guns to their heads, they cannot outrun bullets. Slowly, her heart shuddering through her rib cage with each beat, Miranda climbs toward the men. Perhaps Mukhtar has sorted something out. Some kind of agreement. They could just apologize and promise never to walk here again.

But when they reach the group of men, it doesn't look that way. Mukhtar is arguing with the turbaned man, who is the obvious leader of the group, and the others join in, everyone talking at once. The old man has seated himself on a rock, clutching his rifle with two hands like a walking stick. He is small, with a faceful of concentric wrinkles.

"They think you are all spies," Mukhtar tells Miranda. "And that you are here to look for treasure on their land. To look for gold."

"Gold?" echoes Miranda. "There is gold here?" Surely a country this poor didn't have secret reserves of gold.

"I told them you were all doctors," Mukhtar continues. "French doctors. But they want to know why you have a guard. Doctors don't usually have guards."

"What did you say?" Mukhtar would not have told them he was a guard. But it is fairly obvious. His fatigues, the heavy pack, the suspicious bulges under his shirt. The fact that he is the only Mazrooqi man with a group of foreign women.

"That your company requires you to have a guard."

Miranda hardly has time to assess the situation before Mukhtar takes her arm and leads her directly toward the old man on the rock. "Mira, let me introduce you," he says. Mukhtar is the only one of the guards who calls her Mira, mimicking Finn. He knows she speaks some Arabic. This is his attempt to humanize me, she thinks. She has no time to become nervous.

"*Salaam aleikum,*" she says, looking the old man in the eyes. He won't look back at her. His greenish eyes are hard and remote, trained on the air above her right shoulder. He does not return her greeting. The silence closes cold fingers around her heart. Never, since she arrived in this country, has anyone ever failed to respond to this greeting with "*aleikum salaam.*" Every Arab knows that a person who refuses to return this greeting intends harm.

"She said '*salaam aleikum*' to you," Mukhtar prompts the silent old man in Arabic. "Respond to her. Show some respect."

Avoiding the sheikh's eyes, Miranda stares at the gold paisleys on his turban. *Paisleys.* Which she associates with hippies, with peace. The old man mumbles something under his breath, clinging tightly to his gun. The countryside around her falls away. The rocky hills, the puffs of dust rising from the trails, the spiky shoots of aloe plants fade from her periphery. There is only this man before her.

"*Kayf halak?*" Miranda continues. How are you? No response. "I am a friend," she tells him in Arabic. "I want no problems."

"She's a *woman,*" says Mukhtar, just in case the man has missed this fact. She is, after all, dressed in men's clothing, with the baseball cap covering her hair.

Their entreaties are ignored. When Miranda looks again in the man's eyes, her fear grows. His eyes absorb nothing; he cannot *see* her. They are the blind, decided eyes of a lunatic set on an irrevocable path. Miranda is not a woman to him. She is not even human.

The man begins shouting at Mukhtar again, and Miranda cannot understand what he is saying. As Mukhtar murmurs placatingly, she looks around for the other women. They are huddled a bit farther down the hill, inching away from the confrontation. A willowy young man, not more than eighteen, stands next to the sheikh, his AK-47 pointed at their heads. Slowly, Miranda steps away from Mukhtar and the men, toward the women.

"We're all French," Doortje whispers to her. The two women had tried to pick a benign nationality, a country less hated than America. A language they all spoke.

"That's what Mukhtar told them," said Miranda. "Thank god."

She keeps her eyes on the men and their guns. There are a dozen of them now, all in white *thobes*, like angels in a school Christmas pageant. Bloodthirsty angels. She counts them again. There is one on the ridge above, one standing protectively at the sheikh's shoulder, five in a knot at the top of the hill engaged in fierce debate, and five arranged around the periphery like the points of a star.

She cannot make sense of the situation. What do the men want? Surely they don't want to kill them for trespassing? Do they really think they are spies? Will they search them? And when they find nothing, will they let them go? Or are they among the fanatics who loathe all Westerners and want them dead? Is this what happened to the group kidnapped up north? The whole thing is surreal. Is it possible that all these men want are government concessions of some kind? A few tribesmen sprung from jail? Or are these men—at least their leader—simply crazy? Crazy men with guns. The thought is not comforting.

We still have phones, she realizes. She can call Finn, if she can get a signal out here. She has no idea what he can do to help, but she has to let him know what is happening. She puts her hand into her front pocket, searching for her phone. But it is gone. "My phone," she says aloud. "My phone is gone." She must have dropped it near the old man, but she is not eager to return to him to search for it.

She stands there thinking what a ridiculous way this would be to die. To be shot—on purpose or even accidentally, given the very casual way the men are handling their weapons—by crazy men who think they are spies. The thought that her selfish desire for exercise and fresh air could deprive Cressida of a mother and Finn of a wife nauseates her. How could she have been so careless with her life, with theirs? It was all well and good to be bold and free when she was single, but now there are people who need her, people for whom she is responsible.

These thoughts take less than a millisecond to fly through her mind while she searches all her pockets again for her phone. The other two women stand close, cracking nervous jokes. Neither is panicking, no one is in tears.

Mukhtar is suddenly at her side. "They want you to walk toward that house," he says, pointing to a stone structure across the valley.

"No," Miranda says reflexively. "Not into a house." For some reason she feels that would be the end of them, to enter an enclosed structure. As long as they stay outside, there are escape routes. Still, inspired by the approach of several rifle barrels, the three women begin to slowly shuffle in the direction indicated.

Miranda's hands continue to fruitlessly search her pockets.

"Here," whispers Doortje. "Use mine." She slips Miranda her phone. Turning away from their captors, Miranda flips it open. Thank god she has memorized Finn's number. With shaking fingers, she dials. *Please pick up*, she silently pleads. *Please pick up*. It isn't easy to reach him during the workday. He is often in meetings, and his cell phone doesn't work in the embassy.

But Finn answers immediately. "Sweetheart?" she says, weak with relief. "We're in trouble."

"What's happened?" His voice is steady and alert.

"There are men with guns who have us, they are trying to corral us somewhere—" She struggles to string words together in a way that makes sense.

"Where are you?"

She turns to Kaia. "Do you know where we are?"

Kaia takes the phone and gives Finn directions to the beginning of their hike. But they have been walking into the mountains for more than two hours, and they don't know exactly where they are. Finn asks to speak with Mukhtar. Miranda looks up. Mukhtar is still arguing with the men. She isn't sure she should interrupt. "We'll call you back," she tells Finn.

"I'm ringing the Minister of the Interior," he says. "We'll find you. Tucker knows your route." How could Miranda allow herself to become hysterical when he is so calm? It's as if she has called to give him the weather report or ask what he would like for dinner. Just hearing his voice steadies her.

The tallest man in white moves slowly down the ridge toward them, never lowering his weapon. Mukhtar leaves the group of men and joins them.

"Do not worry, Miranda," he says cheerfully. "You will be okay. You will be okay even if I have to give my life."

"Thank you, Mukhtar, but I hope that is not necessary." Miranda smiles at him. "Would you talk with Finn?" She hits redial and hands him the phone.

A shot suddenly explodes the air by her head. Miranda didn't see who fired it or from what direction it came. But she is facing Mukhtar, and she sees the expression of surprise on his face as a red bloom spreads across his cheek. His ear is gone, the phone gone. Slowly, with a helpless look at Miranda, he crumples to the ground. She stares at him in horror.

"*Yalla!*" a man yells at them. The man in white is behind them now, indicating with his rifle the direction they are to walk. "*Yalla, ilal bait,*" he says. Miranda cannot move her legs. Her knees fold beneath her and she reaches for Mukhtar, touching his face. His cheek is damp and warm. "*Sadeeqee,*" she says. My friend.

Part Two

JANUARY 2007
Miranda

Struggling with several bags of produce, she had turned a corner onto a nameless cobblestone street of the Old City as twilight approached and nearly knocked Finn over. He was just standing there, a still island in the river of humanity swirling past him, conversing with a Mazrooqi in fatigues. Small boys steered their wheelbarrows of mangoes around him with snorts of annoyance and shadowy women shrank toward the limestone walls of the surrounding houses. In a city of white-robed men, he wore a navy pin-striped suit with a sunflower tie. He was hard to miss.

Miranda had been walking with her eyes to the ground, both to avoid the gaze of the men and to keep from breaking an ankle on the uneven stones. The five plastic bags she was carrying, bulging with the heavy orbs of pomegranates, onions, tomatoes, and oranges, had started to cut into the skin of her wrists, and she was eager to get home.

Just in time she saw Finn in her path, though one of her bags, carried forward by momentum, swung wide and hit him in the leg, causing the man next to him to jump and fidget with something underneath his jacket.

"So sorry," she said, curious as to who would choose to shop the Old City markets in a pin-striped suit. "I hope you don't bruise easily."

He laughed. "Actually, I get lost easily, which is why I'm standing in your way. Do you have any idea where I might find the silver souq? I'm looking for a gift." He spoke in English. *English* English, though she thought he'd been speaking Arabic with the man beside him when she socked him with a pomegranate.

"It's kind of impossible to give you directions. There aren't any street names." He looked disappointed. "But I could show you? If you're willing to follow me into the labyrinth?"

"Only if you promise to lead me back out again."

"Call me Ariadne."

"Somehow that's not entirely reassuring."

"Theseus made it out okay."

"But he was such a horrid man in the end. It always made me sad, that story."

It made him *sad*? Greek myths made him *sad*? What kind of man goes around confessing something like that? She liked him already.

Miranda glanced at the Mazrooqi man standing at Finn's left shoulder, who was frowning at her. The intensity of his gaze sent a slight shiver down her back.

"Was I interrupting? You were talking—"

"Oh no, Mukhtar is just . . . He's . . . Well, we have plenty of time to talk. Don't worry about him."

Miranda shifted the bags in her hands and took a step forward. "This way." For a moment they walked in silence, Miranda aware of Mukhtar's presence just behind them.

"Forgive my rudeness," he finally said. "I'm Finn."

"Miranda. Tour guide to the stars."

He smiled. "I'm hardly a star."

"Normal people don't walk around with a bodyguard. Even here."

"Um, *bodyguards*, actually. I think I've got ten with me today."

Miranda glanced around them, but Mukhtar was the only one she could identify. "They must be good," she said.

"Oh, they are."

Miranda turned to study him for a moment. Curly, honey-brown hair, hazel eyes, dimples in both cheeks. "So. Do-gooder film actor, Russian oligarch, or the foreign minister of a Western country?"

"Nothing so thrilling, I'm afraid."

Miranda waited for a moment, but he didn't say anything more. "Come on, you're really not going to tell me?"

"And lose my air of mystery? Never."

"Do you want to actually get to the silver souq, or be left to wander a maze of twisty little passages until the end of time?"

He paused to consider this. "I'm just trying to avoid being written off as boring and stuffy before we've had a chance to talk."

"You have your chance to talk right now. I'll give you until we find your gift, but I'm not leading you home until you tell me who you are."

"Done. That is, if you'll do the same."

"The same?"

"Tell me who you are."

She smiled. "I don't want to be written off as Bohemian and flaky before we've had a chance to talk."

"Fair enough. So. Talk."

She took him the long way. The streets of the Old City were such a maze that he'd never know. She just didn't want the conversation to be over. Her bags were no longer heavy and her exhaustion had lifted, leaving her buoyant and breezy.

"Did you know that the entire Old City is carved out of the same chunk of rock? If you were a giant you could just pick the whole thing up and use it as a centerpiece for your dining room table."

"Or a playhouse for the kids."

"More like a play city."

"I wonder how long it took them. To chisel every one of these." Finn reached out to touch the cold wall next to him. On every side rose similar buildings, tall and immovable.

"Generations. Generations of people who didn't feel the need to see it finished in their lifetime."

"How did we lose that kind of patience, I wonder."

Miranda shrugged. "That's one reason I loathe modern architecture. So rushed. It's all gone downhill since the Romans, in my opinion. I look at this, this million-year-old *sculpture* of a city, and then look at the new condominiums and McMansions outside of town and I think, This is *progress*?"

"I take it you like it here."

"This city has ensorcelled me. So much that I don't seem to be able to leave." What could possibly lure her from a home in a living work of art? She was in awe of a culture that could create this. Mazrooq had its flaws, but it had created this—and preserved it.

"You have rather old-fashioned tastes."

"Medieval," she agreed. "Though not when it comes to politics."

"What politics would those be?"

"Surely you don't want to ruin the afternoon?"

As they walked, Miranda greeted several people she knew: neighbors, grocers, professors from the local university.

"You've obviously lived here awhile."

"Nearly three years."

"On your own?"

"Not even a single bodyguard."

"Very brave."

"I'm very unimportant."

"You must be important to someone."

"Not anymore." Not since Vícenta left, not really.

So engrossed was she in talking with Finn that it took her half a dozen turns before she realized that she kept seeing the same men at intersections. They wore no uniform but were all in pants and long-sleeved shirts and jackets, not the traditional *thobe*, and they carried suspiciously bulky backpacks. A few stayed ahead of them, sometimes just a few steps ahead, and sometimes they would vanish into the crowd only to reappear at the next turning. Since she was leading Finn, she wondered how they knew where she was going. Mukhtar stayed by Finn's side the entire time. Several others seemed to be following them. She admired the grace of their choreography.

When they ducked into Miranda's favorite stall in the silver souq, Finn took over, chatting easily and fluently in Arabic with the diminutive shopkeeper, asking questions about the jewelry, the city, the weather. He looked oversized in the tiny, dark stall, having to fold himself nearly in half to avoid knocking his head on the ceiling. Miranda marveled at his ability to charm, even from this awkward posture; after a few minutes the shopkeeper dove through a curtain of jangling plastic beads into the back room and emerged with two small glasses of tea and a plate of cookies. "You seem at home here," she said, sipping her tea.

Finn smiled, fingering a string of beads. "I'm at home everywhere."

After she had helped him pick out a silver-and-coral necklace and matching earrings for his aunt, he asked where she lived. She gestured through a stone arch, down a narrow alley in the general direction of her house. "You take a left there, then veer right at the bakery, take two more lefts, a right, and then at the square with the best *fasooleah* in town, you turn left again and go straight until you see the blue gate with the bougainvillea climbing over it. You're welcome to come along for tea."

She hadn't meant to invite him home, but the words slipped out. Could you even invite a man with ten bodyguards home for tea? She wasn't sure. Would they all come too? She would need a bigger teapot.

"I'm afraid I can't. I've got a national day of some sort tonight that I am afraid I can't get out of. Perhaps another time? Look." He searched his coat pockets. "Here's my card. I've only been here a week, so I'm sure there's plenty more you could tell me. You are, after all, the only person who has managed to infiltrate my security team to get close enough to wound me."

"I didn't wound you; the pomegranate did. You know weapons aren't properly regulated here. Besides, you aren't limping."

"I'm limping on the inside. I'd better be off; the guys are starting to get twitchy." He gave her his hand, warm, thin-fingered, and dry, and vanished into the crowd.

Miranda looked down at the card in her hand. FINN FENWICK, BRITISH AMBASSADOR.

No one was home when she got there. "Madina?" she called. "Mosi?" Nothing. No one. Good. She put on the teakettle and tipped her bags of produce out onto the counter. The pomegranates were fat and yellow, a shiny blush of pink staining their sides. She rolled one under her palm, feeling the nubs of seeds pushing through the skin. If Madina were home, she would be tempted to tell her about Finn, and Miranda wanted to keep him all to herself for a little while longer.

Ever since Vícenta left, her home had become a kind of hostel for lost and wandering souls. She didn't plan it that way. She had always loved living alone; she wasn't looking for housemates. They just kind of showed up, like stray kittens. Now she can't imagine life without friends wandering in and out of her house all day and night.

She had met Madina at the gym. It was a women's gym up in the ritzier part of town, and it was Miranda's first (and last) visit. Gyms hadn't exactly caught on in this country, and the few that existed outside of the luxury hotels were minimally equipped. She had tried the bicycle and the rowing machines, both of which were broken, before ending up on one of the two treadmills. They were the only things in the gym that worked, aside from a vibrating platform that one of the staff members told her would jiggle off fat.

She was mid-run, watching with great interest a heavy woman standing on the platform, the folds of her thighs flapping up and down as it vibrated, when Madina climbed onto the treadmill opposite. Even had she not been directly in Miranda's line of vision, she would have been hard to miss. Her thick black hair wasn't covered but pulled back in a ponytail. She was very dark, espresso rather than cappuccino, with dramatic cheekbones and enormous eyes. She was beautiful. But that wasn't the first thing Miranda noticed. No, the first thing she noticed was that the girl was wearing a form-fitting black T-shirt emblazoned with the words I AM A VIRGIN (this is an old T-shirt) in white. Which isn't something you see every day on the streets of this or any other Muslim city.

She spoke to Miranda first. "How do you work this thing?" she said in flawless English. "I don't really do exercise."

"You're at a gym," Miranda pointed out. "Exercise is kind of what it's *about*. That platform aside," she said, waving at the vibrating woman.

The girl laughed. "I thought maybe it would be a good place to meet some girls. I don't know anyone." Miranda briefly recalled a

time when she too visited gyms in the hopes of meeting girls but suspected this girl's intentions were less salacious. Still, you never knew.

Panting slightly (the city was eight thousand feet above sea level,
so even minimal exertion resulted in panting), Miranda told her how
to set the controls on her machine and introduced herself.

"Madina," the girl said. "As in the Arabic word for city."

She was nineteen and had arrived just nine days ago from her
home in Kenya, where she lived with her Somali mother and Italian
father. At the moment she was renting a room from a family in the
Old City, but living with Mazrooqis was cramping her style. "I just
want to have some fun," she said. Which wasn't the usual reason
people come to Mazrooq. But, she quickly added, "I also came to
learn a little more about Islam. Or at least that's how I convinced my
parents." She had started attending classes at a local university, which
already bored her. "The teachers are kind of a pain. So serious! And
what's with all the black? At least we African Muslims have a bit of
style. As long as we cover our hair it doesn't matter what color we
wear."

She spoke like an American teenager, though she had never lived
outside of Africa. She spoke Swahili, Somali, Italian, Arabic, and
English, all fluently. Which made Miranda feel rather half-witted for
knowing only English, French, and basic Arabic. Americans were so
pathetic about languages.

They left the gym together, Madina's scandalous T-shirt now hidden under the voluminous folds of an *abaya*, and Miranda scribbled
down her phone number and rough directions to her house. Without
street names in the Old City, you had to use the ubiquitous mosques
as guideposts.

Two days later she came home from the swimming pool at the
InterContinental to find a note from Mosi, a Kenyan friend who
worked for the Ministry of Education and who had moved in soon
after Vicenta left. "Just to let you know, we seem to have acquired a
cat," he wrote, "and a teenage daughter."

Madina had discovered the white fluff ball of a kitten limping
on the streets outside of their house. "She's little," she pleaded to

Miranda. "She won't take up too much space." The kitten was small enough to fit in the center of Madina's dusky palm.

"That's not what I'm worried about." The Old City was crawling with stray cats, almost all of whom were mangy and riddled with disease. This innocent-looking kitten could be carrying enough bacteria and viruses to kill them all.

"Could I at least fix her paw? I'll give her a bath first!"

Miranda thought about what would happen to the kitten back on the streets. Muslims do not keep household pets, which was one reason the country overflowed with stray animals. But it wasn't just that the local children didn't keep animals at home; they seemed to openly loathe them. How many times had she stopped to yell *"Ayb!"* (shame) at a boy throwing rocks at a cat or whipping a dog with a stick? Torturing animals was a popular local hobby. She often wondered what this suggested about how the children themselves were treated at home.

Relenting, she watched as Madina tenderly lathered the mewling kitten in the kitchen sink with one of Miranda's self-imported organic, nontoxic soaps. With its fur slicked down, it was hardly bigger than a mouse. After fluffing it dry with a spare washcloth, Madina held the kitten still while Miranda examined its back left paw. A shard of glass was wedged into it. Using her tweezers, she carefully extracted it and then rinsed the wound.

"That kitten still needs a vet," she said. These were not easy to find. Once a year a man at the British embassy brought a vet in from Dubai to treat expat animals, as there were so few qualified locals. But she let the kitten—and the girl—stay.

Madina, Mosi, and Qishr the cat (named after the Mazrooqi drink made from cardamom and the husks of coffee beans) were often joined by students, poets, and diplomatic interns passing through for a month or three. Yet the house never felt crowded. Not only was it plenty big enough to accommodate them all but they were all so busy they were rarely home. Miranda was there most often, because she worked at home, in the airy *diwan* that made up her top floor. Boy-crazy Madina was out nearly every night with a series of Lebanese, Palestinian, Egyptian, Mazrooqi, and Syrian men. They

went to the city's sole nightclub in the basement of the InterContinental, took all-night drives to the beaches of the South, and threw
impromptu parties at their homes. Rare was the night she did not
come home in love. "I didn't even know there *was* a nightlife here until
you moved in," Miranda told her. She worried over Madina's safety,
but Madina assured her they were all gentlemen; she remained a virgin. And then Madina adopted Mosi as her protector. Every evening
she would model her spangled skirts and tight jeans for him, solicit-
ing his advice, before dragging him out of the house with her. That
she actually got him to leave was impressive; Mosi loathed nightclubs
and preferred to keep his own company. But he loved Madina, taking
a fatherly interest in her well-being. At first, they had invited Miranda
along as well, but she always begged off so that she could work while
the house was empty. It was also the only time she could pay serious
attention to her students' artwork.

The house was peaceful now. The kettle had boiled, and Miranda
poured the water over a cup of green tea leaves and sat down at the
kitchen table. They had only two hard plastic chairs, but on the rare
occasions that there were more than two people in the kitchen, they
sat on the counter or the floor.

Miranda wondered how long she should wait before e-mailing
Finn. Three days? The same number of days she used to wait in Seattle before calling someone she'd met at a party? A ridiculous waste of
three days, really. She would have Googled "how to invite an ambassador for tea" or something like that if she'd had Internet access. But
she did not have Internet access. Wireless did not exist yet in the Old
City, and what little wiring could be strung up in these impenetrable
houses could not be trusted even to keep the lights on for an entire
evening.

To check e-mail Miranda had to walk out of the Old City to
a grimy little Internet café in Shuhadā' Square. She didn't do this
very often. Squeezing in between two adolescent boys both covertly
downloading porn was not her idea of a good time. Every Internet
shop in the country was like this, with the young men doing their best
to hide their illicit searches from each other, shrinking the images of
copulating couples until they were tiny figures in the corners of their

screens. Still, Miranda didn't have to look hard to figure out what they were. All of the fevered and covert behavior around her made it kind of hard to focus on writing to family. Mostly she wrote letters at home and then uploaded them at the café from a flash drive, as quickly as possible.

Why was she so interested in this man anyway? She had no ambassador fetish—the few she had met were terribly worthy and dull—and, well, he was a *man*. Not that she hadn't fallen in love with men before, but not often, and it had been a while. Six years at least. Not since she met Vicenta.

It was, in fact, three days before she managed to get herself to the Internet café to write to Finn. Whether that was due to ambivalence about jumping off this particular cliff or a simple lack of time was anybody's guess. Miranda must have done a passable job with her note, as he wrote her back about seven minutes later to see if she might be free for tea the next day. She replied to say she was, pretty much any day, and would he like to have tea at her place? After all, Finn was new to the country, and had the misfortune of living outside of the Old City.

The next morning, before Miranda had even managed her first cup of coffee, "the guys" or "the team," which was how Finn referred to his bodyguards, arrived at her gates to do a "recce." Miranda's fogged brain puzzled over what *recce* was short for. Reconnaissance? Was that it? Somehow that seemed an odd word to have applied to her beloved home. She panicked when she saw them at her door, worried they would search her rooms and find the paintings. But they merely knocked politely at the gate, made sure the address was correct, glanced around her courtyard, and vanished. Finn arrived several hours later.

Turned out she needn't have worried about the teapot. The guys stayed outside in the courtyard (and at the top of her street, the bottom of her street, and across her street. There may even have been some at a neighbor's window).

"Do you have a curfew?" Miranda asked nervously, peering out one of her tiny slot windows.

"Yes. I absolutely must be at the embassy by seven thirty in the morning."

"Hmm," she said, noting with a glance at her phone that it was only 5:00 p.m.

"I know," he said sadly. "It doesn't give us much time. But I'm free Thursday too."

Miranda laughed. "We haven't even sat down yet! How do you know you'll want to see me again Thursday?"

"I know," he said simply, smiling. "I just know."

So DID SHE. She'd known since the second the pomegranate rebounded and she looked up to meet his eyes. She didn't believe in love at first sight, but apparently you don't have to believe in it for it to happen. The funny thing was, it wasn't merely that kind of physical chemistry buzzy thing that had happened with so many of her previous loves, including Vicenta. It was a calmer, quieter thing, saying *not* (or rather, not *only*) "I want to throw this man down on the pavement and have my way with him" but rather "I want to be doing crossword puzzles with this man on Sunday mornings thirty years from now." That kind of thing. On top of the buzziness.

There was something else that set Finn apart from her previous lovers. She had chosen him. For so long she had simply allowed herself to be chosen. There had been hardly any space in between her romantic entanglements. As soon as one ended, she had always told herself that she needed time alone, needed time to be free. But it never happened. She'd be at a St. Patrick's Day parade and suddenly find herself dancing with a firefighter in an Irish bar. Or she'd be doing volunteer work painting schools and a skinny girl with a shy smile would invite her to her art studio. People kept happening to her.

Granted, she kept letting them in. Miranda had always been more of a why-not? kind of person than a why? kind of person. So when she met someone who was attractive, bright, kind, and slightly eccentric, she couldn't find a reason *not* to get involved. Which was why after Vicenta left she had striven to keep herself unattached for nearly two years, aside from a few minor flings. Solitude, it turned out, was wonderful. She loved not having to report her whereabouts to anyone. She loved eating alone in her kitchen with a book. She loved sketching in her *diwan* over the first cup of coffee of the day. It was an entirely new kind of freedom.

But Finn she chose. She chose him when she led him the long way through the Old City so that they'd have longer to talk. She chose him when she invited him home. She wanted to keep choosing him.

AUGUST 9, 2010
Finn

Cressida is hot and restless in his arms, squirming against his thin T-shirt. She is dressed for bed, in her blue flannel pajamas and fleecy sleep sack. It still gets cold at night, especially in this vast marble-floored monstrosity of a house. Numbly, Finn had somehow managed the bath and bedtime stories. They'd read *Ferdinand*, *Dear Zoo*, and *Giraffes Can't Dance*. Nothing that mentions a mummy. He is thankful for the routine of lifting his daughter into the bath, pouring water over her curls, and rubbing the flannel lightly over her back and bottom. Usually he sings, but that was the one thing he couldn't do tonight. He'd tried, as he brushed her eight tiny teeth and smoothed the lavender lotion over her fat little thighs, but his voice had cracked and died.

He is trying to get her to drink. Along with everything else, he'd panicked over what to give her before bed, without Miranda there to nurse her to sleep. But thank god for diplomatic connections. He'd rung one of the German dads from Cressie's playgroup in desperation, and less than an hour later he had several canisters of imported powdered formula. It wasn't long before Cressie could have cow's milk, he thought, but he couldn't remember the exact age. Miranda has always done Cressida's meal planning. She insists on whole grains, vegetables, and as much organic food as they can import in overstuffed suitcases. She would never have let Cressie drink the milk here. There is hardly any fresh milk available; they drink only the long-life milk that comes in boxes. "By the time Cressie is old enough for cow's milk, we'd better be living somewhere that has organic dairy or I'm buying a cow," she said.

Once he had the formula, Finn couldn't remember whether he was supposed to mix it with boiled tap water or with bottled water. Miranda had said something about bottled water being bad for babies, too high in minerals or fluoride or something. His mind raced now, trying to recall her words, her directions. Why hadn't he paid better attention?

He finally opted for the bottled water, sure that whatever was wrong with it couldn't be worse than the local tap water.

But Cressida isn't having it. Apparently sharing her mother's militant aversion to formula, she spits out the teat every time he tries to press it between her lips. Pushing the bottle away with both hands, she burrows her damp head into his armpit and wails. *"Mummy mummy mummy!"* Her small fingers claw at his chest, pulling down the collar of his shirt.

"You won't find what you're looking for there, sweetheart," he says softly, rocking her. She opens and closes her mouth like a fish, catching the cotton of his shirt. He tries again with the bottle, but it only makes her cry harder. How is he going to get her to sleep if she won't drink her milk? How long will it take her to dehydrate if she keeps refusing her bottle? He catches himself. If she gets thirsty enough, she'll drink. She already takes water with her meals, doesn't she? She'll be fine. Even with no milk, she'll be fine. He lifts her to his shoulder and stands. Walking from room to room, switching out lights as he goes, he finds he is able to hum. And nearly forty-five minutes later, when he has hummed "Scarborough Fair" at least a dozen times, her sobs subside and she drifts off to sleep against the rumble of his chest.

Downstairs, Negasi, Teru, and Desta are huddled in the basement bedrooms they use occasionally after late dinner parties and before early breakfasts, refusing to leave Finn alone in the house. They had wept and hugged his rigid body. He was unable to respond, except by awkwardly patting their warm backs as if it were they in need of comfort. The dinner plates of *hammour* and creamed spinach, the potatoes and rhubarb crumble, meant for the EU ambassadors, were stacked in rows in the refrigerators, uneaten.

Gently, Finn lays Cressida down in her cot and stands looking at her. At least she isn't old enough to understand what has happened. She isn't old enough for him to have to explain. Still, she is old enough to be devastated by the absence of her mother.

The first twenty-four hours are the most vital in a kidnap, as he knows all too well. If the victim—*god*, can he really think of Miranda as a victim? She just isn't the victim type—isn't found in the first twenty-four hours, the chances of finding her diminish rapidly. He's been working all evening, pulled constantly between the urgency of finding Miranda and his desire to comfort his daughter. But even the frenetic activity hasn't been able to stifle the intrusive thought that somehow this is fitting punishment. Doesn't he deserve this? Hasn't he been waiting for seven years for this particular darkness to catch up with him? He had been careful—painfully, lonesomely careful—for so long. Until he met Miranda. Still, if he deserves this, surely Miranda doesn't. Some people might call—and no doubt have called—her past checkered, but he would call it honest. She loved fiercely and freely, without thought of consequence. And she fit an awful lot of people into that tough little heart of hers. "I don't understand this societal obsession with one true love," she said. "How can we be so small-minded? Don't we have things to learn from many loves?" She hadn't tried to hide anything from him. She refused to live a lie. This is what he loves most, and what frightens him the most.

But it never occurred to him he could lose her like this. It was supposed to have been him. This is why he has ten bodyguards; he is the target. The FCO hadn't even been sure that Miranda needed close protection at all. What were they thinking? If an ambassador was a target, surely his wife was at an equal risk? Why has this not occurred to anyone? He cannot stop hearing that shot. It was all he heard. He doesn't know who dialed the phone that second time, Miranda or Mukhtar or someone else. He had answered and heard only the blast of a rifle and some muffled noise before the phone had been shut off. It could have been a warning shot, he constantly reminds himself. The shot itself does not necessarily mean that someone is dead. He cannot contemplate that. Cannot begin to contemplate anything so final.

THE ENTIRE EMBASSY has been mobilized. Tucker and the team set out with both armored cars as soon as the call came in, driving to the area where the cars were parked and fanning out from there along the route the women had taken. Finn had demanded to go with them, but Tucker was unmoving on the topic. "With all due respect, sir, the last thing we need is the distraction of looking after you while we're trying to find her. Not to mention the fact that I cannot knowingly drive you into danger." Tucker could not forgive himself. If only he hadn't allowed Miranda to go. If only he had personally gone with her. He and the men had walked for hours without finding a trace of the women. None of the locals they questioned had seen them. How was that possible? Someone must have seen them. A group of Western women was not inconspicuous, no matter how modestly they were dressed. Mukhtar's radio seems to be working, but no one answers it.

Finn had spent part of the evening meeting with ministers and local police officers, while Leo, his defense attaché, worked with the local military. None of these meetings has filled him with confidence. But he hasn't stopped moving, hasn't stopped calling and organizing and brainstorming strategies. He has not broken down, has not wept, has not delegated any of his duties. It occurs to him that Alastair and the others have only just landed back in the UK. Will they now return? He isn't sure. Sometimes they send different men. Or women. There are women officers these days, though Finn hasn't met too many of them.

Cressie rolls onto her stomach, her right arm curling around Corduroy and dragging him underneath her body. Her right cheek presses against her cot mattress, her bottom in the air. She breathes so quietly that Finn has to lean close to her face to reassure himself that she, at least, is still living. He cannot bear the thought of walking out of this room. To leave this room is to return to the echoing emptiness of the rest of the house. To the devastating tidiness of Miranda's side of the bed. To thinking. And to work.

JUNE 7, 2007
Miranda

It looked *just* like a light switch: a small white plastic square set into the wall next to the bed. The room was dim, and Miranda was tired. So how was she to know? It was Thursday, the start of the Mazrooqi weekend, but Finn had gone into the embassy to finish up some work, leaving her slumbering. She had not woken up in this room very many times, and never alone. So when she slid from the sheets to stand, her sleepy fingers fumbled for the nearest switch, and pushed. A short, piercing beep was the only response. The room stayed dark. That didn't bode well. She stood naked next to the bed, puzzled. But hearing no further noises, she made her way downstairs in search of lime juice. There was no point in getting dressed. She was alone in the house and it was warm. Besides, there was something a little thrilling about walking naked down such an elegant staircase, in a house usually bustling with overdressed people.

Her cell phone rang before she was back upstairs. "Sweetheart, are you all right?" Finn, sounding out of breath, phoning from the embassy.

"I'm fine," she said, setting the glass of pale green juice down on the table next to the bed before she spilled it. "Why?"

"One of the house panic alarms has gone off—"

"Oh no . . ." Her stomach started to curl into itself.

"Did you hit an alarm?"

"Well, um, it looked *just* like a light switch . . ." She wondered how much trouble she was in.

"Well, Tucker is on his way over to reset the alarms, so let him in. Probably useful for you to know anyway."

"I'm really sorry. But you might have mentioned it was an alarm; it really looked so much like—"

"It's all right, but six armed men are about to break down the front door, so you might want to get downstairs."

"Oh god, I'm not dressed!" Just then the house phone began to ring, and she heard a pounding on the front door. "I have to go!"

"Go, go. They are just going to want to check the house, so let them do that."

"Okay, okay. Shit, I'm really sorry."

She put the phone down and reached for the closest things she could find to put on, a green Indian blouse and black skirt left on an armchair. Pulling the blouse over her belly as she ran down the stairs, she reached the bottom just as the front door flew open and several dark men with machine guns stormed the front hall. Immediately, they moved toward the living room and kitchen, their eyes searching the upstairs balcony for intruders. A rosy-cheeked British man with short-cropped blond hair led the team of invaders. This must be Tucker. She hadn't met him yet; he had arrived in Mazrooq only recently, to take over the training of Finn's close protection team. Hell of a way to introduce herself: her clothes wrinkled and twisted around her body, her corkscrew curls standing out from her head in every direction, her face still creased from sleep. And obviously too dim-witted to know what a panic button was. She had so hoped that they'd get along.

"I am so, so sorry!" she said. "I'm afraid this is all my fault."

"No worries!" Tucker smiled at her, his blue eyes still glancing around the house. "At least this way I finally get to meet you. You must be Mira."

"How did you guess?"

"Tucker." He shook her hand before continuing. "Actually, we've never tested that particular button, so now at least we know that it works."

"Looks that way."

"We just have to check the house anyway," he said. "In case there is someone in here making you say things."

"Okay," she said, feeling incredibly foolish. "Go ahead." Not that anyone was waiting for her permission.

He ran upstairs, and she apologized to the CP team as well, in her halting Arabic. They were kind, saying *"mafeesh mushkila"* (no problem!) before going off to search the corners of the house for terrorists. She sat down at the bottom of the long marble staircase, her head in her hands. She obviously wasn't quite prepared for her new life.

Of course, her new life hadn't really quite started. She was still in between lives, in between homes, in between security regulations. And in Finn's life, she didn't officially exist.

AUGUST 14, 2010
Miranda

It is dark when Miranda opens her eyes. Her left hip aches from lying on the earthen floor. She can feel a thin mat underneath her, but it offers no cushion. She wonders how long she has been here. How is it possible that she had actually fallen asleep? As she pushes herself up, her palms pressing into clammy grit, she feels the dampness of her shirt against her skin. Her body doesn't understand what has happened, dumbly continuing to churn out milk. She puts a hand to her breasts, lumpy and swollen under her bra. *Cressida.* Tears prick the backs of her eyes, but she wills them away. To cry would be to admit that this is real, that this isn't just another nightmare. But then the memory of the night before flashes through her in all of its horror. Could it have really happened? But even as she asks herself the question, she knows the answer. Knows that this is what she has been waiting for, ever since she met Finn. How could she have ever for a moment thought she could get away with that life? But then how stupid, how narcissistic of her to think of this as some kind of personal punishment. She isn't the only one who has been punished. Kaia and Doortje. Their husbands. Their children. Mukhtar. Even if they are alive—and they probably are, she tries to convince herself— they may still never make it home. Do the kidnappers know who they are, where they come from? France and the Netherlands generally pay ransoms, but the British and Americans do not. Is this why the other women were dragged from the truck? Why she has been separated from them? Because her homeland won't pay to get her back? While she isn't worth money to them, they could certainly use her to make a political point. *If* they know who she is. Is there anyone terrorists hate more than Americans and the British?

Her stomach drily heaves, as if she could somehow vomit out the shock and sorrow. Slowly, her arms trembling, she pulls herself into a sitting position, her back pressed against the wall of what appears to be a small stone hut. It's cold, and she reaches for the thin blanket that had been draped over her and wraps it around her shoulders. It stinks of male sweat and prickles with some kind of animal hair. She spits a mouthful of sour bile toward the wall and blinks, shapes appearing as her eyes slowly adjust to the darkness. The room is empty, save for a thin, dirt-caked carpet spread across the back. There are no windows, but through the open doorway she can see the pale light of dawn. Just inside the doorstep is a round black lump that Miranda eventually decides is a woman, sleeping. Her guard. She wonders if the woman has a gun, and decides that she doesn't. Surely the men are close enough to run to her aid should Miranda try to make a break for it.

She must try to think, but her brain is a carousel of horror and she cannot make thoughts line up in an orderly fashion. Her mouth is dry and she longs for a glass of water. What happened to her backpack? She tries to remember. There was water in her backpack. Images come to her as she sits, her head tipped back against the stones. Mukhtar, slipping to the ground. The plume, skittering away over the stones. The thin, wispy mustache of the teenager with the AK-47 who had prodded them toward that first house and later into a truck. Or what she assumes was a truck. They had all been blindfolded. The pressure in her breasts is distracting. Miranda reaches a hand between the buttons of her shirt and unsnaps the nursing bra to squeeze out a bit more of the milk. How long will the milk be there, undrunk, before realizing it is no longer needed? She stops herself from pursuing this line of thought. Finn will come for her, or will send someone for her. It is possible that she will be with Cressida again before her milk disappears. It is possible that her life will continue. Isn't it? After all, she is still alive now. Cressie will be distressed without her milk, but this is a relatively minor worry at the moment. Finn is there. Finn will take care of her. He will not let her go hungry. He will sing her to sleep. Miranda has faith in little else, but she has faith in this.

She refuses to think about how Cressida must feel about the absence of her mother, about how long she could be gone. The craving for Cressie's weight in her arms, her petal-soft skin against her stomach, is so fierce it steals her breath.

THEY DROVE FOR most of the night. The men had kept all of them in the small house near their picnic site until dusk, and then herded them onto the back of a truck. A tarp had been pulled over them and fastened. They hadn't spoken. It wasn't possible over the grating of the engine, the flapping of the old, slick tarp, and the wind in their ears. Frozen with terror, they had simply tried to roll close to each other, to touch as many parts of each other as possible, elbows to waists, ankles to knees, heads to shoulders. It was cold, unbearably cold, in that truck after the others were gone.

She doesn't know in which direction they had traveled. They could have gone west, into the mountains, or north, toward the rugged rebel-held province, or east, toward that vast empty desert. Had they gone through the mountain pass, that treacherous gateway to the North? It is possible. It had been freezing in the truck. She doesn't think they have gone south. At some point they had been handed over to different men. She knows this because the voices changed, because the man commanding her into this hut last night was not the man who led her to that first house. There are dark implications to this handover. Implications she doesn't yet feel strong enough to contemplate.

As the sky grows brighter, she inches toward the door to peer out. But when she moves, the woman in the doorway rustles and abruptly sits. She wears both a *hijab* and *niqab*, so her face is almost completely obscured. It is too dark to see her eyes. *"Sabah al-kheer,"* she says, straightening her *abaya* around her.

"Sabah anoor." Miranda is so surprised by the cordial greeting that she responds automatically.

"Feyn ana?" she says. Where am I?

The woman makes a clicking sound with her mouth and shakes her finger back and forth. *No no no.* She follows this with a torrent of Arabic too fast for Miranda to comprehend. Miranda's Arabic is nearly conversational, but only if it is spoken slowly and clearly. Finally, she recognizes a phrase.

"*Ana Aisha*," the woman says.

"Like the wife of the Prophet," Miranda says, holding out her hand. "*Ana*." She pauses. Surely she shouldn't use her real name? "*Ana Celeste*," she says. It is the first name to come to her.

"*Antee Francia?*" says the woman, ignoring her hand. You are French?

Miranda responds a second too slowly. Is that what they had decided? Are the French really hated less than the Brits and the Americans? Figuring that pretty much no one is hated more than the Americans, she finally nods. "*Aiwa*." Yes. Then, too late, she remembers that French nationality hadn't saved her friends.

"Why?" she starts in Arabic. "My friends, why were they taken away?"

This provokes another indecipherable torrent of words. The woman waves her arms and makes shushing noises, so Miranda figures she had better try something more neutral. "Please," she says. "Could I have some water?" She cannot remember the last time she has had a drink. At the picnic? Were they offered anything in that terrible house? Tea, they had been offered tea. Sweet, milky tea that she had accepted gratefully. Besides, you do not turn down tea in this country. She is relieved when Aisha brings her a bottle. Tap water— should any houses nearby contain taps—would be more likely to make her sick and dehydrated than to help her.

No sooner has Miranda finished her bottle of water than she has to pee. She has had to pee for hours, actually, but now the pressure on her bladder is urgent. Aisha finally takes her outside, where Miranda blinks in the dazzling light. They're in the mountains. North or West, she imagines. There are no mountains in the East, only sand. A heavy mist still enshrouds the tops of the jagged peaks rising to either side of her. Rows of stones crisscross their lower slopes, dividing the cultivated terraces into trapezoids of tender green. Miranda doesn't instantly recognize the crop. It could be coffee, or cocoa, or even hibiscus. It's too early to tell, the shoots too young. Around the houses grow scrubby olive-green bushes. If she weren't a captive here, Miranda might even find her surroundings beautiful.

She turns to look at the small stone hut where she has been sleeping. Its roof is a sheet of corrugated tin and the door a scrap of dirty fabric. It might just as well have been built to house goats or chickens. Off to the right, several hundred feet away, are four or five similar buildings.

She doesn't see or hear anyone else. The air is still and silent. "The men?" she asks.

"Sleeping," says Aisha, pressing her palms together and resting her cheek on them, in case Miranda had not understood the word. *And the women?* she wants to add. *My friends? And Mukhtar? Is he alive?* But she couldn't bear to hear the answer.

Behind an especially thick shrub, where a small hole has been dug and obviously used regularly, Miranda pees, the warm stream sending up puffs of dust where it hits the sides of the hole. When she is finished, the woman leads her back to the small house. "We will get water," she says. "Water for breakfast." Back outside, she shows Miranda a small, empty stone cistern.

Numbly, Miranda follows Aisha's instructions while covertly pinching her blouse between her fingers to keep the damp cloth from her skin. It will dry in the sun. The older woman does not seem to have noticed her leaking breasts, the soaking shirt. Its dark color has hidden the stains. Aisha carries two large plastic jugs, and presses two more on Miranda. They are light and easy to carry now, though Miranda isn't sure how she will manage when they are full.

As Aisha leads the way down a rocky path, Miranda places her feet in the woman's footsteps. At least she's wearing sneakers. Thank god she wasn't kidnapped in heels and an evening dress, on her way to yet another national day. That is something for which she can be grateful. She wonders how far it is to water. The women of some villages spend all day fetching water, she knows from her travels as well as from listening to the various aid groups, the British Department for International Development in particular, naturally. This is a country without rivers, without lakes, without working systems for conserving rainwater. It has survived by sucking slowly away at the providentially profound underground reservoirs. But even these are finally running out, and in some places workers have to use oil-drilling equipment to reach the water. The woman shuffles down the *wadi*, her feet picking up speed. Grateful to be moving, to be conscious, to be handed responsibilities to keep her mind away from black holes of despair, Miranda follows.

JUNE 7, 2007
Miranda

After Tucker and his team finished searching the house and left, Miranda ran upstairs, peeling off the blouse and skirt. Her heart was still racing. She wasn't used to so many machine guns so early in the day. Certainly not before coffee. She had better not push any more buttons for a while. Apparently there *were* more; Finn had told her on the phone there was one above the painting of the Queen in the front hall (which the housecleaner, Desta, had set off several times with her duster), one by the bathroom, one in each guest room, one in the kitchen, and one in Finn's downstairs office. Good to know.

As was usual on a Thursday, the house was empty. She glanced around the bedroom. It was impeccably neat, aside from the tousled bedclothes and last night's sundress, which lay on the floor where she had discarded it a few minutes after arriving.

She still hadn't met the household staff—the cook, the cleaner, the housekeeper, the gardeners. Unsure as to how they would react to her spending the night, she always arrived after they left the house at 4:00 p.m. and scurried out the door before 6:00 a.m., when they began their shift. Finn had told her a little about each of them, in preparation for their eventual introduction. There was Negasi, the sturdy Residence manager–housekeeper who had worked at the house the longest, in various capacities, for at least three ambassadors; Teru, the moonfaced cook who had nearly been fired for unpalatable menus before Finn sent her off to study at one of the five-star hotels; and the clumsy but devoted housecleaner, Desta, renowned for regularly setting off the alarms. Semere and Yonas worked in the gardens. They were all Christian, which was significant because a fair amount of alcohol—which would have made Muslim staff uncomfortable—was served at the Residence.

But whom were she and Finn fooling? The staff knew when she was there. Miranda couldn't get in and out of the Residence without passing the guards—who were most certainly aware of her arrival and departure times. And no one gossips like guards. Even before she met Finn, Miranda was a member of the British Club, one of the only bars in town. One either joined the club or became a teetotaler. All gossip eventually reached the ears of the Vietnamese-Mazrooqi bartender Abdullah, who had been a frequent guest at parties she and Vicenta threw in the Old City. On Halloween he had shown up at their home in full drag under an *abaya*. "Is it true," he had whispered, "that in the US there are men who dress like this all of the time?" Having intuited the truth about her and Vicenta, he trusted her with his own secrets.

The property around the Residence was constantly monitored by closed-circuit TV, which meant the guards could zoom in on anyone on the grounds. At the end of the lawn was a pool, used by embassy staff. The guards, whose exposure to semidressed females was limited at best, were perhaps understandably excited by all the bathing-suited Brits.

"They rank them," Abdullah told Miranda. "From one to ten. Want to know who number one is?"

She did. Abdullah named a friend of hers, Sally, a tall, curvy Amazon of a woman with long dark hair who was in charge of the consular section.

"And guess who they call the Potato."

She guessed.

"It's a good thing I don't swim there," Miranda said.

"Yes, but you swim at the InterContinental, and you think those guards aren't rating women?"

Miranda sighed. Arab men, Western men, not as different as you'd think. What else did the Residence guards know about her?

She sometimes thought she was followed when she walked from

Finn's house to the Old City. The same car would pass her seven times, slowing down each time it approached. She'd finally noted its license plate, which was blue, meaning a local registration. "Do you ever send anyone to watch me?" she had asked Finn. "To make sure I get home safely?"

He'd looked puzzled. "No," he'd said. "I'm not really allowed. Do you really think you're being followed? It's not just the usual harassment?"

Miranda wasn't sure. She had grown accustomed to the constant verbal onslaught as she walked down the streets, which ranged from innocuous "I love you"s to the rather surprising (given the dearth of English spoken in the country) "suck my dick." The men here made a big show of their deep respect for their women, which they demonstrated by keeping them wrapped up and locked away at home. But for some reason this alleged respect rarely prevented them from harassing her or even her women—all of whom were completely covered—on the streets. Miranda couldn't be accused of trying to attract anyone's attention. She dressed in long skirts and long sleeves, keeping her curls knotted at the back of her head. Yet the violet-gray of her eyes was enough to invite inspection in the streets. The catcalls in her wake were the kind she might expect back home in Seattle, were she to walk down the street wearing nothing but fishnets and a sequined bikini.

Finn was still looking at her, concerned. "I can let Tucker know," he said. "He'll try to find out who it is."

Miranda shook her head. She was wary of taking advantage of Finn's resources. She'd managed here for years on her own, she could manage awhile longer. "I'm not really worried," she said. "I'm sure it's nothing."

No one at the embassy knew about their affair. It wasn't against policy, but they weren't sure how people would react. "When I first joined the Foreign Office, they gave us a lecture on romance while abroad on a posting," Finn told her one night. "They said,

'Look, you'll be meeting exciting people in all sorts of places, you're bound to play around. Just do us—and yourselves—a favor and *sleep NATO.*' So, I think we're okay."

Miranda laughed. "You only picked me so you'd be sleeping NATO?"

"I'd have picked you no matter where you were from. But then I'd have to keep you secret forever."

"You're keeping me secret now."

"Does it bother you?"

"No. Yes. I'm not sure."

"It won't be forever. It's just that I've hardly started here and I'd rather get to know people a bit better before I begin flaunting my personal life."

"Is it because of the painting thing? My women?"

"I love your painting thing. And your women."

"You haven't met them."

"I love them anyway. I love how you talk about them. I love the paintings you've shown me."

She kept her women's paintings on the fourth floor of her four-story home, where their families had no chance of finding them. No one had ever seen them but Finn. She probably shouldn't have shown them even to him. You couldn't be too careful.

MIRANDA STOOD NAKED again in the middle of the bedroom. The blinds were still drawn, though you couldn't see into the house during the daytime. Finn wouldn't be back until lunch, possibly later. She picked up the cold cup of tea he had made her before leaving and drank it in three swallows. Might as well go to the gym before the embassy people got there. It was still early enough.

The gym was just across the lawn, through a gate at the bottom of the garden. It was a modest, one-room building that housed only one treadmill, one bike, one rowing machine, one stair-climber, and a bunch of free weights. But at least everything usually worked. There was even a boom box and a stack of CDs, most of them belonging to Tucker. He trained here, often with his team. He had them on a strict routine of free weights, running, and crunches. Some mornings Miranda could hear him yelling *"As-raa!"* (faster) as the men did laps around the Residence. Tucker knew only a few Arabic words, but he made a valiant effort to use them as much as possible.

Miranda plugged in her iPod and speakers, climbed onto the treadmill, and fiddled with the buttons. All of it took getting used to. The guards, the constant guards. The absurdly oversized house. The lack of freedom. But what she found hardest of all was the happiness.

She had never been so happy. She had never been so appreciative for every single second of her life. It wasn't just Finn, although he was a major source. The happiness had begun when she moved to Mazrooq, three years ago. For the first time in her life, she had been able to paint whenever she wanted to paint. Every second of the day was hers to fill. She could while away entire afternoons over lunch with Mazrooqi friends. It still amazed her how warm everyone was, how quickly she was invited into people's homes. The Mazrooqis, for all of their weapons, were an unguarded people. Their homes and hearts swung wide open the minute they laid eyes on a stranger.

Here, there was no worrying about preparing for her classes at Cornish College or finishing her grading. There was no worry about money. Rent cost her almost nothing. Before Vicenta left, they had split the expenses of their ten-room home. Vicenta's grant money and Miranda's small savings went a long way here. A dinner of beans and bread cost a dollar. Fish might cost a couple more. Electricity and water were a few dollars a month. Her biggest expense was probably her cell phone, which still cost less than thirty dollars per month.

Living in a poor country set her free, freer than she had ever been.

Plus, with Finn there was none of the awkwardness she had always felt with other men. In the past, only with a woman had she felt her body truly unclench, the result of her politics falling in line with her heart. With men she had always been wary, monitoring every interaction for signs of a power imbalance. Loving a woman didn't carry the burden of the long history of patriarchy. It just felt easier. But then, nothing about Vicenta had been simple or easy. While she had rescued Miranda from the predictable tedium of academia, launched her into this captivating country, and prodded her work forward, Vicenta had inspired as much anxiety as ardor. Her mercurial passions had wrenched Miranda in too many directions at once.

With Finn, she felt instantly at home. It continued to surprise her, how uncomplicated everything was with him. Finn's patience and consistency allowed *her* to be the mercurial one. Nothing frightened him. When she was euphoric because her work was going well, he loved her. When she flew into an irrational fit of rage because she could not find her favorite black cardigan, he loved her. When she wept uncontrollably at the beauty of a painting in the middle of a public gallery, he loved her. Vícenta's love had always felt conditional, contingent, hazardous. Her unpredictability, her extremes, had edged Miranda toward caution and pragmatism. Someone always has to play the anchor. It was a role she had gladly handed over to Finn. With him, she could simply *be*.

There wasn't a room in the house in which they hadn't made love: the front hallway underneath the stained-glass Union Jack and the disapproving eyes of Elizabeth II, the second Finn closed the door on their last guests; the dining room, straddling a chair; the kitchen, over the cold industrial metal counter. They made a point of it. When would they ever have so many rooms at their disposal again? When in their future lives would they ever have such a luxury of space? Her desire for him still astonished her. That she could feel this for a man. Yet she did. Unmistakably, undeniably, she did.

Almost from the start of things with Finn, she had been waiting for this happiness to be taken away. She had always assumed that meeting the person with whom she wanted to spend the rest of her life would be blissful. The search was over, there would be no more broken hearts, and she would be drunk with joy. Wasn't that how she was supposed to feel? She hadn't expected the accompanying terror. The second she knew that she wanted to be with Finn for the rest of her time on Earth, an abyss opened beneath her. Not because she doubted him or worried he would leave her. Their relationship had always been—perhaps bizarrely—free from that particular worry. But because she was newly vulnerable in a way she had never experienced, in a way for which she had no preparation.

It was possible, the world being as the world is, that she could lose him. Almost anything could happen—a car accident, a heart attack, the flu. It didn't help matters that here, he was a true target. This wasn't just her morbid imagination, it was fact.

That Finn had bodyguards should have been reassuring to her, but it had the opposite effect. The fact that he had bodyguards implied that he *needed* bodyguards. Ten of them. This fact didn't create her terror, which was purely precipitated by her overwhelming love, but it fed it.

She didn't feel deserving of this happiness. She hadn't led a particularly exemplary life. She'd been self-absorbed and single and free. She'd put her passion for painting before all else—her family, her friends, her lovers, Vícenta. She wasn't cruel. She never purposefully caused anyone pain; she was kind to strangers on buses; she played with children in coffee shops when their mothers needed to use the toilet; she recycled. But she had never had to truly sacrifice anything dear to her. So how was it that she suddenly came into this happiness? Why her and not the millions of raped and tortured women of the Congo? Why her and not the Bosnian Muslims? Why her and not the millions of babies who died every year in the first few weeks of life? Did they not deserve even a small portion of this joy?

Superstitiously, she hoped that perpetual awareness of her good fortune would somehow ward off tragedy. Free from religion, she had no god to thank. Nor did she see the universe as a benevolent force that arranged things as they are meant to be. But she'd read in a science magazine that gratitude alone, whether to God, cosmic forces, a friend, or family, was enough to improve health and well-being.

Miranda was not constitutionally cheerful; her default take on the world veered toward noir. She viewed with awe her Zen-like friend Moira back in Seattle, who found reasons to be overjoyed every minute of the day. Moira stopped to smell the roses. Moira was flooded with pleasure by the sight of a bluebird, a jar of almond butter, or a stray balloon. Moira believed that everything happened for a reason. Miranda wished she could believe that, but struggle though she might, she could not manufacture faith in the bounty of the universe.

Moira was an acupuncturist, someone who believed that bad moods were simply blocked energy flows. For Miranda, bad moods were the results of reality, by-products of reading the news. Every front-page story sank into her like a voodoo needle. Every day there was another dead child, another natural disaster, another insane politician insisting that gay people could be "cured." She didn't know how not to take it all personally.

Yet the pendulum also swung the other way, filling her with a baseless euphoria that made her skip down a sidewalk, flirt with a pretty girl at a party, or dance on a bar. Her bleak worldview remained unaltered, but she experienced brief reprieves. Which is all to say that this consistent happiness was like a stiff, shiny ball gown rubbing against her tomboy's knees. She couldn't get used to wearing it. She didn't know how to properly inhabit it, how to walk in it, how to make it her own.

The first time she stayed over at the ambassadorial Residence, she'd spent the night throwing up in the marble-floored bathroom. She'd woken close to 3:00 a.m., desperately nauseated, and slipped out of bed in search of a remedy. They kept a stash of organic ginger beer in the upstairs refrigerator. Naked, she'd sat on the cold bathroom tiles clutching the sweating can. She'd been halfway through it when she started vomiting.

She wasn't ill. She had no fever, no pain, and had had only a modest dinner of carrot soup and bread. It was just, she couldn't believe that all of this, that Finn most of all, was hers.

He hadn't stirred. He slept so little that when he did drift off he committed fully to unconsciousness. In the morning when she'd told him what had happened he chastised her for not waking him. "You needed the sleep," she'd said. "And there was nothing you could have done anyway."

"I could have held your hand! Or kept your hair out of your face."

She'd laughed. "Thanks, but it really wasn't a moment for romance. I'm not in the least sad that you missed it."

HER FEET HAD been beating out a mindless rhythm on the treadmill for nearly an hour, her mind lost in a meditation on color, when the glass door of the gym slid open. The sound jolted her back from Ethiopia, where she and Vícenta had traveled during their first year here, and where they were shocked to find themselves in the dazzling palette of Africa after so many months confined to the black-and-white world of Mazrooq. Here, with women dressed as shadows of their white-robed men, any color was subdued, hidden, suppressed. But Ethiopia! Ethiopia was a revelation. She fell instantly in love with the women there, with their bare faces and their lithe bodies dressed in reds, purples, oranges, yellows, and pinks *all at once*. Every woman was a garden unto herself, in radiant full bloom. Traveling from Mazrooq to Ethiopia was like going from Kansas to Oz.

"SALAAMA ALEIKUM," CHORUSED Mukhtar and Bashir politely, looking slightly bewildered at the sight of her in a camisole and shorts. No doubt they were wondering whether to report her unauthorized use of the gym equipment—before remembering that the person to whom they would report her was most likely responsible for her presence. *"Wa aleikum asalaam,"* she said cheerfully, as if it were the most natural thing in the world for them to find her here. Only then did she realize what her iPod was blasting. *That butt you got makes me so horny* ... It was "Baby Got Back," from her *One-Hit Wonders of the '90s* album. "I can turn off the music," she offered, hoping the guards' English lessons weren't going well.

"No problem," said Mukhtar, heading for the bench press. "We like music."

Miranda kept running, praying the next song would be better. But no. *I'm too sexy for my shirt* ... Mortified, Miranda didn't know whether to turn off the music or fake ignorance of the lyrics. The men continued their bench-pressing and biceps curls, seemingly oblivious. She left it on. They didn't stay long, just another ten minutes, before slipping out to change back into uniform. Breathing a sigh of relief, Miranda upped the speed on the treadmill. And the door slid open again.

"Oh!" a female voice said.

It was Antoinette, a chubby blonde from the embassy whose job seemed to be primarily to find furniture for staff housing (Miranda hadn't realized how pedestrian most diplomatic jobs were. Most people in the embassy were not involved in politics at all; they were accountants, housing managers, or personal assistants). She'd never been particularly friendly when they'd seen each other at the club or various receptions, but then again, not many of the British staffers were. They were cliquish and kept largely to themselves, not mixing socially with the local population or even the staff of other embassies. Why be a diplomat then? Miranda had wondered. Why take a job abroad if you want to spend all of your evenings tossing back gin and tonics with your pals from the homeland? Finn was different, of course. Though comparisons were not fair, given that an ambassador had entirely different social and professional prospects from those of his staff. Finn socialized every night, either out or at home, much of it obligatory. Still, he seemed to relish spending time with his local contacts and immersing himself as much as was practical in the culture. He often dressed in a *thobe* for Mazrooqi gatherings, joining in the local dances with gusto.

But the pressing concern at the moment was that Antoinette didn't know about her and Finn. Which meant she would be wondering how Miranda had happened to get access to the gym. Think fast, Miranda urged herself, her feet suddenly getting in each other's way on the treadmill.

"Good morning!" she said brightly. She couldn't hide, so she might as well try to brazen it out. At least there was no chance that Antoinette would ask her directly what she was doing there. The Brits, in Miranda's experience, rarely communicated anything directly. (Again, Finn excepted.)

Antoinette gave a short nod and headed toward the elliptical machine.

She could lie and say that she had come with Sally, one of her few embassy friends, and that Sally had left earlier. She could say Tucker let her in. Or she could say nothing and hope Antoinette just assumed she was there legally. The less said the better, she finally concluded, reaching for the treadmill's controls.

She had increased her pace so that she was nearly sprinting, so she wanted to slow the machine before attempting to dismount. But embarrassment and panic made her clumsy. Instead of changing the speed, her swinging palm swiped the Emergency Stop key. The rubber mat of the treadmill jerked to a standstill. Miranda kept moving, catapulting headfirst over the front of the machine, her hips catching on the display console. For a nanosecond she hung there, draped over the tilted treadmill, her curls brushing the floor. But Miranda's slight form was apparently not quite substantial enough to flip the machine entirely. It slammed back to the ground, dropping her unceremoniously on her head.

Breathless from the impact, Miranda kept her eyes closed. This did not just happen, she thought. *I did not just flip myself over the handlebars of a treadmill in the embassy's gym in front of an embassy employee. A treadmill that I am not officially allowed to use without Finn around. Even I could not be this uncoordinated.*

And yet. There she was. Flat on her back with her head throbbing and her camisole riding up, showing the top of her striped cotton underwear and a strip of her naked belly.

"You all right?" The voice was polite, but not overly concerned. Antoinette hadn't paused the elliptical machine. "Do you need help? I could get off. I just didn't want to stop suddenly and . . ."

And do what you just did, Miranda silently finished for her.

"Oh, I'm grand," she finally managed. "Just getting my breath back. Up in a sec." But she wasn't quite sure this was possible. Cautiously, she tested a few body parts. Her toes wriggled. Her fingers too. Not paralyzed then. She bent a knee. If something were broken, she would be crying, wouldn't she? Slowly she rolled onto her side, conscious of Antoinette's curious gaze, and got to her feet. The lights felt very bright suddenly, and it occurred to her that she might have a concussion. She took a few limping steps.

Halfway to the door she paused. Would Antoinette see her slipping through the gates back toward the Residence? The embassy staffers came in a separate entrance, from the street. Only the ambassador and his guests used the gate from the house. She could avoid questions by going out the staff door and circling around to the main entrance of the Residence. But that posed two other problems. First, there was no way she was going to walk outside of this little compound dressed in shorts and a camisole. She'd give the guards a coronary. Second, she couldn't get in or out of the staff entrance without a key. She'd have to go back to the house directly.

"Bye!" she said cheerfully to Antoinette, who continued to take slow steps on the elliptical machine.

There was no answer. Miranda watched her for a minute before slipping out the door and, glancing painfully over her shoulder to make sure Antoinette wasn't looking, darted through the Residence gates and staggered up the lawn to the house.

Christ, she thought, stepping into the shower in Finn's bathroom. Land mines everywhere.

FINN FINALLY GOT home around 3:00 p.m. She always had plenty of warning of his arrival, as the gates would clatter open and the guards' walkie-talkies would start bleating before his armored convoy finally swept into the yard. She ran downstairs to meet him, still damp from her shower.

"Staying away from buttons?" he said, kissing her. "I leave you alone *one* morning and you managed to get the whole team round."

"Let that be a lesson to you. I got lonely. Besides, I've been wanting to meet Tucker for ages."

"And I'm sure you made quite an impression. What did Teru leave us?" They headed to the kitchen and rummaged around in the refrigerator, finding spinach quiche, salad, and apple-rhubarb crumble.

"I've made a decision," Finn said as he refilled their glasses with sauvignon blanc. They were eating on the front porch, where they could look out onto the garden.

"You're never going to leave me here alone again?"

"In addition to that. I've decided that it's time to tell my staff. It's silly, really, to wait any longer, and it just makes it seem like we're doing something wrong."

"Which we're not."

"Which we absolutely are not. So I think I'll say something at Saturday's morning meeting. If that's all right with you."

"Is there a reason it shouldn't be? Do you have ex-lovers in the embassy who are going to come after me with AK-47s?"

Finn laughed. "I haven't had a girlfriend in five years."

"So you say. I still don't believe you." The five-year gap bothered her. It was impossible for Miranda to envision going without intimacy for that long. Besides, Finn was brilliant, attractive, personable, and single. How many people were there like that in the Foreign Office?

"I've been busy. I've moved quite a bit in the last few years. And I don't manage time well."

"And everyone else is married?"

"Either that or they just didn't fancy me."

"Impossible."

"This is why I love you."

"Well it's not for my cooking."

"Wait—you cook?"

Miranda laughed and choked on a bit of crumble. Finn pounded her on the back.

"Ow!" she winced and pulled away from him.

Finn looked stricken. "I'm sorry. I didn't mean to hurt—"

"No, it's okay, really. I'm just a bit . . . bruised. I had a little incident in the gym this morning."

He raised an eyebrow. "*Another* incident?"

Miranda told him about Antoinette and the treadmill. Finn tried valiantly to keep a straight face but couldn't manage it.

"It wasn't funny!" she said.

"No, no, I'm sure . . . I'm just . . . thinking about the CCTV footage."

Miranda groaned. "Nooooo, seriously? That was on camera?"

"Sweetheart, you're at the ambassador's Residence. Everything is on camera."

"Even here? Even now?" She stretched a toe underneath the table to nudge his knee.

"Especially here. We're on the porch! Someone could try to climb in our windows from here. But we are safe inside. Or so I've been told."

"God I hope so."

"Well if they have any footage of what we get up to inside, we ought to be able to charge people to view it."

"Pay-per-view ambassador porn. Sounds like a promising category."

"Promising at least a better income than I have as a civil servant."

"And more than you'd make as an artist."

"Indubitably. Especially given my complete hopelessness with a pencil. Speaking of which, I haven't seen any new pieces lately. Shall we go to yours after lunch?"

"Are you allowed?"

"If I give the guys an hour's notice."

"Okay. I don't think anyone else is home. But if we eat anything there we'll have to wash our own dishes."

"Heaven forfend. I'll bring them back here."

"Go tell the guys then. I'll head upstairs and slip into something much, much less comfortable."

FINN WAS THE only one who had seen the paintings. Anyone in his position had to be good at keeping secrets, she figured. Besides, if there was anyone as enthusiastic about supporting the local women as she was, it was Finn. More than thirty paintings were secreted in her house, stacked in boxes within an unused wardrobe in a cramped room on the roof. She wondered what she would do with them when she eventually left. Where would her girls be able to keep them? They could not store them at home, where their families would see them. While some might be able to accept a still life or two under their roofs, surely the recent paintings would arouse furor. Or worse.

She sighed. Why was she doing this? Why was she encouraging these women to cultivate talents that they would never be able to use? But she knew the answer. The answer was simple. She was teaching these women to paint because they wanted to learn. They wanted to learn so badly they made up excuses to get to her house. They risked being found out. They kept secrets from people they loved.

"Tell me again how you found all these women," Finn said on their way over. "Tell me how Tazkia found you."

"You already know about Tazkia!"

"I'm getting old. I forget things. And I want to memorize everything that has ever happened to you."

Miranda smiled. "Call me Scheherazade," she said. "Okay. Tazkia."

"Wait, should we change her name for the purposes of the conversation? With the guys up front?"

"They don't speak English. They'll only understand her name. For all they know we're saying Tazkia is the most pious and virtuous Mazrooqi in the entire country."

"Okay," said Finn, though his brow remained creased.

"I'll try to avoid saying her name much. Okay?"

"Fair enough."

"Once upon a time there was a feisty little artist named—well, a feisty little artist. She lived in a stone house carved out of the Old City, with her mother and father and two sisters and two brothers. Our artist was the youngest. During the day, her father ran a tiny store, where he sold batteries, water, sodas, cookies, candy bars, milk, and yogurts."

"No porridge? I feel like there should be porridge in this story."

"Don't be so English. Mazrooqis don't eat porridge."

"What do they have for breakfast?" he asked. "I'm never invited for breakfast."

"Well, our artist's mother baked long, skinny baguettes and stir-fried chicken livers and onions for their breakfast. Two sisters and one brother remained at home. Only the artist had attended university, where she had studied the unwomanly art of geometry, drawn to its logic and relation to her own secret scribblings."

"See, you didn't mention the geometry part before. What else are you keeping from me?"

Miranda smiled and picked up his hand from the seat to give it a clandestine squeeze. "Not a single thing."

Miranda had met Tazkia at German Haus, at Vicenta's first installation. Eager to explore an unfamiliar part of the world and interested rather abstractly in the plight of women in the Middle East, Vicenta had come here on an artist's grant and Miranda had taken a sabbatical to accompany her. Of all the cultural centers in the city, German Haus was the most active, often inviting foreign artists to exhibit their work, usually with the stipulation that they also teach a workshop for the local population. There, Miranda (who spoke exactly eleven words of German, most of them names of foods) had met weavers, batik artists, painters, photographers, writers, and sculptors. Not all of whom were German. It didn't seem mandatory. She had watched presentations on alabaster, mined by hand here, and suffered through countless German movies with only Arabic subtitles. So few places in the city offered any kind of entertainment that she'd become willing to sit through just about anything.

Tazkia had somehow wrangled permission from her parents to stay out past dark that night. She was already perched on the steps of German Haus, waiting for it to open, when Miranda and Vicenta arrived. Draped in black from head to toe, she looked like a small stray phantom. As they started up the steps, she launched herself at them. "I am sorry but is one of you the artist?" Her eyes glinted hopefully through the slit between her *hijab* and *niqab*.

Miranda and Vicenta glanced at each other briefly, smiling, before Miranda said, "Tonight, she is."

"And tomorrow, it's Miranda's turn."

"But privately. I'm only an artist at home here. No public shows for me here." She did not explain why.

Tazkia studied them, frowning.

"And it depends what you mean by *artist*," added Vicenta.

"Vicenta's more of a performer really. More conceptual. More installation arty," said Miranda, noting Tazkia's perplexed look.

"Tonight I'll be showing my installation arty side," said Vicenta. "You'll see."

"Installation art-ee?" Tazkia looked desperate.

"Why don't we go inside?" said Miranda. "Then you can see. We don't mean to confuse you. I'm Miranda, by the way."

"Tazkia. I am so happy to meet you. There is so much I want to ask you."

Vicenta rang the bell, and a blond girl with a ponytail, one of the German Haus administrators, showed them in. The gallery was just to the left of the front door. Vicenta had been here late the night before, finishing up. In the center of the room was a black figure about the size of Tazkia. Only it was truly shapeless; no hint of hips or breasts or neck was visible. It was an abstracted outline of a Muslim woman. A perfect parabola. On the cloth, in tiny white letters, were quotes from women in the Old City that Vicenta had been collecting for several months, some in Arabic, some in English. On the far side was a gap between the *hijab* and *niqab*, where eyes would be. In this gap, in letters of diminishing size, were the words "My soul has no windows."

Against the four walls were small screens playing interviews with Muslim women about the *hijab*. Almost all were completely obscured, but one left her face bare and covered her hair with a flowered purple scarf. It was the brightest spot of color in the room.

When Vicenta had first explained the idea for the exhibit, Miranda had been skeptical.

"Seriously? The *hijab*? Could there be a more hackneyed image of the Middle East?" she'd said.

"Does that mean we should stop discussing it?" Vicenta had answered. "I mean, the women I talked to, they couldn't *wait* to discuss it. Whatever their point of view."

It hadn't turned out badly, Miranda thought. Not her kind of art, but she was seriously old-fashioned in some ways. An oil painter whose subjects were generally recognizable. No wonder she hadn't found fame and fortune.

Also on the wall hung a horizontal strip of black cloth embroidered with gold thread. From afar, the gold simply looked like repetitive geometric or floral patterns. But if you looked closely, very closely, you could make out tiny figures. At one end sat Queen Arwa, ruler of much of the Arabian Peninsula from 1067 until her death in 1138. At the other end sat Bilqis, Queen of Sheba, possibly ruler of Mazrooq in the tenth century BCE. A stream of women spilled across the cloth between them, in dozens of postures. Some carried heavy water containers on their heads; some cringed from menacing husbands; others sat in tattered rags, their hands outstretched. "Once, we were queens," read the tiny embroidered Arabic letters underneath.

Tazkia took all of this in with dark, serious eyes, as Vícenta darted from room to room making final adjustments—snipping a loose thread here, restarting a video there. A trickle of people had begun entering the gallery and milling around. Miranda smiled at them stiffly, feeling extraneous. She still missed the glass of wine in her hand. Here, there would be plastic cups of fluorescent synthetic juice at a bar in back of the gallery, but not until later. She watched Tazkia catch hold of Vícenta's arm and follow her around, avidly questioning her. Vícenta didn't seem to mind (Vícenta never minded attention), chatting as much as she could in between greeting newcomers.

For some reason German Haus seemed immune from local censure. Despite the parade of Western artists exhibiting here, and the occasional mildly racy film, there had never to Miranda's knowledge been any protests. She remembered watching *Perfume* here, and the sharp intake of breath when an exposed breast appeared on the screen. She had been momentarily paralyzed, waiting for a violent reaction. But none had come.

Still, there were limits. Obviously, no nudes were exhibited. So far, no one had been stupid enough to suggest that there should be. And there was no representation of lifelike human figures, a concession to Islam. The art tended toward the abstract and the geometric. Vícenta's work just barely fell within the parameters of what was acceptable; nothing she did was very lifelike. And oddly, video was not prohibited, as long as it was not obscene.

The Islamic aversion to figures pretty much ruled out Miranda's work. Worried about getting herself into trouble (a constant concern), Miranda read many of the *hadiths* that govern the objection to figures. The Quran condemns idolatry, but does not explicitly forbid the drawing of humans and animals; that is left to the *hadiths*, several of which are narrated by Aisha, one of the Prophet Mohammed's many wives. In one, she says: "Allah's Messenger visited me. And I had a shelf with a thin cloth curtain hanging over it and on which there were portraits. No sooner did he see it than he tore it and the color of his face underwent a change and he said: Aisha, the most grievous torment from the Hand of Allah on the Day of Resurrection would be for those who imitate [Allah] in the act of His creation."

Once, Aisha reportedly brought home a cushion decorated with animals for her husband to sit on. Her gesture was met with rage: "The makers of these pictures will be punished on the Day of Resurrection, and it will be said to them, 'Give life to what you have created [i.e., these pictures].' The Prophet added, 'The Angels of [Mercy] do not enter a house in which there are pictures [of animals].'"

That was pretty much all Miranda needed to read. But there were more: "All the painters who make pictures would be in the fire of Hell. The soul will be breathed in every picture prepared by him and it shall punish him in the Hell, and he [Ibn Abbas] said: If you have to do it at all, then paint the pictures of trees and lifeless things; and Nasr b. Ali confirmed it."

She had been warned.

As THE ART exhibition drew to a close, Tazkia found her. "This," she said, sweeping an arm toward the walls. "I find it very wonderful. But I am wanting to learn how to draw. And paint. Do you know an artist like this? It is very hard for me to find here someone like this."

"You just found one," said Miranda, smiling. "You are an artist yourself?"

"No, no. No, but I would like to learn."

"Why?" Miranda leaned on the white door-frame, pressing her tired spine against it and longing once again for a glass of champagne.

Tazkia clutched at her embroidered cloth shoulder bag and glanced around her. "Could we go outside?"

They had stepped out into the cool, dark, jasmine-scented night. A crescent moon cast pale light that seemed just to reach the tips of the bruise-colored mountains in the distance. But even shrouded by the night Tazkia was nervous. A guard sat at the entrance to the small courtyard, where others were beginning to spill out of the building. Stepping closer to Miranda, Tazkia held open her bag, revealing a thick spiral notebook.

"It's my trying," she said. "My trying to be an artist. Would you look at it? And tell me if I should keep trying?"

"I'd be honored."

"Please, no one can know."

"I understand."

Tazkia still looked uneasy. There was something else. "There are figures," she whispered softly. "I can't help it. They just come."

Miranda nodded. "Okay," she said. "Okay."

As if they were conducting a clandestine drug deal, Miranda and Tazkia huddled together, slipping the notebook quickly from Tazkia's bag and into Miranda's distinctly unglamorous backpack. As Tazkia turned to go, Miranda touched her shoulder. "You're not the only one," she said quietly. "Do you know this?" Tazkia's eyes remained blank and questioning over her *niqab*. "Not the only one to paint figures. Not the only Muslim. I will show you." Her eyes still unsmiling, Tazkia gave a faint nod and, tripping over the hem of her *abaya*, tiptoed through the garden until she and the night became one.

DESPITE HER GREAT curiosity, Miranda waited until the next day to examine Tazkia's drawings in the daylight. She sat in her *diwan* with sun streaming through the windows (it was the only room in the house with large windows, as it was far enough from the ground that uninvited eyes could not intrude. The circular windows, like oversized portholes, made Miranda feel that she was in an airborne submarine), turning the pages with mounting excitement. They were extraordinary drawings. She wondered how Tazkia had managed to make them without attracting attention. She could never have sketched them out in the open, where she could be observed. And surely she wasn't wealthy enough to own a camera. Few people here were. Miranda thought about the tiny keyhole windows far up in the tall houses of the Old City, windows that allowed women to look out but no one to look in. Perhaps Tazkia had watched her subjects from there, crouched in a dim stairwell, her secret notebook in hand.

There were sketches of wheelbarrows overflowing with pomegranates; a squat, plain mosque with a cat in its doorway; the city's immutable skyline against its surrounding mountains. More intriguing were the drawings of people. There was a man sitting cross-legged in a *thobe*, sucking on a cigarette in his market stall. Smoke rose from a corner of his mouth, but his face lacked any other features. None of the figures had eyes or noses, and most lacked mouths. It was as if Tazkia thought if she left out these details she wasn't really drawing human figures. There were women wrapped in the blue-and-red *sitarah*, viewed from the back as they climbed a flight of steps. And there were small children playing in an alley, one holding a kitten above his head while the others reached for it. Miranda hated to think of the fate of that kitten.

When she was done, she sat in her *diwan* for a long time, thinking, Tazkia's oeuvre resting on her lap. Then she called Tazkia. "First, you are already an artist. Second, would you be interested in meeting every week for a small class? And third, do you know any other women who would be interested?"

They began the following Friday. It was a good day for the women to slip away. Their fathers and brothers all headed to the mosque for Friday afternoon prayers and then often went to sit with their friends and while the afternoon away smoking shisha and gossiping. Their mothers were busy baking or dancing to music in private rooms with their own circles of friends and relatives.

Tazkia usually arrived first, ripping her veil off the second she was safely within Miranda's hallway. She was Miranda's star pupil, a feisty little ball of hyperactivity and nerves. And there were three others now: Mariam, Nadia, and Aaqilah. That was enough, Miranda thought. Any more and they would become conspicuous. Besides, she was running out of space to store their paintings.

SEPTEMBER 3, 2010
Finn

Finn stands outside the gate of Miranda's former home, holding tightly to Cressida's hand. He has hardly let go of her since Miranda was taken, cannot bear it if she is even in a separate room. He dragged her crib into his room so that he can hear her breathe when he wakes at night. Miranda would laugh to hear that he wakes several times a night now. He, whom nothing could stir before dawn. Now, he climbs out of bed every hour or two to rest a palm on Cressie's stomach and touch his rough cheek to her milk-smooth skin.

Inhaling deeply, Finn knocks firmly on the metal gate. Cressie imitates him, pounding away on the lower gate until Finn stops her tiny fist in his hand. He wonders if anyone can hear from inside. Probably not. He pulls his new phone from his pocket and searches for Mosi's phone number.

"*Salaama aleikum!*" The cheerful voice takes him by surprise. A shrouded form stops by his side and offers her hand. "We've been wondering when you would show up," she said. "We've been worried about you." It takes Finn a moment before he can place the voice.

"Hello, Madina. Cressie, remember Madina?" Cressie clings to his leg, looking with great suspicion at Madina, who is obscured by black cloth. "It's Madina," he reiterates. She pulls aside her *niqab* so that Cressie can see her face. Reassured, Cressie launches herself at Madina's knees.

"Come in." Madina takes Cressie's hand as she slips a key into the lock and swings open the gate.

Once they are settled in the *diwan* and Cressie is busy exploring the other upstairs rooms, Finn explains to her why he has come.

IT DIDN'T TAKE long for the Foreign Office to decide he could no longer be trusted to carry out his duties in an impartial manner. It wasn't anything he had done. Every day he had continued to work tirelessly, coordinating with the US embassy to investigate every angle of Miranda's case (though because a US national is considered at the highest risk, the Americans want to avoid taking a visible lead) while continuing to fulfill almost every other obligation of his post. If anything, he was more dogged than ever in his efforts to medi ate a peaceful agreement between the northern and southern leaders. For months he had worked to assemble his coalition of twelve tribal leaders, six from each side, painstakingly chosen for the respect they commanded in their home governorates, plus a handful of officials from the ruling and opposition parties. He had met with each leader personally, explaining the specific consequences to outright hostilities and conversely the possibilities available to them in peace. The FCO was concerned about the increasing aggression on both sides, not least because of the threat of a new flood of immigrants making their way north to the UK to beg asylum. And now Finn had a personal stake in keeping the country as calm as possible.

But he wasn't surprised when the Office decided to replace him with the very competent Celia Rhodes, fresh from Sudan— temporarily, they had promised, just until Miranda was back. No ambassador would be kept in post under these circumstances. No matter how good. No matter how critical his current projects. There would always be "concerns about his continuing ability to take dis- passionate decisions and to focus on the priorities of Her Majesty's government." Wilkins, his current line manager, has been enormously sympathetic, reassuring him of his continued employment, so long as he returns to London until Miranda is found. He can work on the Mazrooq desk if he wants, said Wilkins. Or do something unrelated if that is more comfortable.

Yet a return to London is unthinkable. How could he go without Miranda? How could he leave her in a country edging toward civil war, especially when he is no longer in a position to help prevent it? How could he ever explain to Cressida a decision to leave the country without her mother? So he requested Special Unpaid Leave, SUPL in FCO-speak. He has some small savings, and it costs almost nothing to live here. He will stay for as long as it takes. This is his fault, after all. It couldn't have been an accident that kidnappers had made off with the wife of an ambassador. But this is not what weighs heaviest on him, not what keeps him staring into the darkness until the predawn prayers blare from the neighboring mosque. He cannot help thinking that he deserves this. This is repayment for Afghanistan, for his deadly naïveté, for Charlotte. This is the world's way of not letting him forget. He has never been a religious man, but he cannot shake the feeling that this is some kind of divine retribution. If there can be such a thing without a divinity.

The Office was deeply unhappy with his decision. You'll be in danger, Wilkins said. We can't afford to pay for protection for you once the new ambassador arrives. People know who you are. You're a target. And don't even think about going after her yourself. You know we need to control the situation. You know the dangers of going rogue. Finn had patiently listened to all of his arguments, had let him present his whole case, and then he had said simply, "Have you never loved anyone?"

MIRANDA'S FRIEND KARIM, who lived near her old house and had often run errands for her and Vicenta, helping them pay electric bills and find a repairman for their capricious washing machine, had found him the house. It was in the Old City, where he had always dreamed of living but which had been forbidden to him as ambassador. Diplomats lived in a wealthy suburb north of town, which was allegedly safer, but which in fact just made them easier to target, with their monstrous guarded homes and conspicuous diplomatic license plates (called CD plates, for *corps diplomatique*). In the Old City, Finn felt he could almost disappear. He still couldn't navigate the maze of streets alone. And while his neighbors stared at him and cried "Welcome, welcome!" whenever he left the house, they didn't appear threatening.

Of course, many people knew who he was. Something like that was hardly a secret. And they were curious to see the ambassador who had moved to the Old City, where no ambassador had ever made a home. The ambassador who had lost his wife. The embassy had not been able to keep that out of the papers, despite their best efforts. How embarrassing it must be for Mazrooq, for those Mazrooqis who cared, to have failed to protect the wife of an ambassador. An ambassador who was here not only to support the country's democratic aspirations but to offer increased food security, water purity, and education for girls. (Not that everyone believed this to be true. There were still many who believed, despite evidence to the contrary, that the Brits were there to recolonize the country. Finn was constantly reassuring tribal leaders that when the UK had pulled out on November 18, 1968, it had meant it.) This man was helping their villages to get sewer systems, and they had allowed his wife to disappear. As soon as they heard the news, all of his contacts in the government had phoned Finn with eloquent condolences. He had no use for their poetry; he wanted their help, which has thus far not been forthcoming.

He had wanted desperately to keep Miranda's identity out of the press, to keep her kidnappers from finding out what a big fish they had hooked. She wouldn't have told her captors her real name. She would certainly not have mentioned that she was—and how she hated the term, how it turned her into a possession, an accessory—*the ambassador's wife*. He is sure of this. But there was no way to disguise her disappearance. He could have made up a story that she was traveling for work, to an artists' residency or gallery opening. But no one would have believed she would leave Cressie behind. And her women would never believe that Miranda had left without telling them. She knew too many people, was expected to be too many places. Then of course there was the fact that two other women had disappeared with her. And Mukhtar. Silence was impossible. It was astonishing the kidnappers themselves hadn't started bragging; an ambassador's wife was a major coup.

Since the news broke, eleven days after the women disappeared, the British press hasn't left him alone. Reporters rang his office, his cell phone, his aunt Mary in Ross-on-Wye, his school friends, his university professors, his boss. They showed up at the gates of the Residence, heaving their cameras over their heads, trying to get an image through the bars. Thank Christ for gates, for security. After the guards had escorted them back to the main road several times, they erected a roadblock to keep the press at bay. Finn hadn't given them a single word. It is always a mistake to speak to the British press, which has never managed to quote him accurately or write a factual story on Mazrooq. Which isn't that surprising, given that not a single British paper has a reporter who actually lives here. Even *The Guardian* and the BBC, which once upon a time he had loved, had trusted, failed to grasp the intricacies of Mazrooqi politics and culture. How could they, when their reporters never spent more than three days in the country? International reporting had essentially died with the demise of most foreign bureaus. Finally, he had switched off his mobile and buried it in the garden under the fig tree. Before pressing the powdery earth down over its shiny black shell, he'd hesitated. What if Miranda rang? What if she needed to reach him and he didn't answer? But she knew the house number by heart, he reassured himself. She could reach him there or at the embassy. Should she still be alive.

At the souq he found a cheap new phone. Only the necessary people had the number. Well, most of the necessary people. All except one.

He had moved to the Old City with the help of Tucker and his team in the middle of a cold, moonless night. The press hasn't found him yet. Soon, they will lose interest and go back to stalking celebrities, spying on the royal family, and occasionally libeling an ordinary person, just for sport. Finn's Mazrooqi neighbors watch his door, noting his comings and goings with Cressie and sometimes with Bashir or Negasi. His devoted bodyguard Bashir had quit the police force and the CP team in order to come sleep in the small shed in the courtyard. Finn had discouraged him, saying that he couldn't pay enough, that the embassy offered better benefits, but Bashir would not be dissuaded. He had sworn to protect Finn for as long as he was in the country and that was that. "If you don't care for yourself, care for your daughter," Bashir had finally said, silencing him. Tucker stopped in at least twice a day, out of guilt and fear that Finn would be next. He had even broached the subject of sending Cressida out of the country. "To whom?" Finn had asked. He had no one left but an elderly aunt; Miranda's mother had wandered off to Mexico or South America, and her father was hardly capable of caring for an active toddler. But even had Finn had a younger brother or sister with the emotional and financial resources to care for his daughter, he isn't sure he could let her go. The house is empty enough without Miranda. If Cressida were not there to distract him with demands to "play bears" or read her Corduroy books, how would he keep his mind from the sharp blade of loss?

Negasi and Teru take turns visiting, always with tubs of Tupperware packed with muffins, quiche, or salads. "I don't think you're allowed to be giving me food," Finn tells them. "I can't take it." But in the end he does, to avoid breaking their hearts. They need to care for him as much as he needs to care for Cressie.

Ordinary things feel like luxuries. He can walk to the grocery store, buy his own milk and cereal. Karim is his ever-ready guide, helping him to navigate the warren of streets and to find the freshest produce at the best prices. He can decide to go out to dinner at the very last minute and walk to a restaurant. He can sit in the garden of the Ahlan Hotel and watch Cressie tear mint leaves into tiny pieces. And then there is the house. Like Miranda's former home, it has four stony stories, tiny windows, and nearly a dozen rooms. He's hired a Somali woman to come clean once a week and kept Gabra to watch Cressie when he is working. But mostly, he and his daughter are alone.

One perk of being out of a job is that he's free to devote all his energies to the search for Miranda without the distractions of diplomacy. Ignoring the FCO's warnings, he recruited enough people to create his own little network of spies and investigators. It is useless for him personally to set out on a quest for her. He knows that. He isn't a fool. He would need permissions to travel through each checkpoint, he would set himself up as an easy target, and people would know he was coming. He is not anonymous here. And there is Cressie. How can he walk into known danger when she is already missing a mother?

Yet this inability to travel drives him mad. He wants nothing more than to walk the mountains and valleys searching every single house for her. Nothing could be worse than this waiting, this endless nothingness. And he knows from long experience that these situations always involve interminable stretches of inaction and patient waiting. There have been a few false leads, spottings of Western women in remote locales, but no real progress. Every trace of Miranda and the other women seems to have been swept from the desert, as if by a broom.

MADINA AND MOSI help him lug the paintings from Miranda's former home—where she had continued to teach her class until they married—down the street to his gates. Before removing them from the rooftop room where Miranda kept them, he seals them into their cardboard boxes with borrowed tape. Mosi and Madina knew what they were, though only Miranda had had the key to that room. Finn had found it in the purse she had left behind in her studio. "If you see the women," he says, "please reassure them that their work is safe. And unseen." Having failed to protect Miranda, the least he can do is try to protect the women she loves.

JUNE 7, 2007
Miranda

When Finn and Miranda arrived at her house, she ran up the stairs calling, "Allah Allah Allah!" in imitation of the local men broadcasting their presence to women in time for them to hide themselves. No one responded. Given the number of housemates she had, it was astonishing that so few were ever home. She extracted a set of keys from the patchwork bag that served as her purse and contained a book, a sketchbook, three pencils, a pack of sugarless Orbit, a camera, and a bag of raisins, and continued up to the top floor. Finn followed her, his long legs taking the stairs two at a time.

On the roof, she unlocked the small padlock on the door of a tiny stand-alone room and pushed open the door. It didn't open very far—the room was nearly full. The stench of linseed oil and turpentine was overwhelming in the windowless space. She turned to the first box of canvases and pulled the light cord.

"This is one of Mariam's," she said, tilting it forward to show Finn. "She's really coming along. Look at her use of texture." The first painting was a still life of *foll*, the chains of jasmine flowers worn to celebrate weddings, Fridays, or funerals. Three chains lay abandoned and entwined in a *diwan*, their petals browning around the edges. The red cushions of the *diwan*, created by rolling paint-soaked rags across the surface of the canvas, were so invitingly velvety Miranda could hardly restrain herself from stroking a finger along their seams. Yet the jasmine petals were silk-smooth. Mariam was in love with the static, but she did it so richly Miranda was loathe to steer her in another direction.

They looked through dozens more paintings, of horses, houses, camels, gardens, and landscapes, before they came to Nadia's wedding series. Weddings were seriously single-sex affairs here. Guests were patted down before entering a women's celebration to make sure they were not carrying a camera or cell phone. Only an official (female) photographer could capture the bride and her guests. Even this was too terrifying for many women, who pulled their *hijabs* back over their heads as the bride and her photographer approached. Nadia worked from her cousin Imaan's wedding album, painting vibrant scenes of revelry certainly unwitnessed by at least half of the population. Her faces were blurred, like those of Degas's dancers, and her style impressionistic. But she painted the bare shoulders and knees, the tilted hips, the long locks of hair tumbling down around waists. Miranda was impressed with how accurately she captured movement, in the reach of an arm and the toss of a head.

"She's an accidental Degas apprentice."

"Wow," said Finn, properly awed.

"I know. I just wish I could *show* them somewhere," she said. They stood together looking at the last painting for several minutes.

"What about in another country? Oman or Egypt?"

"Maybe. I don't know. We haven't really talked about where things will end up, we're still wallowing in the process."

Finn looked up suddenly, cocked his head to one side. "What about Tazkia? I don't see anything of hers?"

"Ah," said Miranda. "Tazkia. Tazkia gets a bit of extra security. Hang on . . ." She stepped deeper into the closet, fumbling in the dim light of the farthest corner until her fingers found a sharp edge of the metal trunk. Pulling her key chain from her purse, she unlocked the clasp with a miniature key. "Stay there, I'll take one out," she called back to Finn, who lingered underneath the bare bulb, watching her with starkly shadowed eyes. Carefully, Miranda freed a recent painting; Tazkia had created it from an old sketch of Vícenta. Cradling it in her arms, Miranda spun on her heel and held it up to Finn without speaking.

For a moment he simply stared. "Mira," he finally said. "Are you sure you know what you're doing?"

"No," she said. "But she does."

By the time Miranda met Finn she had already been working with the women for more than two years. While she had slowly grown closer to all four, her relationship with Tazkia had evolved into a thing apart. Nadia was still so nervous every time she arrived that it took several minutes for her hands to stop trembling. Mariam was a plodding perfectionist—not without talent but without a flicker of fervor in her heart. Aaqilah was their fairy-tale artist, dreamily daubing her saccharine fantasies of romantic love: men on horseback wooing shadowy maidens, poets swooning over their quills, long-haired princesses stroking kittens and looking glazed with lust. The kinds of things one paints when one has no experience of men. Miranda's teeth ached every time she glanced at Aaqilah's easel.

But Tazkia. Her cartwheeling firework of an artist. Tazkia was made of passion; she blazed her way through sketchbooks and across canvases, leaving dazzling color and contorted human shapes behind. She was Miranda's Mazrooqi soul mate. Miranda enjoyed teaching the other women but had no personal stake in their creations. Tazkia she wanted to show to everyone. She wanted to set ablaze her booster rockets and launch her into the art world. And yet, it was her work that was most likely to doom them all.

A SINGLE RAY of sunlight streaming in through a tiny square cut into the roof of Miranda's *diwan* caught the dusty air, exposing the glittering powder with which the women filled their lungs. Atoms of stone exhaled centuries ago that had drifted out windows and down narrow passageways, in and out of mosques, in and out of Mazrooqi mouths. Male and female, adult and child, believer and heretic, sharing breath. Miranda contemplated the light, the tumbling grit, tempted to draw out her own sketchbook. Pieces of the universe, as old as God, rained down on them.

She sat on the floor at the end of the rectangular room, charcoal pencils and pastels fanned out in front of her. The women were still floating onto the cushions, *abayas* sinking down around them like parachutes, two on either side. Aaqilah and Nadia on her left, Tazkia and Mariam on her right. Their faces were bare, *niqabs* flipped back over their heads. As Miranda shuffled through a stack of sketchbooks on her lap, they unzipped bags, curled their bare feet underneath them, and lifted their eyes to her, hopeful, wary, eager, anxious.

They had been meeting for several weeks. Each time, the women were incrementally more relaxed, more confident. But it was slow. Their fears were too well founded to be vanquished entirely. In her first class, as if to make sure Miranda understood what they risked, they had told her—in turns, interrupting each other in their imperfect English—the tale of Aila. Instinctively the girls who doodled in the margins of their school notebooks were drawn to each other and formed a kind of protective secret society. Tazkia, Aaqilah, and Mariam had met as children, scribbling with their fingers in the dust of the alleys near their homes until adult arms finally descended to restrain them. Nadia and Aila, who came from villages in the North, had moved to the city later, as teenagers. Rarely did they meet all together, afraid of discovery. But in pairs they encouraged each other, rationalized away their sins, offered the comfort of shared guilt.

Aila had been among the boldest, sketching caricatures of their teachers and friends, which she shared only with her fellow artists before tearing them into confetti or setting fire to them in an unpopulated alley. When her father discovered one such drawing on the back page of a textbook, he had taken Aila by the hand without speaking and led her to the room where her mother was ironing their sheets. "Go," he'd said to his wife. "I have a lesson to teach to your daughter." As soon as the woman was out of sight Aila's father had turned the iron on its side and stood behind the girl, holding her wrists. With slow deliberation, he had pressed her palms against the scorching metal. Her mother had responded immediately to her daughter's screams but had been unable to pull her husband's arms away. Aila had been hospitalized with third-degree burns for thirteen days before she died of septicemia.

The story had a dampening effect on Miranda's professorial passion. While she hadn't been cavalier in inviting the women to study with her, she had insufficiently grasped the peril in which she placed them. Never had such responsibility been laid on her shoulders. Yet, here they were. Four hungry souls, gathered before her, their passion overwhelming their terror. Did this not have to be honored? Knowing what they dared, how could she *not* teach them?

"I have some extra sketchbooks and pencils," she said carefully, passing them around. "In case you would like them." Sketchbooks and pencils were never extra, never in danger of going unused. But none of the women—whose parents were shopkeepers, taxi drivers, or unemployed—could afford to buy them for themselves. They had been drawing and painting on pages torn from school notebooks and magazines, in the margins of textbooks. She had to find a way to give them what they needed without it looking like a gift, like charity. They touched the thick new paper with wonder. Tazkia bent to inhale its woody scent.

"I have a new exercise for you to try today," Miranda said. "So I'm not going to waste time talking. First, I want you to draw an object from memory, from your imagination. It will be something you can find in this house or in the courtyard, but not in this room. It could be a plant, a teakettle, a chair. Think about this object. Summon it. You will have thirty minutes to work. This is the first half of the exercise."

"We can pick anything?" asked Tazkia.

"No. Here . . ." Miranda picked up the cloche hat lying upside down beside her. Vicenta's hat. "I've written the names of four objects on scraps of paper and put them in this hat. You will each pick one piece of paper, and draw what is written on it. Okay? Any questions?"

The women were silent. Tazkia stared at her anxiously while the others glanced at each other or the carpet. "It's not a test. You're just drawing." When no one spoke up, she passed the hat to her left, to

Aaqilah. Tazkia pulled out a piece of paper, frowned at it, crumpled it in her hands, smoothed it against her sketchbook, and crumpled it again. There was a clatter as the women reached for their pencils, the creak of their stiff new books, and then nothing but the scratching of pencils on paper.

Miranda turned to look out the windows, forgetting she had covered them. All of her portholes were obscured by scarves and sheets, to conceal her women from view. It was unlikely that anyone would be able to see in here, on the third floor of the house, but her students' paranoia was contagious. The only uncovered source of light was that small square in the ceiling. It was still bright outside, still enough light burned through her makeshift curtains to illuminate their work. But it wasn't ideal. Sighing, she flipped open her own sketchbook. What could she do? Not Vícenta, not any woman. Their bed. It was the first thing that came to her.

The alarm on her cell phone startled her back into the room. "Okay, stop," she said to the women. "Turn the page."

"But I'm not done." Mariam's chubby, round face gleamed with a sheen of sweat. She was the slowest of Miranda's students, an artist constantly losing sight of the forest because she couldn't take her eyes off the pine needles.

"You are for now. Forget what you have just done and find a new page. Everyone there?" The women nodded. Tazkia and Aaqilah stroked their clean pages with eager fingers.

"Now, go find the object you just drew, and bring it back here if you can. Or draw it where it is. I want you to draw it from observation. Look at it closely as you draw; notice everything about it, every little detail. Don't make any assumptions, just draw exactly what you see in front of you."

With a rustle of rayon, the women stretched their legs. Tazkia shot out of the room first, followed by Aaqilah and Nadia holding hands. Mariam lingered, looking anxious. "What is it, Mariam?"

"I drew a teakettle . . ."

"You can go take our kettle, it's all right." Relieved, Mariam smiled and slipped downstairs.

Miranda followed them, turning off at the bedroom she shared with Vícenta. She looked at their mattress on the floor and then back at her sketch pad, smiling. It wasn't anything like what she had drawn. The blue felt blanket wasn't pulled up neatly but tossed in a heap at the foot of the bed. White sheets had been ripped from where they were tucked underneath the mattress and lay twisted, damp, and mangled. Vícenta's pillow was halfway across the room, where she had flung it that morning when it became lodged between their two bodies. In the corner, Miranda's squashed pillow held on to the vague outline of Vícenta's profile. Her head had been turned to the left, her cheek pressed on the embroidered roses of the pillowcase, her teeth gripping a fold of the cotton as Miranda took her hips between her hands. Even standing here, Miranda could still smell her, the dark, wintry forest pine of her.

The bed she had drawn was the kind of bed you might see in a children's first words book, an illustration of a generic bed. But it wasn't this bed. Quickly, she sketched their sex-tossed sheets, feeling a tug of longing in her gut, before returning to the *diwan* and her women.

As they continued scratching at their pages, she wandered the room, looking over their shoulders. Aaqilah drew her pencil along the stem of a potted plant, the basil Miranda grew in the courtyard, perhaps disappointed that she hadn't been assigned to draw Princess Barbie. Mariam huddled over her sketch of their ancient tin teakettle, erasing and redrawing its spout. A spiderweb spun from Nadia's now-steady pencil—it hadn't been difficult for her to find one in their several unused rooms. Tazkia was the last to return to the *diwan*, having drawn the bicycle that rusted against the walls of their house.

"Time's up," Miranda announced. The women looked at her, slightly dazed, coming back into their bodies. "Tear out the first drawing so that you can lay it alongside the second, and tell me what you see."

The air stood still as the women examined their work. It was unusual for the city to fall this silent, as if it were holding its breath. It was long after the clamor of lunchtime but before the muezzins' calls for evening prayers.

"Wow," said Tazkia first. "Very completely different."

"Different how?"

Tazkia squinched up her face, wrinkling her stubby nose. "More detailed?"

"Not so boring?" This from Aaqilah.

"And why is that?" The girls simply stared down at their two pieces, as if waiting for them to speak. "Because when you draw things from memory, you tend to set things down as symbols. Like the cocktail glass signs in airports." Whoops, bad example. "Or like the airplane symbols you pass on signs on the way to the airport. They are recognizably planes, but not specific planes. Only when you observe an actual plane, and put down its specific lines on paper, can you see." None of them had ever been on a plane, but they saw them overhead with alarming regularity, government planes on their way to the North.

Miranda leaned forward on her hands, pulling Tazkia's drawings across the carpet and holding them up. "Look at the first bicycle. It's a generic bicycle, a two-dimensional illustration of the word. We know what it is, but there is no personality there. But here—" She put the first one down and held up just the second. "Suddenly her bicycle has three dimensions. The handlebars are turned sideways. They have thick rubber grips on them, and tassels on the ends. The tires are slightly flat. The seat is banana-shaped rather than triangular. There is a screw coming loose behind the seat, hanging off of it. The basket on the front has a hole. You couldn't make this bicycle up; you couldn't imagine it."

Miranda set down the drawings and turned Nadia's spiderweb sketches so that they were facing the women. The first was neat and geometric, a perfect hexagon. The observed spiderweb was larger, sprawling, an octagon with a small tear on one side, a thread hanging from the top. "Do you see? When you actually look at things, weird things happen that you would never know about were you not observing."

Tazkia was kneeling, pulling drawings closer to her, inspecting them all. "Magic," she said. "Like magic."

"No." Miranda shook her head, smiling. "It is only that there are more interesting things in this world than you can imagine. You must go out. You must explore. And you must keep your eyes wide, wide open."

AUGUST 18, 2010
Miranda

Several uneventful days pass before Aisha notices the state of Miranda's shirt. No one else has come near her. The men keep their distance from the hut; Aisha is the only person who speaks to Miranda, usually in monosyllables. Each day they walk through the slanting mountain sun to fetch water, eat their meager meals squatting in the dust, and crouch silently in the dark of their hut. Miranda tries to question the old woman about why she is being held, what plans the men might have for her, but Aisha only shakes her head and looks fearful.

"And Mukhtar?" she is finally desperate enough to ask one morning as they huddle over their tin plates of beans. Her need to know his fate has overpowered her terror of the answer. "My . . . my friend?" She almost says the word *guard.* But if they don't know who she is, she doesn't want to give it away, that she is a person deemed worthy of a guard.

Aisha's face shifts nearly imperceptibly. But there is something, a shadow crossing. Bile rises to Miranda's throat; please, let him not have died for her, because of her.

"Is he alive?" she persists. "Is he here?" When Aisha remains silent, she leans forward and touches the woman's rayon-sheathed arm. "Please, Aisha, is he alive?"

"You are asking too many questions. I do not know. I know nothing of this man."

For a few minutes, Miranda falls silent. Either Mukhtar has been left in the mountains for dead or imprisoned somewhere else. He cannot have gotten away, not with blood streaming from the side of his head. She misses Mukhtar. In the last few years she has come to think of him almost as an overprotective brother, the brother she had longed for and her parents had not been inspired to produce.

Out on the team's practice range in the desert, he had taught her how to fire a Sig Sauer and an AK-47, never losing patience with her no matter how many times she missed the target entirely. Miranda was not a gun enthusiast, nor did she get any kind of macho kick from wielding deadly machinery, but she loved Tucker and his team and thought it wise to understand their weaponry. When she had fallen ill with typhoid (despite having been vaccinated), it was Mukhtar who took her to Dr. Jay, the embassy's doctor. When she had walked to Baskin-Robbins, Mukhtar carried home the pints of chocolate-chip-cookie-dough ice cream and lime-pomegranate sherbet. She had become accustomed to having a shadow.

"Are we in the North?" she asks, changing tack. She wants desperately to know where she is. "Is this Zajnoon's land?" She is only guessing, but Aisha looks up sharply at the mention of the sheikh's name.

"I'm right? Is he here? Is this one of his camps?" Her pulse speeds into hyperalertness.

Aisha stares at her as if she isn't sure what to say. Then, "Zajnoon is dead."

"Dead?" Miranda's mind somersaults. Surely this is good news? Will the violence end without the vicious, fanatical leader? She feels a surge of hope, though she knows Zajnoon's people are not the only rebel tribe in the North. Her thoughts fly to Finn; is he still working with the sheikhs? No, no, impossible. He would probably have been removed from post, if not by now then soon. Removed from the work he loves, from the project he initiated. And it is her fault. Is he even still in Mazrooq?

"The last government bomb. It destroyed his house, his wives, his sons." Aisha's voice catches, as if she is holding back tears. This is the most information she has imparted thus far. Miranda wonders how many of Zajnoon's followers are still alive.

"But our struggle will not die," says Aisha, with renewed vigor. "In his name, we will fight to our deaths."

Miranda's hope fades quickly in the wake of this pronouncement. So it is Zajnoon's people who have her. What could they possibly want, other than a ransom? And how organized are they, suddenly left leaderless? She is still puzzling over this when Aisha demands her shirt. "I will wash," she says. "Here is a new one, a clean one." She holds out a long-sleeved jersey emblazoned with the name of a British football team. Has it come from a former prisoner? Miranda hesitates before handing over her shirt, all she has of Finn's. *"Yalla,"* says Aisha impatiently. Slowly, Miranda unbuttons the shirt and slips it from her shoulders. The front is wringing wet. Desperate to maintain her milk supply in the wild hope Cressida could still profit from it, Miranda empties her breasts as often as possible. But still when she wakes, her shirt is drenched.

She holds out the soggy shirt to Aisha. "Milk," she says. "I have a baby at home." Perhaps this information will encourage leniency. Surely a woman would understand what it means to be separated from a child?

Aisha stares for a moment and then reaches her left hand toward the shirt. She pinches it and lets it drop. "Milk?" she says. "Son or daughter?"

"A daughter." Miranda isn't sure she should be giving this information away, but she cannot think of anything else to say. She pulls the jersey over her head.

The woman clucks again in disapproval. "Maybe next time you will have a son," she says.

Miranda bites back an instinctual defense of her daughter. When she was pregnant, the guards had constantly blessed her belly, wishing her a boy. But Miranda had wanted a girl for as long as she wanted a child at all. After the amniocentesis in London, when she and Finn told the guards they were definitely having a girl, the men still resisted the idea. This is not a country that rejoices at the birth of girls. *"Insha'allah* it will be a boy," they repeated. Miranda and Finn tried to explain that they already knew the child's sex, but this just confused the men. Finally, Miranda gave up, though she could never resist saying, "But I don't *want* a boy. I *want* a girl." It was important to her that they know that somewhere, by someone, girls were *wanted*.

Aisha adjusts her *niqab* one more time and disappears. Miranda assumes she has gone to fetch her something else to wear, but when the woman returns a few hours later, she is carrying a tiny parcel

wrapped in a dirty pink blanket. "You feed," she says. "Feed her."
She thrusts the blanket toward Miranda, who gingerly takes it in her
hands. It weighs almost nothing. In the dim light it takes her a second
to discern the top of a tiny head covered with fine black hair. Kneeling, Miranda lays the baby on the floor in front of her and slowly
peels back the blanket. Nausea wrings her stomach when she sees the
tiny infant. Its ribs are clearly visible, propping up the skin like tent
poles, its arms and legs wasted almost to bone. Its stomach is bloated
and round. Miranda slips a finger around the edge of the filthy piece
of cloth pinned at the tiny hips. A girl. The child watches her with
large dark eyes, quiet. She doesn't have the energy to cry, Miranda
thinks. It may be too late.

Aisha is watching her impatiently. She flips the blanket closed
again, covering the child's shriveled form. "Feed," she says again.

"Where is her mother?"

"*Mayyitah.* Dead."

"And her father?"

"They were both killed. Government bombs."

"She has no one?"

"No one is left."

Miranda lifts the featherlight child, shifting her into her left arm
as she lifts her shirt with her right hand. Queasiness at her disloyalty
almost overwhelms her. But chubby little Cressida doesn't need this
anymore, even if she could get to her. She presses the child's face to
her nipple, but the tiny girl doesn't drink. She simply continues to
stare up at Miranda, her cracked lips slightly open.

"What has she been eating?" asks Miranda, stroking the girl's
cheek.

"Tea."

"Tea?"

"That is all we have to give her."

Carefully Miranda takes her nipple between her fingers, holds it
over the child's lips, and squeezes gently. A few drops of watery milk
spatter onto the girl's lips. A tiny tongue darts out, searchingly. The
taste is sweet. She opens her mouth wider. Miranda squeezes more
milk into her mouth. For nearly an hour she repeats this, alternating

breasts and continuing to try to get the child to suck. She licks her own finger to clean it and gives it to the girl to suck, then transfers her to the nipple. The child doesn't have the strength to suck for more than a few seconds, but Miranda is patient. Her body relaxes as her breasts are slowly relieved of their stores. She does all of this mechanically, trying to calculate its significance. If her captors need her to feed this child, surely they won't kill her now? Is this girl her salvation? But before this morning, they hadn't known she was breast-feeding, hadn't known about Cressida. So why have they spared her?

Aisha watches for a while before beginning her morning prayers, prostrating herself on the dirt floor. Miranda wonders how old the child is. She doesn't even know her name. She waits for Aisha to finish her prayers before she asks.

Aisha isn't sure of the girl's age—no one here is ever sure about anyone's age—but thinks she is not more than a few weeks old. She has no name. Or rather, no one knows her name. But Aisha had passed by the ruins of her house and heard the crying. The child had been lying under an inverted V of mud bricks, surrounded by splintered plaster and stone. "I could not just leave her there when Allah had spared her," she says. "Though we have nothing to give her. The women left here are either too old or too young to have milk." The girl had been staying with one of Aisha's sisters, who fed her tea.

I don't have enough milk for a newborn, Miranda thinks. Perhaps her body will adjust to the child's needs, but she has no idea. Aisha squats, anxiously watching Miranda.

The frail child has fallen asleep in her arms. Miranda rewraps her in the dirty blanket and places her on the mat. They had swaddled Cressida until she was three months old and could wrestle her arms and legs out of her blankets. "Like the Incredible Hulk," Miranda had said. Finn had looked at her questioningly. Another cryptic pop-culture reference.

Aisha stands. "*Haasna*. Now we get the water."

"But the child," Miranda starts. The woman nods and disappears into one of the other houses. When she returns, she carries a long bolt of red-and-black striped cloth. Together, they fashion a sling so that Miranda can carry the infant close to her chest. Miranda pays close attention to the way Aisha folds it. To think she had paid nearly fifty dollars for a custom-made sling for Cressida. That amount of money seems ludicrous to her now. The baby smells faintly of fecal matter, though Miranda imagines it has been a long time since she consumed enough calories to trigger a bowel movement. Miranda is surprised to find herself trusted with the infant. Aisha could just as easily have carried her, but she seems to have abdicated responsibility.

The girl sleeps all the way to the spring and back, exhausted from her efforts to nurse. When the water is stashed by the fire and the women have settled on the ground to eat their beans again, the baby opens her eyes and lets out a feeble howl of hunger.

"Well, that's a good sign," whispers Miranda, setting aside her tin plate and picking up the child. "Let's try this again, shall we?"

AUGUST 30, 2007
Miranda

Miranda stood in front of the mirror and groaned. "*Nothing works!*" The silver-and-black sundress, which had always felt so modest back home in Seattle, made her feel exposed and slatternly. Sighing, she slipped the straps from her shoulders and let it fall to the floor. "Everything makes me look either Amish or prostitutional," she said, stepping out of the puddle of polyester at her feet.

"Prostitutional?" Finn watched her with amusement from across the room, where he was adjusting his tie. He was wearing khakis and one of his many long-sleeved, stripy shirts.

"You men have it easy. You can wear pretty much the same thing in any culture. It's a minefield out there for us."

One of the things she loved about living here was that every day she had only to throw on one of her three floor-length skirts with one of her seven cotton Indian blouses. That was it. No agonizing over which pants worked with which shirts, or which dress was most flattering. Further abbreviating her morning routine, she wore minimal makeup and kept her hair tied up in a ponytail or knot at the back of her head. It was so freeing to shed all of the accoutrements of vanity. Yet, oddly, she received more male attention on the streets here than anywhere else she'd ever lived. "I look like Laura Ingalls Wilder in mourning," she said to Finn, "and they treat me like I'm Dolly Parton."

Now everything had changed. When she went out with Finn, they were just as likely to mix with Western diplomats as they were to mix with the locals. And at Western homes, the women *did* pay attention to fashion. At least, certain women did. The wives of ambassadors, for example. The thing was, Miranda didn't own anything remotely chic. She traveled light. What on earth would she do when she and Finn had to host dinner parties together?

Tonight they were stepping out together for the first time, to the InterContinental for a dinner and dance celebrating the launch of a new adventure tourism agency (for very brave tourists, willing to wander into lawless lands to scale monumental walls of rock). Miranda found the agency's optimism about its prospects refreshing. Few diplomats thought anything could succeed in the grim political and economic climate of Mazrooq. She felt like wearing something cheerful, something red. But while the hotel was certainly quite Western (and as fancy as it got in this city), there were certain to be Mazrooqis there as well. So did she deck herself out in bright Western wear and risk shocking the Muslims, or wrap herself up in modest lengths of cotton and risk being thought dowdy by the international community?

At last she found a suitable compromise: a long, polka-dotted black skirt topped with a sleeveless, embroidered black blouse. For safety, she added a black pashmina shawl to cover her shoulders. Her black leather sandals were scuffed and gritty with embedded sand, but the skirt was long enough to hide them. Finn, who had just finished straightening his green flowered tie, inspected her selections lying out on the bed. "What?" she said. "You don't like them?"

"They're fine," he said. "It's just . . . would you mind terribly if I ironed them? And give me those shoes." Wordlessly, she handed him the shoes, and he disappeared downstairs into the utility room, emerging twenty minutes later with freshly pressed clothing and shiny sandals.

"Wow," she said. "Full-service ambassador."

"Attention to detail, darling. It's part of the job."

"You're almost as useful as Negasi," she said, admiring her improved feet.

Brushing her hair, Miranda wandered over to the window. The fanciful metal grating, all swirls and curls, somewhat limited the view of the drive. But she could see the massive armored car just beneath the bedroom window, all four of its doors standing open, surrounded by men gripping AK-47s as they surveyed the surrounding rooftops.

"The guys look ready," she commented.

"Always," said Finn. "Usually about an hour before I am."

THEY SLIPPED OUT the front door just after seven. Mukhtar, who had been lurking in the shadows of the bougainvillea bush beside the stairs, emerged to shield them from the possible bullets of possible snipers on the way to the car. Would she ever get used to living steeped in hypothetical menace? Finn strode past her to the far side of the car. He was required to sit on the right, directly behind his bodyguard, something Miranda had learned when she once tried to climb into his side of the car. She hadn't yet earned the right to her own bodyguard, so her protection wasn't officially important.

Climbing up into the armored car was impossible to do gracefully, but finally Miranda managed to haul herself and her trailing skirts through the open door. Not until their seat belts were fastened did Ali start the car. *"Masa al-kheer,"* he said politely. *"Masa anoor!"* she and Finn chorused back.

Finn was cheerful in the car, chatting in effortless Arabic to Ali and Mukhtar. Miranda's Arabic was slowly improving, but she still understood only about half of what was said. She caught "sun" and "England" and "weather." Apparently some of the men had just returned from a training course in the UK. "There was sun in England, but it had no heat," Finn translated for her. She smiled.

Miranda was preoccupied. This was the first time she and Finn had ever been out in public as a couple. It felt momentous. Almost as momentous as Finn telling his staff about her earlier in the week. Miranda had been sitting on the edge of his bed, watching him change out of his suit after work. "What did you say?" she asked. "'Just in case any of you were worried, I'm finally getting laid'?"

"Um," he said, turning from the closet lined with dress shirts organized by color and fabric, looking slightly embarrassed. "I'm afraid I told them we were engaged."

Miranda looked at him, startled. "We are? You've known me what, five months?"

"Six. Nearly seven. About as long as you've known me."

"It's just—I don't remember a proposal. Did you do it while I was sleeping?"

"Well, it just seemed the easiest way to say it."

"Huh."

"Huh?"

"It was *easier* to say we were engaged than to say we were seeing each other."

"I wanted them to take it seriously. I don't want to look like I'm behaving frivolously." He looked at her anxiously. "Are you cross?"

Miranda was quiet for a moment, studying him as he stood before her in plaid boxers and a slightly creased white dress shirt. His pale, bare legs made him look terribly vulnerable. "No one even knew you were seeing me, and now you tell them we're *engaged*? Don't you think that's bound to strike someone as odd?"

"Not anyone here—the Mazrooqis regularly marry people they haven't ever met."

"But the Brits don't. At least, not as far as I know.... Aren't you going to look rash? Or if not rash then secretive, for not having disclosed our alleged courtship?"

Finn frowned. "I hadn't thought of that."

"Hadn't you?"

"I'm sorry, love, I thought I was doing the right thing." He came and sat beside her, taking her hands in his.

Miranda sighed. "Well, what did they say?"

"*Mabrouk,* for the most part. Congratulations. The local staff said *mabrouk.* I don't think it struck any of them as odd in the least. And my British staff were all very polite about it."

"Of course they were. You're their boss."

"Are you sure you're not mad?"

"It's just . . . Would you mind letting me know if we've set a date? I mean, just so I can get it on my calendar?"

"Miranda . . ." He pulled her down onto the bed so they lay side by side, facing each other. "It's just, I know already. I've never felt this way. I know I will marry you. That is, if you're willing."

"Is this a proposal?"

"Absolutely not. I'd like to try to arrange something a bit more elaborate. Think of it as a kind of pre-proposal. A testing of the waters."

Miranda smiled. "Well, I'd hate to make you a liar. . . . I guess you could say the water's warm enough for wading."

The ride to the hotel felt endless. Through the window she watched the oversized mansions of the elite fly by, their heft squeezing out any hope of gardens. The Mazrooqis had an odd aversion to outdoor spaces; they built their homes with neither yards nor courtyards. How ugly it was here, in the wealthy end of town. Yet the Mazrooqis were proud to live here, proud to have escaped the claustrophobia of their city's ancient, rocky heart. Nadia once confessed that she had never been to the Old City before she began visiting Miranda. Unfathomable, to live so close to perfect beauty and to shun it.

Her mind strayed to who would be there tonight. Some of her friends from the Old City, certainly, as most of them were so desperate for evening entertainment they would attend the launch of a paper airplane. Mosi and Madina might come. But she didn't know who else was invited. Many ambassadors probably had more prestigious things to do with their evening. Or maybe not. It wasn't such a hopping town that there were swank social gatherings every night. They had chosen the event carefully. It wasn't political, wasn't diplomatic, wasn't high-profile. It was a low-key celebration of a local company, a comfortable place for them to come out as a couple.

The guard at the entrance to the hotel's parking lot waved them right through. This didn't happen when Miranda arrived by taxi (as she had many times, to swim at the pool or meet a friend for lunch). When she arrived alone, the guards stopped the car for ten minutes or so while they ran mirrors attached to the ends of sticks under the engine, checking for secreted explosives. Not that she minded; she was all in favor of security measures. But it was fairly time-consuming, so eventually she just had taxis let her off down the road from the hotel and walked the rest of the way.

Tonight they were driven right to the entrance. A doorman ushered them from the car through the revolving doors, directing them to a small herd of white-robed men who surged toward Finn, kissing him and shaking his hand. Miranda had never felt so invisible. *"Sa'adat assafir! Ahlan wa sahlan!"* Your Excellency! Welcome! Finn vigorously resisted being called Your Excellency, but the Mazrooqis clung to honorifics. They surrounded them, picking them up in their current and wafting them toward the elevator. Finn made an attempt to introduce her but was interrupted by new arrivals slipping in at the last minute and thrusting their hands at him.

She was relieved when the elevator disgorged them on the eighth floor, opening into a small front room lined with buffet tables. A pair of swans sculpted from butter gazed imperiously down on dozens of salads, spreads, cheeses, and fruit. Miranda looked longingly at the cheese. But they were swept along with the crowd, into an enormous ballroom crowded with people in various forms of evening dress. Mazen, the Lebanese hotel manager, greeted them just inside the door. "Tonight for your special pleasure we have a belly dancer," he said. "From Helsinki!"

"They have belly dancing in Finland?" Miranda wondered if it were ever warm enough in Finland to shed the requisite layers of clothing.

"She has trained in Cairo. She has been working at the Marriott there."

"I'm looking forward to it," said Finn. "I've never seen a belly dancer."

Eagerly, Miranda scanned the faces for someone she knew. Crimson-draped tables clustered around the dance floor, most of them nearly full. *"Ahlan wa sahlan!"* A man dressed in white slacks and a blazer made his way to her from across the room.

"Halim!" She smiled, relieved to see him. The owner of a resort on one of the Red Sea islands, largely responsible for the launch of the new company, Halim was an old friend. She and Vicenta had met him during their first year, when they'd stayed in one of his grass huts. He kissed her on both cheeks before turning to Finn. "You must be the ambassador," he said, his round brown face radiant with welcome.

"How did you know?" Finn and Halim had never met, and Miranda had confessed her romance to no one but her housemates.

"This is a small country," he said. "Everyone knows everything."

"God, I hope not!" said Miranda, immediately regretting taking the Lord's name in vain. But Halim didn't seem to have noticed, or if he had, didn't care. The two men chatted happily while Miranda continued to gaze around. She spotted Morgane, a friend from her weekly treks, whose husband, Sebastian, worked for the German development organization. They were sitting with Kaia and Stéphane (here courtesy of BNP Paribas), who were also avid hikers. Morgane and Kaia spent their time exploring, mountaineering, and studying Arabic. Suddenly, Miranda was excited to introduce them to Finn. Finally, finally, they could stop hiding. He could know all of her friends, and she could know his. This was marvelous. She tugged at his sleeve.

"Halim, would you mind if I borrowed Finn for a moment? I want to introduce him to some other friends."

"Only if you promise to come stay with us. On the house! We will be so happy to host you."

"Thank you, Halim. But you realize that if we come, you'll be getting ten extra guys with guns. You may want to think about that."

Halim stretched his arms wide. "You are all welcome! But there is no need for protection on my island. We are peaceful there."

"I'm sure you are. I've been there, remember? But ambassadors have an awful lot of rules."

"So you will come?"

"We'll come, Halim. Someday." She kissed his cheeks again and led Finn away.

IT WAS AT least an hour before they got to the buffet. After chatting with the French and Norwegians, Miranda had introduced Finn to Mosi and Madina, who had settled into a back table, where Madina was busy flirting with some young Arabic students while Mosi sat in his customary regal silence, smiling indulgently. Madina had given Finn her most dazzling smile and talked nonstop at him until Miranda finally led him away to the food. By the time they joined the buffet line the butter swans were beginning to wilt, their long necks drooping toward the basket of flour-dusted rolls. Miranda blissfully filled a plate with cheese and accepted a glass of red wine from a passing waiter. By the time she was on her second glass, the band had started and the belly dancer had begun a slow slither across the floor.

Somewhat predictably, the belly dancer was pale, a chalky white. Slender and narrow-hipped, she lacked the grounding heft of the belly dancers Miranda had seen in Egypt. Still, there was enough fat over her belly to jiggle as she shimmied. Miranda found it more entertaining to watch the men in the audience, who stared fixedly at the long-haired girl, their mouths hanging slightly open. "I wouldn't say it's my favorite dance form," said a disappointed Finn. "But maybe it's better in Egypt?"

When the belly dancer had left the stage, the band struck up "Come On, Eileen," and there was a stampede to the dance floor. Miranda was about to pull Finn into the fray when across the room she caught sight of Leslie, Finn's deputy, with his wife, Camilla. Miranda had immediately liked Leslie, a stout, warm man with a hearty laugh. He had arrived in the country a month before his wife, and Miranda had enjoyed chatting with him at parties. She was less sure about Camilla, a tall, stork-like woman with short, straw-dry hair and liver-spotted, leathery skin suggestive of a life spent by the side of a pool clutching a gin and tonic. She and Leslie had done postings in Kiev, Sierra Leone, Athens, Zimbabwe, and Tortola, places with no shortage of sun or alcohol. As far as Miranda knew, Camilla had never had a job. She had been friendly enough when first introduced to Miranda, but in that high-pitched, overly polite British way that doesn't convey true warmth. They must have seen Miranda and

Finn, but they hadn't come over. She tugged Finn's sleeve. "Shouldn't you say hello to Leslie?"

"Oh, is he here? Of course." As they walked over, Miranda tried to remember if Leslie and Camilla had seen them together. "Does Leslie know?" she asked.

"I told him earlier this week, before I told the rest of the staff. Um . . ." Finn paused for moment.

"What?"

"It's just, they'll be polite I'm sure, but I wouldn't expect Camilla to be overjoyed that you're on the verge of outranking her."

Miranda raised an eyebrow. "I hadn't thought of it like that."

"Sweetheart, if all goes according to plan, you're going to be an ambassador's wife. That may not go down well with women who have been waiting thirty years, suffering through innumerable posts in uncomfortable places, for their husbands to be made head of post."

"I see."

"You kind of cheated."

"It never occurred to me that women actually *aspired* to be ambassadors' *wives*. As if that were a profession in itself. I mean, I can see aspiring to be an *ambassador*. But an ambassador's *accessory*?"

"Do me a favor? Don't say anything like that to anyone but me?"

"Are people going to hate me?"

Finn hesitated. "Well, *hate* is kind of a strong word."

Anxiety clutched at her abdomen. "I think you had better fill me in later on the various expectations people will have of an ambassador's wife. Perhaps before the wedding."

"Certainly. Right. Are you ready? Deep breath . . ."

"As I'll ever be."

Camilla stood up as they approached, still clutching her glass of white wine. She was at least three inches taller than Miranda, and slightly unsteady on her feet. "Hello, *darling!* I hear congratulations are in order," she said, with a wide smile that didn't quite communicate joy. Her lips were dry, flaking lipstick the color of orange sherbet. "That was *quick*, wasn't it? We hadn't even known you two were a couple! Though of course, there have been rumors . . ."

Miranda smiled back. "Yes. Well, thank you."

Leslie stood and gave her a warm hug. *"Mabrouk,"* he said. "And good luck."

"Will I need it?"

"Every married couple needs it."

"I hope you know what you're getting into," said Camilla, her smile stretching even wider.

"I'm sure I don't," said Miranda. "But isn't that the fun of it? Come on, *darling*," she said, turning to Finn. "They're playing our song." They were, in fact, playing something in Arabic she'd never heard before. But it would do.

On the dance floor, Finn surprised her with his abandon. He took her hands and spun her into his arms and back into the fray. At first, the floor was crowded with other couples and groups of people, laughing and swaying. Through the crowd, Miranda could see Finn's team watching them, their hands ever-ready at their waists. Was there a chance that he'd be offed by a sniper on the dance floor? She closed her eyes and shook the thought from her head. Sweat ran down the sides of Finn's face and drenched the back of his shirt. Miranda shrugged off her shawl and felt grateful for her bare arms. She could not remember the last time she'd danced like this, felt the visceral delirium of disappearing into the music. When Finn spun her close again, she responded instinctively, kissing him. The moment their lips touched, he drew back quickly. "Not here," he murmured. "We shouldn't . . ." The cheese and wine curdled in her stomach. She had forgotten, for a fleeting moment, where they were. "I'm sorry!" she said in abject apology. He smiled and said it was all right, but she wasn't sure it was. She didn't feel like dancing anymore. It was late anyway, and the band would soon be stopping.

They gathered their things from their table and started to make their way to the door, stopping every few steps to say good-bye to the dozens of men stretching their hands to catch Finn and kiss him. "I'm beginning to get jealous," she muttered. The guys followed them, unsmiling. She tried to remember if they usually smiled when they were working. Mukhtar helped her into the car without speaking. That was definitely unusual. No one said a word for the entire ride home. Miranda stared out the window, feeling miserable. Finn reached for her hand and pressed it.

As soon as the heavy door of the Residence had swung shut behind them, Finn turned to her in the hallway, under the watchful gaze of Elizabeth II at her coronation. "How bizarre!"

"What?" She slid the shawl off her shoulders and stepped out of her shoes, sticky with spilled wine, leaving them by the hall table.

"The close protection team. They were so quiet the whole way home. Completely taciturn."

"Because we were dancing?"

"I don't know. They usually natter away the whole journey."

"Was it because they saw us kiss? Is that why Mukhtar wasn't speaking to me?"

He shrugged. "Maybe. I had better make an honest woman of you fast. They'll get over it."

"They will?" She looked up at him, worried. "You'll tell them how lovable I really am?"

"I already do, all the time. Eventually, everyone will love you. I promise."

OCTOBER 2010
Miranda

Miranda does not try to keep track of the time. She doesn't want to know how many days she has been apart from her daughter. She doesn't want to know how long it has been since Finn slept beside her, since she had to roll him over in his sleep to stop him from snoring. If she doesn't count the days it deprives them of a sense of reality, of solidity. Time is measured out only in the hours she spends feeding this nameless child. Unable to do anything of use to herself, she does this. She narrows her world down to filling up this tiny girl, this sparrow of a person. It is difficult. The child is slow to learn to suck properly, to build up the strength to drink for an extended period of time. Miranda is grateful for the massage techniques she had learned to make her milk come down for Cressida. She feeds the baby almost every hour, unless she is walking to fetch water or doing the other menial tasks required of her. In her real life, this would have felt a terrible burden, an interruption of her painting or reading or time with Finn. But here, it is her connection to sanity. The child has not gained a significant amount of weight, but her eyes have started to brighten and she waves her hands with more vigor. Her cries too have grown louder. The breast milk seems to have reawakened an appetite she had forgotten she had.

Miranda's breasts have swollen with the increased demand, but she wonders at the quality of her milk. Her diet here is dire, consisting mainly of sweet, milky tea, beans, and bread. She remembers reading that a breast-feeding mother's body will deprive itself of nutrients in order to ensure enough nutrients end up in the milk, that even a malnourished mother can nourish a child. She wonders if this is true. And she wonders how long this is so, before the mother's body has no stores left to drain. She is always thirsty, always seeking extra water.

At night, Miranda sleeps curled around the tiny girl, breathing the smoky scent of her head, a luxury she had rarely allowed herself with Cressida. She had read too many stories about parents rolling over on their children and accidentally suffocating them. But children here all sleep with their mothers. Tazkia had been horrified when Miranda told her that Cressie slept in her own room, down the hall. "What if she gets sick?" she had said. "What if she needs you?" "I will hear her," Miranda had responded, confident of the lightness of her slumber. Now, it occurs to her that babies sleep with their mothers in most of the world's cultures. It is only the West that sees this pressing need to separate the child. Miranda wonders if she has somehow damaged her daughter, leaving her to sleep alone in those early months, without even the comfort of a plush animal (another suffocation risk). Is this why Cressida is so uncuddly? To punish them for having slept apart?

At every thought of Cressida, which is nearly every waking moment, there is the twist of pain and guilt and longing around her solar plexus. Every night Cressida goes to sleep motherless, while this silent child borrows her warmth. Miranda wants the anchor of Cressida's plump, well-fed body in her arms, the light, soapy scent of her scant hair. She wonders what Cressie would smell like without her daily bath, if she would smell more like the child at her side. Or if every baby has her own particular scent, crafted to appeal to the olfactory organs of her particular parents. At first Miranda had found this dark baby's scent mildly repellent, redolent as it was of excrement and animal. But now she smells nothing but the child herself, a warm, bread-like odor. Bread cooked by a smoky fire.

When no one is around, she washes the child with her drinking water, using a scrap of cloth torn from the makeshift sling to squeeze water over her sharp little ribs and tiny fingers. Aisha does not approve of this washing. The baby will get sick, she tells Miranda. Babies should not get wet. Miranda has given up trying to explain that she only washes her in the warmth of the afternoon and dries her immediately. That the water keeps the girl's bottom free from rashes and infections. There is no soap, but the baby is too young for soap. Every few days Miranda rinses the child's only outfit, a long grayish dress, keeping her wrapped in a blanket until it is dry. It doesn't take long. The air here is so thirsty that it takes less than two hours for the garment to be drained of moisture.

Miranda is almost grateful for the sleepless nights, for the night feedings. She wants to be too tired to think. It has always been so for her, constant activity and work buffering a troubled heart.

Sitting in the shadow of the hut, this feather of a girl pressed to her breast, Miranda feels her heart swell and grow heavy, making room. It is not something she has hoped would happen. It is not convenient. Her captors have chained her with this child more effectively than if they had strung her from the wall in shackles. It occurs to her belatedly that if she tries to run, this girl will almost certainly die. But when she had first unwrapped that scrawny, barely living child, she had not hesitated.

While vigilantly protective of the girl, touching her with something approaching reverence, Aisha remains resolutely unmaternal. Perhaps she knows too well the hazards of opening her heart too wide to such a fragile life. She has five sons living, she has told Miranda. And two who died before their second birthday.

Miranda runs her fingers over the girl's short, spiky hair. Cressida had been bald for most of her first year, only recently growing a strip of curls down the middle of her head. But this child already has a full head of straight, black hair. "You need a name, little one," she says in English. "It's time we gave you a name."

Aisha looks up at the sound of her voice. "You speak English?" she says sharply. She has been peeling potatoes with a knife, and she stops, mid-stroke, a bit of brown skin dangling from the blade.

Miranda freezes. She has been so careful, speaking only in Arabic or French when talking with the baby. Never English. How could she have been so stupid?

"Only a little," she says in Arabic. "I learned some in school. I thought maybe I would teach the baby a few words."

Aisha's dark, ageless face creases. "You're always talking to her," she says. "Why do you talk? She is just a baby, she doesn't understand."

Miranda smiles at her. "I think she does." She had talked to Cressida from the day she was born, a running monologue from morning until night, interrupted only by Finn or Gabra. Aside from the stimulation she hoped it provided her daughter, she talked to stave off boredom. So much of that first year is boredom, if you aren't creative. Now, she doesn't talk to the baby to alleviate boredom; she talks to the baby to fend off terror, grief, and insanity.

She gives the child a finger to grasp and looks back at Aisha. "Could we give her a name?" She doesn't know why it has taken her so long to ask this question. Is it because neither of the women had thought the child would live? We grow attached to those we name; they are ours forever.

"An Arabic name," says Aisha.

"Of course."

"An important name. This child is—" Aisha falls suddenly silent and sits for a moment in thought. "Kanza means hidden treasure. Or Sawdah? A wife of the Prophet, Peace Be Upon Him. Kawkab? That is the name of my mother. Fatima? One of my sisters. Abrar? Means devoted to God. Is a good name. Luloah?" She counts the names off on her fingers.

"Luloah." Miranda tests the word on her tongue. The baby looks up at her, dark eyes wide. "What does Luloah mean?"

"Luloah. Like the jewel that grows in a shell. A seashell."

Pearl. Miranda almost says it out loud. She is astonished she is allowed to help choose. She has no right to name this child. "Luloah," she says again. A child born from the sand. "Luloah?" She looks hopefully at Aisha.

"We give her two names. Luloah Abrar."

Miranda looks down at Luloah and smiles.

NOW AS SHE sits, with no paintings to create or ponder, no book to read, and nothing to keep her thoughts from their wild rambles, Miranda remembers Nasser. Her first year here she had taken a solitary holiday to Egypt. Vicenta had been finishing work for her show and needed some time alone, and Miranda had been feeling restless. But Cairo had completely overwhelmed her. She had not anticipated the noise, the endless shriek of car horns, the greasy, unbreathable air. At least in the Egyptian Museum it had been quiet. There were more people sitting outside in the front garden, talking or sharing sandwiches, than there were in the cool, dark building. Standing in the foyer, she was unsure which way to go. Thousands of years of history confronted her all at once, and it was too much. There was no possible way she could wade through a past as long as Egypt's. The cards on the exhibits were tiny, and she had to strain her eyes to read them. The names all ran together. So many kings and pharaohs. So many gods and goddesses.

After peering into the first few glass cases, she had been on the verge of giving up when Nasser appeared. He was the fifth guide to approach her. The others had accosted her outside, descending upon her as soon as she had her ticket in her hand. *"Laa, laa, laa,"* she had said reflexively. *"Laa shukran."* No thank you. It had become a mantra, something she said so often here that it gained a melody, became a song. Only as Nasser launched into his pitch—he was an Egyptologist offering her the one-hour highlights tour or the two-hour in-depth tour, for the low, low starting price of one hundred Egyptian pounds—she asked herself if it was really necessary to say no to him as well. She had been so appalled by the way the men followed her on the streets, clicking their tongues and sucking their breath in noisy whistles, and by the constant demand for baksheesh that rejection had become reflex; it hadn't occurred to her that any of them would have something she could possibly want or use.

She looked at Nasser. He was probably close to sixty, with graying hair, crooked teeth, and brown eyes stained with an ancient grief. Tall and thin, he wore a card around his neck that announced him as an accredited museum guide. He wasn't funny in the aggressive way so many of them were with tourists, trying to entertain. He spoke simply and clearly. And he expected her to disappoint him. "All right," she finally relented. "Please show me the highlights." It was a good decision. Nasser spoke briefly about each of the more significant statues and treasures, moving on before she had time to get bored or restless. One reason she hated group tours was the long periods of standing they always involved. But Nasser seemed to sense her need for flow. His English was fluent yet still littered with charming idiosyncrasies. When they came to King Tut's tomb, Nasser explained that the walls within his chamber had been "dismantled so they could be removed, and then mantled again."

What comes to her now as she sits looking down at Luloah's sharp little face, her translucent eyelids trembling as she nurses, is the last item Nasser had shown her. "This is the last judgment," he had said, "the weighing of the heart." Miranda had looked at the scales, the scales of Libra (Vícenta's sign), balanced in the middle of the drawing. On one of them rested a small human heart, on the other, a tiny image of Maat, the goddess of truth. Or so spake Nasser. "If the heart is heavier than the goddess, then it belonged to a good man and he should go to Heaven. But if the heart is lighter, he did not take enough into his heart and he should go to Hell." This is what stays with her. Not the golden trinkets of Tut's tomb, not the hermaphroditic pharaoh with the wide thighs of a woman, not even the desiccated faces of the royal mummies. But that a heavily laden heart was the entrance ticket to Paradise.

SEPTEMBER 17, 2007
Miranda

The third Monday of every month was Quiz Night at the British Club. Miranda loved quizzes and was getting desperate to leave the house. All week she had been painting steadily, struggling to work her way out of reality, out of narrative, taking time off only for meals with Finn. He was often out in the evening, at dinners for visiting American dignitaries, meetings with the Foreign Minister, or in strategy sessions with the intelligence community. While Miranda missed his company, most nights she didn't mind being alone in the house. It felt luxurious, all of that space to inhabit, to fill. More important, it meant she could work without distraction, eat only when she felt hungry, and wander around half-dressed. But solitude's charm was fading. There were days in the hollow, soulless Residence when Miranda could not stand the isolation, moments when she was tempted to run through the kitchen and downstairs to bang on the door of Negasi's room and beg her to talk with her. About anything. Miranda wanted stories about Ethiopia, about her son who died mysteriously years ago, about Negasi's family. But she had never been down to that room. It was Negasi, Teru, and Desta's only completely private space in the Residence, and Miranda felt that to enter it would be a violation.

Finn didn't have an evening engagement on Quiz Night, but he had stacks of work to finish at home. "Go, darling," he said. "You'll find someone you know."

Normally Miranda wouldn't need someone she knew. Normally she was completely happy to fling herself at strangers. But chatting up the still-frosty embassy staff was hard work. She craved nondiplomats. Graceless artists with no manners and articulate philosophies. Bipolar poets. Self-aggrandizing actors. Anyone but the Professionally Polite. She called Mosi and Madina, but Mosi said he loathed the British Club and Madina had two Mazrooqi girls spending the night with her. Miranda could hear them shrieking in the background. Everyone else she called was also busy. Well, she thought, it's no crime to go out alone. She was a paying member, after all. Had been since long before Finn.

The guards at the club were very smiley. She had always been able to rely on the kindness of the guards. Not once since her first visit had she ever had to show identification at the entrance, discreetly unmarked in the front wall of a flat-roofed, cinder-block house. Abdullah—the one and only Mazrooqi bartender—was also welcoming, walking to the end of the bar to kiss her cheeks as soon as he saw her. "I'm hearing things about you," he said, slapping down a paper Heineken coaster.

"Oh?" she said, nodding at her favorite gin.

"Like I hear you're moving next door." Abdullah took down the dusty bottle of Hendrick's and poured a generous shot.

"Says who?"

"Says just about everyone in the room."

Miranda turned to look around. The club was busy, with clusters of embassy people gathered around the circular tables of its main room. Several oil workers leaned on the bar, their faces creased by age and sun, their hands clutching sweating pints. A group of Westerners she didn't recognize sprawled across the overstuffed beige sofas under the oversized television screen, laughing at someone's joke. Outside, several smokers stood gazing at the abandoned tennis courts. Everyone showed up here eventually.

She pushed her chit toward Abdullah and picked up her glass. "Don't believe everything you hear." For a moment, she stood there, sipping her drink and feeling awkward. Should she join one of the embassy tables? Was that the correct thing to do? She tried to catch the eye of one of the women from the political section, who studiously looked away.

"Miranda?" She was rescued. It was Karl, who worked for Save the Children. Miranda didn't know him very well, but she had met him and his wife, Sabina, several times at the German Haus and the French Cultural Centre, where they had chatted about art and censorship and the plight of Mazrooqi children. "Looking for a team?"

"Yes, *please!* I tried to round up some friends, but it seems everyone had plans."

"Well, we're a few short, so join us. On the sofa over there." He gestured toward the massive sofa crammed with at least seven people. Karl introduced her around. There was a Swiss woman newly arrived in the country; a pregnant Norwegian and her husband, who worked for a German development organization; an Indian named Moon and his pregnant wife; a young Frenchman; and the Italian head of the World Food Programme. No one Miranda knew, no one British. Perfect.

She wasn't much use during the sports, music, and entertainment rounds, but when an art history round came along, she triumphed. Her teammates kept her glass refilled and generously credited her with their eventual win. When they asked where she worked, she told them she was an art teacher. How relaxing a few hours of anonymity could be!

The quiz broke up around ten, and people wandered outside to smoke or sat with their teammates for a few more pints. No one from the British embassy spoke to her all night. In fact, no one would look at her. Once, on her way back from the bar with a round of drinks, she said hello to two of the management section women, but neither responded. Jesus, she thought. Seriously? Stealing their ambassador's heart was that terrible a crime? Well, she wasn't going to force herself on them. She had other friends. But still, it bothered her. They didn't know her. They'd never had a conversation with her. She could not help but be hurt that they didn't have a crumb of curiosity. Maybe they thought they already knew. That was the problem with gossip. But perhaps she was too hard on them. How much fun would it be for them to hang out with the boss's girlfriend, watching every word they said, lest something untoward reach his ears?

Restless, she wandered into the back room to watch a game of pool. The oil company guys were playing, lining bets up along the side of the table. Next to them was a small bookcase stacked with shabby paperbacks. Miranda picked up a few and flipped through them. Romances, thrillers, naval history. She put them back on the shelves and returned to the bar. She was waiting for Abdullah to notice her when a tall, honey-haired man with military posture sitting on a nearby stool introduced himself. "Leo," he said. "I don't think we've met."

"Miranda," she said. "I'm—"

"I know who you are," he said, smiling and offering his hand. When he stood, she noticed he was at least two feet taller than she was, taller even than Finn.

"Oh dear."

"Oh, nothing to worry about. I just thought you'd be a good person to talk to as rumor has it you've been around for longer than any of us."

"Nearly three years. Wait, you're Leo? The vegetarian defense attaché?"

"Guilty as charged."

"I could tell by the glow of your complexion."

He laughed. "Oh, that's just the chemical peel I had last week. Buy you a drink?"

"Thanks. I'm okay though."

"So you're the mysterious painter."

"Not so mysterious."

"But no one's ever seen your work."

"Finn has. And no one else has asked. It's not exactly Mazrooqi-friendly."

"I'm not Mazrooqi."

"I might let you see it sometime, if you're really interested."

"I am." He asked her what it was like to live in the Old City, where she had traveled in the country, and whether she had seen any Mazrooqi art. He was relaxed, charming, and genuinely happy to be in Arnabiya. This was not necessarily a common reaction to the capital city.

They were laughing together at one of her taxi driver stories when the Overseas Security Manager, whose name she'd forgotten though she had met him several times, stopped beside them. Swaying with drink, he glared at Miranda with slightly unfocused eyes. "Watch it with her," he said to Leo.

Miranda's smile froze on her face. Was he joking? She wasn't sure how to react. But then he leaned in a bit closer, so she could smell the whiskey on his breath.

"I thought we weren't your type?" he sneered insinuatingly. "Or does rank trump sex?"

Even without moving, Miranda could sense ears turning in her direction. Camilla, top-ranking wife in the embassy until Miranda married Finn, was sitting at a table to her right; Miranda could hear her trying to stifle an equine snort of laughter. The conversations around them subsided to an attentive buzz. Was this some kind of a test? Let's see how the American girl reacts to binge-drinking British men? She didn't trust herself to speak; she could not risk insulting this man. Paralyzed by uncertainty, she tried to think what she might have done to provoke him.

"*I know what you really are,* you lezzie, status-seeking American cunt," he whispered, poking a finger toward her chest. "You might fool the ambassador, but you don't fool me. I don't like you. I don't like you *at all.*" His voice grew louder, filling the sudden silence in the bar.

Leo was on his feet, his expression grim. "Go easy, mate," he said. "That's no way to talk to a lady."

Miranda couldn't move. Her usual impulses were reined in by fear of aggravating the situation or embarrassing Finn. As she studied the man's buzz cut and bloodshot eyes, something fell into place. *Norman.* The name finally came to her. And suddenly, she remembered where they'd met before. They'd been at a buffet dinner at someone's house—who was it? One of the EU people. He'd cornered Miranda as she balanced a plate of hummus and tabouli on her knees, regaling her with stories of his glorious security career as she shoved food into her mouth as quickly as possible. As the evening dragged on, she had had to keep pushing his hand off of her knee. *Any minute now, he's going to tell me how lonely he is here,* she'd thought. *Any minute now, he's going to tell me how he and his wife hardly have a relationship anymore.* And he had. "And so I'm hardly married at all," he'd started, before Miranda had cut him off.

"I'm sorry, but I must get home," she had said as politely as she could manage. "My *girlfriend* is expecting me back."

Now, he stood before her, still fuming, unsteady on his feet. "*Lady?*" he sneered. The wife, *with whom he hardly had a relationship at all,* lurked dourly behind him. She was massive, with vast, drooping but-tocks and pendulous breasts resting on the mound of her belly. When Norman—she wouldn't forget his name again—shook his finger at Miranda, his wife let out a piercing giggle.

He turned back to Leo. "I'm serious," he said. "You watch it with her."

And he and his wife turned and waddled out the door.

Miranda looked down at her drink. I am not going to cry, she told herself. I am not going to cry in front of the entire fucking embassy staff.

"Hey," said Leo softly. "That was *despicable*. That was unbelievably rude. He had no right to do that." His face was kind. He was young, Miranda thought. Probably younger than she was.

"I'm okay," said Miranda. "It's all right."

"It's not all right. There is no excuse for that kind of behavior."

"It's really okay," she said, slipping off of her stool. "But I think I need to go now."

"I'm sorry. Do you need a lift?"

Mutely, she shook her head. She had no intention of going any-where but next door to Finn. She gathered her *abaya* and shawl, and without looking around the bar, slipped out the front door. In the dark street, she started to run before she remembered the security cameras. She didn't want to look like a terrorist about to charge into the Residence. The tears trembled just behind her eyes, but she could not let them come yet. She first had to get past the guards.

Finn always knew the second something was wrong. He read every fleeting expression on her face, often sensing distress before she had fully experienced the emotion herself. "What is it?" he said when he opened the door to her. "Has something happened?"

Miranda opened her mouth to speak and burst into tears. Finn took her in his arms before leading her into the living room. "Tell me what happened."

Sobbing, she told him, watching his expression morph from ten-der concern to rage—and strangely, fear. "Mira, this is terrible. He had no right to do that to you."

"That's what Leo said." And she told him about Leo, how solicitous he had been.

"He's a good man," said Finn. "And I've got a serious conversation to have with Norman tomorrow. I have made it abundantly clear to him and to my entire staff that you are my partner, and for him to treat you like that is disrespectful of my position, of me, and of my choices. It was totally and completely inappropriate." He paused for a moment. "Do you think it could be jealousy? Did you ever—I mean, before I got here . . ."

"God, Finn! No! Are you serious?"

"I didn't really think so," he said quickly. "But I can't help wondering if he has some kind of infatuation with you."

"Intriguing way of expressing it."

"Lustful men are irrational creatures."

"Don't I know it."

Finn studied her for a moment. "It's just. Well. I shouldn't say."

"Finn?" Miranda pressed a palm against his denim-clad thigh. "Please tell me."

"It's just that—and you didn't hear this from me—it wouldn't be the first time he strayed from home."

"Ah."

"In fact, he's rather notorious for it."

"And his wife hasn't left him?"

"She may not know."

Miranda raised an eyebrow. "Come on, Finn. Wives *know*."

"I presume she doesn't want to rock the boat. They have a comfortable life, a position of respect. Why would she throw that away just because her husband is a jackass?"

Miranda shuddered. "Save me from a life so comfortable I would settle for a dishonest relationship."

"There's a gentlemen's agreement about this sort of thing," Finn said, flushing. "It just isn't done to tattle on your fellow diplomats. No matter how naughty they are."

Miranda withdrew her hand from his thigh. "And you're all *naughty*, are you?" Her heart thudded heavily, rattling her rib cage.

Why did so many grown British men still have the vocabulary of schoolboys?

"No. Not me. Not in that way. Oh, Miranda, you have nothing to worry about, please believe me!"

"I'm no hypocrite, Finn. I'm not expecting to marry a virgin. But I would hope you'd trust me enough to tell me any of your past indiscretions. I really don't mind however many women you've seduced, as long as you're mine from now on."

Finn looked down at his hands, his curling lashes golden in the lamplight. "I do trust you."

"And?"

"And I'm yours from now on."

"Okay." Miranda leaned forward to find his eyes, forcing him to look at her. "So what do we do about Norman?"

Finn sighed. "I wish we didn't have to talk about Norman."

"Leo said that it was a firing offense." Miranda looked hopefully at Finn, who was quiet for a long moment.

"Miranda," he began, and fell silent again. Then, "I can't fire Norman."

She simply looked at him.

"He did something for me in Afghanistan—"

"He was in Afghanistan with you?"

"Yes."

"And you didn't think this worth mentioning to me?"

"It didn't come up. Look, Miranda, I promise I will explain all of this to you someday. But please, not now."

"Why not? I have time." Miranda crossed her arms over her chest and stared at him. He had never spoken to her at all about Afghanistan, deflecting all of her questions. She had been patient, not wanting to force him into talking about what was obviously a source of trauma—who returned from that country unscarred?—but now she felt a burning need to know.

"*Don't,*" he said, filling that one word with quiet desperation. "Please."

Miranda lifted a hand to his face, touched the side of his cheek, rough with a day's stubble. "Sweetheart. Can you really not trust me?"

He took her hand in both of his, squeezing her fingers until she feared for her bones. "It's not about how much I trust you."

"Then what is it about?"

He was silent for a moment, his eyes turning toward the windows at the far side of the room. "I made a mistake," he finally said. "A mistake that will live with me for the rest of my life. And I don't want *you* to have to live with it. Not yet."

A flutter of fear rippled through Miranda's stomach. What terrible thing could Finn have done? He wasn't capable of terrible things. And how bad could it really have been if he was still an ambassador? She had a dozen new questions.

Still, sensing that this was as far as he was capable of going tonight, she softened. "But someday." It was not a question.

"Someday," he said. "I promise."

Upstairs, Miranda climbed into bed while Finn rummaged through the top drawers of his dresser. "It's not quite your birthday yet," he said. "But maybe this would be a good time to give you this."

She slipped a finger under the flap of the envelope and pulled out a reproduction of a painting she didn't recognize. A dark-haired woman leaned over the balcony of a square, mosaic-covered villa, stretching her arms above her head as a bearded man on a camel tucked his hands just above her ribs, like a parent lifting a child from a crib. Behind the house stretched an improbably (given the camel) green landscape, more reminiscent of England than of Arabia.

Inside, in his tiny, immaculate handwriting, Finn had written:

To my darling Miranda, my camel is on order. I have never before felt so profoundly and passionately about anyone. My love for you is unequivocal. You fill me with joy and inspiration and give purpose to my existence. I cannot wait to share the rest of my life with you, and to join you in the adventures and success that await you in the years ahead. With all my love, Your Finn
xxxxxxxxxoxxxxxxxxxx

"You see?" he said as Miranda started to cry again. "No one can hurt us. No one can really hurt us."

SEPTEMBER 17, 2007
Finn

After Miranda had finally fallen asleep, her eyelashes and cheeks crusted with salt, a tissue still clutched in one hand, Finn found himself unable to stay in bed. That ugly guilt had risen from its shallow grave, wrapping his heart in its clammy fingers. Did he have any right to marry Miranda without telling her this story? Did he have any right to remain next to her in this bed? He padded down the hall to the bathroom and pulled on his robe. No shortage of places to pace in this house. Still, even the enormity of the Residence felt claustrophobic. Pocketing the key, he pulled on his slippers and walked downstairs to the heavy front door.

Outside, he descended the stairs and stepped onto the spongy lawn, his slippers instantly soaked with dew. A warm breeze caressed the back of his neck, sending a shudder down his spine. It was a kind night, a soft, jasmine-scented, moonlit night. A night that nurtured dreams and calmed fears. A night he in no way deserved. The city was uncommonly silent around him, no growl of cars from the main road, no whining muezzins, no shouting vendors. All around him good Muslims slept peacefully in their beds, awaiting the signal to rise for morning prayers. And here he was, he with a guilty conscience and no god. The only thing in the world that meant anything to him at all was Miranda. And he wasn't sure that he would be able to keep her.

Where was Afsoon now? Was she still living? Or had he ultimately been responsible for her death too? It was too dangerous for him to try to find out. Or that was what he told himself. Perhaps he simply could not bear to find out. Even now, that night in Afghanistan, March 19, 2003—a date he would never forget—returned to him easily, instantly, indelibly. The sounds and smells of that country, not so unlike those of Mazrooq. The blaring muezzins, leaded exhaust fumes, bleating goats, frankincense, the haunting absence of feminine laughter, burning rubbish, the twang of the *rubab*, perspiration, rose. And the taste of hot, metallic dust in his mouth.

"SLEEP NATO," FINN murmured to himself that night, rolling over in his narrow bed. "Sleep NATO. NATO, NATO, NATO." There was no shortage of women in the twenty-six member countries; why could he not fall in love with one of them? Yet here he lay, dreaming of an Afghan girl with wide, dark eyes and the slender ankles and wrists of a dancer. Every day he saw her in the office, and every day she grew the slightest bit bolder, crossing her long legs so as to reveal a tantalizing stretch of brown calf, perching on the edge of his desk, so close he could smell her Iranian rose perfume. Afsoon wasn't your average Afghan woman, if there was such a thing. As a child she had traveled extensively with her diplomat father and been educated at Durham, reading French and Chinese, which she spoke as fluently as she spoke English. It was entirely possible she was the cleverest person in the embassy, wasted in the Siberia of the visa section. God knows why she had come back to this hellhole. If he were a woman he couldn't get away from this country fast enough.

In his first few months she had been an invaluable guide, helping Finn sort through the strands of tribal politics and wade through government bureaucracies. She was patient with him, drawing charts of tribal ancestries and geographical diagrams, filling in the holes in his historical knowledge—none of which was part of her job. He had people to do these things for him, but none of them explained things as lucidly as she. He had not wanted to flatter himself that she treated him any differently from the others, but for no one else did she make herself as available. Slowly, they became real friends, drinking tea together cross-legged on the floor of his cell-like pod while analyzing the latest news. They were careful not to be seen together outside of work. Even an innocent friendship could ruin a girl here. Finn wanted to be cautious.

He had always been careful, perhaps too careful. As a child he was shy and bookish, nervous around the opposite sex. Not until he was assigned Claire Henderson as a lab partner in chemistry class in third form had he developed a friendship with a girl. A scrawny, dark-haired sprite, Claire was nearly as timid and earnest as he was,

and probably smarter. Throughout high school they had been insepa-
rable, competing in class, editing each other's papers, and taking the
train to London on the weekends to go to the theater or the movies.
He adored her unreservedly, painfully, loved the light in her pale blue
eyes when she laughed, the smallness of her feet, the tiny bones of
her white wrists, even the thick black frames of her glasses. He had
never dared to touch her. It would have been irreverent, disrespectful.
He told himself that his love for her was on a higher plane than the
"love" he witnessed in the school corridors, boys backing girls against
their lockers, forcing their meaty tongues down their throats. And
ultimately, he couldn't face the prospect of her turning away.

His friend Charlie hadn't had such compunctions. In their final
year he had wrested Claire away, seducing her with his easy confidence, casual athleticism, and a keen scientific mind. They ran off to
Cambridge together to read physics and were now married and settled
in Dorset with two children. Would things have been any different
if Finn had had the courage to act? It was impossible to know. And
the truth was that she and Charlie were happy, he could see it every
time he visited, in the way she smiled at him over the heads of their
children, stroked the back of his hand when she asked him a question.

There had, perhaps inevitably, been a few romances at university,
but not love. His ardor for Claire took years to wither, to recon-
cile itself with reality. Only during his first year in the Foreign and
Commonwealth Office had he fallen in love again. Cordelia was a
fast-tracker, an Oxford-educated, ginger-haired diplomatic rock star
who spoke more languages than he did and had once played cricket
for England. They met on their first posting, to Amman, where they
courted in the Roman amphitheater, countless coffee shops, and the
ancient ruins of Petra. Lying on their backs in the sands of Wadi
Rum, they watched summer stars shower toward Earth while they
plotted their meteoric careers. Now that she had mastered Arabic,
Cordelia wanted to learn Mandarin and Thai. Thai? Finn said. Who
learns Thai? Hardly anyone, said Cordelia. So I won't have a lot of
competition. Everyone wants China; I need a backup.

Finn hadn't known what he wanted to do. He never thought that
far ahead. Only by accident had he become a diplomat at all. Having

finished a degree in contemporary Arabic and Spanish literature, he had assumed he was destined to teach. A professor of his convinced him otherwise. "You're an Arabist," she said. "We need you working on world peace."

He'd found himself surprisingly well suited to the work. He had the patience to endure the impoverished slog of the early years, a curiosity about the world that increased with each foray beyond Britain's borders, and most of all, an ease with and expertise in languages. It exhilarated him to shed both his mother tongue and his country. In a new land, with new vowels and verbs, he slipped into unfamiliar alphabets like a second skin, like an alternative persona. He could be anyone; he could reinvent himself. Clothed in a novel idiom, he brimmed with confidence.

It helped that he listened. *Really* listened. In meetings with ministers, military leaders, or even with lowly receptionists, he never took his eyes from the face of the person to whom he spoke. (Unlike so many other diplomats, he wasn't constantly glancing around the room for someone more important to approach.) People instinctively trusted him, for his ease with their language, his attentiveness, his concern for their concerns.

While he loved each language for its unique idiosyncrasies, Finn had a special fondness for Arabic, for the way it unfurled backward from his pen, looking like the kind of secret code he'd invented to write to boyhood friends in dull classes. And how could anyone understand politics today without a knowledge of Arabic, with its indirect, poetical digressions, its cryptic grammar, its ancient resonances?

He supposed he would continue in the Middle East as long as the FCO was willing to send him there. He and Cordelia were briefly back in London together while she completed language training for a posting to Beijing (she hadn't needed Thai after all), and Finn applied for other Middle Eastern posts. They managed to stay together through her four years in Beijing and his eventual posting to Beirut. But ultimately, Finn didn't want a girlfriend a continent away. He had a long attention span when it came to love, but he wanted someone at his side, in his bed. Marriage was not on Cordelia's to-do list, nor did she want children. An only child from a quiet home, Finn was unwilling to rule out the prospect of a family. So regretfully, amiably, they split. Cordelia surged ahead of him, becoming an ambassador before she turned thirty-nine—a couple years before Finn won his first ambassadorship, to Bahrain.

It was difficult for diplomats to find domestic bliss together. One had to give up a career, they had to coordinate their postings, or they had to settle for spending most of their lives apart. In fact, it was difficult to have a partner with any professional life. After Cordelia, Finn kept finding himself dating women—in London, Beirut, pretty much anywhere he spent time—who turned out to have purely domestic aspirations. It took only a few dates for him to be bored witless. An alarming number of the world's women seemed to think nothing—not even a career of their own—could be more glamorous than to appear at cocktail parties on the arm of a diplomat. But why would any man *want* a housewife? He had never understood this. He needed a woman with whom he could share thoughts about his work. Someone with ideas of her own, a drive of her own, someone who could introduce him to other worlds. Without this two-way exchange, where was the partnership? What was there to engage him? He didn't need anyone to follow him; he wanted someone to take turns leading. Finn was doomed to be drawn to intelligent, ambitious women whose passions took them away from him.

He had lost himself in work after that. When abroad he was often wooed by local women, but he knew better than to believe their affections sincere. Unmarried diplomats were unnervingly popular with the female natives of almost any developing nation. Smelling the chance for a Western visa and an easy life, women cornered him at national day receptions, charity fund-raisers, and once even at a coast guard training exercise, fluttering their heavily mascaraed lashes and unspooling their tragic circumstances. They were in love with his nationality, his security, his prospects. He himself had nothing to do with it. He had a horror of becoming one of the too-numerous unremarkable and aging white ambassadors wedded to dark-skinned beauties half their age. Surely they knew why these women had married them? Had they not also been urged to sleep NATO? He pitied these men. For they would never be loved. Or was he being unkind? Perhaps there was a kind of love involved, the kind of affection one would feel for a fatherly patron.

But his customary caution blew out into the desert sands that first night Afsoon came to his room, slipped in with the moonlight. She stood there, just inside the door, breathing. He could almost hear her heart beating from the bed where he lay, its metronomic thwack drowning out his precautionary mantra, *Sleep NATO.* "Tell me if I should go away," she said.

"It is not for me to say what you should do," he answered, English suddenly feeling like a foreign language. He couldn't encourage her, but neither could he summon the discipline to send her away. It had to be her decision; it was she who had everything to lose.

She stood silent, unmoving, hesitant. And then slowly, deliberately, began unpinning the scarf from her hair.

HE HAD LOVED her, as much as he knew how to love anyone then. He had thought he could rescue her, marry her and take her somewhere she would be safe. Afsoon wasn't like the other diplomat hunters, he reassured himself. She was just two years younger, had a profession of her own, refused any expensive gift, and had ultimately refused to marry him. No one could accuse her of gold digging or status seeking. And she had laughed when he talked about taking her back to England. "To die of loneliness?" she said. "Away from my family in a country where it takes three years to make a single friend?"

"It doesn't have to be England; it could be anywhere."

"I don't know how I feel about *anywhere,*" she said. "And what will happen to my country if every educated woman leaves? There are few enough of us as it is."

It was a decent point, and Finn did not argue. But finding a way to lure her abroad kept him awake at night, during the few hours he actually spent in his bed. Work kept him up late most nights, not least because it took him so long to complete all the paperwork. Someday he should perhaps learn to type with more than two fingers.

"Why do you not dictate?" Afsoon asked him. "You have a PA. Use her." But he couldn't think the same way out loud as he could when he formed the words on paper himself. He might be slow, but the time it took for his thoughts to travel from his brain to his fingertips and be transformed into pixels improved the end result.

Recently it had been more than paperwork and Afsoon keeping him up nights. Charlotte Fernsby, a British aid worker, had disappeared with her translator-fixer on the road between Lashkar Gah and Musa Qala. Two weeks later the embassy had received the ransom request, presumably from Lashkar-e-Jhangvi, the terrorist group linked to the murder of the journalist Daniel Pearl. There was no question of paying the ransom. But there were debates on whether to attempt a rescue mission and if so, how soon. Rescue missions had an unfortunate tendency to fail. Dramatically. Which was why attempts at mediation were usually the first course of action. But in this case, requests for meetings with a mediator had been ignored.

When intelligence finally informed him that they knew where Fernsby was being held, Finn was tempted. The ambassador was out of country, leaving him as chargé. The impulse to rescue, despite the risks, was strong. He held meetings. He talked through every detail with intelligence, with the political staff. And finally, illegally, desperately, he talked with Afsoon. He had been young back then and in his first posting as deputy head of mission. But not young enough to excuse what had happened.

SEPTEMBER 18, 2007
Miranda

Miranda teetered on the spiky heels as she sauntered across the worn pink carpet of the small bedroom, dressed in a fuchsia, sequined gown that clung to her legs like plastic film. Tazkia and her two sisters lay sprawled across the rose-patterned velour blankets of their double bed in jeans and T-shirts, laughing at her ungainliness.

"Go on," said Hind, the youngest sister. "Dance for us. Show us how models walk in America."

"But I'm not a model! I can barely dress myself." The sisters had yanked off her dowdy blouse and pulled the dress down over her hips as if she were a giant doll. Usually when she visited they performed comic skits for her, but today they had insisted Miranda take a more active role.

"But models are on television all the time. Aren't they? Like in Egypt? We can get some Egyptian stations." Hind was even more outspoken than Tazkia, taller and slightly chubbier, with enormous dark eyes and auburn hair curling to her shoulders. Though only sixteen, she was already engaged to one of her first cousins, a man in his early twenties who worked with their father in his grocery stall. Next to her on the bed, their middle sister, Sehr, sat quietly brushing her hair. She worked as a math teacher in a neighborhood school, an unusual occupation for a woman here. Sehr and Tazkia remained unmarried at the old-maidish ages of twenty-one and twenty-three, but Sehr didn't want to stop working, and Tazkia claimed she would settle only for love—though how love could spontaneously occur in a culture that prevented the two sexes from ever coming into contact mystified Miranda.

"We never had a television. But okay, I admit I've seen models. It's kind of unavoidable." Miranda got the feeling Hind expected Americans to be a little more glamorous than she evidently was.

"So do the walk. Like on the catwalk."

"Wait!" cried Tazkia. "We need music!" She ran to the plain wooden dresser the three girls shared and picked up a small cassette player. A few seconds later, the wail of an Arabian love song filled the room. Miranda posed, one foot forward, hands dangling as she looked haughtily down her nose at the women. Then, swinging her hips in exaggerated motions, she strutted across the room, not even remotely in time with the music. At the end of the room, she attempted a complicated turn, catching a heel on the hem of the dress and launching herself onto the edge of the bed. "You *Americans*," Tazkia said in dismay as her sisters convulsed with laughter. "You don't know what to do with your hips." She leapt up from the bed and launched into the pelvis-swirling dance Miranda had admired at many Mazrooqi weddings. Twisting her hands in the air like a pair of charmed serpents,

Tazkia smiled up at Miranda through lowered lashes. The effect was more seductive than anything Miranda had seen in a Seattle club. "I know!" Tazkia said, abruptly dropping her arms and breaking the spell of her dance. "Let's all do a show!"

In a corner of the room rested a familiar hand-painted metal trunk, its lid thrown open to reveal a slithering mass of lace, feathers, and polyester. This was where the sisters tossed the flamboyant dresses they bought at the discount store DinarMax to wear to weddings. Rarely did a dress get more than one outing—they liked to impress each other anew at each celebration (and the dresses were not sturdily made). But on Thursdays, the women often spent the long afternoons after lunch playing dress-up and acting out little dramas. Tazkia and Hind would pretend to be Egyptian soap opera stars, smearing on thick coats of lipstick and gluing on false eyelashes. "You!" Hind would cry, with a dramatic flourish of her arm. "Don't you think I don't see you making eyes at my husband!"

"Lies!" Tazkia yelled, jumping onto the bed. "How dare you slander my honor!"

"I knew your father should never have let you go to university. All you learned there was how to impress boys!"

"You are just jealous because you were too stupid to go to school. Did you know your mother dropped you on your head when you were still a baby?"

The sisters could rarely get through a whole scenario without dissolving into giggles. Miranda watched them with a mixture of amusement and envy. They so obviously adored each other; she had never heard them utter a cross word that wasn't in jest. Not only did Miranda covet their easy camaraderie but she also envied them their mother, a smiling, apple-shaped woman devoted to her children. She always welcomed Miranda with a flurry of kisses, clinging to her arm as she led her to the *diwan* for lunch. "Can I believe this? An ambassador's wife in my home?" she had said in wonder after Miranda first moved in with Finn (technically, they weren't married yet, but once they were living together all the Mazrooqis just assumed they were). "I'm the same Miranda you've always known," she had said, embarrassed at her sudden rise in status. To her relief, after a few more visits, the awe had worn off. As far as Tazkia's family knew, she had become an ordinary housewife.

Miranda knew the costume trunk well. As a special homework assignment, she had asked Tazkia to draw the same object every single week for six months. It hadn't been easy, as Tazkia was rarely alone in the room. But somehow she had found time to make a rough ink sketch of the trunk most weeks. She hid the drawings in a suitcase full of old clothing underneath the bed until she could get them to Miranda. When the six months were up, Miranda pinned up the sketches across three walls of her studio in the Residence. "What do you see?" she asked.

Tazkia stepped back and stood still, looking at the series with anxious eyes. There were pictures of the trunk locked shut, thrown open, empty, overflowing with dresses, and one of a doll sitting atop the closed lid. "Different details," she said. "Like the metal hinges on the corners. I didn't paint that the first time. Maybe I didn't see it?" Miranda remained quiet. "I guess I didn't see the little flowers on the lid the first few times either. There are more details toward the end. It seems more alive, later."

Miranda nodded. "Every drawing you did, you discovered something you hadn't seen before. Or you drew it from a perspective you hadn't used before. It wasn't the trunk that was changing—your vision was."

"The ones at the end are better, aren't they?"

"Because when you look at something so many times, run your pencil over it so many times, you become braver, attempt things you might have found hard to draw at first. You reconnect with it a different way." This was one reason Miranda liked to return to places she had once painted, return to people and objects that had inspired her. She had worked on a similar exercise while Tazkia was working on her trunk, every day tracing the bars of their upstairs kitchen window, the leaves and flowers that obscured it. In fact, she couldn't stop drawing those bars, would likely draw them until the day they left the country for good.

"Mira," Tazkia said as Miranda sat on the bed struggling to extract shoe from sequins, "you be in a show with us now."

"I don't know how." She didn't feel at home enough in their culture to parody it the way the sisters so often did.

Tazkia was already scrambling into a dress made entirely of white and blue feathers, while Hind tugged a silver minidress down over her soft belly. "You be the man," Tazkia called through the feathers. "Pretend you want to marry one of us." Marriage was a popular theme.

"But I'm wearing a dress." Miranda felt lost in their games, clumsy and out of place.

"Pretend it's a pink *thobe*." Tazkia's head emerged from the feathers, and she settled herself on the carpet, legs curled demurely to the side.

Miranda drew herself up, standing with legs apart and hands on her hips. "Most beautiful Tazkia, I have come from a faraway land just to seek your hand in marriage—"

"No, no!" Tazkia cut her off. "First of all, I would never marry someone from a faraway land. Our friend Naveen married a man from Dubai, and now she has to live there, with his family. You have to be Mazrooqi."

"You wouldn't move to Dubai?"

Tazkia wrinkled her nose. "Of course not! My family is here. I could never live where I couldn't see my mother every day. And my sisters."

Miranda thought about her mother. It would never occur to her to pick a place to live based on its proximity to her parents. Most of her friends back home wanted to live as far from their parents as possible. Was there something they had gotten wrong, something they were missing? Why did they not feel this easy, daily affection for their families? Why were they so comfortable with distance from people they loved?

"But, Tazzy," she said, falling out of character. "You could be freer somewhere else. Not Dubai, maybe. Somewhere you could—" She stopped herself.

"I wouldn't, though." Tazkia frowned at her. "Not if I went there with a man."

There was so much Miranda wanted to say. But instead she looked beseechingly to Tazzy's little sister. "You're engaged to a Mazrooqi, Hind. Will you show me how it's done?"

OCTOBER 19, 2010
Finn

Finn is in the kitchen with Cressie when the first notes arrive. His sleeves rolled up to his elbows, he is kneading bread dough, folding it in half and pushing it into the tiled counter with angry thrusts. Two months. It has been two months now, and his embassy seems to be getting nowhere. He rings every day, aware of the staff's growing reluctance to take his calls. At least once a week, Celia updates him on the progress of the case. *Progress.* If you can call a flurry of false leads and lies *progress.* "We're keeping an eye on the chatter," said Celia in one conversation, meaning the mysterious phone and e-mail networks used by terrorists. It isn't just Al Qaeda here. In a country this poor and desperate, there are all kinds of terrorists with all kinds of causes. But no one has stepped forward to claim responsibility for this one. It is inexplicable. Often there is at least a ransom request, or a demand for prisoners to be released. But they have heard nothing.

"And the mediations?" Finn asked Celia. "They're continuing?" After locating his wife, this is his main preoccupation. The country must not disintegrate. Not now. Not ever, if that is possible. He had met with Celia several times to bring her up to speed on the mediation he had been conducting with sheikhs from the North and South, but how could she truly replace him when he had personal relationships with these men? When this project had been *his* from its inception? When the other EU ambassadors had looked to *him* for leadership?

"It's slow, Finn, you know how it goes. Some of the sheikhs aren't wild about a woman moderator."

"But they're meeting with you?"

"Some of them."

"Christ, Celia. It will never work without all of them. Can I help? Do you want me to talk to them?"

She sighed. "You know what the Office would say about that."

"Celia, this doesn't count as 'going rogue.' I *know* the sheikhs, they trust me. These negotiations are too important to fail now."

"I'm sorry, Finn, but you're going to have to trust me to do the job. We don't have a choice."

Finn was gripping the phone so tightly he was surprised it hadn't crumpled in his fist. "But the other ambassadors? They're being helpful?"

"As much as they can be. I promise I'll ring if I have questions. You've been a *star*, Finn, I know how hard you've been working on this. And I do understand what is at stake."

"*Do* you? Because—"

"Finn. I've got to take this call from London. I promise I'll call if there is news."

Finn glared at his phone, listening to the drone of the dial tone, before hurling it across the kitchen.

HE HAD NOTIFIED Miranda's family and close friends immediately after her disappearance, before the news had a chance to break. Every Sunday night Finn phones Miranda's father, Lloyd, with updates; the two men had met on a monthlong holiday in Seattle and bonded immediately over a shared affection for the works of Carl Sagan. Lloyd had absorbed the news of his daughter's disappearance with a stunned silence. Then, his voice faltering a little, "Miranda is gone? Not her too?" Finn hasn't been able to locate her mother. But he'd found Vícenta; her number was in the worn address book Miranda kept on her bedside table. At first, he hadn't been sure whether or not to ring her. It wasn't as though she could do anything to help, should she even want to. But he knew that she and Miranda still wrote to each other regularly; Vícenta at least deserved an explanation for her sudden silence.

"Vícenta, this is Finn," he'd said when she answered. "I'm, um, I'm—"

"I know who you are, Finn." Her voice had been low, almost gravelly.

"I'm afraid I am calling with some bad news." As simply as he could, he'd explained what had happened.

Silence. Finn had waited. Then, "I'll come."

"No," Finn had said quickly, panicking. "Don't. Miranda would never forgive me if you put yourself in danger. I promise I will tell you if there is anything you can do."

"I can't just sit on my ass here in Seattle and do *nothing*."

"You have to. Please, Vícenta."

"Have you talked with her women?"

"Just to tell them the news."

"Talk to them, Finn. They have many relatives. They adore her."

"Right." But he had remained unconvinced. He had plenty of his own sources. "Listen, I promise to keep you updated. And if you think of anyone else we might contact . . ."

Silence again. And then, faintly over the long-distance line, he could hear her stifled sobs.

"It would be naïve to promise you that I will get her back," he'd said softly. "But we will do everything humanly possible."

Kaia's husband, Stéphane, and Doortje's husband, Alfons, come round to the house at least once a fortnight to compare notes. They vary the times and days, not wanting to alert their respective embassies or anyone else. But their respective embassies, it is agreed, are turning out to be fairly useless. The French, British, Dutch, and American governments have already wasted valuable time sparring over who is best equipped to lead the negotiations, should the kidnappers make themselves known. (There is no doubt in Finn's mind that the Americans have more resources than the other three combined, but it is impolitic to point this out.) All four governments officially refused to entertain a financial resolution, but Finn is skeptical, at least about the French and Dutch. Alastair, Gazza, and Mick, who had returned to Mazrooq when Miranda first disappeared, had been sent home yet again, having failed to track down any hostage takers with whom they could negotiate.

Fortunately, specialized security consultants had stepped into the breach. Both Kaia and Doortje had kidnap insurance through their husbands' companies. Dutch and French insurance consultants had already arrived and set up crisis management cells in separate wings of the InterContinental. How much they actually talked with each other was anyone's guess.

The most influential Western embassies in the country, thinks Finn, and they are coming up with bugger all. Finn has long harbored a prudish objection to swearing, considering it the sign of an unimaginative intellect, but recently some surprising things have been falling from his lips. He makes an effort around Cressida, but when she is out with Gabra or asleep, he can curse without stopping or repeating himself for at least seven minutes.

He manages to control himself around his former colleagues—just. He feels sorry for Celia. He likes her. She is smart, driven, and exceedingly capable. In any other circumstances, he would relish working with her. But his missing wife is just one of the many disasters that have been dropped at her feet.

Yet knowing all of this fails to make Finn more forgiving. His wife, the woman for whom he has spent his life searching, is at the mercy of terrorists. She could be starving or tortured or— He stops there. He still cannot consider the possibility of her death, despite the embassy's diminishing hope in her survival. The only reason to keep prisoners alive is to collect a ransom. When no ransom is demanded, one can only assume that the kidnappers have no reason to keep their captives alive.

At least the American spooks seem to be doing something. Dax, the UK's own agent, meets with them regularly, and when he hears a lead of interest he turns up on Finn's doorstep in the middle of the night. He texts a line from Robbie Burns's "Tam o' Shanter" whenever he is on his way over, and Finn pulls on a sweater and jeans and meets him in the courtyard. They never speak indoors.

———

FINN THWACKS THE bread dough again so hard it startles Cressie, and she stops smacking her own little ball of dough long enough to look up at him reproachfully. She sits on the counter, close enough so Finn can catch her if she falls, her prison-striped vest flecked with flour. "Been inside for nine months," it reads. Once, this had been amusing. Now, it is simply the only clean vest available.

Finn has never been much of a cook, let alone a baker, but it fills the time. He also has a child to feed. He tries to make things Miranda would approve of: vegetable soups, hummus and bread, beans and rice, slices of tomato and cucumber (carefully washed in vinegar and bottled water). Gabra helps him, making lentil curries and the spongy injera bread Cressie loves, though Gabra fails to understand why she isn't allowed to feed the little girl chicken or beef. Miranda was adamant that Cressida be raised vegetarian. It's funny, Finn had always thought that he would be slipping steak and sausages onto Cressie's plate as soon as her mother wasn't looking, but he can't bring himself to do it now. He has become almost as vigilant as Miranda, despite remaining an enthusiastic carnivore. After all, he thinks, when Miranda finally turns up, I don't want the first words out of her mouth to be "You are feeding my child *what?*"

Chopping, kneading, and sifting often help keep despair on the perimeters of his consciousness, though it isn't exactly working at the moment. The silence has become too ominous.

That's when he hears the pounding at the front gate and a rattling of the lock. Bashir has gone to the souq to pick up tomatoes and cucumbers, so Finn and Cressie are alone in the house. Brushing his hands on his jeans, Finn lifts his daughter down to the floor. "Don't move," he says, handing her the bread pans. "Make some music."

He runs down the two flights, listening to the carefree clatter of tin pans above, and crosses the courtyard to find no one at the gate. He sticks his head out, peering in both directions, but sees no one other than the usual gangs of filthy children. *"Qalam?"* a small, barefoot boy in a ragged *thobe* and oversized suit jacket politely inquires. "Later," Finn answers in Arabic. "I've got some on order."

He is about to give up and close the gate when he sees the envelope under his foot. It must have been slipped under the door. Dusting it off, he uncovers red and white hearts and flowers. "A bit early for Valentine's Day," he mutters, picking it up. It is addressed to HIS EXCILENCY THE AMBASSIDOR. It occurs to Finn that he should probably have someone scan it for poison or explosives, but he's too anxious about the contents to wait. He locks the gate and runs up to the kitchen, catching Cressie trying to wrench open the oven door. He sets the envelope on a high shelf while he quickly lights the stove, sets his loaves in greased pans, and slides them into the oven. Cressie's grubby ball of dough gets its own small pan.

Only after he has set Cressie in her crib, handed her Corduroy, and sung her a few verses about the doomed Molly Malone does he finally sit down at the kitchen table—a square plastic card table, no fancy furniture here—with the envelope. Using a butter knife, he slits the top. Several pages of flowered stationery tumble onto the table, each written in a different hand, in varying levels of English. Most are addressed to HIS EXCILENCY or AMBASSIDOR OF GREAT BRITAIN, but the one on top is addressed simply to AMBASSADOR FINN. He turns it over, searching for the signature, and is not surprised to find Tazkia's name. She is the only one of Miranda's women he has met, the only one who knows him well enough to use his first name. He had phoned her the first week Miranda disappeared, so she could hear the news from him. She had taken it stoically, coming as she did from people accustomed to death and disappearance, but she had sent a card to the office with a yellow plastic bag full of tiny green raisins for Cressida. "I will help find her," she had written. Finn had appreciated the sentiment without taking it to heart. How could she help? She didn't even have a car, and women rarely traveled alone. This was a puzzle for intelligence services and diplomats, not for naïve young women constrained by custom and culture.

"You know that our hearts are bleeding like yours," she began.

I tell you over and over but you know how Miranda has helped us and how we would do anything for her. The girls are shy to write you but I encourage them because we think we can help you. You being ambassador cannot go places and maybe do not know the right people. We maybe can help. Maybe not but we need to try. No longer is it tolerant for us to sit while you and Kresida are so suffering. The girls do not know you so they are not trusting yet but I say to trust you as they trust Miranda because you are the same. You know we cannot come to you for the obvius reason but my brother he will help us. He can take you to a place we can talk. Send him a message to his phone and tell him when you can come.

One by one, Finn reads through the rest of the letters from Miranda's pupils. Their expressions of grief are eloquent in their simplicity. "Miranda she cut windows in our lives," wrote Aaqilah. "We will cut through mountains to find her."

SEPTEMBER 18, 2007
Norman

Norman woke with a splitting headache and the dull, nagging sense that he had done something stupid. He rolled onto his side, away from the mountainous bulk of his still-sleeping wife, reaching for the glass of water on his nightstand. The water slid coolly down his throat, failing to remove the bitter taste from his tongue. He swung his pajama-clad legs over the edge of the bed and sat for a moment paralyzed with self-recrimination. How could he have been such an ass? The first thing that little cunt would have done was run and tell Finn. Which meant he could expect to be called into the boss's office for a little chat this morning. Fuck. Fuck fuck fuck. Double fuck.

Still, Finn wouldn't fire him, would he? He wouldn't risk it. Norman would probably just get a stern talking-to. If only he hadn't saddled himself with this man. But what alternative had he had? He needed this posting, needed this promotion. If he proved himself here, he had a good chance at getting another posting. God knows they needed one; every time he got stuck with a London job they nearly went bankrupt. The Foreign Office had it all ass-backward when it came to allowances. He got all this extra cash to come to this third-world country, where they had a free (and enormous) house, free utilities, staff, and where groceries cost a whopping thirty pounds a month. But when they were stationed back in London, what did they get? Zilch. In London they were *stuffed*, stuck with astronomical rent, exorbitantly priced groceries, and scrubbing their own dishes. There was very little incentive to spend any time in London. And he had needed Finn to get this job, had needed that dazzling performance review for Afghanistan. Finn needed him too, he reminded himself. He needed Norman to keep his mouth shut about that girl.

But why, why did Finn have to go and pick Miranda? The one woman Norman could not evict from his mind? Granted, Miranda had rejected his advances before Finn even arrived in country. But to see her at his side, to see the two of them so visibly happy, it burned. It meant the end of hope. He had suffered infatuations like this before, some of them unrequited, but usually a change of country or position had eased the agony. Oh, Mira, Mira, beyond high walls, why do I still want you most of all?

He stood, his knees creaking as he straightened up. He was getting old. Still, he was no older than Finn, who unerringly managed to pull the most interesting women. Half his staff seemed to be enamored with him, finding excuses to linger in the doorway of his office, asking his advice, bringing him tea. Had Miranda ever really had a girlfriend, or had that merely been her way of fending him off? Because look at her now. Little ambassador fucker. Just like that bird in Afghanistan, whatever her name was. Apsoon? Agoon? Some fucking Arab name. She'd turned him down too, for his religion, the fact that they worked in the same office. But somehow those objections hadn't applied to Finn. He didn't get it. What was so special about Finn? Norman staggered to the bathroom mirror, speckled with dried toothpaste, and took a long look.

He wasn't in sparkling form, he was forced to admit. The pale expanse of his belly hung over his striped pajama bottoms, advertising his excessive bar tab. His eyes were bloodshot, puffy, the flesh on his arms loose and soft. He ran his fingers through his hair. At least he still had that. Hadn't lost a single strand and it was still brown. Maybe it wasn't too late. Maybe he could start going to the gym, doing a little swimming. He looked out the bathroom door, back toward the bed. Was that what he was stuck with for his remaining days? That moaning lump of a woman? She was devoted, that much could be said. She took good care of the house and kids and made muffins twice a week for the entire embassy staff. But then, who else would have her now? She'd gained more than eight stone since their marriage twenty years ago. It weighed on her personality as much as it weighed on her bones, dragging her into chronic depression and complaint. She smelled funny, like something had curdled between the folds of her flesh. They hadn't made love in years. Their kids had left home, and he wasn't quite sure why he hadn't left himself. He'd had his chances, when he was younger, before this belly and these arms. But leaving had seemed too complicated then, too messy. Please, he pleaded with his image in the bathroom mirror, I'll try to pull myself together. I'll be a good boy. Just please, please don't tell me this is as good as it gets.

OCTOBER 2007
Miranda

Miranda was at home, cutting photographs out of magazines, when Finn called to tell her about the assault on the American embassy. Early that morning, a small group of men had attacked with truck bombs, grenades, and automatic rifles. Nineteen Mazrooqis and Mazrooqi-Americans were killed, most while standing in line to renew their visas. None of the expatriate staff was harmed.

She stared numbly down at the stack of colored envelopes on her worktable. It was Finn's birthday, and she was nearly finished making him forty-seven cards, one for every year of his life. She had missed so many of his birthdays, she wanted to make up for lost time. It was his first since they had been together; she wanted it to be memorable. But not this memorable.

Nauseated by the news, Miranda pushed away the carrot muffin she had been nibbling as she worked. She had stood in that same line at the embassy just a month ago, to get pages added to her overstuffed passport. "Please tell me there weren't children."

"All right. I won't tell you."

"Oh, Finn, *no*."

"I know. I know, sweetheart."

They were silent for several minutes.

"I'm really sorry, but I am guessing I'll be late home," he said finally. He had to reevaluate the security of his own embassy, as well as the safety of his staff. He'd already arranged a meeting with the US ambassador, both to offer his condolences and to find out the details of the attack. The embassies often pooled intelligence and were frequently the targets of the same people.

Tucker texted her almost simultaneously, asking her to let him know if she had any plans to leave the Residence. Miranda thought it would appear insensitive to go to the gym when so many were mourning. But she didn't have any other way to cope with terrible news; exercise was her drug, her therapist, her most reliable friend. Besides, whom would it help for her to spend the morning pacing around the house? Idleness made everything feel worse. Twenty minutes into her run on the treadmill, the head of an American oil company called her cell phone to ask if Finn had any information about the attacks. He hadn't been able to reach the US ambassador and was concerned for his staff. Miranda called Finn with the message. As soon as she had hung up, an American friend called to say that immigration wasn't letting her leave the country, and did she have any idea why? A few friends from the Old City also called her to find out what she knew. Which was pretty much nothing. Finn wouldn't tell her anything until he got home. Finally she dove into the pool just to get away from her phone.

After her swim, clean, dry, and with nothing else to do, Miranda went back to work on her cards. Many of them were made from postcards or photos in travel magazines of places she and Finn had gone together. There were postcards of the Bosporus in Istanbul, the skating rink at Somerset House in London, the Sofitel Hotel in southern Mazrooq, and paintings they both loved, such as *Farewell*, Remedios Varo's painting of two lovers disappearing down diverging corridors, just their retreating backs visible to the observer. Stealthily, their lengthening shadows have stretched back, their lips moving together for one last phantom kiss. There were photos of more mundane pleasures, such as Christmas pudding and Hendrick's gin. And there were cards made from *New Yorker* cartoons and from Miranda's own artwork. On the back of each she wrote something she loved about Finn. "You read plays out loud with me in bed"; "You keep your mother's recipes"; "You can tell me you love me in seven languages"; "You make lethal gin and tonics"; "You have never uttered an unkind word about Vicenta (or, for that matter, any of my legions of past lovers)"; "It doesn't scare you when I say things like 'my legions of past lovers'"; "You help me with my Arabic homework"; "You made me an art studio even before I moved in"; "The way you say 'articulated lorry'"; "You think my Mazrooqi women are brilliant"; "You let me cry on you and don't get all freaked out about it"; and "You sing along with eighties pop songs."

After she sealed each envelope, Miranda wrote a number (in Arabic) on the front of it. She didn't think Finn would feel like celebrating his birthday on such a grim day. But she wasn't exactly throwing a drunken party and tossing confetti out of the windows with whoops of joy. She simply wanted to make her love visual, tangible, to turn it into a gift. This could not be wrong, no matter what the state of the world outside. Having thus reassured herself, she gathered up her envelopes and headed downstairs. She taped the first card to the front door, the second and third to his office door and wall, and the rest throughout the house, from the front hall to the tiny *diwan* perched on the top of their home. Recently renovated, it had never been used.

The household staff watched her curiously as she fixed cards to the wall in the kitchen. When Miranda explained what she was doing, Teru ran back to the laundry room, returning with a box of Lindt truffles. "The ambassador, he likes chocolate, no?" And she took the roll of tape from Miranda and attached a truffle to each card in the kitchen.

With Desta's help, Miranda then set up the roof *diwan* for dinner, with a tablecloth, paper Winnie-the-Pooh birthday napkins (the only celebratory napkins to be found in the stores), plates, wineglasses, candles, and enormous bunches of flowers that her driver had picked up that morning. She had wanted to choose the flowers herself, but Tucker refused to let her leave the grounds.

In the bedroom, Miranda peeled back the comforter and laid a towel over the sheets. Candles and massage oil stood at attention on her bedside table. In their private kitchen she sliced cucumbers and limes, lined up the bottles of Hendrick's gin and tonic water, and chilled a bottle of champagne. She found an ice bucket, filled it, and stuck it in the freezer. Thus she was able to keep danger and grief dancing on the periphery of her consciousness. The succession of small tasks occupied her until Finn arrived home, at the miraculously early hour of 6:30. For a moment—and only a moment—she considered waiting upstairs while he followed the trail of cards. But she couldn't keep her feet from the steps. After all, he had thirty cards to read before he even got to the bedroom; it could take a while. He was just setting his briefcase down in his study, the first card open in his right hand, when she came in. "Thank you, sweetheart," he said, hugging her. "Beautiful card."

"Rough day at the office."

"Not as rough a day as the American ambassador had."

"Did you talk to the Americans? How is the staff?"

"I've done everything I can do for the moment. The Americans are as you would expect them to be. I promise I'll tell you everything as soon as we sit down."

"Okay, but did you read the instructions? There are a few more cards . . . if you don't mind? Are you up to it?"

Finn looked again at the card, which contained a clue leading him to the next one. "It's a little bit of a relief to be told what to do for a change," he said, walking back out into the hallway.

Miranda followed him as he discovered each card, peeled it from the wall, and read it slowly. He stopped after each one to take her in his arms or to kiss her, so they progressed slowly. After the fifteenth card, when Miranda edged him forward again, he said, "Oh, there are *more?*"

"Well, sweetheart, how old are you?"

When he looked at her with brimming eyes, she knew her efforts had not been wasted.

On the wall next to the kitchen table was a crossword puzzle, which they religiously completed together on weekend mornings. A postcard of Kati Horna's 1937 photograph from the Spanish Civil War *Woman from Madrid in a Refugee Centre in Velet Rubio,* of a stout woman breast-feeding a child standing and gazing into the distance, both fear and determination etched in her eyes, hung in the hall between kitchen and laundry room. On the staircase they followed a series of Meret Oppenheim shoe photographs: elegant, ivory high-heeled shoes trussed up like a roast turkey (Miranda's idea of a joke; she still loathed heels although Tazkia's lessons had made her slightly less likely to shatter an ankle). Near the top was Jim Warren's surreal *Sexual Explosion,* its ecstasy-shattered woman flinging her head back in erotic surrender.

In the bedroom, he followed the instructions on the violet, heart-shaped Post-it notes stuck to their headboard, which read, "Remove clothing" and "Rest here."

"Drink?"

"A gin and tonic would be wonderful," he answered predictably, struggling to balance on one foot while removing a black sock. "Hendrick's?"

"Would I ever use another gin?"

"Forgive me."

"Oh, wait! I forgot the Finn's Birthday Music!" Miranda ran to the iPod, and the initial notes of the Magnetic Fields' "It's Only Time" drifted into the room as she mixed their drinks. "Why would I stop loving you a hundred years from now? / It's only time. . . ."

The ice crackled in the gin as she set the glasses down on the nightstand and shrugged her sundress to the floor. Naked, they sat on the towel together.

"So tell me," she said.

Reaching for her hand, he described the morning's horror and its aftermath. "There are too many days like this," he said. "Too many."

Tomorrow morning he would hold a staff meeting to discuss increased security at his own embassy. "And I hate to say it, sweetheart, but we'll have to discuss the possibility of sending spouses and partners home."

"Home?" Miranda echoed. She no longer had any home other than this, other than Finn.

"I'll do everything I can to keep you here. But not at the expense of your safety, or the safety of others at the embassy."

"I'm not going," Miranda said, gently tipping Finn over onto his back and straddling his hips. "You can't get rid of me so easily." And slowly, her eyes pinning him to the sheets, she bent her mouth to his.

AFTERWARD, THEY LAY silently, listening to Wilco's "Reservations." "I was supposed to give you a massage first," she finally said.

"It's not too late."

She smiled. "Where shall I start?"

"Here," he said. "And here."

WHEN FINN'S BODY had gone limp underneath her prodding fingers, Miranda slid down beside him.

"I'm so glad it wasn't you," she whispered. He rolled onto his side and pulled her toward him.

"I wish it wasn't anyone."

TO THEIR GREAT relief, Miranda (and every other spouse) was allowed to stay. But after that day she began to imagine things. When she stripped off her gym shorts in the bathroom and climbed into the shower, she had a sudden vision of the men who attacked the US embassy. They were dead, missing arms and legs and heads and viscera, but still pondering their fate. No virgins had welcomed them to the afterlife. No god had commended them for slaughtering innocent people. No reward awaited them except for the slowly dawning realization that they had been had. "Why don't they come back from the dead and *tell* people?" She said this aloud, turning on the tap and letting the water run through her hair. By the time she was pulling on socks and shoes, she was rigid with fury that these ghosts had failed to appear.

The anger came out in strange bursts now, when she was not

expecting it. The day after the attacks she was absorbed in a painting when the next-door mosque began its midday wail. "How *dare* you?" her reptilian brain cried out, before she had time to moderate her response. "How dare you pretend to be holy when you *massacre* people?" It was not a just anger. It was clumsy and blunt. She was not angry at Islam itself, but angry about the way Muslims were too often manipulated. The threatening missives that regularly arrived on the desks of Finn and other Western ambassadors always began with praise for Allah, and just after that, praise for those who had murdered in His Name. When she read a copy of one of these threats late one sleepless night, her heart staggered with rage. These never-ending crimes committed in the name of God, of religion. Wouldn't a just god want nothing more than peace?

One crisp autumn evening, as she and Finn (and the team) walked the three blocks to the home of his deputy, Leslie, where they were hosting an *iftar* to break the Ramadan fast with local staff, she found that even the ordinary details of their life had begun to take on an ominous cast: the absence of cars in front of the Iranian embassy, a white van turning down a side street, a sudden violent gesture made by a black-robed woman sitting on the sidewalk. There was menace everywhere, even in the purple flowers swaying in the evening breeze, thick enough to hide a body. If I saw someone about to take a shot at Finn, she thought, if I saw him raise his gun, which way would I move? The scene unfolded in her head. She saw herself lunging for Finn, wrapping herself around him like armor. Finn had an entire embassy depending on him. He was the most thoroughly decent person she had ever known. He needed to be alive. It took less than a second for all of this to run through her mind, less than the time it took her sandaled foot to take the next step. And with the *next* step came fresh hypothetical horrors.

These were the things she fantasized about now. When she was waiting for Finn to come home from work, it was hard to believe that he still existed. That *they* existed, that she hadn't dreamed their entire life together. "He wears striped shirts," she would remind herself. "He comes back to bed every morning smelling of lemon shaving cream. He has the funny, slump-shouldered walk of a tall person. The first thing he will do when he comes home is ask me if I want a cup of tea."

At home without him, she watched for signs. A garbage truck went by one mid-October morning, stopping near their door. She watched from their bedroom window, pulling aside the curtains that their security manager insisted they keep shut. A man with longish, curly hair stood on top of the refuse in the back, catching plastic bags of garbage. If it was garbage. There was no way to know what was really in that mound. Why couldn't it be explosives? She wondered if the guards had searched it, or if they had decided they would rather not explore trash. The curly-haired man hauled up a bag from in front of their gate. She could not see who handed it to him, whether it was one of their guards or someone else. He tore it open, let the garbage tumble on top of the heap, and bent to retrieve something. As he stood, polishing an empty wine bottle with his sleeve, staring at the label, Miranda's stomach clenched in fear. We're doomed, she thought. He knows we were drinking during Ramadan.

The anger erupted even in her Arabic class, with her sweet, gentle teacher, Mahmoud. She arrived one morning sweating under a long-sleeved black blouse, long skirt, and *hijab*, her Mazrooq drag. *"Antee mareedha?"* one of the teachers asked when she walked in, pulling off the scarf.

"No." She hadn't thought she looked that bad. She rethought her decision to forgo lipstick.

"Ta'bana?" She was neither sick nor tired but finally admitted to the latter, so he had an explanation for her apparently unhealthful appearance. She couldn't very well say, "No, I'm enraged and terrified and *nothing helps.*"

She was happy to see Mahmoud. Which was why she was surprised when she sat down at the desk to work and burst out with "Why aren't people taking to the streets? Why are there not newspaper headlines condemning this as against Islam? I don't understand! If someone were using *my* religion to murder people, and my religion were as central to my life as it is to the lives of most Mazrooqis, I would feel a desperate need to publicly say, 'This is not Islam! This is against the Quran!' Why are religious scholars not racing to be quoted in newspaper headlines condemning this, so as to prevent others from following in their footsteps? Why are they letting their religion be disgraced? Why are they not outraged when these murderers use God as their excuse? Do they secretly approve or *what*?"

Mahmoud was calm. Mahmoud was always calm, and he knew her. He had been subject to passionate outbursts before. He looked at her with his tranquil brown eyes and nodded in sympathy.

"And why is it that when something like this happens, everyone I know outside of this country sends me immediate e-mails to find out how things are here, how I am, but not one of my Mazrooqi friends contacts me? The Mazrooqi response to terrorist attacks seems to be something along the lines of 'Oh.'"

Mahmoud bowed his head. "I don't know," he said. "You are right. I wanted to call you, but I thought I would talk with you today. I think we are just quiet because we don't want to make trouble."

Was that it? she wondered. Were they just cowed? Afraid of drawing attention to themselves? Perhaps they thought that to step forward was to put themselves in the sights of the next bomber. It didn't occur to them that they could change things. She had forgotten the learned passivity of a people accustomed to their powerlessness. She had forgotten their religious fatalism. She had forgotten that for them, change had always been violent.

Her anger was gone, as quickly as it had overtaken her. She felt deflated and sad. Pulling her textbook toward her, she switched into Arabic. She hadn't yet learned to manage her outbursts in Arabic. Mahmoud tilted his new pen toward her so that she could see the purple circle on the cap. *"Banafsaji!"* she said. Mahmoud knew that purple was her favorite color for writing Arabic. "It's yours," he said. "After this lesson."

ON HER WAY home, she passed a woman's pink leather shoe, its inside worn and blackened, its outside still shiny, with rhinestones winking in the sun. Someone had loved it, someone had danced in it. And now it lay at the side of the road, without a partner, near a dead orange cat and a handful of plastic water bottle caps. Bougainvillea petals had sifted down on top of it all, as if they had decided they were garbage too. Somewhere a would-be Cinderella was waiting in vain.

It was funny how often boredom and terror went hand in hand. How much they both made you notice. She was overwhelmed now by the infinite details of the world. Her world, here. Times like this, she spent all day at the easel, just to stay sane. Otherwise, her brain swelled with fearful fantasies, rages with no outlet, and images of AK-47s laid out on prayer mats, and she ended up not being able to do anything but stalk the house, a caged panther.

Every evening, when the garden outside her studio window darkened and dissolved into the night and she switched on her lamp (never, ever before pulling the shades, as per security instructions), the familiar fear started up in her belly. Every time she heard the gate clank open, she started from her easel and ran to the window. At least a dozen times it was a false alarm. The guards walked in and out of the gate all day long. She sat back down and tried to work, but when she was waiting, it was impossible. She made herself cups of tea and tried not to imagine the countless ways to die between the embassy and the Residence. At last she would hear the blare of the Mazrooqi police car horn that augured Finn's arrival. There was one long honk, followed by the growl of two armored cars sweeping around the corner of their house and whipping into the gate. This was followed by the unmistakable clatter of the bodyguards leaping out of the car with their AK-47s and scanning the rooftops, escorting Finn for the final leg to the house.

She willed herself to wait upstairs; he liked to find her at work. But at the sound of his cheery "Hiya!" echoing up to her as he took the steps two at a time, she shoved her easel away and started for the door. He was in her arms, he was real, he was smiling. "Fancy a cup of tea?" he said.

Worry always seemed foolish then, until the next morning, when he picked up his red cloth bag of sandwiches and kissed her good-bye. That was when the movies started up again in her mind and she didn't know how to stop them. All she could do was to somehow pin her fears down in paint and hope they stayed there.

JANUARY 4, 2008
Finn

Miranda was in her studio, daubing the final streaks of paint onto a canvas before preparing to meet her students at Mosi and Madina's, when Finn knocked on the frame of the open door. "Could I have a word?" He wore khaki shorts and a blue polo shirt with the logo of his Afghani CP team, his weekend outfit. On Friday afternoons while she was painting or at class he usually read by the pool or played tennis with the US ambassador, if he didn't have too much work.

"Hang on, just finishing." She stepped back to consider her canvas, still unsatisfied. It was crowded with naked women, as usual, but these women had gaping holes riddling their torsos. Some had voids where their lungs should be, or their hearts, wombs, breasts, bellies, livers, spleens. In each of these holes something rotten had begun to grow, a fat worm, shiny roach, or long-toothed rat. *Nature Abhors a Vacuum*, she wanted to call it.

"I have class, but not for an hour or so." Wiping her sticky hands on a damp rag, Miranda turned to Finn. Her eyes burned, from either the paint fumes or the hours of intent looking.

"I'm not interrupting a burst of inspiration?" Finn was always fearful of disrupting her work and so rarely came to her studio, though he had created it. As soon as she had agreed to marry him, he'd stripped the front corner room on the second floor of its mismatched, overstuffed furniture and Persian carpets, leaving the wood floor bare. Somewhere in the Old City he'd found a carpenter to make two easels for her, to the same specifications as the one she kept in her former home. In the far corner was a plain blue sofa and round wooden coffee table, next to a long wooden bookcase. Along the back wall was a worktable Finn had covered with the full range of Michael Harding oil paints, boxes of charcoal pencils, and a stack of new sketchbooks. Next to those were cans of Zest-it (she preferred its citrusy scent to the toxic fumes of turpentine) and gesso. Rolls of unstretched canvas leaned against the table. He'd made her walk from the bedroom with her eyes closed, leading her by the hand. She had looked around her, at the paints, the easels, and the space—all of the space!—and wept.

"I wish. Take a look if you want."

Finn stepped into the room and tilted his head. "Holy women?"

"Ha ha. But yes. In a way. How are the accounts?"

"Do you really want an answer to that?"

"I guess not."

Finn looked uneasy, his eyes uncharacteristically lusterless. Something twitched in Miranda's stomach. "What is it?"

"Could we sit?" He gestured to the sofa.

"What is it?" She was alarmed now. "Are you breaking up with me?"

He laughed. "Nothing like that, sweetheart. There's just a few things I think we ought to talk about. Before next month."

Miranda stayed where she stood. "You used to be a woman?"

"Um . . ."

"You're addicted to online porn?"

"Sweetheart . . ."

"You're still married to someone else?"

"Miranda, will you please listen for a minute? It's nothing that serious."

Demurely, she sank onto the sofa, folding her hands in her lap.

"I'm not sure that you're fully aware of how much your life is about to change."

She waited, silently. Finn sat down next to her, taking her left hand between both of his.

"You know that once you are official, you'll have your own bodyguard, for one. Once that happens, you will not be able to leave the house without him. You will not be able to spontaneously meet a friend for coffee. You cannot run to the corner store for butter without giving him an hour's notice. You can't go on your long rambles around town unless your guard knows your entire route in advance."

Miranda frowned at him, nodding. "Okay. I think I get it."

Finn sighed, a hopeless little gust of air. "Think this through, Mira. Today you can go to class on your own. We're not married yet, protection is still optional. But come February, you're going to have a mandatory escort. Everywhere. And that means to your class."

Something tightened around her solar plexus, a serpent of fear. "But a man can't come to class. He couldn't. He's——"

Finn searched her face, waiting for some realization she had yet to make. "He wouldn't need to come into the house with you, into your class. But he would be outside. He would see every woman who arrived, every woman who left. Even if they are covered, they won't want to be seen."

Clarity arrived, like a slap in the face. "You want me to stop my classes."

"It's not what I *want* . . ."

"But that's what you're telling me, isn't it. I can't do the classes anymore. *Jesus.*" She leapt to her feet, paced to the far end of the room before spinning back to him. "Finn, those classes are the only reason I stayed here. Those women are why I am here. Without those women I never would have even *met* you."

"I know." Finn didn't move, he just watched her, a helpless sadness creeping across his face.

"*Fuck,* Finn!" He hated it when she swore, but she couldn't help herself.

"You'd be putting them at risk."

"And I'd be putting you at risk too, right? Isn't that what you are saying? That I could ruin you too? The wife of the ambassador, teaching scandalous things to the natives."

"I wouldn't have put it like that."

"No, you wouldn't." She studied him. This wasn't something she had ever wanted to do, to balance her love for Finn on the scales against her passion for her women, for the thrill of witnessing their little leaps forward, the opening of their eyes.

"So what am I supposed to do with myself? Hold tea parties for the other wives?"

"Only if you want."

"I *don't* want. I want—"

"You can work. Your own work."

"I have plenty of time for that already."

"You can still see them, Mira. It's just, the classes . . ."

"They could come here?"

"Not all at once. And as you know, some won't want to."

"Tazzy can come?"

"Of course Tazzy can come. Just—you'll need to be careful."

She turned away from him, toward the window. Looking out at the slices of garden visible between the bars, she felt a sudden impulse to reach her hands through the glass, letting its splintered diamonds rain around her, and take those iron bars in her fists, to shake them until they came loose. With a jerk of her head, she cast off the vision. These bars were here to keep danger out, not to confine her. She had come to this palace freely, locked herself in with joy.

Across the lawn, Semere trained a long green hose on his roses. The water arced out, catching the sun in an ephemeral rainbow shimmer. The thing was, Finn was right. Even if he weren't worried about his own reputation and security, her women were at risk. They were at risk already, but the watchful eyes of a Mazrooqi bodyguard could only further imperil them. Even had she wanted to continue teaching with an armed man in tow, the women were not likely to show up. A feeling of safety was critical for them to be able to work.

She turned to look back at Finn, slumped and defeated on her sofa, his hands limp on his lap. "I'm sorry," he said. "I'm so, so sorry."

And she realized there had never been any decision to make. Finn was her home more than anyone or anything ever had been. "Well," she finally said. "They've had me for more than three years."

"Almost a university education. You should make them diplomas." Light tiptoed back into his eyes.

"Diplomas that they can't hang on their walls, or show to their parents and grandparents? Diplomas they will have to hide, along with everything else?"

Finn's face crumpled. "Right. Sorry." He unfolded himself from the sofa and came to her, his long arms wrapping around her waist from behind. "How about this," he said. "When this posting is over, we'll follow you for a bit. You pick the next country."

"And your work?"

"I can take a leave of absence."

"And what would we live on, while we gallivant around Tanzania? Do you know what artists make? How do you feel about lentils and rice?"

"I have savings. Enough for a year anyway."

Miranda twisted in his arms to see his face. "Are you serious?"

"Deadly. I just don't want you to get fed up with me. To feel like you're stuck playing second fiddle all the time."

She laughed. "I don't want to play the fiddle at all."

"Stick with me for a couple more years, love, and you can be the conductor."

JANUARY 11, 2008
Miranda

For her last class, Miranda chose an exercise on releasing control, a lesson she needed perhaps as much as her students did. She had begun to catch herself thinking of these women as her own creations. Tazkia was to be her masterpiece, the culmination of years of sculpting, her Galatea. Had Miranda not taken her untamed talent and given it form, purpose, freedom? Yet it was, ultimately, the women who did the work. Who stood over their own easels and sketchbooks, illustrating their own dreams. Perhaps it was not altogether a bad thing that the classes were coming to an end, before she lost all perspective.

Miranda stood at the end of her *diwan*, clutching a bundle of meter-long sticks. They hadn't been easy to find in this tree-impoverished city; she had been forced to strip still-green branches from fig and pomegranate trees. But she needed only five. On the floor in front of her, the women were staking out their spaces, pouring black ink into pie tins scattered across the plastic tarp Miranda had spread over the floor. The whole *diwan* was encased in plastic; she wanted her women free to be messy.

It was difficult to get them to shut up these days. Now that they had relaxed into the routine of these classes and come to trust each other, they almost never stopped talking. Yet today, Tazkia was—most uncharacteristically—the exception. She sat in a corner by herself, knees drawn up to her chest and eyes solemn. Her sketchbook lay in front of her toes, opened to a blank page. Mariam and Aaqilah sat with their heads bent together, laughing over one of Aaqilah's romantic tableaux. "He looks like a girl," Mariam says. "Look at his hair!" Nadia watched them, making a rough sketch of her friends and smiling to herself. She looked tired. Nadia was often in charge of looking after her five younger siblings; she could rarely get any of her own painting done until they were all asleep.

"*Khalas!*" Miranda clapped her hands, and the women turned their eyes to her. Mariam and Aaqilah drew apart and picked up their pencils. None of them wore *hijabs* inside anymore, and their dark hair—uniformly long and thick—spilled across their shoulders and down their backs. "Each of you take one of these." Miranda began handing out the sticks. "You know what to do. Pick a brush and use the masking tape to fix it onto the end. Make sure it's secure. I don't want the brush to be able to move. It should feel like an extension of the stick." They have done this exercise several times before, but not for many months.

"We're going to start with the bush." Miranda gestured to the potted plant on the floor next to her. "Then I'll let you do a few of me. Since it's your last chance." She had already explained that this would be their last class, had already offered endless reassurances that they could still contact her, that she wasn't disappearing entirely. Only Tazkia seemed to take her abandonment personally, tears occasionally appearing in her reproachful eyes. Madina and Mosi had offered to let the women use the house without Miranda, to work in private, and Miranda was glad that they would still have each other. If they wanted to continue.

One by one, the women began dipping their brushes into the ink and dabbing them onto the paper clipped to their small easels. "Don't be fussy about it," Miranda reminded them. "Remember that just a suggestion of a leaf or an ear is enough for us to recognize it. You don't need to paint every swirl."

The first time she had done this exercise with them, Mariam and Nadia had ended up in tears. It was impossible to have complete control over the brush when it was so far away from a guiding hand. The inexactitude of their marks frustrated the women, drove them to tear up their pages. Aaqilah had refused to do it again for nearly a year. "You have to stop being so precious with your brushes," Miranda had exhorted. "Let go of your need to control. Freedom is letting go of control. Go with where the brush lands, make something from what is there, not from what you wish were there. Be fearless." Slowly, over the years, they had grown comfortable with the exercise, even found delight in unexpected strokes across their pages.

Miranda watched Tazkia's hand, waving the stick like a conductor's baton. Her potted plant looked electrified, fuzzy. Even her melancholy didn't dampen her painterly zeal. Nadia's plant spun on the page like a dervish. Even timid, laconic Mariam swished her brush with vigor, dabbing oversized leaves onto her paper. Perhaps they didn't actually need her anymore; perhaps she had given them enough.

When fifteen minutes were up, Miranda switched places with the potted plant, standing before her women with her arms raised to the sky and feet apart. She was clothed, in black jeans and an oversized T-shirt. It had never felt appropriate to model nude for them. There had to be some kind of boundary between teacher and student. "Go now," she said. Watching their serious faces, Miranda wondered—not for the first time—what was possible for them. If any of them wanted to be an artist, a professional artist with a gallerist, exhibits, and catalog, she would have to leave the country. So what was it she had been doing? Training women to be capable of leaving their country behind? Surely that wasn't what she had set out to do. She had wanted to make *this* country better, to help the women living here. Yet she had given them skills that were useless in Mazrooq. Worse than useless—dangerous.

"Mira, look." Tazkia turned her easel around, derailing Miranda's train of thought. It was a good likeness, a few squiggles suggesting Miranda's hair, loose strokes delineating her form. But what drew Miranda's eyes more than the work itself was the glow of confidence on her student's face. *I put that there,* she thought. *At least I've done that.*

OCTOBER 2010
Miranda

Miranda squats in the dust outside her small hut, Luloah a warm, sleepy ball against her back. Cautiously, as though she is doing something forbidden, she pushes a finger through the dirt. A line. Just a line. But that is where everything begins. Looking up to make sure she is free from observers—only the mountains gaze sternly down—she extends the line, curves it, adds another.

Of all the privations, the absence of books, paper, and drawing materials is the worst. In her real life, rarely does she leave home without a sketchbook and a pencil. She hardly knows how to think without a blank page reeling images from her mind down through her elbows and wrists to her fingertips. Unable to think through her hands, through color and shape, she feels semiconscious, almost brain-damaged. How foolish was she—in the free and privileged life that feels a decade away—to believe those gallery openings constituted the most thrilling part of her career. The anxiety and adrenaline, the desperate craving for praise, the euphoria of receiving it. But here, now, this is not what she hungers for, not what is missing. She has hardly thought of those champagne-soaked evenings in uncomfortable shoes. It's surprising how quickly the trappings of her career have ceased to feel important. What she is left with, what courses through her more strongly than anything except her longing for her daughter, is a craving for the process itself: setting ideas on paper or canvas, making them tangible, giving them form. Never in her life has she been denied access to the tools of her trade—not since she could hold a Crayola crayon steady and drag it across a sheet of construction paper.

And how desolate is a life devoid of a drawing pinned to the wall, a watercolor, a painting, even a graphic novel. A life without a portrait's silent gaze, the eloquence of eyes. Without geometry, without color, without the language of shape and motion. Without even the forms of words. She has asked for a Quran, because it's the only book anyone owns, and after all she has been meaning to get through it for years. It's agonizingly slow going, as she struggles to make out the tiny words without her reading glasses. Her Arabic isn't nearly good enough, and she has to keep stopping to ask Aisha for help. This pleases Aisha, who grows uncustomarily animated when attempting to explain the language of the Quran to an uncomprehending Miranda. So far, Miranda finds it rather nerve-jangling reading, dwelling as it does on the unimaginably horrific fates of unbelievers.

But the Quran is also one of the only things keeping her sane, rescuing her mind from its endless dizzying circles. If she had a pencil—and if she dared—she would be tempted to sketch in the margins. It's the only paper she has seen. Though the last thing she needs is to be caught desecrating the holy book. Absently, she continues moving her finger, watching an image unspool itself in the dust. The curve of a breast, the curl of an infant.

The men don't seem to be around today. They never speak to her directly. They shout orders to Aisha, who accepts them with a nod. Miranda isn't sure how many there are. One of the men is Aisha's husband, another is her son. They sleep separately, in the other huts they share with the rest of the men. In the morning she watches them gather for breakfast, squatting around a fire to take their tea and beans and bread, their AK-47s resting across their thighs. She and Aisha eat when the men are through, when Aisha carries over their own small pan of beans. In the late morning the men gather in a rocky stretch of dirt beyond the houses to conduct a mystifying set of exercises, jogging in circles with their rifles pointed to the sky, dropping to the ground, and squirming through the dust on their stomachs. She has even seen them performing push-ups and rigging up makeshift monkey bars. Miranda isn't sure if this is meant to keep the men fit or if it is preparation for some kind of attack. She tries to remember a terrorist attack that had required physical fitness. Walking onto a bus wired with explosives? No monkey bar practice required for that. Flying a plane into the World Trade Center towers? No wind sprints necessary. Perhaps they are simply interested in maintaining good health, so that they may live long enough to carry out their mission.

Miranda looks down at her own wasting thighs and almost smiles. To think that her mornings were once organized around her exercise routines. Now, without the gym or pool or yoga DVDs, she is thinner than she has ever been. Now she is at least as terrified of losing weight as she used to be of gaining it. She needs to keep enough on to be able to feed this child. She needs enough food in her body to turn into the necessary nutrients. When she was nursing Cressida, she had been vigilant about every mouthful. Every day she ate generous helpings of dark green vegetables, orange vegetables, beans and nuts, tofu, whole grains, figs and pomegranates from their garden, and plenty of yogurt.

There are hardly any vegetables here, unless you count beans. If they are lucky there are onions and jalapeños. Once in a while Aisha's husband brings her dates or bananas, which she shares with Miranda. No one ever offers her meat. If someone *were* to offer her a piece of chicken or goat, Miranda is almost hungry enough to eat it. She is always hungry.

It's odd how alone she feels. Almost unwatched. The air is still and silent. She can smell the acrid scent of her unwashed armpits, a reminder she is still alive, that her body is continuing to function. Occasionally she manages a furtive rinse when she and Aisha are fetching water, but it is difficult without removing her clothing. She has never seen Aisha disrobe. After her first couple of weeks she had asked Aisha to cut her hair. Without a brush, showers, or conditioner, it clumped together in dirty dreads and stuck to her skin. Aisha had obligingly hacked it off with a sharp blade, leaving just a curly scrub to cover her scalp. "You are a boy now," Aisha had said. She disapproved of short hair but had finally agreed to cut it when Miranda told her she thought a swarm of biting bugs had colonized it. This wasn't far from the truth. The itchy red bites that appear on her skin at night keep her awake more often than does Luloah.

It had taken more than a week for them to find her a toothbrush. When she first asked, they had given her a slender green branch the length of her forearm and told her to chew it. That is for teeth cleaning, they'd said. Miranda had sniffed it, licked it, and stuck it in her mouth. But she couldn't see how it could be much of a plaque deterrent. She had begged every day, until at last Aisha's husband had turned up one evening with a blue Oral-B he had found somewhere. It is amazing how much saner and more hopeful she feels with clean teeth.

Aisha dozes just inside the door of the hut. Would anyone notice were she to slip away? The men seem awfully confident that Aisha alone is enough to keep her from fleeing. Or is it Luloah they are counting on? Miranda has no idea how old Aisha is—it seems rude to ask and most people here aren't sure of their exact ages anyway—but she moves heavily and slowly, as if in pain. Miranda pays close attention to the landscape on their long walks to fetch water, noting the dirt roads, paths, anything that might lead toward civilization. She would have to be able to outrun Aisha; there is nowhere to hide. No massive trees, no dense greenery. Just scrubby bushes, rocks, and the endless dust. Why hasn't she tried yet? she wonders. Well, there's the fact that she still isn't sure whether Aisha is armed. Then it wouldn't matter how fast she ran. And there is Luloah. She doesn't know how fast she could move holding the baby, and leaving her behind has become unthinkable. Who else does she have? No matter how she feels about the child—and she already feels far more than she can admit—she cannot abandon her to certain death.

Escape also seems a bit less necessary when no one has hurt or threatened her. True, she has been here for many weeks now and there has been no indication that freedom is in her future. But if they wanted to kill her, wouldn't they have done it by now?

Continuing to push her finger through the dust, she completes the outline of the nursing baby and begins to draw a small child standing nearby. She wants to be Harold with his Purple Crayon, bringing her daughter to vivid life with a few deft lines. A little Cressida, watching. Miranda has never been able to draw or paint her daughter. She grows and evolves so swiftly that Miranda cannot capture her face and features before they subtly shift. A few times she began a sketch only to find it completely unrecognizable the next day.

Now, she is drawing in the dust and it doesn't matter. It will be gone in a moment, a memory of a memory. She puts a little dust Corduroy in the child's hand. Abruptly, desperate longing sweeps through her rib cage, erupting in a hoarse sob. She had not thought this would last so long. She had not considered that she could be kept from her daughter for months. She had not believed that she could be the cause of Cressida's first heartbreak. And how long will it be before Cressida forgets her? Squatting, she presses her gritty palms to her eyelids, hot tears mixing with the sand. In the mornings, Cressida always called for her first, knowing her father was harder to wake. "Mummy!" she'd yell down the hallway. "MUMUMUMUM!"

Finn will come for her, she tells herself. Not Finn himself, of course, but someone from the embassy. They have to come. They have resources. They have intelligence. She is surprised they haven't found her yet. Finn will not give up until he finds her. He wouldn't have left the country. Would he? Miranda suddenly wonders if perhaps fear for Cressida's safety would have prompted him to leave the search to others. After all, it isn't likely that he would be able to search for her himself, given that he has probably been removed from post. And remains a target.

Of course, the Americans might come instead. She is registered with the American embassy, which is larger and has vastly greater resources. Finn had insisted on it. "If we ever need to be evacuated," he said, "you'll want to go with the Americans. With all due respect to my own organization, no one does it better."

Then there are the other women, and their respective embassies. Have they been found? Are they alive? She has no way of knowing. Just as she has no way of knowing if her disappearance has made it into the press or if her kidnappers have figured out her identity. If they have, they haven't let on. Aisha still calls her Celeste, and the men don't speak to her.

She thinks of Mukhtar. She thinks of Mukhtar every day. Wouldn't they have found his body by now? Wouldn't someone have reported it? And thus, wouldn't her identity have been revealed? There are no answers. All she hears is the echo of her questions in the distorting canyons of her mind.

Aisha stirs behind her, and quickly Miranda brushes dirt across her sketch. She isn't sure how to feel about Aisha. The older woman hasn't been unkind, but there is a reserve Miranda cannot trespass. She is an unsentimental woman, offering Miranda little more comfort than her daily water, tea, and bread. Never does she lean over little Luloah to cluck and coo. Never does she initiate conversation.

"Aisha," Miranda starts. Could it hurt to ask? "Do you think I could have some paper? Just a bit of paper and a pencil?" Her Arabic still stumbles, and she has to repeat herself several times, with pantomime, before Aisha understands. *"Leysh?"* she replies. Why would anyone want these things?

Miranda hesitates, searching for the verb. "To draw?" she finally admits.

"To draw?"

"Pictures. Pictures of . . ." Not people, she thinks. I shouldn't say people. Or animals. Animals are *haram* too. "Pictures of mountains," she finally says. "Flowers, buildings."

"Why?"

"Because . . . it is what I do. I draw pictures. I have always been drawing pictures."

"No letters. You cannot write letters."

"No. Pictures of things. Mountains. Rocks."

"You want to draw rocks?" Suspicion creeps into Aisha's expression.

"Yimkin," Miranda says. "If they are pretty rocks." She has a sudden inspiration. "I think Luloah would like to see them. Babies like pictures. My daughter, she likes pictures."

Aisha looks at her silently, studying her face. *"Yimkin. Sawfa nashouf,"* she finally says. Maybe. We will see.

A few days later, Miranda is leaning against an inside wall of their hut, feeding Luloah, who now sucks with determination and vigor, when Aisha appears in the doorway, blocking the light. "Here," she says. Miranda reaches out a hand, fumbling in the dark. At last her fingers touch the edges of a book—no, a pad. A small pad of paper. Aisha moves from the doorway, and Miranda can see that the woman also holds a small packet of pencils. "My sister's husband has a store," she says. Miranda sets the pad on the ground in front of her and takes the pencils. "Oh, *Aisha*," she says. "Thank you."

When Luloah has again drifted into the arms of Morpheus, Miranda opens the cover of the notepad and runs joyful fingers across the blank page. She picks up a pencil from the dust. And touches down.

No sooner has the pencil fallen upon the sheet of paper than she feels it straining to delineate a female form. It's a reflex, rusty yet persistent. Women are and have always been her subject, her objects. It was more than a year before she shared her work with her students. After their initial shock, they became curious. No one had ever punished Miranda for this? Artists in the United States were allowed to draw women? Were there lots of these drawings? Lots of women artists? Were there many women in paintings without clothing? Shown in public? And no one tried to hurt them? They were inebriated with the mere thought of such freedom. And ultimately, they could not resist its lure.

The day she finally allowed her women to draw a human form, they fell silent as Vicenta stepped barefoot from behind the Chinese screen in the corner of the room. She wore a thin silk robe, scarlet, knee-length. Miranda had given it to her on their first Christmas. At the middle of the room she turned, looked questioningly at Miranda, and dropped the robe to the candy-apple-colored carpet. "Something simple at first," Miranda had told her. "Just stand there. Catch the light."

For a moment, no one moved. It couldn't have been shock at the nudity; these women saw each other in the bathhouse and at each other's homes. No, it was Vicenta's cavalier attitude, her casual movements, her utter lack of self-consciousness. With her right hand on her hip and her left hanging loose at her side, Vicenta cocked her chin toward the ceiling. She was more than comfortable in her skin, her bones, her stretch marks and moles; she was proud. Vicenta dared you not to admire her.

It had taken a long time to get here. While Tazkia and Nadia had both been clandestinely drawing figures for years, they were initially terrified of anyone finding out, even each other or the other women. Guilt and doubt had become constant companions. We don't ever have to do figures in class, Miranda had reassured them all at the start. We don't have to do animals, we don't have to do humans. I don't want to do anything that makes you uncomfortable. It was the women's own increasing appetites that had driven them forward. You said other Muslims have done this, Tazkia had reminded her. Tell us about the Muslim figure drawers.

And Miranda had. It had taken a fair amount of study, as she had known very little about art from this part of the world before she came here. In a dingy little copy shop in Shuhadā' Square, she printed out articles on the Turkish miniatures of the fifteenth to nineteenth centuries, detailed depictions of Turkish military victories, men on horseback raising swords, elaborate processions, and circumcision feasts, all created for the personal use of sultans. Figures, imagined by Muslims. Then there were the countless works from India and Persia, some of which Miranda managed to print in color. *A Lady Prepares a Meal*, a vivid depiction of a woman in the Himalayan foothills. *Sulayman Enthroned Above the Orders of Mankind and the Jinn*, a Turkish illustration for the Book of Solomon. *An Intoxicated Prince Woos a Chinese Maiden*, an illustration for the *Gulistan*, by the thirteenth-century Persian poet Sa'di.

What had truly shocked her students though, what had sent them home with their worlds upended and certainties shattered, was *Muhammad and His Army March Against the Meccans*. The Prophet, on paper, on the page of a book. His face was veiled and his body obscured by green robes, but it was unmistakably him. The painting came from a much longer work, the illustrated six-volume *Life of the Prophet*. None of her students had heard of this book, of these splendidly rendered, deeply respectful images of their prophet. It was several weeks before they began to believe her and months before they started thinking of what they themselves might do.

Tazkia had been the first to broach the subject of drawing a nude. "Every artist who ever lived has done it," she told her friends. "Since the beginning of time. Miranda has books of them."

And now here they all were. Tazkia was too animated to sit still, rising up on her knees to inspect Vicenta more thoroughly. Her pencils were sharpened and set smartly in a row next to her open sketchbook. Nadia was nearly as fidgety, but Miranda suspected that this was a result of apprehension rather than joyful anticipation. Mariam shuffled her papers, lining up all of their edges, trying to look bored. Only Aaqilah seemed to have mentally left the room, staring vacantly at a corner of the ceiling. Miranda hadn't been sure all of them would come, but they had.

"Before you start," Miranda said. "Here is what I want you to do. Forget, for a moment, that she is a woman. Forget that you are drawing her shape. All I want you to do is to draw the light. Observe the way the light falls on her body, which lines it erases. Notice which parts are shaded, which parts exposed. Keep focusing on the light." They have done this before with objects, with vases and chairs, but nothing real, nothing breathing.

"*Yalla*," said Miranda, smiling at her students. "She's not good at standing still." There was a rustle of sleeves brushing across sketch pads, and the pencils came to life. Miranda sat on the carpet behind her women, drawing her knees up in front of her. She had again covered the windows against prying eyes. A single, naked bulb lighted the room, casting stark shadows across Vicenta's face. Well, it couldn't be helped. Finding a room with both natural light and privacy was impossible. The light flattened Vicenta's forehead, hollowed her eyes, and drew a line down the bridge of her nose. The top slopes of her breasts and belly were bleached white by the glare, her left arm and pubis fading into shadow.

Miranda never got tired of looking at Vicenta. They could be in the middle of one of their fiercest arguments, and Miranda would find herself distracted by the jut of those birdlike hip bones above the waistband of her trousers, the flat expanse of her brown belly, the unusually upturned nipples. Vicenta never wore a bra, not even here, though she draped herself in enough layers not to scandalize their neighbors when she left the house. Vicenta had the sharp cheekbones Miranda had fantasized about as a teenager, eyes the greeny black of a night in the forest, and shiny ebony hair cut chin length, Cleopatra-style. Half-Argentine, half-Italian, she had moved with her mother and older sister from Buenos Aires to New York as a toddler. "My father was never in the picture," she'd told Miranda on their first real date, a sweaty hike up to Hidden Lake. "I think he's on his fourth or fifth wife by now. Sometimes I get a birthday card, but the return address keeps changing." She grew up in the South Bronx, won a scholarship to attend a private secondary school in Manhattan, and studied art at Hunter College. A New Yorker at the cellular level, she had never planned to move away. But after a dispiriting year of trying to interest Chelsea gallerists in her work, she took a year off to travel across the country, stopping to do odd jobs and sell her art on street corners. Which was how she ended up at the Pride march one June in Seattle, sitting on a stranger's front stoop drinking Emerald City lager out of a paper bag. Miranda had been wandering through the crowds, dressed in not much more than pasties and body paint, trying to find a colleague from Cornish when an impatient elbow had knocked her into Vicenta's lap. "Well look at this," said Vicenta, setting down her beer to sling an arm around Miranda. "And it isn't even my birthday."

MIRANDA PICKED UP her own pencil and pad. She wondered how much trouble she would be in if anyone found out. (Not as much trouble as her women, she reminded herself.) At least she wasn't using a male model. Surely that would be the end of everything. But how were they to learn? These women were no different from the women artists of the early 1800s, whose careers were thwarted by their lack of training in anatomy and life drawing. God forbid women learn how their own bodies worked. God forbid their pure minds be contaminated by male nudity. Here, Miranda found women who had no idea where the uterus was, or how ovaries functioned. They bled every month without understanding its significance. She made a mental note to pick up a copy of *Gray's Anatomy* the next time she left the country.

While reading the sparse literature available about early women artists, Miranda had fantasized about going back in time to teach these women how the body worked. Just as when she was very small she had fantasized about touring Laura Ingalls Wilder around the modern world, showing her cars and airplanes just to see the astonishment on her face.

"Cramping," said Vícenta, shaking out her long legs and flexing a foot. "Can I sit?"

At Miranda's nod she lowered herself stiffly to the ground, curling her feet beneath her and leaning on her left palm. Miranda walked around to look at her students' first sketches. Mariam's sketch was surprisingly good, a starkly delineated Vícenta emerging from her tiny, neat cross-hatching. Aaqilah had softened her model, giving Vícenta's tomboy body a few additional curves, and her eyes a most uncharacteristic gentleness.

"Do you see?" Miranda asked, peering at Nadia's sketchbook, which she had drawn up close to her chest. "How the light, how drawing just the light gives the body volume? It's not just a silhouette now, it's a whole person."

Miranda had sketched and painted Vícenta a thousand times. It was one of their early games, drawing each other posing in imitation of women in famous works of art. Miranda drew Vícenta as a narrow-hipped tomboy Gérôme Galatea, a lascivious Bouguereau baigneuse, an elegant Degas dancer. Her favorite was Vícenta as Sargent's Madame X; the lines of her chin and neck were perfect. Once, in response to antigay slogans posted on the message board of a local Baptist church, Miranda and Vícenta had stayed up all night rubbing their pastels on the church's front walk. Together, they had painstakingly re-created—with the help of large flashlights and a print of the original—Courbet's *Le Sommeil*, a dreamy vision of two naked women dozing in an erotic embrace. They had contemplated creating an original work, perhaps featuring the two of them, but hadn't wanted it written off as mere pornography. Courbet was a famous painter. This was a famous work. Legitimate. It had been their best collaboration, and Miranda had regretted that it couldn't be preserved. Still, they had taken photographs, and alerted a local journalist who ran a photo and story in the art section of the *Seattle Post-Intelligencer* the following day. By noon, the sidewalk had been scrubbed clean.

"Mira?" Tazkia squatted by her side, interrupting her reverie. "Like this?"

Miranda looked at her sketch pad. Tazkia had sketched Vicenta's body quickly, simply, but lingered on her face, capturing not only the play of light on her bones but the sensual invitation in her eyes. Miranda looked up at Tazkia's earnest little face and wondered if she even knew what she had done.

"Yes," she said. "Just like that."

NOVEMBER 5, 2010
Miranda

Aisha looks at her quizzically when she straps Luloah onto her front instead of her back. "So I can nurse her more easily," Miranda explains. It's astonishing how quickly her Arabic improves when she hears nothing else. Aisha gives a faint shrug. "As long as you can still carry water," she says.

Miranda's fingers tremble as she winds the cloth around her ribs and the tiny child. She pulls the cloth as tightly as she possibly can without suffocating Luloah and ties a few additional knots. She cannot risk losing her. It is a clear, sunny day. It is always a clear, sunny day. Even once the rains start, the mornings will continue like this, relentlessly bright. The air is sharp and clear, with a metallic smell Miranda normally associates with the onset of autumn. But there is no autumn here.

There is no point in waiting any longer. She is not sure how many months she will be kept here, whether she will be moved, or even whether they will keep her alive. Any day now, her captors will find out who she is, if they haven't found out already. And that will only put her in graver danger. She has been unable to find out anything from Aisha, who simply repeats that she does not know. There is nothing that she knows. Miranda has no idea if a ransom request has been made. She wouldn't even bother asking if a ransom had been paid; she knows it would not have been.

But she cannot simply wait for them to decide to release her. She could keep waiting forever, and it is entirely possible that once Luloah is old enough to eat beans and bread, Miranda will no longer be of use. Though she wonders how much the men holding her really care about the fate of this child. Life is cheap here. Most parents have lost children. And this one has no one to claim her. This is a highly unusual circumstance. In a country where every woman has an average of 6.5 children, there are always cousins, aunts, and uncles galore. Perhaps there are relatives who have escaped the bombings and have sought refuge elsewhere, who have no idea where to even look for the little girl. Or perhaps they are all dead. The bombings had leveled Luloah's home, after all, and many generations often live together under one roof. If Luloah's mother were alive, thinks Miranda, she would have found her by now. A mother would never stop looking.

Miranda has been watching. Every morning when they make their journey along the worn dirt trail to the well to fill their water jugs, she examines the terrain. Most of it is too exposed, there is nowhere to run. Just cracked, flat earth interrupted only occasionally by scrubby olive-green bushes and a few dilapidated wooden shacks that appear uninhabited. But there is a road. She and Aisha cross it every morning, Aisha slowing as they approach, looking anxiously left and right to ensure that they are not seen. Miranda has never seen a vehicle here, though that is hardly surprising. It is more of a track than a road, suitable only for four-wheel drive or a donkey. To the left, the track curves upward into the mountains. To the right, it slopes down, disappearing around a curve obscured by a stand of scruffy trees. Down is her best bet, thinks Miranda. Down might lead eventually to another road, a village. The only question is whether she can make it there fast enough. She knows she has lost muscle mass and endurance but suspects she could still outrun Aisha, who despite their abstemious diet remains stout and slow. For the first time, Miranda wonders if Aisha secretly has access to more food. She still isn't sure that Aisha is unarmed. But if she has a gun, she keeps it well hidden. To Miranda's knowledge, no one ever follows them on their morning walks. Armed men dot the perimeter of their encampment, keeping watch, but none has ventured as far as the well.

For the past several weeks, she has been preparing. When Aisha and Luloah sleep in the afternoons, Miranda does furtive push-ups, squats, and sun salutations. Under her thin rug is a cache of dates. Every time they have appeared on her plate, she has squirreled away one more. She hopes it isn't far to the next village. She hopes someone with a car will give her a lift toward the capital. She needs to get as far as she can as fast as she can. Because she has no idea where she is, she doesn't know if she is among the Shias of the North or the Sunnis of the West. It doesn't matter to her; most people in this country are friendly and intend no harm. *Most* people.

Aisha waits impatiently for Miranda to finish fiddling with Luloah's sling and hands her two large yellow plastic jugs. She will struggle with them on the return journey. Only today she will not be returning. Her heart speeds until she can feel her blood throbbing through her neck, temples, and inner thighs. Luloah stirs on her chest, looks up at her with wide black eyes. *"Kull shee tamaam, habibti,"* she says, stroking a finger down the little girl's cheek. *"N'aie pas peur."* But the child continues to stare, the sparse hairs of her eyebrows rising up her forehead. She's right to be worried, Miranda thinks. I'm taking her into danger.

"Yalla." Aisha is growing impatient. Miranda runs through the checklist in her mind. Small plastic bottle of water, tucked in the sling with the baby, handful of dates wrapped in a scrap of cloth, and Luloah. The lip balm and the thousand-dinar note were taken from her the first day. She looks up at Aisha, whose face is obscured by the *niqab*. Only her dark eyes are visible, urging Miranda to hurry.

Fear catches hold of Miranda's heels, slowing her steps and making Aisha even more impatient. What will happen if she fails? Aisha will never trust her again. But she cannot consider this. "But screw your courage to the sticking place / And we'll not fail," she murmurs, and then chastises herself for quoting the cursed play. The last thing she needs right now is bad luck. The journey is too slow and too fast all at the same time. The sun feels hotter than usual, and trickles of sweat slide from Miranda's armpits down to the band of her trousers. Luloah's body relaxes with the rhythm of the walk, and she dozes against Miranda's chest.

As usual, Miranda sees no one on the way to the road. Aisha

pauses for what feels an eternity, looking around her before crossing the track to the trees on the other side. Miranda allows her to walk ahead, saying she wants to adjust the sling. In the first stand of trees she stops, watching Aisha continue up the path, her water jugs banging against her sides. Miranda presses Luloah closer to her as she glances left and right. The contours of the rocks and trees are sharp against the eggshell-blue sky. Her vision is so keen she feels she could see through walls. One deep, shuddering breath, and she turns back to the road. One foot numbly follows the other, an arm fixes around the child, and suddenly, she is running.

JULY 2008
Miranda

Miranda had been an ambassador's wife for nearly five months before she made it to her first Heads of Mission Spouses Association meeting. Several embossed invitations had been hand-delivered to their guards, but she had always found an excuse not to go: She'd already planned a hike in the western mountains; a new painting was flowing and could not be interrupted; she had agreed to meet one of her women. But it could not be put off indefinitely. Even Finn was beginning to grow impatient. "What are you afraid of?" he asked one morning over muesli. "They're women, not sharks. And they do some good things, things you would approve of. Helping local children's charities and whatnot."

"I know . . ." Miranda felt a little ashamed. What a snob she was. She was reluctant to go to a HOMSA meeting because she didn't want to spend her morning with a bunch of housewives, something she was embarrassed to admit even to herself. Besides, she was making generalizations. Some of the ambassadors' wives worked. And these were women from all over the world. Surely she had plenty to learn from them—even from the housewives.

It was difficult for ambassadors' wives to maintain careers. (It was equally hard, she supposed, for ambassadors' husbands. But there were still regrettably few of those. Many of the women who did make it to the lofty heights of the Foreign Office were single and childless—apparently men were less willing to be trailing spouses.) Many of the wives had had careers before they married, working as lawyers, architects, chefs, journalists, teachers, or scientists. But committing to a diplomatic spouse meant committing to a lifetime of impermanence. Few careers were flexible enough to survive transitions from Britain to Romania to Bangladesh to Uganda to Oman and back again. Miranda was fortunate. She didn't—and wouldn't—have to sacrifice a moment of her painting (or teaching). And without painting she would go slowly mad. Perhaps not so slowly. Would Finn have been such an easy choice if her career demanded that she live elsewhere? But the question is absurd. If Miranda's career had not been flexible, she wouldn't have been here to begin with. She would never have met Finn.

"And sweetheart, I am sorry, but there are some things that are expected of you as my wife. It's inconvenient, I know, but these things do matter."

"I'm sorry." Miranda stirred her cereal, avoiding his eyes. "I'm a crap ambassador's wife."

"It really wouldn't take much—"

"I know, I know. I'll go. Okay? I will go to the next meeting, I promise."

"And you'll play nicely with the other wives?"

"As long as they play nicely with me." Miranda smiled and reached for his hand. He held her fingers briefly, before picking up his coffee.

"It's not forever, you know."

"Do you hear me complaining? I'm a reformed woman! I embrace my wifeliness!"

"Don't get carried away. I won't know who you are."

Of course, there were plenty of women who saw being an ambassador's wife as a satisfying career in itself. It was easy to fill entire days managing staff, hosting teas, planning Christmas parties, counseling the younger staff members, organizing outings for other ambassadors' wives, and planning menus. Many women relished these tasks. But not Miranda. In fact, she felt a reflexive and guilty condescension toward such domestic ambitions. Her conscience wrestled with this prejudice, meanness not sitting comfortably in her psyche. Who was she to judge anyone else's choices? Just because traditional wifely duties were not for her did not make them less worthy. Surely many of these women frowned on Miranda's obsession with her own work, her abandoning of most domestic duties to Negasi. Because Finn had been a bachelor ambassador before Miranda came along, Negasi had assumed many of the duties of an official wife. When Miranda moved in, Finn—aware of her lack of passion for managing household staff—had suggested that Negasi continue with these duties.

Even now, Miranda wore her official duties uneasily. She wanted to be Miranda the Artist, not Miranda the Derivative of Finn. After spending much of her early twenties reading artists' biographies, Miranda had concluded that there was nothing worse than being the wife of a famous or powerful man, condemned forever to the shadows, forever to a supporting role. She had always thought that if anything, she would like a wife of her own—someone to make the meals, raise the kids, and do the laundry while she focused on her art. "You need a wife more than anyone I've ever met," a friend once told her. It was true. When Miranda had lived alone, she'd subsisted on toast, hummus, carrots, nuts, dried fruit, and apples, daunted by the thought of cooking. And while she had always kept her bathroom and kitchen spotless, the rest of her apartment was generally strewn with discarded clothing; books; tubes of paint; rolls of canvas; sticky cans of turpentine; half-stiffened, paint-spattered rags; and endless mugs of tea. Things hadn't been that much different when she lived with Vicenta, who was similarly domestically challenged. Turned out Miranda just wasn't attracted to the kind of woman who wanted to stay home cooking and cleaning. She remembered the jolt of recognition and surprise she felt the first time she read Anna Lea Merritt's "A Letter to Artists, Especially Women Artists."

"The chief obstacle to a woman's success is that she can never have a wife," Merritt wrote.

> *Just reflect what a wife does for an artist:*
> *Darns the stockings;*
> *Keeps his house;*

Writes his letters;
Visits for his benefit;
Wards off intruders;
Is personally suggestive of beautiful pictures;
Always an encouraging and partial critic.
It is exceedingly difficult to be an artist without this time-saving help. A
husband would be quite useless. He would never do any of these disagreeable
things.

How little things have changed, mused Miranda. Thank god Finn liked to cook and knew how to sew. After all, they wouldn't have a staff forever. When his posting ended, they'd likely be living in a shoe box in London and doing their own dishes. This didn't worry Finn.

"The passion you have for your work is one of the things I love best about you," he told her. "I'd never let you give it up for me, even if you tried."

In the end, she had become an ambassador's wife in the garden of the Residence. She and Finn had briefly considered eloping to an exotic country before thinking, What could be more exotic than here? And when would they ever have a home more appropriate for entertaining? So Teru and Miranda put together a wedding menu, Finn ordered the gardeners to set up a tent in the yard with a dance floor, and the bride and groom hastily compiled a guest list. They didn't have to worry about inviting their extended families; most of them wouldn't come. In fact, they could invite ten times the number of friends and relatives they could accommodate and still have a fairly empty house. Most Westerners—particularly those who read the news—found Mazrooq too intimidating a destination. But there was no shortage of local invitees: the entire close protection team, the household staff, Miranda's students, Mosi, Madina, Morgane and Sebastian, Kaia and Stéphane, Doortje and Alfons, the French, German, Italian, Dutch, and American ambassadors, the Omani, Egyptian, Emirati, Saudi, and Tunisian ambassadors, several of Miranda's friends from the Old City, the whole expatriate staff of the British embassy, and a smattering of oil workers. So it wasn't quite the intimate affair they had planned.

The Mazrooqis, of course, assumed they were already married. As soon as Miranda had moved in with Finn, he began referring to her as his wife. Given that marriage contracts and wedding celebrations were normally separate events in Mazrooq, it wouldn't surprise anyone that Miranda and Finn were throwing a party long after they were legally wed.

"So how modest do I have to be?" Miranda asked Finn. They were sitting over a breakfast of scrambled eggs and porridge—they lingered in bed so late on weekends (and not because they were sleeping) that they were ravenous by the time they made it downstairs—at the small round table in a sunny corner of the kitchen, which during the weekdays was monopolized by the staff, working on the Sunday *New York Times* crossword puzzle. A friend of Miranda's in Seattle mailed a collection of them each month. Finn had pointed out that they could probably print them off the website, but Miranda had looked at him reproachfully. "It's not the *same*."

Pouring cold milk over her porridge, she continued, "I mean, there'll be an awful lot of Muslims in attendance. Wondering, no doubt, why we're allowing men and women in the same room. Or same yard. Whatever."

Finn looked up from the puzzle. "Massenet opera?"

"Who the hell is Massenet?"

"It's your wedding," said Finn. "This once, I think, you can wear whatever takes your fancy."

"Nothing you can buy in this country. I don't *fancy* getting wrapped up in polyester. Dear god, Finn, you realize what this means, don't you? I am going to have to *go shopping*."

"I'm sorry, sweetheart, but I'm afraid there's no way around that one. Unless you want to wear one of your sundresses?"

She gave him a hopeless look. "I just don't want to be one of those *bride* people."

"Um, have we not gone over the definition of wedding? Big party, bride, groom, sometimes bridesmaids?"

"Bridesmaids." She looked horrified. "All in look-alike taffeta. I couldn't bear it."

Finn reached for her hand. "Are you sure you want to do this?"

"Of course!" She squeezed his fingers. "If taffeta means that much to you, I will suffer it."

"We can skip the taffeta. Do you think you want bridesmaids at all? Or maybe just one attendant? Maid of honor type of person?"

Miranda thought for a moment. "I want Tazkia," she said. "Can I have her? Though she'll have to be all covered up, of course, with all those men around."

"Of course. Look, do you want to give Marguerite a call?"

"Are you going to have any—what are they called? Ushers? Groomspeople?"

Finn thought for a moment. "I don't think so." He had no siblings, his parents were both dead, and he hadn't been the world's finest correspondent with his friends. He had always had plenty of great mates wherever he had been posted, but he somehow never managed to maintain those relationships once one or both of them had moved on. Claire remained his closest friend in the UK, doggedly continuing to write him at least once a month even in the face of his long silences. There was little chance, however, that she and Charlie would drag their family over here for the festivities.

"If I have Tazkia, won't we be lopsided?"

"Could we both have Tazkia? She could be our maid of groomsman. Our usher of honor."

"I'm sure she'd be flattered."

"Look, I'm going to be doing the accounts solidly through next weekend. Why don't you go to Istanbul or Dubai or somewhere and pick up a dress?"

Miranda looked at him in surprise. "Seriously?"

"You'll want something nice, or at least something you like."

"We can afford it?"

"We have a travel package, love. Among the great perks of hardship postings are all the free airfares."

"Maybe I'll ask Marguerite to come with me."

Finn smiled. "I recommend it." He had been relieved when she and Marguerite began spending time together. While Miranda seemed happy with her merry band of expats and Mazrooqi women, he had fretted about her integration into diplomatic life. Marguerite managed to engage Miranda on an intellectual level—they traded books and argued about postmodernism—while also gently coaching her in the diplomatic arts of managing staff, planning menus, and dressing appropriately. He was careful, however, never to openly express gratitude for this.

"You don't trust me, do you? You think I'll come back with something in patchwork!"

"Well, sweetheart, as much as I love you, I wouldn't say fashion sense is one of your finer points."

Miranda sighed. "No, you're right. I basically resent the fact that fashion exists at all."

Finn picked up the pen. "Okay, so now that that's settled . . . word with 'bum' or 'bunny'?"

"Ski," said Miranda, scooping up a mouthful of her porridge.

"Right. And—"

"*Grisélidis? Bacchus? Cendrillon?*"

Finn looked up at her. "What?"

"The opera. Do any of those fit?"

He counted the squares. "No."

She pulled the page toward her. "Oh," she said. "It's *Ariane*."

Finn leaned back in his chair and crossed his arms. "Didn't you just say, 'Who the hell is Massenet?' A few moments ago?"

Miranda sighed. "Okay," she said. "I dated an opera singer."

"I should have guessed. So that makes an opera singer, a fireman, a burlesque dancer, an artist, a saxophonist, a composer, a poet, and a choreographer."

"Look, I told you. When I said I have slept with half the planet, I meant it. I just want you to know everything. You know, before we're married. So you don't feel I've misrepresented myself in any way."

He laughed. "And I appreciate your honesty. It's quite refreshing."

"How would I know who to marry if I didn't try everybody first?

But you, you are special. You are the only person for whom I am willing to brave the bridal boutiques."

"And your only civil servant?"

"Of course! Repetition is so boring."

"Is there any profession you haven't slept with?"

Miranda thought for a moment. "Yes," she said. "I have never, to my knowledge, slept with a banker."

Finn

February 21, their wedding day, much like the other 364 days a year, dawned sunny. The guests, duly checked off security's list at the gate, milled around the spongy lawn, sipping mango juice or champagne. Miranda was still locked up in their bedroom, where she'd spent the night alone, suddenly superstitious. "You're not supposed to see the bride on the wedding day," she'd told Finn. "You can have the Minister's Suite." He hadn't argued. What was one night apart before a lifetime of a shared bed?

Now he stood in front of the rows of chairs (tilting on the uneven grass), nervously exchanging inanities with the consul, Sally, Miranda's one close friend within the embassy. She chose wisely, thought Finn. Everyone loved Sally, a tall, striking woman who laughed easily, spoke beautiful Arabic, and adored entertaining. She was also one of the two people in the country who could legally marry them. Finn and Miranda had written their own vows and selected several short poems and readings, none of which were from the Bible. He worried a bit about the reaction to an utterly secular ceremony. Muslims could relate to Christians and even Jews, who shared with them a monotheistic tradition, but they struggled to wrap their minds around a life devoid of any religion. "You must be *something*," they would say on the rare occasions Finn confessed that he was neither Christian nor Jew. But he wasn't. He wasn't anything. And his wedding was no time to pretend.

Nervously, Finn adjusted his cuff links, tiny silver daggers Miranda had given him for his birthday the year they met. He had discarded his well-worn dinner jacket in favor of a morning suit with blue waistcoat and pinstriped trousers. The pinstripes wouldn't have been his choice, but Miranda liked them.

"Is this part of your unfulfilled desire to date a banker?" he'd asked.

"I just like how they look. You look so pretty in stripes. Why should we let the conservatives have all the good clothing?"

He had chosen the tie, patterned after *The Hunt of the Unicorn*. It was one of the few ties he had actually purchased himself, at the Cloisters during a business trip to New York. The unicorn's refusal to stay dead appealed to him, as did the persistence of the tapestries over some five hundred years.

Negasi came bustling down the aisle. "Ambassador, Madame she almost ready. Do you want I should ask guests to the chairs?"

"Yes, please, Negasi. Wonderful. Is Teru okay in there?"

"Yes, Teru she is fine. Everything is ready." The circular tables had miraculously appeared throughout the first floor sometime during the night, and by the time he descended for breakfast, they were set with silver and crystal and scattered with jasmine petals. Finn had eaten quickly at the small table in the kitchen and sent a tray of tea, pomegranate seeds, and porridge up to Miranda.

He wondered if he should be more worried. He, a lifelong bachelor, was about to marry a woman many men might consider a bad bet. But for some reason nothing in Miranda's past gave him pause. The fact that she had had relationships with so many others before him was oddly comforting as well as intriguing. He didn't have to worry that she would spend her remaining years wondering if she should have sown a few more wild oats. And he didn't have to worry that she would obsess over his own past, though it has been far tamer than hers. Other than the series of unfulfilling or lopsided relationships, there has been only the one serious miscalculation.

He sensed that Miranda was almost disappointed in the lack of passionate complications in his past. Someday, he would tell her about Afghanistan. Someday, but not just yet. He could not risk losing her now. A ring would not be enough to irrevocably bind her to him, but that plus time, and perhaps someday a child . . . then he might feel safe enough to confess.

The next time he turned toward the house, she was there, cautiously teetering down the slippery front steps in ivory lace shoes. Heels, even. He felt honored. A strapless gown of sea-green silk clung to her torso before spinning out to just below her knees. In a slight concession to local custom, she had covered her shoulders with an ivory lace bolero. Her hair fell in ringlets down her narrow back. Aside from a circlet of jasmine flowers in her hair, she was unadorned. "A wedding ring," she had told him, "is jewelry enough." Finn stood staring at her, as though she were a mirage, until she waved her small bouquet of jasmine in his direction. "Come help me!" she called, "before I sink into this lawn!"

They walked each other down the grassy aisle, Miranda thinking it silly to have her father give her away when she had been living apart from her parents for more than twenty years. She didn't like the idea of being delivered into the keeping of one man by another. Better she and Finn process as equals, mutually submitting themselves to each other's keeping. Not that her father would have come anyway. He was terrified of flying. Which Miranda always thought was an odd fear for an astronomer. "You're a man of science," she told him. "You know it's the safest way to travel. And the closest to your favorite stars." He simply agreed with her and stayed behind his telescope. Miranda worried about him living alone. Her mother had disappeared years ago, fed up with her dreamy, absent husband. As soon as Miranda was off to art school, her mother had packed her paints and paintings and gone south, first to Mexico and then to Costa Rica. She had no phone, but Miranda had sent her a wedding invitation pasted to a postcard of the Old City at twilight. In the margins, she had penciled in, "spectacular place to paint." But she hadn't heard anything back. Either her mother had moved again or she was too wrapped up in her own work to respond.

Miranda hadn't seemed to take this personally. "Weddings aren't really her thing," she'd said and shrugged when Finn attempted to console her. "It's okay. She's been a good mother most of my life, I don't mind if she does her own thing now." Finn could not fathom this. His mother had died of cancer when he was seventeen, and his father had died of a heart attack just a few years ago, and not one day went by when he did not long to hear their voices. Because Finn was an only child, his parents had always been his best friends. Among his favorite memories were reading *The Wind in the Willows* with his father when he got home from school and helping his mother with her translations in the evenings. She was Quebecoise and worked translating poetry from French to English or vice versa. She was the reason Finn had a head start with languages. His English father bartended in a pub close to their house in Acton, always dressed in a clean white shirt and bow tie, even as his clientele grew shabbier over the years. He would have liked Miranda, Finn thought with a pang. Like all the best bartenders, he was a terrible flirt, but the harmless sort, the sort that came home every night to the same woman. He especially appreciated intelligent women, women willing to argue with him. Like Finn's mother.

"Don't feel sorry for me," Miranda had warned. "I'm not a neglected child. My mother made my lunches and picked me up after school every day. She went to PTA meetings. My father helped me with my math homework. Ultimately though, we're three people without much in common." Finn had never met Miranda's parents, but he was curious. Someday he would surprise her with a trip to Costa Rica. He wondered if she would like that, or if it would just annoy her. It was hard to tell.

As they stood behind their guests, awaiting their cue, Finn squeezed her fingers. "Sure you want to be an ambassador's wife?"

Miranda turned to him and smiled. "I have a feeling I should have asked you earlier more about what this involves . . ."

"The FCO gives lessons. If I had met you before I came out here, you could have had classes."

"And now I have to wing it."

"You'll be fine. As long as you learn to suppress your strident, feminist political opinions." Miranda swatted him with her bouquet, sending jasmine petals showering to the ground.

"Do I have to learn how to play bridge or garden or anything?"

"Mah-jongg. And I'm afraid you'll be required to host coffee mornings."

"As long as they don't interfere with my gym routine."

"One of the sacrifices I am sure you'll gladly make for love."

The music changed and Sally began plucking out the initial notes of "Believe Me, If All Those Endearing Young Charms" on a guitar. Finn reached over and brushed a petal from Miranda's hair. "Last chance to make a run for it."

She sighed. "You had better be worth it," she whispered, as they took their first unsteady steps across the springy turf of the garden that was only ephemerally their own.

Miranda

And now here she was, modestly attired in an ankle-length dress and linen blazer, buckled into the backseat of her own car, heading to the home of the Mauritanian ambassador for her first HOMSA meeting. She had her own driver now, a slender nineteen-year-old who was the son of one of the guards. Altaf was polite, courtly, and like few others in this country, a cautious driver. This was the crucial quality for Miranda, given that traffic laws were mere suggestions and most drivers plowed through intersections without a glance to either side. There were no child car seats, a fact that alarmed Miranda even though she did not yet have a use for one. But when she saw a mother driving with an infant in one arm, or a small boy kneeling on the front seat with his face pressed to the windshield, she wanted to chase down the drivers and thrust the statistics on child fatalities on the road into their reckless hands.

Miranda had told the staff she would be back in time for lunch, just in case she was ejected from the meeting before anything had been served. But why was she expecting unkindness? These women were diplomatic spouses. At the very least they would *fake* kindness. She wished Marguerite could be there, but Marguerite had to host a lunch for some visiting French dignitaries. Miranda wondered how many of the wives knew about Vícenta, knew about her former life. The Western ones probably wouldn't care, but would the Arab ambassadors' wives? Or would they secretly be plotting to have her burned at the stake for perversion? Suddenly, she realized she didn't care. Wasn't there enough in the world to worry about without fretting about the approval of ambassadors' wives? Besides, chances were that any Westerner who knew about Vícenta would be discreet with that knowledge. The stakes were too high.

She had barely reached the top of the steps when the front door swung open to admit her. A smiling Filipina woman showed her down the vast, carpeted front hall and into a gilded *diwan*. Almost everything—mirrors, framed paintings, pillows, sofas, plates propped up on little gold stands, ceramic jugs, glass coffee tables—was trimmed with gold. Miranda was surprised that the enormous flat-screen television didn't have a golden frame. Olamide, the Mauritanian ambassador's wife, a woman nearly as wide as she was tall, rose to greet her in a rustle of rayon, kissing her cheeks. Miranda tried to remember if they had met before. A few others were already settled on the cushions. Miranda recognized Chrysantha, the wife of the Egyptian ambassador, and was introduced to Adinda, the wife of the Indonesian ambassador, and Alena, the wife of the Palestinian ambassador. They smiled and greeted her warmly. "We haven't had a wife of the UK ambassador in a while," said Chrysantha. "We weren't sure you were getting the invitations. We are happy to have you, Madame Fenwick."

"I'm happy to be here!" Miranda smiled brightly as she tucked her bare feet underneath her on the cushion. She resisted the urge to correct her name. She hadn't changed her surname when she married Finn, and she had no intention of doing so. Nor would she ever claim the title Mrs. Besides the fact that it made her feel middle-aged, she felt strongly that a title should not betray marital status. Ms. would do nicely, as it had done for most of her life. Finn had no objection, but envelopes still regularly arrived addressed to Mrs. Finn Fenwick. No sign of Miranda at all in that name; it erased her utterly. It was maddening, but there were battles more worthy of her time.

Before she had time to say anything else, another group of women arrived: Algerian, Malaysian, Omani, Kuwaiti, Lebanese, Cuban, and

Russian. The women kissed each other and chattered away in a variety of languages, mostly Arabic. Miranda felt small and a bit lost, but she didn't mind. It underscored what she already sensed, that she was a spectator more than a participant. The Spanish ambassador's wife arrived last, impeccably dressed in a Calvin Klein pantsuit and chiffon scarf. She sat next to the bottle-blond Russian wife, and the two immediately began complimenting each other's outfits and complaining about their respective staffs. "I asked Fana to make deviled eggs stuffed with salmon filling for the party last week," the Spanish wife said. "And instead of mixing the salmon in with the yolks and the rest of the filling, she stuck a chunk of it on top! I mean, the cookbook has *photos*. She could *see* that the salmon should have been pureed with the rest of the filling. I was *mortified* when she brought around the tray."

"Well, our Kayla puts my stockings away in a different drawer every time she washes them. I can never find anything when I'm hurrying to dress for dinner," answered the Russian. "And why does it take a week for clothing to return from the laundry to the dresser? The washing machine only takes forty minutes!" Both women sighed. "It's always something, isn't it?"

"You can't ever relax, not for a minute. Now I don't just hand Fana recipes, I explain them to her and then try to check on her every few minutes to make sure she hasn't done something idiotic. Like stick canned tuna on top of the salads instead of fresh tuna steaks. Which she has done."

"It's funny, isn't it? People think, ambassadors' wives, we have it so easy."

"I know—my friends back home think we live like royalty."

Miranda listened incredulously. "But we *do* live like royalty," she interrupted. "Other people wash our clothing, make our meals, polish our shoes, mix our drinks, serve our guests. It's true that we have to pick menus, host a few teas, tell a few people what to do—but then, so do queens, no?"

The Spaniard and the Russian turned to stare at her with hardening eyes. So much for making new friends. Miranda wondered if over time she would develop the same sense of entitlement, the same nitpicking complaints about the people who worked to make her life as effortless as possible. Would a lifetime of privilege soften her body and sharpen her tongue? Silently, she vowed vigilance against this peril.

To her great relief, further conversation was forestalled when Chrysantha clapped her hands to call the meeting to order. She began by passing around sheets of paper—in Arabic and English—detailing where the proceeds from a charity luncheon would go. The money would support two organizations. One was a home for children with cerebral palsy, the other was a home for blind women. "Many children, they are forced to lie on the ground because they have nowhere to sit," said Chrysantha. "The money will buy for them things they need." Miranda was instantly queasy with concern for the children and chastised herself once again for not having come to a meeting earlier. She would visit this home for children with cerebral palsy, she promised herself. She would find a way to help.

She was distracted from her self-flagellation by the angry voice of the Omani, Alya. In a torrent of Arabic, she was chastising Chrysantha for something. Or so Miranda gathered from the few words she understood. It seemed a bizarrely outsized response to an announcement of charitable intentions. Several others joined the fray, and soon everyone was shouting. Amazed, Miranda tried to follow what was happening, but the Arabic was too fast for her. She looked helplessly at Adinda, whom she knew spoke English.

"Stop! *Khalas*, you are making me frightened," Adinda told the women. "And switch to English; not everyone understands Arabic."

"Yes, English please," said Stefania the Russian, who spoke no Arabic. While Miranda also wanted to understand what was going on, she noted that the majority of the women in the room spoke Arabic. It was hardly fair to expect everyone to use English when there were only a handful of people who spoke it. Not to mention the fact that they were, after all, in an Arabic-speaking country.

Eventually, it became clear that Alya was criticizing Chrysantha for not having invited all of HOMSA to go to these organizations and see their conditions for themselves. Apparently, she had visited with just a few of the other wives. Alya thought they should all have a chance to visit the organizations before any decision was made.

"Everyone was notified," Chrysantha protested. "I sent a fax!"

"I did not get a fax," said Adinda.

"You see?" said Alya. "The rest of us did not know."

"It is not my fault if your fax machine does not function. Most embassies, they have a fax."

The conflict escalated until the women were once more shouting across the room. Miranda watched in fascination. It seemed such a ridiculous debate. Why couldn't they all just go visit the places this week and then make a final decision, if more people wanted to see them? Why yell at each other? Were they not supposed to be diplomatic wives? Were they utterly unschooled in the gentle art of persuasion? This was not the meeting she had envisioned.

Intriguingly, most of the women addressed their comments directly to Miranda, as if pleading their case with her. They overestimated her understanding of Arabic, barraging her with proclamations and questions, to which her only response was to smile and shrug her shoulders. When phrases were translated into English, the women glanced at her to check that they had said them correctly. She was, after all, the only native English speaker.

Finally, after another incomprehensible burst of Arabic, Chrysantha hauled herself to her feet and stalked out. A few women made a show of begging her to stay, but no one actually stood up to stop her.

After this, things descended into chaos. No one seemed to know how to properly hold a meeting. "Who is our vice president?" Olamide asked. "Don't we have a vice president?"

"Adinda," Stefania offered.

"No, I am the treasurer!" said Adinda.

"Adinda should be the vice president!" said another.

"No," said Adinda, laughing. "I don't even have all the information I need to do my job as treasurer!"

Nothing was resolved. No one proposed a way to go forward. No one suggested a plan of action. Miranda might have suggested one, just to get things moving in some sort of clear direction, but she wasn't sure that her first meeting was the best time to try taking the reins.

Olamide abruptly stood and began shepherding the women into

the other room. Bewildered, Miranda followed the others into a dining room full of white-clothed tables. A buffet table was heaped with
food: cheeses, meats, salads, and breads. Miranda wished she were
home, eating alone with *ARTnews*.

"Eat, eat!" said Olamide kindly, taking her arm. "You can sit by
me." Feeling trapped, Miranda scooped a few spoonfuls of salad onto
a plate and perched on one of the chairs. She sat quietly, listening
to the other women speak in Arabic, trying to follow the conversation. She caught the words for children, home, and sick. Noting her
confusion, Adinda took pity on her and translated. "We're going to
an orphanage next week," she said. "We go every Tuesday to visit the
children."

"All of you?"

"No no, just a few. Otherwise it is too much for the children. Too
many people."

"Of course."

"This Tuesday, it is just Marguerite, but she could use company.
Do you want to go?"

"Yes, please! Would that be okay?"

"Of course! You can see the babies and then the older children.
They are in a separate area.

"For an orphanage, it is not too bad," continued Adinda. "It will
only half break your heart."

NOVEMBER 19, 2010
Finn

It is an unusually quiet Friday afternoon in the Old City when
Finn sets off from the house, Bashir at his side. Cressie is home with
Gabra, who has strict instructions to allow no visitors until their
return. Tucker will also check on them, as he still does several times
a day, in addition to the hours he spends organizing Celia's protection. Finn doubts that Tucker ever sleeps; if work didn't keep him
awake, guilt would. He cannot forgive himself, holds himself person-

ally responsible for Miranda's loss. Despite the bright sun, a chill has settled into Finn's bones. He has done his best to make himself inconspicuous, dressing in a long white *thobe* and suit jacket, a black-and-white scarf tied around his head. Yet inevitably, people stare as he and Bashir weave their way through the maze of streets toward the Grand Mosque, where Tazkia's brother Hamid is to meet them. Finn received the text from Tazkia yesterday. The girls needed to speak with him, but they had to be careful. Would he please meet Hamid at the mosque? He would take Finn to a place where it was safe.

Finn holds out no real hope, but he is not in a position to turn down any offer of assistance. His local network has not yet turned up even a rumor of Miranda's whereabouts. Or those of the other women. Or of Mukhtar. From the various embassies, there has been only silence.

As they approach the mosque, Finn scans the crowd. He hasn't met Tazkia's brother before, but he knows it won't take long for the boy to spot him. He is easily the tallest, palest, and lightest-eyed person for blocks. Dozens of men loiter near the mosque. Friday afternoon prayers have come and gone, and most of the men are on their way to a quiet place to gossip over miniature cups of sticky-sweet tea. A diminutive, dark-haired youth flicks his cigarette into the street and stands abruptly from where he has been squatting on a stoop with a friend. His outfit matches Finn's, with the addition of a decorative dagger dangling from a thick leather belt. He smiles, gestures to Finn to follow him, and swiftly disappears down a side street.

Quickening their pace, Finn and Bashir follow him for a dozen or so turns deeper and deeper into the city. At last they arrive at a small, blue, battered Ford truck and the boy turns to look at Finn. "Apologies, *sa'adat as-safir*," he says. "I am only protecting my sister. I am Hamid."

"*Fursa saeeda. Fahimt.*" Understood. "Please call me Finn."

"*Yalla?*"

Finn nods. The boy opens the door of the truck and Finn slides in, wedging himself between Hamid and Bashir. As the truck rattles through the streets, narrowly avoiding wheelbarrows and small children, Finn notices he can see the cobblestones through a hole in the floor by his feet. The noise of the engine makes it hard to speak, though Finn isn't sure what to say anyway. "Your sister is kind to want to help me find my wife," he says finally.

Hamid nods. "She loves your wife," he shouts in Arabic over the engine's rumble. Taking his right hand off the wheel, he rummages between the seats for his cigarettes. The truck swerves, nearly brushing a corner of a building. Finn wants to ask where they are going but isn't sure he should.

It doesn't take long for Finn to discern their destination. Hamid has driven them to the outskirts of a ruined village, abandoned decades ago. Many of the stone houses still stand, but their insides have been scooped out and filled with rocks, soda cans, plastic bags, and other detritus of picnickers and passersby. Finn has visited the village before, on a hike with Miranda. They had climbed up from the nearest wadi and sat on the crumbling wall of the village looking out over the countryside while they ate a picnic of bread and palm fruit. A small boy, not more than six (though it was hard to tell when so many children were stunted by malnutrition), had trailed after them as they climbed, chattering about the history of the village while he collected the palm fruit for them to eat. "This was all Jews," he'd said proudly, waving his hand at a row of modest stone houses. He had peeled the spiky orbs for them, holding out the dripping yellow flesh in his filthy palms. "The Jews, they made the silver jewelry," he'd told them. "The best, with the best designs." Miranda had asked the boy if he had ever met a Jew, and he'd said, "No. They are gone long ago." ("No doubt chased out by his ancestors," Miranda had muttered under her breath to Finn.)

Now, Hamid climbs out of the truck and scans the horizon before letting Finn and Bashir out to follow him. They walk toward one of the larger ruins. "I brought the girls here earlier," he tells Finn. "They wait. In the city, there are too many eyes."

When Finn first ducks into the stone building, he is blinded by the darkness. Slowly, the dim shapes of about a half-dozen women emerge. Completely swathed in black, they are nearly invisible. Yet he recognizes one, the only face not obscured by a *niqab*: Madina. "Madina!" he says, offering and then withdrawing a hand.

"We've been meeting at my house," she says. "They needed somewhere they could talk without a man. No offense, Finn."

"None taken. I'm glad."

One of the smaller, dark shapes jumps up and runs toward him. "*Sa'adat as-safir!*" It is Tazkia. She stops just short of him.

"*Kayf halikee?*" he says, grateful for the warmth of her voice, familiar and kind.

"*Al haamdulillah,*" she says. "Come, sit."

Finn settles himself on the cool earth, moving aside a few sharp pieces of rock. "I appreciate you wanting to help," he begins.

"*Sa'adat as-safir,* we *must* help. Listen . . . ," and squatting beside him with the grubby tips of her sneakers jutting out from under her *abaya,* she begins to talk. The women, like almost everyone in this country, have extensive families with numerous branches. Each of these families originates in an area beyond the capital city. The half-dozen women here have roots in at least as many far-flung villages. "And we have been talking with our cousins, our aunts, our nieces and friends," says Tazkia. "We have sent messages to our families everywhere. And now, *sa'adat as-safir,* we think we may have an idea of where she is, your Miranda." Tazkia pauses, waits for her words to take effect. "Or at least, we think we know where she has *been.*"

Finn has to stop himself from grabbing her shoulders and shaking the information out of her. "Tazkia, are you sure? How do you know? What do you know? Tell me everything."

"Wait," she says, as Finn's heart speeds with reckless hope. Leaning behind her, she takes a bag and reaches inside. It takes years for her to find what she is looking for. And then she extends her hand to Finn. "Take it outside to look at it," she says. "Tell me if it is Miranda's."

Finn's fingers tremble as he takes hold of the crumpled sheet of paper Tazkia has given him. Moving closer to the door, he smoothes it against the ground, until in the light creeping in he can at last make out a familiar image.

SEPTEMBER 19, 2008
Miranda

It was the booze order that began to change things. It had been held up for ages, on account of Ramadan. That was the excuse the government officials gave, although the embassy's alcohol shipment had arrived weeks ahead of the holy month. Every six months or so, staff were allowed to order their fill from a liquor and wine catalog, to get them through diplomatic soirees and their more desperate days. The country was tough enough without having to constantly deal with it sober, Tucker said.

By the beginning of September, everyone was running dry and beginning to panic. The British Club ran out of white wine, Leslie ran out of beer, and Finn had served the last of his Bombay Sapphire. The situation was dire. During Ramadan, not even the Sheraton or the InterContinental would serve a glass of wine. So it was a shock when the booze order abruptly showed up before the last week of the holy month. The customs authorities had refused them their crates of sin before Ramadan but decided to release them during the month itself? Maybe all that fasting was taking a toll. Still, no one complained. No one was about to question this particular bit of local perversity, least of all the Brits.

"I told Camilla that you'd help unload it tomorrow morning," Finn said to Miranda the night before the big day as they undressed for bed. "It should arrive around ten a.m."

A ribbon of dread wove itself around Miranda's rib cage. Camilla, dipsomaniac wife of Finn's deputy, first thing in the morning, was not her idea of a bright start to the day. Camilla had a habit of cornering Miranda after having tossed back one glass of chardonnay too many in the club or at a party and peppering her with pointed questions, usually of an ominously personal nature: What was the name of that girl Miranda used to live with in the Old City? Her *roommate*? What kinds of things did she paint? Wasn't it nice that she had a lovely *hobby* like painting? What charitable work was she doing? Did she get the invitation to the Spanish ambassador's wife's coffee morning? (No, she did not.) Did she need any advice about her new life? (Yes, but not from Camilla.) Or she would say things like "It must be so hard, coming from a country everyone here hates so much." And so on, until Miranda feigned desperate need for the toilet.

But it was important, in these early days, to show herself willing. Besides, she had been trapped in the house for several days. With terrorist attacks escalating, staff members were banned from using the pool or the gym, despite the fact that they were right at the end of Miranda and Finn's garden.

"You'll at least get a decent workout hauling all the boxes." Finn smiled, reading her mind, as usual. It was a testament to how desperate Miranda had become in her fancy prison that she could suddenly think of nothing more thrilling than hauling boxes of bottles around town.

"Plus it's a good bonding opportunity." Some of the staff might actually be forced to speak to her.

"Thought that too."

Finn also wanted to help with the shipment, but he had more pressing concerns than the lubrication of his employees. Before 7:00 a.m., he headed to the embassy to ensure new security measures had been put in place, while Miranda pulled on her cargo pants and one of Finn's shirts and pinned up her hair with a slender paintbrush. All the boxes had been unloaded at Leslie and Camilla's, so she walked the two blocks to their house with Mukhtar, her guard du jour, trailing after her.

Leslie's guards recognized her and swung open the black gate, admitting her to what looked like the festive preparations for a summer picnic. Almost everyone from the embassy had shown up, clad in jeans, polo shirts, and sunglasses, milling among leaning towers of crates of beer, gin, wine, whiskey, and a fairly wide array of other spirits. It was a bacchanalian's wet dream. Leslie's manic dog Tetley was hanging half out of a bottom-floor window, howling his opinion of his exclusion from the proceedings.

"Wow," Miranda said. She had never seen so much booze in one place. No one seemed particularly surprised to see her there. Smiling brightly, she wandered around saying perky hellos, avoiding the creepy Norman and his porridge-faced wife, who were hovering over their cartons of gin and London Pride. The others were divided into their customary cliques. Political staffers, who worked with Finn on strategic planning, human rights, development issues, and who cultivated close relationships with Mazrooqi officials, tended to be snobbish toward the management staffers, who toiled at the more mundane yet no less essential tasks of accountancy, housing maintenance, and day-to-day running of the embassy.

"Finn's stuff is there," said Lydia, the head of the management section, who was holding a clipboard. "But don't take any of it until we've checked it all off."

Miranda nodded. Finn had asked her to be especially kind to management staffers, who had been feeling surly and unappreciated. Apparently the political section had been excluding them from their near-nightly parties and game nights. Given that house parties were among the few entertainments available to staff these days, this stung. "Thank you, Lydia," she said. "This looks fantastic!"

Miranda and Finn had one of the biggest mounds of boxes, as they were responsible for quite a lot of official entertaining at the Residence. There were several cases of Bombay Sapphire and Gordon's gin; five bottles of Hendrick's for personal use; a dozen crates of Old Speckled Hen bitter; a dozen more of Heineken; several cases of wine from Chile, New Zealand, France, and California; two cases of Veuve Clicquot; and a large box packed with bottles of tequila, ginger wine, Belvedere vodka, Campari, Wood's Old Navy Rum, and a dozen bottles of single malts.

"I am a little embarrassed that my stack looks a bit bigger than yours," said Tucker, gesturing to a pyramid of boxes about the width of a city block.

"We'll know where to head when we run dry."

"Shall we?" Lydia hovered nearby, pen ready.

Miranda nodded and pulled a crumpled list from her pocket. Tucker read off what was in each of the crates, and Lydia checked them off her list.

"How many boxes of Caliterra do you have?" said Sally, leaning over to peer at their stack. "We're missing some." Her black hair was pulled back in barrettes, and she looked like a teenager in jeans. A very tall teenager. Miranda had liked Sally long before she met Finn. Sally had no time for cliquishness; she was good-humored and kind to everyone, including the management section and Miranda. But all of Finn's Caliterra was accounted for on Miranda's list, so Sally wandered elsewhere. "It's great stuff," she called over her shoulder. "Cheap as chips and eminently drinkable."

No one was in a hurry. The embassy was officially closed until the new security measures were in place, and there was little else anyone could have been doing, especially given that most of them hardly left their houses since the last attack. The sun was warm but not hot, and there was a breeze. Another delicious autumn day.

"Who on earth drinks this much chardonnay?" said Leo, the vegetarian defense attaché and her defender at the club, leaning over a pile of boxes.

"What's it to you?" said Lydia, rushing to defend her stash. "No one's asking you to drink it, are they?"

Miranda smiled. "I hope she isn't asking me to drink it either," she whispered to Leo. "Not that there's much chance of that happening."

Leo touched her elbow, gently nudging her toward the house and away from inquisitive ears. "How are you?" he asked, with genuine concern. "Has anyone else been horrid to you? I confess I'm a little surprised Norman is still with us."

"I'm fine," Miranda said, as convincingly as she could manage. "Everyone has been very polite, which is about as friendly as I expect anyone to be with the boss's wife. And I'm sure Norman just had a bit too much to drink. Thank you again, though, for rushing to my defense."

"Defense is a bit of a specialty of mine." He hesitated, frowning. "I'm sure Finn has his reasons for keeping him around. And I have every confidence in his ability to protect you . . ." He let the sentence dangle, his ruddy face uncertain.

"Leo, you know I have a bodyguard, right?" She wanted to say more. She wanted to ask what had happened to Norman's other fixations. She wanted to ask why decent men would protect such an asshole. Even more, she wanted to ask what hold Norman had on her husband. But not only was she unsure that Leo knew, she also didn't want to admit her husband kept any significant secrets from her.

"Sorry, I don't mean to go all big brotherish on you. I just know how tough a crowd we can be to an outsider, and I want you to know that I've got your back."

"Thank you. I appreciate that." Miranda searched his earnest face. There was clearly more he wanted to say too, but he wouldn't. That gentlemen's agreement again, no doubt.

"Leo, not to sound paranoid or anything, but has he ever actually hurt anyone? I get that you all protect each other's indiscretions and all, but is that really all it is, that he's a player?"

Leo tilted his head toward the corner of the house, and they moved farther away from the others, who fortunately were far more interested in counting up their boxes than eavesdropping.

"I didn't tell you this, but he was short-toured from Manila—supposedly for health reasons, but rumor has it he was spending a little too much time with the bar girls."

"And that's an issue? For the FCO, I mean?"

"A huge issue. It's a major security risk. And because he's married, it means he's also blackmailable."

"Oh." That hadn't even occurred to Miranda. "So he's been good since then?"

"Well, there aren't any bar girls in Mazrooq."

"Or Afghanistan, I guess."

Leo looked slightly surprised. "Was he there?"

Miranda nodded. "The same time as Finn."

Leo's face stilled, as if it was trying not to give away his thoughts.

"Well," he said finally. "I'm sure you'll be fine as long as you don't accept his invitations to come upstairs and take a look at his etchings."

"He doesn't strike me as an art collector type."

"Depends on your definition of art. He's got a few framed portraits of dogs playing poker." Miranda laughed. "But to answer your question, no, I don't think he would hurt you. He wouldn't have the job he did if he was really a threat to anyone. He's good at his job."

"That's comforting."

"Glad I could be of use." He smiled at her.

"You're not just being nice because you caught a glimpse of our single malt collection, are you?"

He laughed, the lines of his face slackening. "I'm being nice to you because you're the boss's wife. But I won't deny that the Glenmorangie caught my eye."

"Why don't you come round for a drink Friday? Since you're intent on defending my honor and all. We thought we might have a few people over for cocktails. Tucker, a few other armed men."

A shadow still flickered behind his eyes, but he smiled. "Consider my arm twisted."

BY THE TIME Miranda was finished organizing Finn's order, people were starting to shift boxes through the gates and into cars and trucks. Momentarily abandoning her stash, Miranda helped Sally fill her Land Cruiser with Scotch, gin, and the no longer missing boxes of Caliterra. "How've you been?" asked Sally. "They letting you out at all?"

"This is the first time I've left the house in six days."

"I've done it, mate. I can't think of any other time in my life I've actually not left the home for several days running. Can you imagine never leaving your flat in London?"

Miranda couldn't. Not that she'd ever had a flat in London. But she cannot remember spending even one entire day in her Seattle apartment, the small loft she and Vicenta shared in her former life. It was, of course, a bit easier to stay home all day when one had fifteen or so rooms at one's disposal, as well as a cook, yoga videos, and a vast library. She'd never painted and read as much in her life as she had in the past few months. The mornings were spent at her easel, and her afternoons methodically working her way through her back issues of *ARTnews* and an assortment of unfinished artist biographies. This was the kind of thing she'd dreamed about, back when she worked fifty hours a week teaching and preparing for teaching while trying to keep up with her own painting.

When Sally's car was full, she and Miranda helped the others haul their boxes into waiting vehicles. Though no one but Sally, Tucker, and Leo addressed Miranda directly unless it was about Finn's order, she kept smiling inanely at people and lugging their boxes until they were forced to offer grudging thanks. An hour or so later, when all the staff cars were full, she joined the assembly line of management staffers passing boxes into Land Cruisers destined for the club. The weight of the boxes felt satisfying in her arms. Yoga and swimming had kept her fairly strong, and her limbs craved movement. "I'm grateful for the exercise, actually," she said to no one in particular, "given that the gym is closed."

"Can't *you* go?" This from Violet, the freckled, deeply suntanned floater temporarily filling in for a management staffer on vacation. Miranda was intrigued by the idea of a floater, a diplomat who spent part of her career filling in for absent staff, moving to a different post every few weeks. A terrific way to see the world, and a terrific way to kill any chance of long-term romance, Violet told her. A relative stranger in their midst, she was probably the only person who would openly ask Miranda if she were obeying the ban on gym visits.

"I'm not allowed!" She spoke loudly, wanting people to know that she did not consider herself above the rules, despite the fact that the embassy gym and pool were in her backyard.

"Yeah, but who would know if you sneaked over?" teased Violet. "Who would see you?"

"The neighbors," said Miranda, a bit defensively. "The guards. But I haven't gone!"

"It's your house." Violet shrugged. "I imagine you can do what you want."

It was the first time anyone had referred to the Residence as her house. Anyone other than Tucker and Finn, that is.

"Well, I don't," said Miranda. "Frankly, I don't think I'm in any position to be bending the rules."

"I'd go, if it were me," said Violet, swinging a box of Speckled Hen into Miranda's waiting arms. "I've been doing kickboxing videos, but they just don't cut it."

Leo backed the car they'd been loading into a parking space and pulled up another next to the boxes.

"Why is it suddenly just the women left?" said Antoinette, witness to Miranda's treadmill incident. Miranda glanced down the assembly line. It was true, the only men around at the moment were Leo, who was getting out of the car, and Tucker. Norman had vanished hours ago. And where was Camilla? Miranda hadn't seen her since she'd offered everyone lime juice early in the day. "Where'd everyone else go?"

"Club?"

"Bishops Finger?" said Miranda as Antoinette handed her a box. "That's the real name of a beer?"

"Careful, that one leaks."

"I can smell it."

"The Bishops Finger stinks!" said Violet, and everyone giggled.

When two cars were full, Leo and Tucker drove them to the club while the women walked. Mukhtar, who had been sitting in front of the gate with Leslie's guard, trailed behind them. A few more men reappeared at the club, and it didn't take long to unload both cars, especially given that the men were showing off their incredible strength by balancing towers of four crates at a time in their arms as they staggered to the storeroom. Miranda could manage two, but she wasn't interested in risking injury or damaging anyone's machismo by attempting more.

They carried a total of six carloads of alcohol into the club. Abdullah, her cross-dressing, teetotaling Mazrooqi-Vietnamese bartender, helped them carry the crates, sweating profusely.

"Abdullah, you're fasting!" said Miranda. "Why don't you just let us do it?"

But Abdullah would not be dissuaded, puffing alongside them until the entire shipment was unloaded. All without food or water. When their cars were empty, he let them all into the refrigerators behind the bar, to pull out water and Cokes.

There was a brief conference about what to do next. "Let's do the Residence, then load Leslie's things into his house," said Leo.

"And then let's have a beer," said Leslie.

Miranda was elated. She had thought that she and Tucker would have to load in the entire order themselves, unable to imagine any of the staff wanting to help her. To have all these people from the embassy coming along with her to help her move their boxes flooded her with gratitude. Lydia came, and Leo, Tucker, Violet, and Antoinette, though Leslie disappeared somewhere along the way. Miranda ran ahead to warn the guards and unlock the door, and they formed a chain into the house. Their gardeners, Yonas and Semere, rushed to join them. In no time at all, they'd erected a boxy tower of happiness in the middle of the hallway carpet.

They practically sprinted to Leslie's, poor fasting Mukhtar panting along behind them. Damp and streaked with grime, they didn't sit in the white-upholstered living room but crowded around the kitchen counter, leaning or sitting on stools as Leslie passed around Heinekens. The beer was warm, having sat in a warehouse on the coast for the last couple of months, but they sipped it as ecstatically as though it were Veuve Clicquot. Miranda twirled on her stool next to Leo, giddy at drinking in the same room as people who had been avoiding sharing space with her for more than a year, listening to them talk about cars, housecleaners, and holidays in France. And for the first time, she felt that she deserved to be there.

Almost simultaneously, she felt an acute pang of nostalgia for the parties she and Vícenta had thrown in Seattle, their Belltown loft overflowing with painters, sculptors, musicians, actors, writers—gay, straight, transsexual. There was always someone playing the guitar, tipsy girls shedding half their clothes and dancing, a messy-haired poet earnestly explaining Rimbaud to a wide-eyed student. When they got tired of their company, she and Vícenta would retreat to their bedroom and play Exquisite Corpse, pretending to be Surrealists, pretending to be Remedios Varo and friends. She loved the happy chaos. The lack of a dress code. The creative endeavors hatched over a 3:00 a.m. glass of whiskey. The total impossibility of shocking anyone. She wondered now if someday she and Finn could have parties like that. Someday when he was no longer an ambassador, when they had found a home in an exotic yet affordable land, and were no longer subject to Islamic or Foreign Office restrictions. There were artists everywhere, after all. It was possible, wasn't it?

NOVEMBER 2010
Miranda

Miranda stares up into the darkness of her new prison, unable to close her eyes, unable to sleep. How can she ever rest again? She welcomes the discomfort of the rough stone beneath her back, the throbbing pain in her head and ankle; she deserves nothing softer. Her arms flop empty at her sides, and her damp shirt sticks to her skin. A despair that she has managed to keep at arm's length over the last months has descended, has filled her with its poison, has begun to consume her mind. How could she have been such a fool? Of course she and Aisha had been watched. Of course they had.

She had made it only a few yards before she felt the blast hit her ankle like a hammer blow. When she landed on that foot the pain had brought her down, her legs folding underneath her as she twisted to keep from crushing Luloah. A cry had gone up, a man's voice and then Aisha's. Then pounding feet and hands grabbing at her, dragging her back down the road and toward the camp. Aisha's voice had risen in a wail. "What have you done?" she'd said over and over. "What have you done?"

With rough hands, Aisha had loosened the sling enough to pull the wailing Luloah free. "Take her away," the man had ordered. *"Please,"* Miranda had begged. "Please, she needs me. Please, don't take the baby. She will die."

"If she dies it is because of you." The man was slight, with a faint mustache and tattered turban. His eyes were glittering and cold, unreachable. "You would steal her from her home."

"You have stolen me from mine." Any caution Miranda had had left dissolved when the bullet struck her ankle. She had wept, wept with her lungs and her heart, wept with her shoulders and belly. Unmoved, the man had prodded her with the butt of his rifle. "Get up," he'd said. "Move now." When she had failed to rise, her body limp on the ground, he had lifted the rifle and struck the back of her head. And then she was unable to rise even had she wanted.

She doesn't know exactly where she is, though it cannot be too far from Aisha's hut, as the old woman still comes to bring her food and water and change the rags wrapped around her swollen ankle. The room is tiny, made of cinder blocks, airless and dark. Now there is a lock on her door. She is not allowed outside, not even to shit. Aisha has given her a tin bucket for that purpose; it festers in a corner. Gone is the pad of paper and the pencils. Even Luloah is not allowed to stay for longer than the length of a feeding. Only now does Miranda realize how Luloah had protected her, insulated her from isolation and loss. Without the child, she is left with nothing but the outrage of her body and the stark horror of her situation.

The men want to kill her. She has heard them say it, scream it outside her hut, arguing with Aisha. *Laa laa laa!* Aisha responds. No no no! She is worthless to us, the men say. We can't get money for her. Why should we feed her when we can barely feed ourselves? She is *haram*. She is pure evil. We need to make a point. Yes, Aisha concurs. Yes, but wait. Wait until the baby is older. She still cannot survive. We need her for the baby. We must keep the baby alive. And finally, grudgingly, the men agree to a little more time. An unspecified amount of time.

What point are they trying to make? Have they chosen her because she is American, or because she is Finn's wife? Which is the greater crime? Or—is it possible they know about Vícenta? And then something even worse occurs to her. Could they know about the women? Or about her private sessions with Tazkia? After all, the guards had seen Tazkia entering and leaving the Residence. She was always completely covered, but Mazrooqis are good at identifying each other by details Westerners might overlook. A characteristic gait, the shape of a purse, the nervous tic of a wrist. It is entirely possible that although Tazkia never gave her real name at the gate, the guards knew who had been visiting and what she might have been taught.

Until Finn, Miranda had told no one about the girls. Telling even one person was too big a risk. And no one, *no one*, was privy to her sessions alone with Tazkia. These had started before her marriage to Finn, after one of their last classes. At the end of class, Tazkia had lingered, kneeling up on the velvety red cushions, pressing her palms against the cool circular glass as she watched the limestone of her hometown turn from gray to a gilded rose in the sunset. "We don't have windows like this," she'd told Miranda. "Our rooms, they are closed." When the sun had slipped below the buildings, dripping down their sides like the yolk of a cracked egg, she had turned toward Miranda, blinking. "Could I have some tea?"

At first they had talked only about their work—materials, theory, color, balance, frame, light. Tazkia always wanted to know everything all at once. Miranda hauled out the small collection of art books she had managed slowly to accumulate, importing a few in her suitcase every time she returned to Mazrooq from abroad, and the two women bent their heads over the images for hours. At first, Miranda was cautious. There were artists and paintings she skipped. But Tazkia protested the censorship, gripping Miranda's wrist with her stubby but strong fingers as she tried to quickly turn a page. "You are the only one I trust not to keep things from me," she told Miranda sternly. "Do not protect me. Do not be like everyone else in my life." Miranda looked at her, at the earnest brown eyes fixed on hers, and slowly nodded.

When they began meeting in the Residence, tucked away from prying eyes on her office sofa, Miranda showed Tazkia everything: portraits, nudes of both sexes, embracing couples. Tazkia was fascinated by the variety of the human form. When Miranda showed her Michelangelo's *David* and other male nudes, she didn't flinch, only gazed with interest. She was curious about the models, about their relationships with the artists. Were they prostitutes? Were they the painters' wives? Where did they come from? Miranda explained that anyone could model for a painter. Nakedness in front of another person did not necessarily suggest a sexual relationship. And modeling was uncomfortable. Miranda told Tazkia about her years as an art student, when she had modeled several times a week to help pay her tuition. She was often cold, cramped, and bored. "It's very unglamorous," she said.

"These women," said Tazkia, waving a hand at Delphin Enjolras's *Nude by Firelight*, "they look so comfortable naked."

"You forget that your body is your body. It's hard to explain. I sometimes used to forget my body was there at all. Except when it hurt."

"But she looks like she enjoys her body. . . . I don't know that women enjoy their bodies naked like this here."

"Are you sure? Even married women?"

"Maybe. Married women talk about these things to each other. But my friends, they are ashamed of their bodies. We are taught that we are ugly down there." She gestured between her legs. "We are told that our bodies are disgusting and never to look at them—or to let a man look down there. Any man that would put his head between your legs is thought a weak man. This is a problem part of the body."

"Have you never looked in the mirror?"

"Not—not down there."

"Never?" Miranda struggled to absorb this. Natural curiosity was apparently no match for religious dictates.

"We are forbidden from looking at ourselves naked in a mirror."

"Even alone?"

"*Aiwa.*"

"Okay." Miranda studied Tazkia's face, the deep sadness rising behind her eyes. "Are you forbidden to look at yourself in a painting?"

Tazkia frowned. Then, a slow smile creeping into the corners of her mouth, "It's not exactly addressed. I guess it's what you call one of your 'beige areas.'"

"Gray areas," Miranda corrected automatically. "Let me show you something," she said. Uncrossing her legs, she rose stiffly and crossed the *diwan* to pick up another book. Sitting once again next to Tazkia, she turned its pages until she arrived at "L'Origine du Monde, Courbet."

"Let me show you," Miranda said. "Let me show you how beautiful you are."

AND THEN ONE night in the stifling dark of Miranda's prison, her thoughts tumbling around in her skull, she wonders if instead there could be any connection with whatever it was that happened in Afghanistan. That mysterious something Finn would never discuss. Was that even possible? But that was more than seven years ago, she reminds herself. And there are different terrorist organizations here. It is pointless for her to dwell on it when she has no idea what Finn is keeping from her. She should have made him tell her before they married.

Even more than the men's words, more than this death sentence to be carried out at an undetermined time, the silence terrifies her. To keep it at bay, to protect her heart from the sharp edges of memory, she talks and sings to herself. Not too loudly, in case anyone can hear, but loud enough for it to fill her ears and stop them against the emptiness. She speaks mostly in French and Arabic, fearful of being overheard. She wishes she knew the words to more songs. Her repertoire is woeful. But she remembers Christmas carols. These are what have stayed with her over the years. Not the pop songs she sang along to in her bedroom, dancing herself dry after a shower. Not the alternative rock songs she listened to on long car journeys. But the carols, she remembers. She tries to translate them into French or Arabic as she goes along, never managing to get all the words (*manger, Hark!* and *yuletide* proving particularly tricky) or to make them scan quite right. But it gives her something to do. Something to keep her mind from turning on itself.

It is amazing how close to the surface insanity rises when you are left alone with yourself, thinks Miranda. How quickly that membrane between sanity and madness threatens to melt away. She feels lunacy's dark pressure in her skull, urging unfamiliar sounds from her mouth, strange prostrations from her body. Every day she has to develop new tactics to keep it at bay, to keep it from closing down around her. Music is one such tactic. It's slightly harder to go insane while singing "Rudolph the Red-Nosed Reindeer," though obviously not impossible. She thinks of Ophelia afloat on that flower-choked river, singing the names of plants. Wait, was she singing? Or was she just reciting? Miranda thinks of Ophelia as a singer, perhaps simply because of the position of her parted lips in the painting. She has seen *Hamlet* only once, but the image of Sir John Everett Millais's *Ophelia* was burned into her brain through countless art history slides and trips to the Tate Britain. But Ophelia was not a real person, she reminds herself. She needs frequent reminding that the subjects of paintings are not always living. To her they so often are. Well, she thinks, if singing doesn't keep a person from slipping from reality's grasp, then at least it adds grace to the fall.

Why is it that keeping our own company drives us mad? Why is solitary confinement such a harsh punishment? How feeble our brains must be, to turn on themselves so easily. She can feel her mind salivating to cannibalize itself. To stop this, to distract this monstrous masochism of the brain, she creates schedules for herself. In the morning, she makes herself sing seven songs (or poems) before breakfast. They must be different songs and poems each day. Her selections include nursery rhymes, "O Little Town of Bethlehem," Shakespeare, "Deck the Halls," Tom Lehrer, "It Came Upon a Midnight Clear." She then does a few dozen abdominal exercises, push-ups, and yoga positions to slow the disintegration of her muscles.

Relief comes when Luloah arrives, often wailing with hunger. Miranda lives for the moments the baby first sees her, her small face radiant with undiluted joy. She draws out the nursing as long as possible, keeping Luloah at each breast, those dark eyebrows knitted together in concentration, until she falls off with exhaustion or satiety. When Luloah is there, Miranda narrows her focus to the child. She strokes the thick black hair, the velvety cheeks, the pinkish yellow soles of her feet. She sings. She tells her stories. And until the child is taken away again, she plays with her: patty-cake, peekaboo, raspberries on her tummy. Luloah is only just starting to laugh, bursting into delirious chortles when Miranda hides her face under her shirt and then emerges again. "Lucky girl," Miranda tells her. "To forget how little we have to laugh about."

When Luloah is gone, Miranda returns to her exercises, mental and physical. She tries to remember something, at least one thing, from every single year of her life, starting with her earliest memory. But chronology is surprisingly hard. The images of her childhood jumble together like photographs in a cardboard shoe box, shuffled all out of order. There is the house itself, of course, an airy blue-gray Craftsman bungalow, with a steeply sloping roof and wide front porch. Was her first memory of standing at the edge of their handkerchief-size back lawn behind their manual lawn mower, straining her plump little arms to push its two rusting wheels forward and failing, until her father placed his hands on either side of her and helped her to push it along the tiny patch of green? Or was it the awe-inspiring population of her ceiling? Surely the ceiling came first, given how much of her childhood was devoted to lying on her back, imagining alternative realities.

Her mother, Leonora, who normally produced artwork as abstract and opaque as possible, had covered Miranda's pitched ceilings with all twelve of the gods and goddesses of Mount Olympus. It was a concession to her daughter's interest in identifiable images, this spasm of realism—if painting goddesses can count as realism. Miranda was so absorbed in the lives of the archaic gods that she shelved her Greek myth collections in her nonfiction bookcases. Those quarreling, humanlike deities were more familiar to her than any of her friends from school.

Nearly every night, her father had read to her from Ingri and Edgar Parin d'Aulaire's illustrated *Book of Greek Myths* as Miranda sat in the bathtub until the water turned cold. She developed a morbid obsession with the illustration of Argus, with his eye-spotted body. How did he bathe when half of his hundred winking eyes were open at any given time, keeping watch over Io? When her father came to that part of the story, she would close her eyes, trying to shut out the distressingly eye-studded body, but curiosity always won out. She'd open one eye and squint at the drawing as she soaked in the fragrance of Leonora's organic gardenia bath beads. How could he lie down, with eyeballs on every part of him? Were there eyes on the soles of his feet? On his bottom? Didn't they get dirt in them? What would it feel like to get soap in fifty eyes all at the same time? She shuddered to imagine such vulnerability, and was very glad that Argus had been left off her ceiling.

Because Miranda had already read Aesop by the time she was started on Greek myths, she was conditioned to seek morals in literature. The Greek stories confused her. What, after all, was the moral of Argus, bored to death by Hermes' soporific storytelling? Never to listen to a dull story? Never to close your eyes? Decent principles, she thought, though difficult to heed. Miranda's father was unhelpful on the topic. "It's just a story," he'd say. "There doesn't have to be a lesson." But Miranda thought that there did. If you didn't learn anything at all from a story, then what was the point? She wanted something she could take with her when she walked away: a compass. She still feels this way about painting, that every square of canvas needs to help somehow in the living of life.

As a teenager she painted over the gods and goddesses on her ceiling, smearing on pure black, as though to erase her mother's influence. She needed to start again, start from nothing. At first she simply retold fairy tales, painting Snow White marrying a dwarf; Hansel and Gretel building a cottage from carrots; and Rapunzel climbing down a rope she had made from her own hair, no prince in sight. I realized I was bisexual, she later told friends, when I wanted to be both Rapunzel and her rescuer.

Is painting helping her now, in the living of this half-life? No and yes. No, in that Magritte's *Attempting the Impossible* is not about to spring the lock on her door and guide her to safety. But without the catalog of artwork in her brain, her arsenal against madness would be greatly diminished. At night, lying on the thin mat, she summons her favorite images, the phantasmagoria of Remedios Varo. She imagines a *Catedral Vegetal* over her head, a ghostly companion in her carriage, sails like dragon's wings propelling her forward. She can remember the day she first discovered Varo in her local library, the way her heart staggered with an almost erotic enchantment. On those pages she watched boundaries fall away, rules of physics alter, and women summon mystical powers. Her mother had found her obsession with the solemn, hollow-cheeked women macabre, but Miranda had defiantly covered the walls of her room with prints of *Woman Leaving the Psycho-analyst* (depicting a robed woman dropping a man's decapitated head into a well), *Exploration of the Sources of the Orinoco River* (a woman sailing alone in a ship fashioned from a waistcoat), and *Encounter* (a seated woman opening a chest only to find her own face peering out at her).

When her mind wanders from childhood memories, she returns to her first art history class, mentally flipping through the slides. Should she begin with the Paleolithic cave paintings of South Africa? The Sumerians? The Egyptians? It doesn't matter. Today, she starts with the Venus of Hohle Fels. What is older? It hadn't been part of her art history syllabus, of course, given that it hadn't yet been discovered when she was in school. But it's definitely the oldest. She closes her eyes and sees the swollen belly and stumpy legs, adds the strangely gravity-defying orbs of the breasts, imagines the person who first saw this image in that woolly mammoth tusk. For some reason, she thinks the sculptor must have been a woman, despite the belief-straining breasts. Miranda imagines the fat, headless woman as a kind of demigoddess. Perhaps wearing the zaftig female as an amulet increased fertility? But why no head? Was this purposeful or had there been one long ago, a head that had left no trace of its existence? These questions were the parallel bars around which her mind flipped and twisted, kept itself limber and strong.

Amulets and ritual appealed to Miranda's love of the occult, of magic, of the unexplained, though she had no specific faith. The closest thing to religion Miranda was exposed to as a child was her parents' unswerving belief in the moral obligation to recycle, buy organic vegetables, and vote in every election, no matter how minor. While Miranda has more or less adopted these tenets, the only thing in which she has true, passionate belief is painting. Only when sitting at an easel, funneling her mind's images through the tip of her brush, does she feel the possibility of the divine. And now that has been taken.

AT NIGHT, WHEN Luloah is returned to her, she remembers the lullabies she would sing to Cressida. Cressie's favorite was "Hush,

Little Baby." Miranda had never known all the real words, so she made up rhymes as she went along. "Hush, little baby, don't you cry, Mama's gonna sing you a lullaby. And if that lullaby won't calm, Mama's gonna buy you some Tiger Balm, and if that Tiger Balm's not divine, Mama's gonna buy you a green grape vine. And if that green grape vine won't juice, Mama's gonna buy you a friendly old moose, and if that friendly old moose runs away, Mama's gonna buy you a brand-new day . . ." And so on. No matter what other verses she sang, she couldn't help eventually arriving at a brand-new day. And then she would have to stop, rather than go on to say, "And if that brand-new day won't dawn . . ." She could not bear to think of a day refusing to dawn for her daughter. Sometimes she got through forty-seven verses before coming to the brand-new day, sometimes it popped up after only nine. At least she does not have this problem when singing in Arabic or French.

Only when she sings these songs, to herself or to Luloah, does she allow herself to dwell on the memory of her daughter. She closes her eyes and wills the words back to the city, or to wherever Cressida and Finn are now, as if she still has the power to comfort her daughter. I will come home to you, she insists in the dark. I will come home. I will come home.

JULY 4, 2010
Miranda

Miranda was dressed for the firing range an hour before Tucker was scheduled to pick her up. He was always early. He had taken her with his team several times now, teaching her to fire a series of increasingly powerful arms. She began with a pistol and an AK-47, and worked her way up to an MI6 and the Heckler & Koch G3 7.62 mm, with a recoil so powerful she had to fire it lying on her belly. In spite of her pacifist nature, Miranda went to the range because Tucker had asked her and she was grateful. In the first year, few people from the embassy had asked her to do so much as have a cup of tea.

Tucker was different. True, it was his job to protect her and Finn.

But it wasn't his job to befriend and entertain her. This was something he did of his own free will, and Miranda loved him for it. She would have loved him anyway, for the simple fact that he kept Finn safe from harm. Both he and his wife, Paige, had spent their entire careers in the armed forces, managing to spend only about half of their time in the same country. At the moment, Paige was in Iraq, and Tucker worked tirelessly so as not to feel her absence so acutely. In his rare off-hours, he worked just as tirelessly boosting everyone else's morale. He hosted barbecues and costume parties and taught them all how to shoot. Always the first on the dance floor at a party, in a wig and miniskirt, he was also the last to go home. Men in the armed forces, it hadn't taken long for Miranda to discover, were the most likely to cross-dress.

Today's visit to the range was not optional. The CP team was going to try a "live extraction," a series of maneuvers they would perform in the event of an attack on Finn or Miranda, in order to remove them from danger and get them to safety.

"You might want kneepads," Tucker said when she opened the door. "I'm afraid we're going to rough you up a bit."

When she climbed down from the car an hour later, she gazed around her feeling—as always—like a visitor to another planet. Planet Men. Planet Guns. Bruise-colored mountains curved around them like a theatrical backdrop. The skies were the postcard-blue of the dry season, the sun having vaporized the last of the clouds. In front of her stretched an empty expanse of sand and dirt, heat rising from it in waves. No life in sight; no plants, no trees, no animals, no humans. This was the range. "You could close your eyes here, and open them in Kabul, and it would look exactly the same," said Tucker. It sometimes seemed to Miranda that she was the only person in the country who hadn't been to Afghanistan or Iraq. Even Finn had been posted to both places. The way the men talked about the dangers, the wild parties, and their cramped pods all in the same breath made Miranda feel she had missed out on something life-altering. She envied the bond among those who had survived.

While they waited for Finn to arrive from the embassy, the team scurried around setting up a long row of targets, black-and-white prints of a generic enemy with dramatic five o'clock shadows and a more than passing resemblance to Richard Nixon, crouched over his gun and glaring from under his helmet. The pictures were stapled onto sheets of plywood propped up in front of a vast sandbank, which absorbed the bullets after they passed through the targets.

Tucker put his men through a pistol drill with their SIG Sauers, blowing a whistle and shouting out, *"Shimal!"* or *"Yameen!"* (Left! or Right!) or *"Khalf!"* (Behind!) In response the men cried out, *"Ado Shimal!"* (Enemy left!) or *"Ado Yameen!"* (Enemy right!) and fired.

After each drill, the men sprinted to the targets to watch Tucker count and chalk the number of bullet holes that would have killed the enemy—those that hit either the center of his body or his head. Most of the team could kill the enemy twenty-three out of twenty-six times. Mukhtar and Yusef were the best, but even tubby little Bashir was a pretty good shot. It gave Miranda confidence that they might actually be able to nail a terrorist targeting Finn—if they saw him first.

When it was her turn, Mukhtar helped fit her with a pair of noise-canceling headphones, reminded her how to load the magazine, and handed her a SIG. It felt light in her hands; a machine capable of a baker's dozen murders in the space of a few seconds should have more heft. She fired six rounds, her heartbeat swooshing in her ears, hitting the target with about every third shot. Her aim was worse with the AK-47. Her first shot not only missed the target entirely *and* the board it was stapled to but also missed the entire sandbank, sailing up into the sky behind it.

"What's behind there?" worried Miranda.

"I don't know, but whatever it was is dead." Mukhtar grinned at her.

"Want to try it on automatic?" asked Tucker.

No, thought Miranda. *I really don't.* But she nodded and allowed Tucker to shift the appropriate lever. It took nearly all of her strength to hold the gun steady as it sprayed bullets; it was like trying to hold a jumping rabbit. A hot, homicidal, steel rabbit. The movies make it look way too easy, she thought. The targets remained unscathed.

"Ana mish tammam!" I'm not good!, she cried. The men rushed to

reassure her. *"Laa! Antee jayyida,"* said Mukhtar. "You could kill some-one!"

"WOULDN'T WANT TO meet you in a dark alley." Finn's car had pulled up while she was firing, and he was standing in his pin-striped suit at the back of the range. Her headphones had muffled the sound of his arrival.

"You'd be fine in a dark alley," said Miranda, lowering her weapon. "I couldn't sight for shit in the dark." Damn. She'd managed to swear in front of the team again. She wasn't sure how much of it they understood, but she had been trying to avoid shocking them more than she already did on a daily basis. Fortunately, the men were all busy loading their weapons or rolling old tires onto the range to create an obstacle course. Miranda handed her gun to Mukhtar and took Finn behind the car to give him a pair of his jeans and a work shirt.

The new guys and Bashir (who had arrived with Finn, looking very smart in one of the new suits and ties Tucker bought for the men; they had to blend at diplomatic events, after all) clambered up a rocky mountainside for a better view.

It worked like this: Finn began striding through the obstacle course the men had erected—his bodyguard glued to him—as if he were heading to a meeting. One man was always assigned to be imme-diately beside him (putting the "close" into "close protection"), while the rest positioned themselves strategically ahead and behind. The tires represented bushes, stumps, or trash cans behind which Finn could hide. Probably bushes would be too porous. But anyway. Six of the guys were spread out, three on either side, alert for threats. Their elbows jutted stiffly out at their sides as they swung their heads left and right. They reminded Miranda of a cluck of wary chickens prowling a farmyard. Bashir beckoned to her, and Miranda clam-bered up the rocks to the ridge overlooking the range. "Nice suit," she said to him. He smiled, turning toward her so she could see her face reflected in his mirrored sunglasses.

A whistle blew, signifying enemy fire. Yusef, operating as Finn's bodyguard, grabbed Finn around his waist, arresting him midstride, and shoved him down into the dirt behind one of the tires. Then, yanking Finn up by his belt, he propelled him forward, running him through the gunfire to the next hiding place. Finn's legs cycled through the air at the end of Yusef's arm as if he were a marionette pantomiming a sprint. All the while, Tucker's team was shooting live bullets at the "enemy," covering Finn and Yusef while backing away. Their goal was to allow Finn to be safely extracted, rather than to chase the enemy. Miranda could see Yusef shouting in Finn's ear, but the gunfire made it impossible to hear anything. Even from the ridge it made her ears ring.

Miranda watched as Yusef shoved Finn into the dirt again. She worried about his glasses. Her eyesight blurred for a moment, and she realized her knees were trembling. Yusef yelled at Finn as he hauled him up again. Was it the manhandling of the person she cared most about in the world that brought up the waves of nausea? The fact that live bullets were flying around him out here in the desert? Or the reminder that this wasn't just playacting, that Finn could actually face such an attack? *I will not cry in front of the men*, she willed herself. *I will not cry in front of the men.*

"The guys have to get used to being rough with him if the situation calls for it," Tucker said when the exercise was over. "Being too respectful in a situation like this could get him killed."

Miranda nodded and tried to smile. Finn strolled toward her, flushed and smiling, his forehead slick with sweat and his jeans streaked with dirt. "You survived," she said weakly.

"Sorry!" Finn squeezed her sweating hand.

"Okay, Madame Ambassador, your turn." Tucker slipped a hand under her elbow and steered her down the slope. "Let's show the guys how to treat a woman."

Miranda walked with him to the course, where he turned her over to Mukhtar. Her legs felt strong again, and she wasn't afraid. Only things utterly beyond her influence terrified her. Keeping Finn safe, for example. She never feared for her own safety; her own safety felt more within her control.

A wave of euphoria struck as she walked alongside Mukhtar into the imminent ambush. She felt a temptation to laugh. "Walk faster," said Mukhtar. "More purposefully. You're strolling." She quickened her pace. Where might she be rushing? To a meeting of the Heads of Mission Spouses Association? The thought of any of the designer-suited ambassadors' wives waddling at speed made her want to laugh again. No one except Finn ever walked quickly and purposefully in this country.

The whistle shocked her from her reverie. Explosions erupted in every direction, the men opening fire. Miranda suddenly forgot every-thing she was supposed to do. "Get DOWN!" shouted Mukhtar, pushing her into the dirt behind the first tire. He held her to the ground with a hand on the middle of her back while she breathed iron-tasting dirt into her mouth. While watching Finn, she had imagined how she would do it when it was her turn, how fast she would run, how she would throw herself into the dirt. But now there was no time for her slow responses. All she could do—and all she was intended to do—was blindly submit. Not something with which she had much practice.

A few seconds later she was dragged up by the waistband of her trousers and shoved in the direction of the next tire. Mukhtar's mouth was next to her ear, shouting, "MOVE, MOVE, MOVE!" But she couldn't make her legs pedal forward fast enough to keep pace. It was like running in a dream, where her legs became heavy or diffuse, unable to propel the body forward. The next time she hit the dirt her knee struck a sharp rock. She felt the indent it made in her skin but couldn't register the pain. As they sprinted for the last tire, a muscle in the back of her right thigh gave a twang of protest. Yoga and swimming were apparently poor preparation for the rigors of dodging terrorist fire.

By the time she and Mukhtar reached the end of the course, Miranda was suffused with adrenaline. She smiled at Finn as he trot-ted toward her, holding his camera aloft. "I got photos!" he said. "You were fantastic."

Miranda limped beside him to the car. "Nothing but glamour, the life of an ambassador's wife."

An hour later, as they rode back to the Residence in their armored car, Miranda's mood tumbled down around her like a house of cards. Discreetly squeezing Finn's hand on the seat beside her, she found herself fighting back tears again.

"You were good with that SIG Sauer," said Finn. "I'm thinking about putting you on the team."

Miranda smiled, not at him but out the window at the endless beige horizon, so he couldn't see her eyes. "Well, at least if you're attacked and someone drops a pistol, I know what to do with it," she said at last.

"Let's hope I have a clumsy abductor."

"And that he has a SIG. Otherwise, we're fucked."

NOVEMBER 18, 2010
Finn

Finn sits at the tiny card table in his kitchen, staring at the drawing. Even Cressida seemed to have recognized its authorship, grabbing a corner in her damp fist while babbling "Mummmmumummy!" Or perhaps she had somehow recognized herself, and deduced that only a mother would create such an image. For it clearly was Cressida, a version of Cressida. Miranda had always said she couldn't draw her daughter properly, and Finn understood what she meant. Their tiny girl changed too quickly to pin to paper. But though the child in this drawing wasn't a perfect resemblance—she had less hair, more fat on her thighs—she retained an essential Cressidaness. Cressidity. The shape of her eyebrows, her long, sweeping lashes, her tiny bowed lips.

How long ago had Miranda drawn this? He had no way to know. It was Nadia who had produced it from beneath her *abaya*. Her family lived in the mountains a few hours north and west of the city, she said. Just outside her cousin Imaan's village was a small training camp. Everyone knew what the men were training for, but it wasn't openly discussed. Someone at the camp might have heard something about a Western woman taken hostage, thought Nadia. Surely these kinds of men talked with each other. She and the other women had been systematically—and cautiously—contacting relatives in their home villages, taking advantage of their vast networks.

Nadia rang Imaan, one cousin she was sure she could trust. When they were still in school, Imaan had caught her scribbling pictures in her religion notebook several times and had never told on her. She made Nadia tear up the sketches of their various relatives, but more from fear of punishment than from fanatical fervor. She didn't want to see Nadia in trouble. Imaan hadn't heard anything about an American woman but said she would pay a visit to her eldest aunt, who lived out at the camp, where her husband and son participated in the mysterious exercises. Aisha's hut was far enough from the training grounds that she wouldn't have to see any of the men. Imaan didn't know any other women who lived out there, just Aisha, who cooked for the men and looked after them.

With her fifteen-month-old son, Kabir, Imaan sat with this aunt in a small, dark hut. On a mat in the corner lay a small baby, waving its feet and hands. "I'm looking after her for her mother, who died," Aisha said, without further explanation. Imaan wanted to ask who the mother was, but Aisha's tone did not invite questions. She wondered what Aisha fed the child, who was surely too young for solid food. It was thin, though not as thin as most babies here. It didn't look unhealthy. Obviously, it was eating something. The baby caught hold of its foot and stared at it with amazement. Imaan remembered that age, remembered Kabir's astonishment at discovering his hands, that they belonged to him and could be commanded to do things. She hadn't realized that babies were not born knowing that their hands are theirs.

A slow walker, Kabir was still slightly unsteady on his feet. While his mother drank tea with her aunt, gossiping about upcoming weddings, he crept slowly around the inside wall of the hut, clutching his small fingers around the protuberant stones. As he neared the baby, it began to cry, whether from fear of the towering toddler or hunger or discomfort, it was difficult to tell. After a moment, Aisha rose to pick up the child. "Tch tch tch," she clucked at the baby, jiggling it in her arms. The baby wailed more loudly, clutching at the folds of

Aisha's *abaya*. Turning its head toward her breast, it opened its mouth in a fishlike pucker, searching for a nipple. Imaan watched this with interest. Someone must be nursing this child, and it couldn't possibly be old Aisha. *"Dagiga,"* said Aisha, taking the child outside.

Imaan looked back at her son, who continued his investigation of the hut's walls. He stopped for a moment as his hand touched something unusual, a sharp fold of paper. Intrigued, he pulled at it, until it slid out from between the stones where it had been hidden, the force sending him backward onto his bottom. Waving it triumphantly, he struggled to his feet and started inching back toward his mother. "What have you found?" she said, opening her arms to her son. Kabir staggered over and pressed the paper against her knee. It was difficult for Imaan to make out the image in the dim light of the hut, but she could see it looked something like a child. A tremor of fear shuddered through her stomach. A heretical image. An actual person. It couldn't be Aisha's, could it? Could Aisha draw? She had never seen her hold a pen for any reason. The only person she knew who could draw was her cousin Nadia. She should tear up this image. But something in her maternal heart resisted damaging the depiction of a toddler. Even this odd-looking, unusually chubby little toddler. No one in this impoverished region had children so fat!

When a rustle of *abaya* announced Aisha's return, Imaan's initial impulse was to ask her about the drawing. But then suddenly she remembered something Nadia had said. The missing American was an artist. "She doesn't draw people," Nadia had been quick to reassure her. "Just flowers and mountains and things." The woman might say that, Imaan thought, but it didn't make it true. Quickly, she folded the paper and slipped it into her left sleeve before looking up to smile at her aunt in the doorway. Now, at least, she wouldn't have to arouse anyone's suspicions by asking about the American.

Once home, she rang Nadia. "I found a drawing," she said. "In a house out there." She had to be careful on the phone. Some of the camps had ways of listening in. Nadia couldn't conceal her excitement. What did the drawing look like? Nadia asked. Did the child have hair? Was it fat? "I will come Friday," she said. "Please save it for me." Only once Nadia had arrived and the two women were alone, walking with the plastic jugs to fetch water, could Nadia speak privately with her cousin. "There's something else," said Imaan. "There is a baby out there." She described what she had seen, and Nadia looked thoughtful. "Miranda has a little girl in the city," she says. "Maybe she was still feeding her." The two women stared at each other in silence. Then, it was very important that she go back to Aisha, Nadia said. She must ask her what happened to the woman who drew the child. Was she still there? Could she be somewhere in the camp?

Impossible, said Imaan. Then everyone would know she had some connection to the woman, and her own family would be in danger. Those men would do anything. Aisha would wonder why she was asking, why she hadn't asked about the drawing as soon as she found it. And they didn't want to arouse the suspicions of the men, did they? Come on, you're smart, think of something, said Nadia. Think of some indirect way to ask. Imaan looked at her cousin despairingly. "I don't know," she said. "What if these men find out we are asking? What will become of us?"

When she returned to the city, Nadia rang Tazkia, who had her brother arrange the meeting with Finn outside of the city. Maybe the drawing could help him. At least they knew now one place Miranda had been. It was possible she was still there, although Imaan had said she saw no trace of any woman, other than the unusual health of the nameless baby.

Finn had been grateful that only Tazkia saw his face when he opened the picture of his daughter. Choked by sorrow and disbelieving gratitude, he could not speak for several minutes. "Where was this?" he finally said. "Where is she?"

AUGUST 11, 2009
Miranda

The first time Miranda ever left Cressida with a babysitter for more than a half-hour was the day she finally went to the orphanage. She had been planning to go for more than a year but something always got in the way: teaching, national days, work, pregnancy complications. There was no reason for her to be nervous about leaving Cressida; the baby adored Gabra, and there were three other women in the house to watch over her. "This baby, she has four mothers," Negasi was always saying. But a nagging guilt persisted as Altaf steered her through the half-paved, litter-strewn streets. Should she have taken Cressida with her? Surely it would be fun for her to play with some other children. Or would it aggravate their parentless state, to see her caring for a child? And then there were the diseases to consider. Cressida had been shot up with as many vaccines as possible in London before they had flown back here to resume their lives, but she was too young to be fully vaccinated against the bacteria harbored by the less fortunate children of this country.

This train of thought was derailed by her arrival at Marguerite's. Miranda's friend was waiting in the driveway, jingling her car keys, her blond hair braided and pinned up, her eyes concealed by enormous dark glasses. "Am I late?" asked Miranda, climbing down from her car.

"*Non, pas du tout,*" said Marguerite, kissing Miranda three times on her cheeks. "I just wanted to be ready when you arrived. *On y va?*"

"*Oui.*"

"*Suis-moi.*"

It would have made things so much simpler if the two women could have driven together, but Miranda was not allowed to travel in any car but her own, and Marguerite, who had no bodyguard, said she had errands to run afterward. It wasn't far to the orphanage. Fifteen minutes later they were parked outside of a walled complex and striding toward the entrance. Miranda fervently wished she could leave Bashir (today's escort) behind. She didn't want him to scare the children. She hoped his guns weren't visible.

At the entrance to the courtyard, they were greeted by a flock of *abaya*-clad women. With a chorus of birdlike chatter, they welcomed Miranda and Marguerite, leading them through a series of courtyards to the buildings where most of the children lived. Marguerite had been coming every week for several months and so knew many of the children. "I'm glad you're here," said Marguerite. "I don't speak Arabic, and I don't have any idea what they are telling me half the time."

Miranda had expected something out of Dickens, a crumbling, derelict structure crowded with dirt-smeared faces and starved, stick-thin limbs. But that wasn't what she discovered. The children's rooms in the sturdy cinder-block structures were airy and spotless, with two or three single beds per room. Not mattresses on the floor but actual wooden beds. They were all neatly made up, with a folded blanket on top of each mattress. In fact, they were far lovelier rooms than Miranda had seen in many of the homes she had visited. There was also a living room, and a television in the foyer.

In the first building, the boys all ran to shake their hands, clutching her fingers with a gratitude Miranda felt she hardly deserved just for turning up. The boys were clean and neatly dressed in long pants and pressed green shirts. A woman in charge of the house came to the front room holding a tiny child wrapped in a pink polyester blanket. This was Abdul-Malik, said Marguerite. He had a thatch of shiny, dark hair and chicken pox scars covering his face. The woman handed the baby to Miranda. Immediately she could feel the unnatural heat of his body through the blankets. "Fever?" she asked. "Yes," said the housemother. "But he is getting better." The child felt as light as a kitten in her arms, and stared at her with blank brown eyes. "He is about two months old," said Marguerite. "Though no one knows for sure. His mother died in childbirth." So where is the father? Miranda wanted to ask. And the aunts and uncles and brothers and sisters and grandparents? Usually there was no shortage of these here. Where did the mother die? How could this child end up with no one? But she said nothing. Where did you start?

As she cradled the limp child, the crowd of boys, who ranged in age from two to twelve, surrounded them. "*Salaama aleikum!*" they cried. Where were the women from? How old were they? What did they think of their country? They had endless questions, none of which were Where are my parents? When Miranda told them the name of her hometown, they savored it on their tongues. "See-ah-tull!" they cried. "Pretty name for a town." They asked the questions any child would ask. Did she like soccer? What did she like to play? Did she have a television? When Miranda said that she and her husband had no television, they stared at her with sudden sympathy. She was obviously worse off than she looked.

One of the women said that there were two other babies, and Miranda asked if she could see them. Before Cressida, Miranda had had no interest in babies or children. When friends came around to her apartment with an infant, she had to force enthusiasm, feeling bored and burdened. She had never been a natural babysitter, and as a teenager she had dreaded the nights she had to spend tucking other people's children into bed. So she hadn't been in any particular hurry to have children of her own. Not until she met Finn had the thought even crossed her mind. But watching him play with the children at their first embassy Christmas party, Miranda had caught herself thinking that raising a child with him might actually be *fun*.

Now, she hardly recognized herself. Something odd had happened, some tap opened in her soul, so that she could not see a baby without wanting to wrap herself around it and protect it forever. She had stopped reading the newspaper for fear of encountering a story about terrible things happening to infants and children. There were always terrible things happening to infants and children: wars, starvation, abusive parents, pedophiles, accidents. Finn would come home and find her weeping over a piece she had heard on BBC Radio 4, which she streamed onto her laptop. She had feared that coming here would have the same effect, that the suffering of the children would overwhelm her. But if these children were suffering terribly, they hid it well.

One of the little boys took them back through the courtyard to a neighboring building, called Dar al-Ikram. There, on the top floor, they met tiny Shafia, just six days old. Swaddled in a white cloth and cradled in the arms of another housemother, she peered out at them with large, curious eyes. Her face was still covered with downy hair. "Where is her mother?" Miranda asked. *"Mayyitah,"* the woman said. "Dead." And the father? "No father." Another mother who had died in childbirth, another missing father. Could these children have been born out of wedlock? It seemed impossible in this country. Maybe they just all had terminally ill fathers? Miranda took the child and held her while her surrogate mother prepared a bottle of formula. She watched the woman measuring powder and water, fighting the impulse to simply pull down the front of her shirt and nurse the little girl. You can't save everyone, Finn was always telling her.

"What are the chances someone will adopt her?" Miranda asked the woman measuring out the formula. "Is it easier for the babies than the older children?"

The woman looked up and frowned at her. "None," she said. "No adoption."

Miranda looked at Marguerite with surprise. "No adoption?"

"It's illegal here," Marguerite explained. "It is assumed that there will always be blood relatives to take in a child. Since the families are so enormous."

"But obviously that assumption is wrong," says Miranda. "Or they wouldn't need this orphanage."

"Well, I'll let you explain that to them. I think it's some kind of Islamic thing. There's something called *kafala* that means you can take care of a child, but not be its legal parents. Of course I might be mixing it all up."

Miranda was bewildered. Why on earth would anyone want to keep a child from finding a home? Why was it better for them to be here than with a couple who couldn't have their own children? She wondered if the Quran really addressed this issue. She should look it up.

They were then taken to another baby, the month-old Badai. She also had plenty of dark hair and enormous eyes. While Miranda and Marguerite cuddled the babies, small girls ran in and out of the room, staring shyly before dashing away. In this building too the rooms were tidy and clean. The girls had neatly braided hair and pretty dresses. Miranda wanted to speak with them but found herself at a loss for words. She asked the girls their names and ages—the youngest was five and oldest fourteen—and was unsure where to go from there. All the things she most wanted to know she couldn't ask. Were they happy? Did they ever know their parents? Did they worry about their future? Were they well educated? Had anyone ever hurt them?

Before leaving, Miranda and Marguerite visited one more house of boys. Miranda held another feverish child, a two-year-old who also had chicken pox. She supposed that once one child had it, it swept through the orphanage. The boys gathered around her, asking their endless questions. Did she know the Quran? Did she know it in Arabic or English? Did she pray? One of the housemothers was cradling an older boy who was so disabled he could do nothing but lie prone. His name was Rahman, and he was seven years old. He had pretty, thick-lashed eyes and rotting teeth. Miranda wondered if the children were given toothbrushes. Maybe she should have brought some? This boy would require someone to brush his teeth for him. He was skinny, with chicken pox scars on his toothpick legs. But he smiled and looked cheerful, lying on a couch. Miranda squatted next to him and stroked his hair. He looked up at her and beamed, displaying all of his brown teeth.

"Come," said another of the women, who introduced herself as Leila. "We are going to sing for you." She led Miranda and Marguerite to the courtyard near the entrance, where most of the older children were gathered, standing in neat rows. When they saw the women approach, they opened their mouths in unison and began to sing. Miranda looked at the little girls, standing so straight in their green-and-white checked dresses, and the little boys with their arms held tight to their sides and their hair combed back. And while she couldn't grasp the words of the Arabic song, the sound of the children's voices rising together above the dust of the afternoon wrung her viscera like a rag.

As the song ended, Miranda became aware that Marguerite had disappeared and returned with a box full of packets of cookies. As the children filed past, she handed each of them a packet. Delighted, the children tore them open and stuffed the cream-filled cookies into their mouths. "I got them from the embassy," Marguerite told Miranda. "They were left over from something."

Suddenly one of the housemothers was shaking Marguerite's arm. "Look!" she shouted in Arabic. "Look! These are expired! No good!" Miranda picked up a packet and looked at the date. The cookies were seven months past the sell-by date. "Do not give them to our children," said the housemother. "Do not give them your leftover gar-bage!" She shook with fury. Marguerite flushed with shame as the woman tore the packets of cookies from the children's sticky fingers, leaving them bewildered and tearful. Once all of the packets, opened or untouched, were collected, she dumped them into a trash can.

"I'm sorry," Marguerite said helplessly to the woman. "I am so sorry. I didn't know." Her big blue eyes filled with tears. Miranda felt sure that she hadn't. "Next time," she began.

"No next time," said the woman. "We don't need anything. We take care of the children. They do not need your trash." Haltingly, Miranda translated this for Marguerite.

"We are sorry," said Miranda to the woman. "She really didn't know. Please tell the children we are sorry." But the woman just stared at them, her arms folded across her chest as she watched them slowly turn and walk away.

NOVEMBER 29, 2010
Finn

"I think we should involve the Americans." Dax doesn't look at Finn as he says this, keeping his eyes on the road ahead. They are pacing along the ramparts encircling the Old City, next to deafening, obscuring traffic.

Finn nods. "But the local spooks, can we avoid telling them?"

"I don't know. It could be hard. How do we explain why we didn't share the information on her whereabouts? It's not likely we'll be able to rescue her very discreetly."

"Certainly not if the Americans do it."

Dax laughs. "They aren't that bad," he says. "In fact, they may be better than we are."

Icy fingers suddenly grip Finn's heart. "Dax," he says, slowing his footsteps. "You know how risky a rescue operation is, and even more so if the locals are involved. I don't know—are there any other options?" He doesn't need to remind Dax what had happened to the group of tourists who were kidnapped several years ago down south.

Government forces had come to the rescue prematurely, despite ongoing mediation, resulting in the death of three hostages in a shoot-out.

"You mean, should we send up a card politely requesting the return of the ambassador's wife?" says Dax.

"Sorry, I'm being stupid. It's just, there is no chance of mediation with these guys?"

"They haven't made contact with us. There has been no ransom request. I don't need to tell you that is not a good sign. Given that, we definitely don't want them to know we know where she is. That is, if your information is good."

"I trust my source."

"Look, Finn, I trust you. But I am going to need to know who your source is."

"No."

"Finn, I cannot in good conscience go to the Americans on your say-so. With all due respect, I'll look like an idiot."

"No one must contact my source. My source is vulnerable and would be in serious danger. More than one person would be in serious danger."

Dax is silent. The crunch of their shoes against the grit of the road is unusually loud, punctuated by the frequent blasts of car horns.

"If I promise to keep the name of your source from the locals, can you tell me? I can swear the Americans to secrecy. I trust them."

"Completely?"

"My American contact, yes."

Finn considers this. "If the Americans head up this rescue, can you keep them from notifying the locals?"

"Honestly? No. I am not the boss of the Americans. Telling them is a risk. But she's an American, Finn, she's their girl. And they're better equipped."

"If it were your wife . . . ?"

"What are our options? It's either tell the Americans and attempt a rescue or sit around waiting for a ransom note or a body. Is that what you want to do?"

"You'll talk with Celia?"

"I'll talk with Celia."

Finn pulled a copy of *al-Ayyam* from underneath his arm. "Something I want to show you in here," he says. "It's hers." Dax takes the paper and glances at the front-page headlines before slipping the rolled-up newsprint into a deep front pocket. And as they continue to circle the Old City, sucking in the exhaust of the cars rattling past, Finn tells Dax who found it, and where.

MARCH 17, 2010
Miranda

Tazkia hadn't called to say she was coming. Her unexpected arrival naturally alarmed the guards, who were given a daily list of visitors. They called Miranda, who slipped on shoes and ran outside to reassure them that the five-foot-tall woman with the suspiciously bulging purse was not a threat to her security. "Why didn't you call?" Miranda said. "I could have had Teru make you quiche." Tazkia had never tried quiche before her first luncheon with Miranda. "Is this a pizza?" she had said, her mouth crammed full. Now she demanded it regularly. Tazkia was their only guest who actually called ahead of each visit to request specific foods. Miranda took an amused pleasure in indulging her. She hadn't met anyone else in this country who was willing to try new foods. When she had first taken over menu planning for their dinner parties she had chosen spicy, experimental dishes—curried broccoli, Vietnamese salads—until she realized that the Mazrooqis would never touch a food they didn't recognize.

"I had to come before I changed my mind," Tazkia said, hurrying to the door. At the threshold, she paused. "Finn isn't home?"

"He's at the embassy."

Miranda remembered the evening Tazkia had first met Finn. Miranda had been showing Tazkia the garden when she heard his convoy approach. As the massive gates swung open to admit the three armored cars, Miranda had grabbed Tazkia's hand to pull her back. The car doors had flown open all at once, releasing a dozen bodyguards, weapons in their hands, eyes sweeping nearby rooftops.

"Oh my god, what's happening?" Tazkia had said, cringing as the CP team spread out across the lawn.

"It's nothing!" Miranda had cried, trying to reassure her. "It's just Finn coming home! It's always like this!" But it took Tazkia several minutes to get over the shock, before she started laughing.

Upstairs in Miranda's studio, Tazkia impatiently tore off her *hijab* and *niqab* and threw herself on the sofa. "I'm getting married," she said, without preamble. Her hair was damp with sweat, and a few strands clung to her cheeks.

Miranda just looked at her, waiting.

"It's my choice," she added reassuringly. "I love him."

Miranda was immediately wounded. How could Tazkia be in love and not have told her? And how could she not have known? Surely there was some sort of sign she should have recognized, some special flush of excitement? And hadn't she told Tazkia about Finn, before anyone else? And even, eventually, the truth about Vícenta?

"I *couldn't* tell you earlier," she said, as if reading Miranda's mind. "You know I couldn't tell anyone until I knew we would be married. You know how things work here. We are not free to feel love without being married."

"But *me*? You didn't trust me? I wouldn't have told anyone! You've trusted me with your paintings." Miranda realized she sounded like a petulant child, but she couldn't help it. Tazkia was her closest friend.

Tazkia nodded. "*Aiwa.* I had no choice with the paintings, if I wanted your help. If I wanted to learn. But it was just safer for me to tell no one about this. Not even my sisters, not even you."

Miranda felt ashamed of her reaction. "Okay," she said. "I get it."

"You'll come to the wedding," Tazkia said. "Do not worry. You will love him as I do; he is a good man."

Miranda had so many questions she wasn't sure where to start. "Who is he?"

"A professor at the university. He is a poet."

"Ah. A poet."

"A very brilliant poet! He is famous here."

"But how did you meet?"

"He was a friend of my brother. But this is not why I come." Tazkia sat up abruptly.

"No?"

"I need you to paint me." No one came straight to the point like Tazkia. Even Vícenta was oblique by comparison.

"Paint you," Miranda echoed.

"Yes. Without this—" Tazkia swept a hand down across her *abaya*.

Miranda studied the serious, dark eyes of her student, weighing her words. "But, why? And this is not a problem for you? Because of . . . your beliefs?"

Tazkia leaned forward. "My belief is that Allah would not make us ugly. My belief is that our bodies must be beautiful if so many artists want to paint them. Your Vícenta, she was beautiful. And before I marry I want to see myself. I need you to show me that I am not disgusting before I show myself to my husband. I need to *see*. I need to see what an artist sees. What my husband, *insha'allah*, will see."

For a moment, words failed Miranda. "You are not afraid?" she finally said.

"It is *you*," Tazkia said. "How could I be afraid? You I would trust with my life. You will protect me. You see, I do trust you."

Miranda nodded slowly. "Still, this is risky, Tazkia. What if someone finds out? What will we do with the painting? Will you be able to get here without anyone knowing where you are going?"

"Yes," said Tazkia, leaning back as if the matter was settled. "Can we start now, or is Finn coming home soon?"

Miranda studied her favorite student, flushed and eager. "On one condition," she said. "We set a date to burn it." It would be insane to keep such a painting, capable of causing incalculable damage to her friend should it ever be discovered.

"Yes!" Tazkia looked relieved. "This is the best thing to do. We will set a date."

Miranda stood and walked to the desk, picked up her daily planner. "When do you think?"

Tazkia thought for a moment. "June sixth but next year. The day before my wedding."

"That certainly gives us plenty of time."

"I don't want to rush."

"Okay." Miranda uncapped her pen and scratched the date into her book. "June sixth, 2011."

DECEMBER 3, 2010
Finn

Finn stares at Celia, not wanting to absorb her words. "Gone?" he says, trying to keep his voice from breaking. "But she was there?"

"We think so." Celia fiddles with her spoon and teacup, without lifting either to her lips. They sit on the wide porch of the Residence, on the worn blue cushions of the wicker chairs Finn had been trying to get replaced for the last year and a half, where he and Miranda and later Cressie had eaten their mango and pomegranate seeds together every morning. How strange it is to be back here, as a guest. As a supplicant. *Please, my wife, could you find my wife?* How many times has he sat here, or on the fat white sofas inside, listening to the urgent pleas of others. *My father is being persecuted, please get him a visa before the government has him killed. My son is missing and I know what tribe has him. Please, could the UK recolonize the country, so there would be jobs and security?* The stream of misery has no end. Now it is his turn.

"We?"

"Us and the Americans."

"Who knew we were coming?" Only once the words are out of his mouth does Finn wonder if he still has a right to the pronoun *we.*

"We had to tell local security," she says, tucking a wisp of blond hair behind her impossibly small ear. "There was no other way to do it. Not without some kind of an incident."

Finn looks at her. Her blue eyes are kind, intelligent. She is hating her job right now, he knows. He nods, slowly. "I see." It isn't surprising there was a leak. That was one of the reasons they were in the country to begin with, to try to improve the security forces, law and order.

"I'm sorry. The Americans did a good job. If she had been there I think they would have got her out."

Finn's hands lie limp and useless in his lap. Sunlight presses relentlessly through the leaves of the surrounding trees, winking on the silver. He had never thought there could be too much sun, too much light, but it has become oppressive, like a jolly uncle constantly telling you to cheer up.

"Cold comfort, I know." He nods. "But on the bright side, they think she's alive. They found some more drawings."

"Where?"

"You'll have to talk with them."

"Can I have them?" The thought of Miranda's work, even if it were only doodles, being in the hands of anyone else makes his whole body hum with anxiety.

"I presume so. The Americans still have them at the moment. I imagine their forensic people want a go first."

"What do you think it means that she's in the North?" Finn is thinking out loud. "Is it the separatists who have her? Or AQ? Or who?"

"We think there is some AQ activity in the area, but it's been hard for us to get in because of the bombings. And because the mountain pass is so often closed by landslides."

"Which will only get worse next month, when the rains start." The main road to the North runs through that pass. If Miranda is there, it will soon be even harder to get to her.

"Correct." Celia's blond eyebrows draw together as she searches for something reassuring to add. "I wouldn't think it's an ideal place for AQ training, what with the government constantly attacking. This camp was small. We think they are more likely to be plotting against the government than planning attacks on Western interests. Though naturally these guys are no fans of the West."

"So they don't seem like the beheading kind of terrorists?"

"Not yet, anyway."

Finn tries to find a way forward through the 973 questions and doubts swirling in his skull. "So they think she was there and then she was moved? How long ago? And why the hell are they keeping her if they aren't going to demand a ransom or chop off her head?"

Celia shrugs, her thin shoulders dropping helplessly. "I don't know," she concedes. "Shall I set up a meeting for you with the Americans?"

"Please, Celia." Finn looks at her and then down at the cold cup of tea in front of him, the dull, rigid whiteness of the teacup suddenly an affront. For an instant, he hears Miranda's voice, teasing him. "You couldn't even drink your tea? Now I almost believe you were really worried."

Something still nags at the back of Finn's mind. "And the others? They were with her? Is there any evidence of them?"

Celia twists her hands in her lap, looking profoundly uncomfortable. "No . . ."

"What is it, Celia? There's something else."

"It's classified." She looks up at him, pleadingly. "It's not to do with Miranda."

Finn just stares at her, rage rising slowly from his rib cage. "If it's anything about the other women, it *is* to do with Miranda. You know what? *Fuck* classified. This is my fucking *wife* we're talking about. How can you justify withholding anything from me? Not as a diplomat, but as a *human being*. Christ, Celia!"

Startled momentarily by his uncharacteristic language, she hesitates.

Unaccustomed to being overtaken by emotion, Finn rises, trembling. His knees catch the table, and without taking time to think about it, he grabs the edge and upends the entire thing—teapot, teacups, silverware, pistachio cookies—into the garden. The glass tabletop shatters against the edge of the porch. *Fuck* tea. Tears prick the backs of his eyes.

Celia doesn't move. "The Dutch and the French have received ransom requests."

Finn falls back into his chair. "When? From whom?"

"About a month ago. We're not sure from whom. They're using an intermediary, a local sheikh."

"A *month* ago? And no one thought to tell me?" Why hadn't Stéphane or Alfons let him know? Were they feeling guilty that they had some hope for the return of their wives, whereas he had nothing?

"We wanted to wait until we confirmed that the requests came from the actual kidnappers. You know how this works. Proof of life and such."

"And did they?"

"We think so."

"But they haven't been paid yet?"

"Not yet. It took a while for the exact amount to be negotiated. Apparently the kidnappers had high expectations of the worth of bankers and oil workers. Not erroneously, of course. But they've agreed on five hundred thousand dollars per woman. They're only wives, after all, not the executives themselves. The drop could happen soon."

"Why did it take them so long to make the ransom requests? Odd, no?"

"No idea. These aren't the most predictable of people. But it could have taken them some time to figure out Kaia's and Doortje's net worth."

"I'm surprised the French have waited this long. They're usually the first to pay up."

Celia just nods. "They'll pay. So will the Dutch. Thus putting all their other countrymen in greater danger."

Finn nods, staring down at the puddle of tea staining the expanse of white stone between them, considering where this leaves him. "If the other women are ransomed, they may be able to help us," he says, allowing himself a glimmer of hope. "But I don't understand. Do we think they are being held separately from Miranda?"

"We haven't received a ransom request for her. I promise you, Finn, we would tell you that. The people with whom the Dutch and the French are negotiating claim they have no idea where she is."

"Why would they separate her from the others? Because she is my wife? Because she is American? Because they have other plans for her? Did they sell her to AQ or what?" Finn doesn't expect answers, he is merely thinking out loud.

"We'll tell you whatever we find out."

"Celia, you *will* let me talk with the women before they are evacuated?"

"I'll find a way. I'm sorry, Finn." She does look sorry, and so helpless that Finn finally says, with genuine contrition, "I'm sorry about the tea."

Celia waves an arm dismissively. "Entirely understandable under the circumstances."

FINN WALKS ALL the way home to the Old City, his mind churning with guilty questions. No matter what the reason for Miranda's capture, it is his fault. He placed her in the dangerous position of being his wife, failed to properly protect her, and is failing hopelessly at tracking her down. For the millionth time, he wonders if this is some kind of reckoning. Would he feel any better had he trusted Miranda with the story of Afsoon? She loved him, didn't he believe that? Apparently he didn't have faith that her love would survive hearing that particular tale, every detail of which tattooed his character with dishonor he could never erase.

That fateful night in 2003, Finn had been working at the child-sized desk in his sterile little pod, his knees knocking against its underside as he wrote up a security report, when there was a rap at the door. He had paused momentarily to rest his eyes on Afsoon, curled up in his bed, sound asleep with her long black hair splayed out on the pillow. He checked his watch: 3:15 a.m. Who on earth? Quickly, he bent over Afsoon. "*Habibti,*" he whispered. She stirred sleepily, inky lashes fluttering against only slightly paler skin. "*Habibti,* wake up. Someone's at the door."

She sat upright with a start, her eyes wide and frightened.

"The bathroom. Quick."

She didn't need the prompting; she was already halfway there. Finn waited until he heard the door click behind her before unlatching the door of his pod.

"Am I waking you?"

"At three fifteen in the morning? Of course not."

Norman looked exhausted. The skin of his face hung gray and loose, and deep lines tunneled across his forehead. He ducked through the doorway and perched on the edge of Finn's bed, his hands folded on his knees.

Finn twirled a pen in his fingers, waiting for him to speak, his heart in his throat.

"I'm afraid there's been a leak."

"A leak?"

"Charlotte Fernsby. . . . She's dead."

It took a few moments for the words, their terrible significance, to worm their way into Finn's brain. "You mean, this evening's— yesterday evening's—operation—"

"They were expecting us, Finn. There's no other explanation." The rescue team was ambushed as they approached the compound where Fernsby was being held, Norman said. Only one man survived to report that Charlotte's headless corpse had been strung up in the entrance to the compound.

Mutely, Finn stared at him. *No* was his first response. *No no no.* Dead. Charlotte Fernsby, dead. And a leak? Jesus Christ no. On his watch?

"Finn, I need to know who knew about the operation. Everyone who knew anything at all."

Slowly, Finn nodded, but he still didn't trust his voice. He would have to speak with Charlotte's family. And the families of the team members who went in. With the ambassador out of country, the rescue operation had been his decision. He had known the odds against success, but thought they were worse if they did nothing. He had been wrong. He picked up a glass of water from his desk and took a shaky sip. "Me, of course," he finally said. "The ambassador. Nigel. Sophie. Defense. SIS, of course. One or two of the senior political staff. How did you hear so quickly?"

"Lucky enough to be on call in the kidnap cell tonight."

"Ah."

"That's all?"

Finn stared at the gray linoleum floor as he mentally flipped through the names of the rest of the staff: Colin, Spencer, Isabelle, Terrence, Rupert, Gordon, Emily, Daisy, Olivia. And Ben. Was that it? Yet even as he worked his way through the embassy, he knew it was an exercise in futility. It hadn't been any of the expatriate staff.

"And Vicky," he added hollowly. His PA. He'd needed her to help with communication with London.

"Finn, think. Was there anyone else? Any friend you might have spoken to in confidence?"

"Of course not!" He wondered if Norman could see the acceleration of the pulse throbbing in his neck. *Just the woman hiding in the bathroom.* "Jesus, Norman."

He looked up to find Norman staring at his back. Or rather, at the back of his chair, where a bit of pale blue lace had caught his eye. A bit of pale blue lace belonging to a female undergarment, slung across the plastic seat in an earlier moment of passion. Finn flushed, heat rising to his face and soaking his underarms. Could Norman have guessed whose they were? Slowly, Norman looked back at him, one eyebrow lifted.

"With all due respect," he said, "I would consider giving this a little more thought. A woman and eleven men are dead. Good night, sir." He stood, wrenched the handle of the door so that it flew open, banging against the outside of the pod, and was gone.

Finally forcing his paralyzed limbs into action, Finn yanked open the bathroom door to find Afsoon crouched on the seat of the toilet, sobbing into her hands.

"Who did you tell," he said flatly. She refused to look at him, pulling her knees into her chest, wiping her running nose on her wrist.

"Get out." Finn stood rigid as she climbed down from the toilet. Stretching out those lovely long arms, she reached for him, encircled him.

"Please," she whispered into his neck, the scent of roses rising from her smooth skin. "I didn't mean any harm."

He forced himself to keep his arms by his sides. Twisting away, he shrugged off her embrace. "You're bloody well going to tell me," he said. "A woman is dead. A woman and about a dozen others whose lives I am responsible for." He backed away from her, toward the bed. Crying, she followed.

"Tell me, and I might not have you prosecuted," he said. "Tell me, and you might not spend your life behind bars." Listening to his words, he didn't recognize himself. The Finn he had always been didn't threaten people. But he also didn't whisper state secrets to honeytraps. He was only too aware that he would never be able to punish her without punishing himself. But would she know this?

"It was just my brother," she wept, sinking onto the edge of the bed and gazing beseechingly up at him. "He said you didn't take me seriously, that I was nothing but a diversion. I just wanted to show that you did—" Again, she reached for his hands. Again, he drew them away, his heart folding itself into smaller and smaller shapes, a muscular origami.

"To my infinite regret." He picked up the panties from the back of the chair and handed them to her. "Your brother must have some unsavory friends. Get dressed. I want you to go home and never come back. Tomorrow you will call the embassy and tell them you found another job. But I never want to see your face again. Do you understand me? Never. You are not to contact me in any way."

Miserably, she nodded, jerking the lace panties up along those fatally alluring thighs.

"You understand how much trouble you will be in if you ever say another word about this to anyone? You are a murderer. You as good as murdered those people."

She nodded again, tears streaming down her face. "I'm sorry," she whispered. Swiftly, she pulled on the rest of her clothing and slipped out the door as easily as she had slipped in. Finn stood for a moment, contemplating his rumpled bed, the scent of her rose perfume still in his nostrils. He was sick with rage and self-recrimination. She had made a girlish mistake, a naïve, stupid mistake. Or perhaps she had actually played him. He would never know. But he, he was the murderer.

An hour later, Finn unlatched his door once more. Fully dressed, he walked across the compound until he found a pod identical in almost every way to his. He knocked quietly, and the door swung open. "Norman," he said. "Could I have a word?"

DECEMBER 1, 2010
Miranda

Miranda is sleeping when they come for her. The voices wake her, the voices of several men, directly outside her prison. She sits up, pulling her crumpled blouse down over her stomach. She never bothers to undress anymore. There is no way to wash and she rarely receives other clothing. She had thought she would grow accustomed to the fetid smell of her body, its festering funk, but she still feels a wave of nausea when a sudden movement releases her scent on the breeze. Only Luloah seems oblivious, clinging to her skin when she comes, chortling with joy.

A loud rapping at the door, followed by *"Allah Allah Allah!"* She is surprised that they bother making sure she is modest. Do they really imagine that she strips down to sleep on the unforgiving stone of this cell? In these desert nights? Instinctively, she looks around for her possessions—a notebook, a pencil, a key ring—before remembering that she has none. Something heavy, a shoulder, a gun, lands on the door, shoving it open. Miranda blinks, trying to see the men, but can make out only dim, hulking outlines.

"Get up," says one. "Move." No *salaama aleikum.* For the second time since her kidnapping, the traditional greeting was omitted. At least Aisha managed this basic reassurance.

For a moment, Miranda contemplates pretending not to understand, before realizing how futile that would be. Slowly, she struggles to her feet, stiff and cold. She has to pee. She should have thought of that before they burst in on her. She might have had time to use the bucket. Whatever these men want, she hopes it won't take long.

"Feyn Aisha?" she asks. *"Feyn Luloah?"*

None of the men answer. Instead, one comes toward her and prods her with the barrel of his rifle. *"Yalla,"* he says.

Ducking her head as she walks through the small doorway, Miranda is stunned by the purity of the air outside, clean and soft like the breath exhaled by laundry as it is shaken out and folded. How long has it been since she has taken a free breath? One month? Two? She gulps the cool, dry air as if she can store it up.

Again, the cold metal pressing against the thin cotton shielding her rib cage. They probably just don't want to touch her, Miranda reasons. Good Muslims, even as they prod her along with their weapons.

She walks. It is too dark to see anything in front of her—or to the sides of her, for that matter. And because she was moved to her latest prison when she was unconscious, she is not even sure where it is, in relation to her old hut with Aisha and the huts of the men. There is no moon, and she sees no lights that might indicate nearby buildings. Though it is the middle of the night; why would there be lights? Her legs are heavy, difficult to move. She feels a burning in her quadriceps, but is relieved to find that she can put weight on her ankle without too much pain. The wound was slow to heal, but miraculously she had developed only a minor infection, a reddish swelling around the hole from which Aisha had pried the bullet. Nothing had ever been so painful, not even childbirth. She would have screamed had Aisha not stuffed a rag in her mouth before she started. Instead, she simply passed out. It is possible that the bone in her ankle is shattered. She sometimes feels a sharp stab when she stands, like a needle in the joint. When she is free, she should see a doctor about it.

She shakes this thought from her mind. Is she really still imagining that someday she will be free? In her weaker moments, Miranda ephemerally wishes she were German. They pay ransoms. But bad enough that she had been taken from Cressida, she couldn't wish this fate on another parent. Or child. Or on anyone. Crime must not pay. She reflexively recalls the debates in her Art and Ethics class, during her undergrad years at the University of Washington, over whether financial rewards should be offered in the pursuit of stolen artworks. Wouldn't such compensation simply reward criminals? Or should art be preserved at any cost? She had argued against compensating thieves. Otherwise, wouldn't every artwork be at risk? Now here she is, a Turner painting, lost indefinitely.

Finn had always been firmly against ransoms; she wonders if this has swayed him. She hopes it hasn't. One of the things she relies on most is Finn's utter consistency. There is something relaxing about knowing what kind of tea he wants every single morning (Earl Grey), what he always wants for breakfast (muesli—unless they are in France, when he will eat a plain butter croissant), what kind of tea he wants before bed at night (chai), and what kind of face cream he uses every day (Body Shop for Men). These are the small things, the insignificant details, but he is consistent in the larger things as well. Like love.

He is slow, methodical, a perfectionist. He could not be rushed, which meant he pulled as many all-nighters as a college student, trying to keep up with his work. Miranda had long ago given up trying to get him to come to bed before he was finished with a project, though there were a few nights when she crept downstairs at 3:00 a.m. and found him asleep facedown on his keyboard, and he allowed himself to be led upstairs. Her heart staggers at the thought of Finn, of the way his face crumples in sleep, and she feels the emptiness of her arms.

She hears a rumble of voices ahead of her. The men are speaking quietly, for Mazrooqis. *Did you tell Aisha?*

No, she is sleeping. She would try to stop us.

Alarmed, Miranda's feet slow. They are taking her from Aisha? From Luloah? From sanity? Not wanting to alert the men to her comprehension, she forces her feet to move forward.

She wouldn't try to stop us if she knew they were coming, the first one said.

She still worries the child won't survive.

No one will survive if we don't move her. We don't have a choice. They could be here any time now.

Maybe she'll feel more at home up there. For some reason, this strikes the men as funny and they emit a joint snort of laughter. *Anyway, they're more likely to actually do something with her than the lazy dogs here.*

Bile rises in Miranda's throat. Luloah has not saved her after all. Nor has she saved the child. But—who is coming? Help?

Her body trembles as she walks, alert now. They haven't blindfolded her, perhaps because it is simply unnecessary in this unrelenting dark. Her mouth is dry, and the pressure on her bladder is growing urgent. Abruptly, her shin hits something cold and unyielding. "Get in," says one of the men who have been shadowing her. Miranda takes a step backward. "Why?" she asks. "Where are you taking me? Where is the baby? Where is Luloah?"

They do not answer. "Get. In." A rifle butt provides the punctuation.

"No." Miranda is trembling violently now. "Please, tell me where is Luloah."

There are two guns now, prodding at the flesh above her ribs. "The child is no business of yours," one says.

A flash of liquid rage courses through her blood. "No business of mine?" Her voice is raw and hoarse, unrecognizable. "She is my business as much as anyone in the world is my business. I keep her *alive*." Immediately she regrets her outburst. "Please, punish me, but don't punish Luloah. She still needs me. She won't survive. She won't—"

Suddenly hands grip her sides and she finds herself hauled into the back of what can only be a pickup truck, cold and gritty beneath her knees. The tailgate slams shut behind her. "She doesn't need you anymore," a man says. He walks around to the driver's side while the other two vault into the back with her. One holds her wrists together while the other binds them with a thick, scratchy rope. A new panic wrenching her insides, Miranda doesn't even think to resist. When the men have similarly trussed her feet, they roll her onto her back with a shove. A moment later, her view of the stars is obscured by a blanket. She turns her head to the side so she can breathe, inhaling some kind of rank animal scent. Rigid with grief and too frightened to cry, she remains motionless. Are they selling her to another group? Is that why they are moving her? Or are they simply fleeing possible rescuers? But how would they know of a possible rescue? Her brain won't stop spinning with the possibilities. Exhausted but far from sleep, she tries to imagine escape. She wiggles her fingers and feet, but they are tightly bound. Even if she could rise somehow, could launch herself over the side of the pickup and out onto the road, she would not be able to free herself. On one side of her she feels the heavy presence of the two men.

Rage rises and floods her body; she can feel it pressing outward against her skin. But there is nowhere for it to go, no escape valve. It is a useless and most certainly dangerous emotion. She has worked hard to stifle her fury at these men, at their delusions. She must try to stay calm. And alert. Watch for any opportunity to flee. But in the unlikely event that she frees herself, where would she go? Would she first search for Luloah or try to find a ride straight back to Arnabiya, to Cressie and Finn? How could she return home, knowing the fate to which she was abandoning Luloah? And how could she go first to Luloah, knowing that she was risking never seeing her own daughter again? Either choice would eviscerate her. At the moment, however, there are no choices to be made.

It is getting lighter. Soon it will be dawn and Luloah will be hungry. She is not old enough yet to go without any kind of milk. How long will she survive without Miranda? They would be feeding her dirty water and sweet tea. She might not last a week.

JUNE 23, 2007
Finn

Miranda and Finn had been (officially) living together for less than two weeks when Finn decided it was time to host their first dinner party. Actually, it wasn't much of a choice. The Middle East editor of *The Guardian* was in town, and expecting to be appropriately feted. Dinner parties weren't exactly an optional part of the job. They sounded glamorous to friends and family back home, but dinner parties were how much of the business of diplomacy got done. And they were hard work. Particularly for him. There were speeches to be made (in Arabic), alliances to be formed, uncomfortable subjects to be broached, dragging conversations to be prodded along. There were the endless courses of soups and meats and salads and puddings, followed by tea and coffee in the parlor and brandy and port on the veranda for the lingerers. Few of these night owls ever seemed to consider the fact that their host had to be back in the office by 7:30 the next morning, and that he could not go to bed until they did. Not that he always went straight to bed. Often, he still had hours of work to do in his home office, managing to slip into bed just as the muezzins were sounding their calls for morning prayers.

He wasn't actually sure that Miranda should be present. Changes in partner status were to be reported first to Protocol, and he hadn't gotten around to that yet. He was a busy man. But Miranda lived with him now; she was his life. He wanted her there. Besides, it was likely to be a friendly crowd, mostly locals. The *Guardian* editor was rumored to be an intelligent enough bloke, and Finn wanted to make sure he connected him with sources who actually knew what was going on in the country. This place was an onion, layer after layer of tribal loyalties, political maneuvering, half-truths. God knows he was still trying to peel back the first several layers himself.

When Finn returned from the embassy a half-hour before their guests were expected, he found Miranda standing in the middle of their room in her underwear, surrounded by discarded dresses. "I'm going like this," she said, a touch of frustrated toddler in her voice. Stepping carefully over the puddles of rayon and lace, Finn leaned in to kiss her. "That's one way to ensure a memorable evening," he said. "But I thought you wanted me to keep my job?"

"My Western dresses are too Western, my Middle Eastern wear is too ugly. I don't want to shock anyone, but I also don't want to be hideous." Finn suppressed a smile. With her hair curling loose past her shoulders, her face flushed and still bare of makeup, and her breasts barely concealed by lace, she had never looked lovelier. He was not a religious man, but every time he saw her unclothed he wanted to fall to his knees and thank someone.

"Hmmmm, not hideous. There's a challenge," he said. "Let me see if I can help." He strode back to her dressing room and opened a closet door. A few minutes later he emerged with a tailored black skirt and jacket, and an aquamarine lace camisole. "What about this?" he said. "Modest with a touch of the feminine? Defiantly not housewifely? A little business looking, but I think you can live with that."

Miranda stared at him. "Are you sure you're not gay?"

Finn looked at his watch. "Do I have time to prove it to you?"

CHARLOTTE, SECOND SECRETARY Political, arrived first. Conscientious in the extreme, she always arrived early and stuck to Diet Coke until the meal was served. Miranda had answered the door, looking only slightly rumpled, and Finn was relieved to hear them chatting away in the parlor like old friends. Why had he worried about Miranda? She could make friends with a hedgerow. He headed to the kitchen to check on the staff, though he wasn't sure why he bothered; they were pros. Glass dishes of pistachios, cashew nuts, and almonds already dotted their coffee tables; silver trays lined with white napkins and empty cocktail and wine glasses stood ready on the steel countertops of the kitchen; and Semere was hacking away at the ice, breaking it into usable sizes.

The guest of honor, Aubrey Lewis, arrived next, looking pale and exhausted. "I'm very grateful," he said, shaking Finn's hand. He'd arrived in the country that morning on the early flight from Dubai and didn't look as though he had had time to nap. The rest of their guests, all Mazrooqi politicians, professors, NGO workers, and ministers, predictably arrived late. Last through the door was Foreign Minister Abbas al-Attas, a short, smiling man with a shining bald head. Miranda told Finn later that she had touched up her lipstick peering into the back of his head. Finn wasn't sure she was joking.

It was a lively evening, livelier than he had expected. Al-Attas was loquacious and expansive, which wasn't always the case, and the Minister of Commerce, Tawfeek al-Kibsi, and political science professor Adil al-Ahmar spoke passionately about their country and its promise. So far Miranda was holding up admirably. After drinks on the veranda she had led the group to the front hall to sign the guest book before escorting them into the dining room.

While Miranda and the others were still in the front hall, al-Attas had followed Finn into the dining room, circling the table reading the name cards like a buzzard seeking out prey. He stopped at Miranda's seat. "Miranda Taluma?" he read, a question in his voice.

"My partner." There was no need to use the word *wife* with a man who was educated in the UK and kept a second home in Surrey. Still, Finn's hands were sweating, and he wiped them surreptitiously on his handkerchief.

Al-Attas looked at him, one graying eyebrow cocked. "Long-term?"

Finn smiled. "Absolutely. Presuming she'll have me."

Al-Attas nodded slowly and patted the sleeve of Finn's suit. "*Mabrouk,*" he said. In his pockets, Finn's hands unclenched.

Just when Finn had completely relaxed his guard, the Foreign Minister had to go and mention freedom of expression. He complained about the way the press was handling the conflict with the North, prompting Finn to point out, with just a touch of frustration, that al-Attas couldn't expect the media to report accurately when the government didn't allow any journalists into the region. "When the government decides to completely block the media from somewhere, it instantly arouses suspicion," he added. "I don't understand why the government has failed to grasp this."

"We *have* let journalists in," protested al-Attas. "Just last week we took a bus full of them—"

"That's just it," said Finn, smiling to soften his words. "You put them all on a bus and told them what they could see. Why don't you let them roam freely?"

Al-Attas frowned. "It isn't safe," he said. "And you must know that our journalists are not professionally trained. We cannot trust them to report the truth."

"Can't you get them training?" said Miranda. "Surely there is no shortage of journalism trainers in the world who could come and teach them?"

Al-Attas bowed his head respectfully toward Miranda. "Perhaps," he said. Then, perking up slightly, he added, "But even without training we have freedom of expression here. Our journalists are free to write what they want even when they are wrong."

"Are they?" Finn raised an eyebrow. "So they're free to criticize the president by name, are they?" Aubrey stayed bizarrely silent throughout this exchange, simply observing. Finn had the feeling he was simply too exhausted to ask the questions himself. But Finn hadn't expected a newspaperman to be so passive.

The Minister of Commerce wiped his mouth and replaced his napkin in his lap with a cough. "They are free enough to commit libel," he said. "I am suing someone for libel, a journalist who wrote that I hired some members of my family and put them on the government payroll."

"Did you?" Miranda leaned forward with interest.

"Miranda!" But Finn couldn't help laughing. Fortunately, the Minister smiled as well.

"I'm just asking!" said Miranda.

"No," said the Minister. "This is why it is libel."

INEVITABLY, THE TALK turned to terrorism and the issue of increasing radicalization. "So what's the main cause *here*, do you think?" asked Aubrey, abruptly setting down his wineglass and coming to life. "Is it poverty? Unemployment?"

"I don't think you could say there is one main cause," replied al-Attas, dabbing at the curried shrimp soup on his chin. "It's certainly much more than poverty."

Finn turned to Aubrey, who was seated next to him. "I'd say— correct me if I am wrong, Minister—I'd say that a sense of injustice and unfairness contributes hugely."

"That's right," said political science professor Adil al-Ahmar. "Unequal distribution of wealth as a result of government corruption. It's the same thing that drove Europeans to socialism in the nineteenth century. We see our world exploited by rich—often foreign—companies and governments. We see our country being run by another country. Or oppressed by it."

"But isn't it also an education issue?" Miranda looked at al-Attas. "I mean, you have a system focused on rote learning. People aren't encouraged to think for themselves. If you had an educational system that actually taught people critical thinking, taught them to challenge what they are told—wouldn't that change things?"

"That's one of our working premises. Which is why education reform is a development priority, alongside political reform," said Finn.

"Ah, but development assistance as a cure for radicalization is a delicate thing," said al-Attas. "Yes, ultimately you need an enlightened education system, young people need access to a dignified livelihood, and the West can help with vocational training and curriculum reform, but—"

"But as soon as a Western presence is involved, the whole project becomes imperialist or colonialist—or at least that's the perception," finished Finn.

Al-Attas nodded in agreement.

"So what should we do? Shut down our development programs? Do we try to deal with these root causes at all, or do we just keep trying to kill off the terrorist leadership?" Aubrey slid a notebook onto the table.

"Killing off the leadership clearly isn't working," Miranda said, abandoning her attempts to saw a leathery aubergine in half. "Every time a US drone attacks, it kills one terrorist and creates five hundred more. Isn't that right?"

Al-Attas nodded slowly. "In a way. It depends whether the radicalization results from a grassroots movement fed by the people's common frustrations, or whether a few charismatic leaders are manipulating the people."

"Could be a bit of both," added Minister of the Interior Mohammed al-Bayaa, who had thus far remained silent.

"So if it's more a leadership thing than a grassroots thing," said Miranda, "by cutting off the head of the movement, do you kill the movement?"

"Yes—but you have to kill the right people," said al-Bayaa. "It doesn't stop it from being a terrorist movement, but it stops it from being a threat to the West. Which is why we allow the American drones to attack known leaders."

"But the drone attacks make people hate the West more than ever," said Miranda, her face flushed and voice moving up an octave. "Even some of my friends here, they have grown to hate the US because of the attacks in the North. I just don't understand why you support them, especially when they always manage to kill off a bunch of civilians in addition to their alleged target. How can you let them slaughter your own people?" Finn found her foot under the table and gave it a firm nudge. She glanced at him distractedly but continued. "Don't drones just anger tribal leaders and exacerbate the whole situation?"

"Well, maybe," answered al-Bayaa cautiously. "But what are five hundred people without direction? A nuisance to their own country, perhaps, but not organized enough to attack abroad."

"But isn't it possible one of those five hundred people would then rise to be the new leader? And what if it wasn't the leadership that had radicalized them after all, what if it had been a sense of common frustrations? And it just keeps spreading, this need for justice?"

"If there's enough of them," said Finn grimly, "you get civil war."

DECEMBER 7, 2010
Miranda

From darkness to darkerness, thinks Miranda. You don't think you could survive anything blacker than your current reality, and then you must. She lies on a cement floor in another stone house, some hours from her last confinement. Alone. Already, her painfully engorged and leaking breasts protest Luloah's absence. Or Cressida's. This undrunk milk mourning two unbearable losses. Cressie is her first love, always and forever, but tiny, fluffy-haired Luloah has made herself some space in whichever atrium or ventricle is responsible for the agonies of maternal attachment.

An image floats into her field of vision, illuminates her despair. An exhausted-eyed woman sits in a small, windowless room, grinding a steady stream of stars into a mush that she spoon-feeds to a caged crescent moon. Varo had probably meant the painting *Celestial Pablum* to say something about the way that women crush their stellar selves, sacrificing their unique light to the hungry demands of their children. Something about the soul-crushing, blue-collar slog of motherhood.

But now, that image for Miranda is an unattainable paradise. For now she would give anything, pulverize any star quality she has left, for the privilege of feeding her two moon children again.

She wrenches her mind from the girls before the fear and grief engulf her. Nothing is more soul-strangling than contemplating her child and little Luloah, when she is helpless to go to them. Her lips are dry and cracked; no one has yet brought her water. It occurs to her that she could drink her own milk if she had a cup. She sits up, presses a little into her right palm, and laps it up. Her hands are filthy. That was probably a bad idea. No one has yet thought to bring her a pot, so she has urinated into a drain in the corner of the floor. Her room has one tiny window, set so high in the wall she cannot reach it. Not that she could squeeze out of it if she did reach it; it's the size of a lunch box. Why do we measure everything with food? she idly wonders. When she was pregnant, the baby websites had informed her that Cressie was the size of a blueberry, then a walnut, a plum, an orange, a melon. Bigger than a bread box. Better than sliced bread. The game of free association has become a way of life. Her mind leaps about in the emptiness, seeking order. The images of food keep coming, garish, taunting. Still life after still life of gleaming apples, dusty plums. A faint burning in her abdomen suggests she is hungry, but she cannot imagine swallowing. She cannot swallow this.

The three tiny stars and crescent moon she can see through her window are fading. Again she thinks of Remedios Varo, her crescent moons in the windows of the tiny rooms where isolated women work—or step from the walls. Her crescent moons brought inside, where they glow like lamps, like sculpture. She thinks of her father and wonders if Finn has told him. Her poor father. For the trillionth time, Miranda wishes she had a sibling, someone left for him. Her mother apparently didn't need anyone. (Or that was the impression she gave.) Her father had tried to hide his fear when she told him where she and Vícenta were moving. "Oh," he had said, turning his glasses over in his hands. "I thought something like this might happen." She and Vícenta had already taken several long trips together, accepting grants and residencies in far-flung locales they hoped would take their work in new directions. They'd begun in Italy, working in separate studios in a stone farmhouse in the foothills of Mount Subasio outside of Assisi, and spent subsequent summers in Senegal and Peru. It was one of Vícenta's German cousins in Buenos Aires ("the Nazi side of my family," Vícenta called these descendants of refugees from postwar Germany) who had told them about the German Haus grants in Mazrooq. "It's one of the last untouched cultures of the Middle East," she'd said. "One of the few places that hasn't yet caved to materialism and malls." Neither Miranda nor Vícenta had traveled to the Middle East, and they shared a craving for novelty. No one they knew had ever been to Mazrooq. "Let's go exploring behind the veil," Vícenta had joked. "Find out what they're hiding."

"I've already got a name for my first painting," Miranda had said. *"The Mazrooq Mystique."*

Vícenta's mother hadn't been quite as resigned as Miranda's father. "Are you fucking NUTS?" she had said over Skype to New York. "You'll fucking die over there, Vícenta. You and Miranda both. You claim you love her and you are taking her back to the fucking dark ages?"

Yet oddly, once they were there, Miranda and Vícenta had stopped worrying that the true nature of their relationship would be discovered. It wasn't in the least bit unusual for Mazrooqi women to share a bed or hold hands on the street. Miranda's students slept in the same bed with their sisters and friends every night; countless times both women had been invited to stay over with Mazrooqi women. It simply didn't occur to anyone that anything sexual could be going on. (Miranda and Vícenta had heard rumors of clandestine lesbian activity in the *hammams,* the local bathhouses, but they hadn't ever witnessed it.) In a way, it had never been easier to live in a lesbian relationship.

Still, the country had been their undoing. While Miranda became more and more absorbed in the culture, in the lives of her students, Vícenta found herself more and more repulsed by its misogyny, unable to see beyond it. By the time Vicenta's fellowship was up in February 2005, her bags were already half-packed.

"Mira?" she asked, as their departure date loomed.

"Mmmmm?" Miranda was sprawled naked across their bed, a fat king-sized mattress that took up most of the floor of their room, her head resting on Vicenta's warm stomach. Half-asleep, she breathed in Vicenta's sharp scent, damp earth and evergreen. "It's like I'm making love to Christmas," Miranda used to tell her. She was dreaming up a new painting, a landscape composed entirely of women's bodies. She had never done anything *entirely* composed of women's bodies. An Amazonian rain forest (made of actual Amazons!)? The Cascades? Or what about Jordan's Petra? Petra could be fun . . . so many different temples and canyons and tombs. She could paint a whole series of Petras . . . Somewhere she still had the photos she and Vicenta had taken on vacation there. Woman as a tomb. Life springs from women. Could it also end there? Sometimes it does, she thought morbidly.

"Have you talked with your women yet?" Setting aside *Body Art/ Performing the Subject,* Vicenta twirled a finger in Miranda's curls.

"What do you mean?" But Miranda jerked awake, knowing too well what she meant.

"Do they know you're leaving next month?"

"Ummmm . . ."

Vicenta pulled her fingers from Miranda's hair and rolled onto her side, letting Miranda's head topple onto the mattress.

"Come on, Mira, you're not being fair. Give them a little notice before you disappear into the sunset." This was the last month of Vicenta's fellowship, and she couldn't wait to get back to Seattle. She was fed up with being harassed on the street, leered at by taxi drivers, and trying to understand why the women did not simply rise up and revolt.

Miranda pushed herself into a sitting position and pulled her knees into her chest, her heartbeat suddenly deafening. "Well, it's just . . . I've been thinking."

"Oh?" Vicenta slid from the mattress and stood up, turning to look down at Miranda with her arms folded across her bare chest, as if protecting herself from whatever words were about to come.

Miranda took a deep breath and looked into Vícenta's eyes, opaque emeralds in the dim light from their one tiny window. "I don't think I am ready to leave."

"Oh Jesus. I was afraid of this."

"You were?" Miranda was surprised. It was unlike Vícenta to be particularly perceptive of the internal lives of others.

"You don't like to disappoint anyone. It's your fatal flaw."

"It's not just that." Miranda had only just begun to feel at home in this strange land. She had learned her way around the labyrinthine Old City, figured out where to find black-market bourbon, and sorted out how to pay their electric bills. She enjoyed living in a three-story house she could never afford in Seattle. But most of all, she had grown to love her women, her artists.

"Vícenta, I feel useful for the first time in my life. These women, they need me more than the rich kids at Cornish. Who else do they have? What will happen to them when I am gone?" She was talking around the only real issue here: Whatever she felt for Vícenta was not strong enough to pull her away. Yet she was too cowardly to say this, too afraid of losing Vícenta completely.

"That's not your problem, Mother Teresa. I don't want to sound harsh, but you could sacrifice your life a million times over to women in the developing world and what would be the result? A bunch of paintings that never see the light of day. A bunch of women still held hostage by their families, their religion, their society, their—"

"True." Miranda thought for a moment. "But they want to learn. They are desperate to learn. They don't know how to live without drawing or painting, without creating something. Like *us*. They are happy when they are painting, happy when they are getting better, even if no one ever sees the result. Is it possible that this is also a valid way to live as an artist? To create for creation's sake, and not for an exhibition, for an audience?"

"No. No, it's not fucking *valid*. What happened to communication? If art fails to communicate something to someone then what is the fucking use of it at all?"

"Maybe they are communicating with themselves."

"Great. So we're teaching a bunch of women to mentally, to artistically masturbate. To monologue in paint. Fabulous. And how exactly does this change their lives?"

Miranda sighed. "I don't know if it does."

"So?"

"I just feel like I want to stay a little longer, see what happens. Give them all of the tools I possibly can and then see."

"How very lofty of you. How very *noble*. But all this idealism of yours, that isn't what this is really about, is it? Could it be that you've become particularly attached to one little apprentice?" Vicenta had backed against the wall, leaning away from her.

Fury rose in Miranda's chest. "I cannot believe you just said that. *You*, of all people."

"Well, who have you spent more time with in the past month, me or your little painter? What am I supposed to conclude?"

"Why do you have to sexualize everything? It's possible to care about someone and spend time with her without wanting to fuck her. Not that I would expect you to understand that."

"Sorry, but wasn't it you who confessed to having slept with half the planet before we met?"

"And wasn't it you who slept with half the planet *after* we met?"

"Not fair, Miranda. Just once, and I was honest about that."

"Were you honest about our waitress at the Daily Grind or that reviewer from the *Times* . . ."

"Those were just flirtations and you know it. You *know* nothing happened with them. Didn't you want that reviewer to like your show?"

"And you thought that was the best way to convince her? Because my paintings were such crap she needed your magnetic sex appeal to sway her? Maybe she wrote a good review because she pitied me for having such a faithless girlfriend. God. You know, I think one of the reasons I thought it was a good idea to come here was that at least the women wouldn't all be making passes at you. Or vice versa."

"No, that seems to be your role here."

"That's *absurd*. Why do you have to misconstrue everything? Why can't you just try to understand? There isn't a single woman here I would sleep with even if I could convince her. Tazkia's like a little sister to me."

Vicenta fell silent, turning her gaze to the floor, something broken in her eyes.

"I'm sorry, Vicenta. I promise I'm not doing this because there is anyone else. I'm not doing this because of something you have done." This was not entirely truthful, but was there any point in hurting her even more? She tried for a lighter tone. "And I like it here. We spend no money, we have endless time to work, and it's one of the friendliest places I have ever been." Her own painting had flourished here; she could scarcely stay away from her easel. But this she didn't say; how could she suggest she was putting her paintings ahead of her heart?

Vicenta lifted her head. "And one of the most depressing. If I have to spend another week around all of these *abayas* I am going to lose my mind. I am going to strip down and walk around the Old City singing show tunes."

"I'd like to see that." Miranda attempted a smile, but Vicenta was unmoved.

"What I really don't get is, how can you want to stay in a culture that treats its women like this? How can you stand it? How can you not go insane with rage every single day? I read these stories about these child brides and I want to go tear all of the men's throats out. I can't live at this level of rage all the time. If I am always at boiling point, eventually I'll just evaporate and be nothing but angry currents in the breeze." Vicenta's hands rose to her hair, tugging at the thick black strands as if she could uproot unwelcome thoughts. It was so like her to take up something—a country, a project, a relationship—with all-consuming, white-hot passion and then abruptly abandon it or her when she got bored or frustrated. Of course, she had finished her own work here, but still. To Miranda, everything felt undone.

"But it's because of the women I want to stay. How can we just do nothing? Isn't it better to do something tiny, something that a few women so passionately want, than nothing at all? And maybe just by seeing us, by seeing the way we live our lives, free of parents and brothers and uncles and choosing our careers, maybe that will change their concept of what is possible for them."

"Nothing is possible for them. Not here. And what do they see of our real lives? Can you tell them the truth about us? Can you chat with them about the virtues of strap-ons and feathers? Their heads would explode."

"You're missing the point."

"I'm not. Your point is entirely clear. You don't care enough to come home with me. To our home, our friends, our lives. Not to mention your job. Have you thought about your job?"

"This has nothing to do with how much I love you."

"Don't lie to me, Mira. *Clearly* you don't love me enough. You can't seriously think I'm going to just twiddle my fucking thumbs in Seattle until you decide you've enlightened enough women here?"

"I don't know, Vicenta. I haven't thought it all through."

"Obviously." Vicenta turned away from her to walk to the dresser, pulling out drawers and slamming them shut. Even now, the sight of Vicenta's long brown legs and the curves of her back made Miranda tremble with renewed desire.

"Please," said Miranda, still curled in a ball on the bed. "I just want to see what happens."

"I'll tell you what fucking happens," said Vicenta. "What happens is that your nights are about to get pretty fucking lonely."

"Don't," whispered Miranda, rocking back and forth on the sheets. *"Don't."* Unfolding her legs, she stretched herself out on the mattress in her *Le Long du Chemin* pose, leaning back on her elbows with her head thrown back, her thighs inching apart. When Vicenta turned to look at her, eyes still incandescent with rage, the black lace bras and panties she intended to pack slipped from her fingers to the cold stone. "That's so unfair, Mira," she said.

"All's fair—"

"No," said Vicenta, sliding to her knees in front of Miranda's prone form. "All is *not* fair . . ." She dropped her head to Miranda's belly, her body quaking. "I'm scared for you," she said, her voice finally breaking. "You get this tunnel vision when you're all excited about something, and it scares me. It's like you don't even hear me. Like I'm not even here."

"I do. I *do* hear you."

"Then *listen*, Mira. Don't be an idiot, okay? Don't go getting yourself killed."

Reaching for her, Miranda cupped a hand around Vícenta's warm head and felt hot tears run down her thighs.

THE FUNNY THING was, everyone back home had seemed to relax when Miranda moved in with Finn. Not only was she in a safe, heterosexual relationship but she was locked up in a house with gates, guards, and a bevy of armed men to protect her. Her father was downright cheerful at the prospect. Now he could go back to pondering the infinite heavens without the nagging worries about his daughter's safety. Her mother had also sent a congratulatory note, though she couldn't help adding, "How *conventional* of you, dear! I hope you're happy."

But Miranda had never felt in danger until she moved in with Finn. When you're tailed everywhere by a man with an automatic weapon, you start to wonder when he will need it. Life with Finn took place in the middle of a dartboard. The Bull's-Eye, that's what they should have named the Residence. The day after she moved in, Tucker had come by with his laptop to give her a lesson on how a close protection team worked, as well as her first lesson on personal protection. Using PowerPoint, he'd explained the importance of awareness of her surroundings and what to do if she felt she was being followed. There was an acronym involved—SAFER. What did it stand for? Situation, Awareness . . . she can't remember the rest. She and Tucker had made it through a substantial amount of gin that night. Obviously she had been a shit student to end up here.

They just hadn't taught her the right things. At the annual security training for staff and their partners at the embassy, she had learned how to work the radios they all kept in their homes in case the phones went down; what to avoid saying on a cell phone; and how to check a car for explosives. In the parking lot of the embassy they had stood around one of the Toyotas, practicing looking under the car, above the wheels, and in the engine. "Look for clean places on the car, where someone may have recently touched it," Tucker had said.

"Good reason not to wash the car," Miranda had whispered to Finn.

"Sweetheart, we leave armed men in our cars. At all times. We might not have to check our own vehicles."

Still, Miranda had been fascinated. She'd watched carefully as Tucker showed how to open the door just a crack, standing away from the opening, and run a piece of paper around the edge of the door, to detect wires.

"And if we find a wire?"

"Get as far away as possible as fast as possible."

Tucker had tested them, hiding a fake bomb in the car for them to find. Not one of them had managed to discover it. To Miranda, it had looked a lot like a car part. She should have taken that auto mechanics class in high school.

But in the end, none of it was of any use to her.

In the years before Finn, she had wandered freely, under any official radar, unregistered with any embassy, expecting hospitality and receiving it. She loved traveling alone, loved stopping in to visit her neighbors for tea, loved her daily conversations with taxi drivers. They were her best Arabic teachers. From them she'd learned her numbers, how to give directions, and the critical sentences "Five hundred dinars? Are you out of your mind? I won't pay it! Two hundred maximum." Bizarrely, they'd never guessed her nationality, running through nearly every country full of white people and giving up before they got to the United States. It didn't occur to them that an American would be wandering around a land where her government was so unpopular. She remembers her last taxi ride, the day before she moved in with Finn. It's not that it was particularly remarkable. She had had similar conversations with innumerable drivers. But she remembers it because it was her last one. Once her final suitcase had been dragged up the steps of the Residence, taxis were forbidden territory.

"*Antee Allmaneea?*" Are you German? This was usually the first guess. The Germans had a lot of development projects in Mazrooq.

"*Laa.*"

"*Francia?*"

"*Laa.*"

"*Al-Roosiah?*"

"*Laa.*"

He gave up. "*Min wayna antee?*"

"*Ana min New York.*" She always said New York because no one had ever heard of Seattle. And she and Vícenta had spent a lot of time there, after all.

"*Ah, New York! Amreekah!*"

"*Aiwa.*"

"*Amreekah wa Mazrooq very friends! Very friends!*" He was wildly excited, slamming his hands together to show how friendly Mazrooq and America were, turning around in his seat to look at Miranda. In fact, he did this every time he said something to her, which meant that for at least fifteen minutes of the half-hour drive, he was not watching the road. And Mazrooqi cars do not have seat belts. You're lucky if they have floors.

"*Aiwa.*" It was easiest simply to agree. What she wanted to say was, In what sense are our countries friends? Friends as in "the enemies of my enemies are my friends"? Friends as in You need the US to keep pouring development money and military assistance into the country? Or friends as in Your president desperately needs American political support?

He didn't clarify. "*Mazrooq kwayis?*"

"*Aiwa,*" she said again, sighing. "*Mazrooq kwayis.*" She said this at least nine times a day. They all had wanted to hear how much you loved their country. And she did, she truly did. But it was wearying to have to express it so often.

He was quiet for a bit, then thought of something else.

"*Antee maseeheeah?*" Are you Christian?

She paused for a moment. She wasn't a Christian. She wasn't anything. But while the Mazrooqis could understand someone being Christian or Jewish, they simply could not fathom someone not having any religion at all. The absence of God was imponderable. For Miranda, the opposite was true.

"*Aiwa,*" she finally said. "*Ana maseeheeah.*"

"I need to know something," he said, twisting around again. "*Isa, leyshe Isa yusawee Allah?*"

At first Miranda didn't recognize the Arabic name for Jesus. "*Laa aref,*" she said. I don't know.

"*Isa! Isa! Ibn Miriam!*" The son of Mary!

"*Ah. Jesus?*"

"*Aiwa. Jay-sus.*" He carefully mimicked her pronunciation of the word.

"*Aish?*"

"*Leysh in Christianity, Jesus yusawee Allah?*"

"*Laa laa laa,*" she said. "*Isa laa yusawee. Isa ibn Allah.*" He is not Allah. He is the son of Allah.

"*Ah, ibn,*" he said. "But Allah have no son!"

Miranda sighed. "Maybe not," she said.

"*Lithalik leysh?*" Why you say son? I want to know everything about Christianity, he told her. He wanted someone to teach him. Could she teach him?

You picked the wrong gal, Miranda wanted to say. I don't really have a strong opinion on whether or not God has a son. Had a son. Whatever. Frankly, he should have had a daughter. Maybe we'd all be better off.

"*Laa aref,*" she said as he pulled into her street. I don't know. Before he could ask her anything else, she thrust a handful of dinars into his hand and leapt from the car. "I'm sorry," she called back. "I'm sorry I don't know."

LYING ON HER back, the bristle of her cropped hair her only pillow, she lifts thin arms above her and claps her palms together. "*Mazrooq wa Amreekah* very friends!" she says with a hollow laugh. "*Very friends.*"

That is when she hears the cry from next door, a low howling sound. Scrambling to her feet, she presses her palms against the cold plaster of the wall. Where has it come from? Is there another prisoner here? She wants to call out to him. The thought that she is not alone fills her with abrupt euphoria. Surely it is a man, though the voice had been distorted by pain. When it comes again, that desperate keening, she hears another voice with it, aggressive and punishing. Miranda clenches her bottom lip between her teeth to keep herself from crying out. Several thuds follow the shouting of the second man, followed by more cries of pain.

Miranda slides down the wall, letting the rough surface chafe her skin. She wants to press her fingers in her ears to block the sound but feels an obligation to listen. Somewhere on the other side of this wall is a man being tortured. Perhaps she is the only person aside from the jailer who knows this. Who is he? A Westerner? Or a Mazrooqi traitor to the cause? She cannot make out the language, only indistinct sounds. After what feels an eternity with her ear pressed against the plaster, the building falls silent. All night she curls close to the wall, forcing herself to bear aural witness should there be more. It is all she can do.

DECEMBER 12, 2010
Finn

A banging at the front gate makes it suddenly difficult for Finn to hear the voice on the other end of the phone. It's London calling, again. He paces the third floor, from his bedroom to the *diwan* to the bathroom, fingers tight around the mobile, agitated, restless. It's been nearly four months now, and his bosses are growing increasingly impatient. "We can't hold the job open for you indefinitely," Wilkins says. "We need a full-time head of mission there. It's a critical country, we know you understand this. Celia is doing a fine job, but she's due back for language training in a few months. You heard she's going to Islamabad?"

Finn has. But he is having a difficult time trying to work up a panic over losing his job when something—someone—so much more significant is missing. He speaks seven languages; he understands development issues; he is knowledgeable about trade and business. If all else fails, he can teach etiquette classes. He will never go hungry. At the moment, working on anything other than finding his wife and raising his daughter is inconceivable. There will be no other work for him until Miranda comes home or her remains arrive in a body bag.

"I understand your predicament," Finn says. "And I am in no position to tell you what to do. But we're getting close; you heard we just missed her. The Americans think she's alive. It may not be long now."

"Finn. Listen to me. I'm going to be frank with you. Even if Miranda does turn up, we're going to send her straight back to London. Chances are good she'll need some kind of treatment, medical or psychological. Things won't just go back to normal. In fact, the chances of you being reinstated are infinitesimal."

Finn holds the phone away from his ear, as if to keep the words from reaching him. He stares at the bare walls around him, longing for distraction. He hasn't hung anything on the walls, save for a few of Cressie's drawings in the kitchen, because he didn't plan to stay here for long.

"Hello? Finn?"

He moves the phone fractionally closer. "Yes."

"Think about these things, Finn. We don't know what shape she will be in, should we find her. You know I hate to bring this up, but we owe it to you to be honest."

"Yes." Finn doesn't trust himself to say more.

"You would be better off waiting for her in London, Finn. Think of your daughter. Think of her safety."

A flicker of rage ignites in his sternum. "Do you think that I don't?"

"Finn. Please."

"I'm not coming back, Wilkins. Not without my wife."

There is silence on the other end, then a sigh. "Another month or two at the most."

"Thank you. I appreciate it." The banging at the gate is growing more frantic. Finn walks downstairs to Cressie's playroom, keeping the phone at his ear. The room is empty, the bare stone floor littered with stuffed bears and rabbits, colored plastic cups, Richard Scarry books, beads from broken necklaces. "Gabra?" he calls, returning to the hallway.

"I'll go, sir." Gabra emerges from the bathroom carrying Cressie and hands her to her father. Finn sets the phone down to settle his daughter on his left hip bone. She is getting too heavy to carry for long. With his right hand, he picks up the mobile. "Can I ring you later? There's someone at the door."

"I hope you're being careful who you let in, Finn. It's not like you're inconspicuous there."

"I'll speak with you tomorrow, Wilkins." He flips the phone shut and slips it into his pocket. Cressie wriggles in his arms, protesting her confinement.

"Okay," he says. "Run along and explore." She is getting increasingly reckless now that she is steady on her feet, falling a few more times every day. The bruises and skinned knees do not daunt her; she stubbornly gets back up and charges on. She'd probably hold her own running with the parentless tribes on the streets. He worries constantly about the stone stairs, their lethal edges, their uneven heights. He still trips going up them at least once a day. Safety stair gates don't seem to exist here; he has looked. Gabra must be his stair gates, his poison control center, the eyes in the back of his head.

Cressie toddles off toward her playroom, no doubt in search of a bear or her growing pebble collection, kept in a discarded Girl-brand ghee can. Gabra has dressed her in another one of her Ethiopian outfits. They are gorgeous, but Finn worries that his staff—his former staff and Gabra—are spending money they don't have to outfit his daughter. She has at least five different hand-embroidered shirts now. He has already increased Gabra's salary twice.

"Sir? Ambassador sir?" Gabra is running up the stairs, breathless. "It's Tazkia, sir. She says please she has only a moment." Behind her, Finn spies the tiny form, familiar to him despite the fact that she is completely covered, even her eyes. He has never seen her eyes covered before.

Tazkia pauses at the top of the stairs, unsure where to go. "Ambassador Finn," she says. "I need to speak quickly. I am not officially here, I am with Aaqilah. But it is an urgent matter."

Finn waves her toward the stairs. "You are not here," he says gravely. "In fact, I'm not even sure who you are."

She skitters up the stairs to the *diwan*, her *abaya* rustling around her like autumn leaves. Without waiting for an invitation, she kneels on the gold cushions, tucking her shoeless feet underneath her. "I know I am safe here with you, but no one else knows this," she says. "We are so backward we think men think only of one thing. But I have had to put my fear away because I have a greater fear. Ambassador Finn, Miranda, she was doing some paintings with me. Paintings of me."

Finn nods, sinking onto the cushions opposite her, careful to keep a distance. Sitting on the floor, or this close to the floor, is always difficult for him. His legs are too long, too stiff. Unable to sit cross-legged, he bends one knee to the ceiling and one to the side.

"She told you?" There is alarm in her voice.

"Only that she was doing some paintings of you. I know nothing about them, I promise you. She never showed them to me. I swear, Tazkia, she would never violate your privacy."

"I didn't think so. She knows how dangerous . . . We were going to burn them, we set a date. Ambassador Finn, I try to be patient. I did not want to disturb you in this time. I hoped that Miranda, we would find her before now. But I cannot wait any longer. I need to get those paintings. I need to destroy them myself. Miranda said the place where they are is so secret she is the only one with a key. So I believe they are safe, but I need your help to get them out so I can be sure."

A current of fear flashes through Finn. Dear god, he had forgotten the secret paintings. Miranda had kept them locked in the safe room near their bedroom in the Residence, and he hadn't thought to remove them when he left, distracted as he was by grief. To be honest, he hadn't even remembered they were there. He would have had second thoughts about opening her cupboard, seeing things not meant for his eyes. But he could have moved them safely, he could have found a way not to see them. He is an idiot. There is little chance Celia would have found them; she is there only temporarily after all, and is staying in the Minister's Suite rather than the master bedroom, communicating her hope that Finn will soon return. Does Tazkia even know she's there? He doesn't want to ask.

Tazkia's hands tremble in her lap, twisting the straps of a small purple purse. Her head is turned toward him, and he is sure her eyes are fixed on his, though he cannot see them. She has not removed her veil.

"I think I know where they are," he says, carefully. "And they are locked up. It is true that only Miranda had a key." He had given it to her. And to the Overseas Security Manager. Norman. Shit. But he would have no reason to be poking around the house. Would he? Finn does not say this. There is no point in unduly alarming Tazkia. "Look, try not to worry. I will find Miranda's key—it must be in her purse with the rest of her keys—and go to the Residence tomorrow."

"But no one must see them, please! Not you, not anyone."

Finn thinks for a moment. "We'll go together," he finally says. "You can take them yourself. We will take a large case for them. Are you able to come with me?"

She nods. "I will find a way to come. But I don't know where I will keep them. I will have to destroy them. It is too dangerous for me. Will you help me?"

"Of course." While the thought of destroying anything created by his wife's hand is almost unbearable, Tazkia's life is at stake. He doesn't have to have seen the paintings to guess at their content. Miranda would have protected her student at any cost; he dimly remembers her saying she and Tazkia had plans to destroy them. But what was she thinking? Nudes, in this country? He'd known this before, of course, on some unspoken level. But it had always been his policy not to meddle with Miranda's work. She was constrained enough by life with him; he wanted her art to be free. But Jesus, maybe not *this* free.

Tazkia stands, fumbles in her purse, and pulls out a phone. "Text me from this tomorrow," she says. "It is my sister's. You can give it back later."

Finn pockets the phone. "Tazkia, nothing will happen to you," he says. "I promise."

DECEMBER 25, 2010
Finn

Finn watches his small daughter push her new car across the carpet and tries to smile. "Daddy!" she yelps with joy. "Look, look!" She has stuffed the car, which Finn had painstakingly carved from the ubiquitous Girl ghee tins (carefully curling down their sharp edges with pliers), with seven of her favorite bears. There are two Corduroys, a black bear, a blue bear on a key chain, and three stiff little brown bears in formal wear. Had he been alone, he would have avoided Christmas entirely. But he has a child. And children must have Christmas.

It was Christmas that made him first want children—many, many children. His Christmases with his parents had been happy but quiet. His father always put on King's College, Cambridge's Festival of Nine Lessons and Carols while they opened presents and cooked his special Christmas breakfast of French toast stuffed with cream cheese, walnuts, and maple syrup (Canadian, naturally). It was pretty much the only day of the year that he cooked. His mother sat in her nightgown sipping tea until about noon, exclaiming with delight over every poetry book and silk scarf he gave her. But Finn had always longed for the happy ruckus of brothers and sisters and cousins that he read about in his books and heard about from his friends. "You're lucky," said his friend Irwin, who had six older siblings. "Only one of us can open a present at a time so we have to wait ages to open all of them." Still, Finn thought it must be wonderful to have siblings, even if they did borrow and break your toys. There would be someone to play with when your mother went back to her books and your father headed out to work a holiday shift to make double pay.

It surprised him to have reached such an advanced age without children, given how much he had always wanted them. But then, it had taken so long for him to meet Miranda. Now they might never have more, even if she did safely return. It had taken over a year for them to conceive Cressida. After the first several months, they had begun to worry. Had they left it too late? Could something be wrong?

Finn had volunteered to be tested first. "But it must be me," Mira had said. "My age. I'll see a doctor for a blood test." They had gone together to the Mazrooqi-German Hospital, Finn heading upstairs (trailed by four hulking shadows) to the urologist and Mira to the Russian gynecologist on the ground floor. Only Yusef had followed him to the door of the doctor's office, the rest of the men spreading down the tiled hallway outside, to protect him from any terrorist who might try to shoot his way into the examining room.

With little preamble, the doctor had handed him a little paper cup, the kind you drink orange squash out of at children's parties. "Take it home," he'd said. "Bring it back here when you're done." Given that the Residence was nearly a half-hour drive from the hospital, Finn had thought this an inefficient way to proceed. Surely the sperm would degrade or something on the ride back? Should they be exposed to air for so long?

"Don't you have a room here?" he'd asked. The doctor had looked up at him, his bushy, dark eyebrows drawn together with concern. This obviously was not a question he got very often. Yet a glance toward the door—and the armed men lurking behind it—had apparently reminded him that this was a patient to be indulged. "Follow me," he'd said.

He had led Finn down the hall and knocked on a closed door. Another doctor, older, with silver hair slicked back from his forehead, had peered out. Behind him, Finn could see a small man clutching a sheet around his naked chest. "We need the room," his doctor had said. *"For the ambassador."* Finn had felt heat rising to his face as the silver-haired doctor swung open the door, took the arm of his patient, and helped him into a pair of slippers before pulling him into the hallway, still dressed only in a sheet. The patient's slack, sorrowful face had showed no surprise. This was the kind of treatment he expected from life.

"*Sa'adat as-safir,*" the doctor had said, ushering Finn into the abandoned room. "Do you need anything?"

Mutely, Finn had shaken his head, his fingers in danger of crumpling the paper cup. Yusef had hovered in the doorway. Gently, he'd touched Finn's elbow. "Take your time, sir," he said.

The doctor had shut the door.

It was hard to imagine a situation less conducive to masturbation, but he'd managed to cover the bottom of that cup. He had to, if only to make the little man's exile worthwhile. As Mira had predicted, there wasn't anything wrong with him. "I knew you had swimmers," she'd said. But there wasn't anything especially wrong with her either. It was probably simply anxiety that had kept them from conceiving thus far. Still, she was older now, and a second miracle might be too much to ask.

She had been shocked that he wouldn't consider adoption, but he honestly felt that he could never love a stranger's child with its alien genes as much as he loved Cressie, child of his flesh. Wouldn't they always be worrying about what might lie hidden in a strange child's DNA? Genetic diseases, antisocial behaviors, inconvenient allergies—the possibilities were infinite. Every day scientists were discovering new ways in which our genes mold our personalities and behavior. At least with their own child there would be no surprises. Or at least fewer. It was the most serious argument he and Miranda had had in their short marriage. "It's just, you're so *good* with kids," she'd said, uncomprehendingly. "At the children's Christmas party, you were like a kid *magnet*. Do you really mean to tell me you don't love those children?"

Of course he loved those children. But not as he loved his own. And it would not be fair to ask another child to live in the shadow of his uncomplicated love for Cressida.

HE HAD DONE his best to create a festive Christmas for his daughter, hanging the stocking Negasi had knitted for her in the *diwan* under the Star of David stained-glass window and helping her to make gingerbread Christmas biscuits to leave for Santa. While Finn's mother had made shortbread smothered in green and red hundreds-and-thousands, Miranda had always preferred gingerbread people. Not only people—she would make dinosaurs and compli- cated flowers and the Snow Queen from *The Nutcracker*, first drawing them on cardboard, then steering a knife through the dough to cut around the shapes. She did this even before they had Cressida, and when their daughter was still too tiny to eat them. It amused Finn that Miranda was so averse to cooking a meal but would spend entire days on holiday cookies. Icing them involved a palette of twenty different colors. No one decorated gingerbread cookies like Miranda. They were miniature masterpieces. Eating them always felt deeply disrespectful. This year he and Cressie had stuck to simpler shapes: bells, stars, trees, little girls.

This was the first Christmas that Cressie could really appreciate; she had been less than a year old for her first one and had slept through most of it, thank god. He and Miranda had hosted a party for all of their friends remaining in the country over the holidays, including not only the obligatory British diplomats but also dozens of Miranda's friends from the Old City and her travels. There was too much food, too much champagne, too much dancing. No one had gone home until long after midnight, and the house had been a minor catastrophe. He and Miranda had fallen asleep on the floor by the faux fireplace, naked and entwined, until Cressida woke up hungry around 3:30 a.m. It was the best Christmas of his life.

This morning, he made Cressida a bastardized version of her grandfather's stuffed French toast, using brown sugar instead of maple syrup. Cressie had been too excited to eat much but seemed to appreciate his efforts, painting her cheeks with cream cheese. Wiping her face, Finn was seized by a spasm of grief; his parents will never know his daughter. She will never know them. In fact, Miranda's father is likely to be the only grandparent in her life. For the millionth time, he wished he came from a large family, with seven siblings, dozens of first cousins, aunts and uncles and grandmas galore. He was too alone in the world.

When Cressie had finished pulling all the small toys and books and a satsuma from her stocking, the two of them had spent the morning patting pastry into tins to make a dozen mince pies. It wasn't Christmas without mince pies. Miranda had her gingerbread cookies; Finn had his pies. While they were cooking, Finn had opened the bottle of champagne Negasi had smuggled over along with a Tupperware box of sausage rolls. By the time Cressie had finished opening her gifts the champagne was nearly gone. Her grandfather had sent a packet of glow-in-the-dark stars through the diplomatic bag, and the Residence staff had all sent over small gifts of clothing and sweets. Tucker had stopped by after breakfast to present Cressie with a tiny bear dressed in the uniform of the Royal Military Police. "Your very own bodyguard," he'd said. "May you never need him."

Now, Cressie drives the car all over the *diwan*, losing and picking up bears along the way. Finn lies on his side, sipping the last of the flattening champagne and watching her determined little face.

"*Yalla! Yalla*, bears!" she cries. "We have to hurry."

"Where are the bears going?" asks Finn idly.

Cressie looks up at him. "To find Mummy," she says. Her voice is matter-of-fact, devoid of sadness or sentiment. Finn wonders what she remembers of her mother, if anything. When she says "Mummy," does she still have an image of Miranda's face? Or has Mummy become an abstract concept? Finn talks to her about Miranda as much as he can, shows her photographs, trying to keep her from forgetting. Unsure of how to explain Miranda's absence, he has told her that her mother went for a walk and became lost. Kind of like Hansel and Gretel. Cressie always greets this story with an expression of such skepticism that he wonders if she believes any of it. "Mummies don't get lost," she'd told him finally. "Ah," he'd said, struggling for words. "But she must be lost, or she would have come back by now to find you. She would never choose to be away from you, therefore she must not be able to find her way home." At this point usually Cressida's attention wandered and she went back to organizing her bears or collecting the tiny green raisins from the cracks of the kitchen linoleum.

Now he is so lost in thought, it takes him a minute to register the sudden silence. Cressida has wandered out of the *diwan* while Finn, heavy with the champagne, feels unable to move from the cushions. Shaking his head to clear it, he stumbles to his feet to find his daughter. It doesn't take long; the minute he steps out in the hallway he can see her little bare feet. She is lying facedown across the threshold of her room, arms akimbo, the new bodyguard bear clutched in her left hand, its beret already coming loose. When he reaches her, he can hear the reassuring sound of her congested snores. What time is it?

Past nap time, evidently. Bending over, he gently lifts his daughter, rolls her limp body toward his chest, and places her in her cot.

HE AND CRESSIDA are eating an early supper when they hear a banging at the gate, followed by the murmur of voices. Whoever it is has met Bashir's approval—a moment later Finn hears a voice calling from the courtyard. He runs down the steps barefoot and opens the door to a breathless Madina, her arms full of packages. "A few things Santa left at my house by mistake," she says.

"Madina," says Finn. "You're Muslim."

"Yeah, so? He's a broad-minded guy. And don't forget my dad's Catholic. I think that entitles me, no?" She starts up the stairs ahead of him, pulling up the hem of her dragging *abaya* to reveal glittering red pumps. Santa, indeed.

"Mina!" Cressie is overjoyed to see their neighbor, abandoning her carrots to launch herself at Madina's knees.

"Merry Christmas, *habibti*! These are for you." Madina carefully sets her stack of packages in the middle of the hallway and picks up Cressie to kiss her. Finn looks at the pile of boxes, all wrapped in glittering red and green paper. Where did they come from?

"They're from the girls," Madina explains. "They left them with me, for all the usual reasons."

Cressie is already investigating the boxes, pulling at the bows. "Open open open!" she says. Finn frowns at her. "Please?" she adds hastily.

"Okay, *habibti*, but upstairs, okay?" He and Madina carry the boxes up to the *diwan* and settle on the cushions to unwrap them. Finn tears off the paper of a square package the size of a place mat to find a small oil painting of a woman. She stands in front an easel, her curly hair held back by a green scarf. Smiling. A smile he recognizes. Finn turns the wrapping paper over to look at the card. Nadia. It's a good likeness. He realizes suddenly that he doesn't have any paintings of Miranda. Vicenta must have masses of them, but apparently she took them all home.

Cressida runs her fingers across the paint and looks up at Finn. "Mummy?"

"Mummy," he confirms.

Together they unwrap the remaining paintings, Finn saving Tazkia's for last. Every single one is a portrait of Miranda. "I had some photos," explains Madina. "So they worked from those." There is a painting of Miranda standing outside of the Grand Mosque, her long white skirt and blouse billowing in the wind; one of her standing by an Old City produce stand, a fat yellow pomegranate in each hand; and one of her sitting meditatively in the *diwan*, almost precisely where he and Cressie now crouch. Tazkia's is slightly larger, rectangular. "Careful," he says as Cressida tears at the wrapping. When he has unwound the layers of paper, he props the painting against a cushion. It's a dancing scene. Someone's wedding. Girls in gaudy sequined gowns populate the periphery, twirling, hands in the air or on their hips, their faces blurred and unrecognizable. In the center is Mira, in a familiar ankle-length emerald dress, holding on to the small hands of her daughter. Cressida, in a white lace dress he'd bought for her in London, is laughing up at her mother, her lips parted to show tiny white teeth. Mira gazes down at her daughter, smiling, as though there were no one else in the room.

DECEMBER 8, 2010
Miranda

It has been six days. She counts them now, unnerved by how unmoored she has become in time. It is so hard to keep track in a country with no familiar seasons. Six days that Luloah has been without her. Six more days plus several months Cressida has been without her. Every morning, afternoon, and evening after she has finished her allotted cup of tea, Miranda compresses her engorged breasts, taking care to keep her dirty hands from touching her nipples, squeezing milk into the cup. She drinks it herself. She has never heard of a mother drinking her own breast milk, but it couldn't hurt. And it will keep the milk coming a little longer. Just in case. Hope is a resilient little beast. You can bludgeon it with reality within an inch of its life, and somehow it drags its mutilated body up from its earthen death-bed and goes on.

The nightmares have returned. It wasn't long after she moved in with Finn that Miranda began dreaming horrors that left her panting and sweaty. They weren't mysterious or difficult to interpret. In the first dream she remembered, she was getting on a plane in Texas, a state Miranda had never had any inclination to visit (except maybe Austin. She wouldn't mind going to Austin someday). Her host, who was to take her to the airport, made her late by taking her on a tour of an oil refinery. By the time she found a clock, she had only an hour to get to the airport and onto the plane to Mazrooq. There was no way she could make it. Her host, a tanned, amiable older man, did not seem worried. But he obligingly hustled Miranda to the airport. As she was checking in with two women at the gate, they conferred with heads bent together before turning to her. "Look, we're not supposed to do this," they said. "But we like you. Don't get on this flight."

She looked at them in alarm. "Suspected terrorists."

They nodded. "And several armed men." The small plane was to be packed with air marshals. Miranda looked at her host, who nodded. She realized he was an air marshal, and was one of the armed men protecting the flight. "This is why you wanted me to miss the plane," she said.

"Yes."

But she got on. Because at the end of the flight was Finn.

IN HER DREAMS she was often naked, her clothing constantly disappearing. She would put on black skirt over black skirt, and they would dissolve into the air. Men were knocking at the door, and she could not cover herself in time. Even in her dreams, she could not protect herself from men. Finn never appeared in her dreams, staying just out of reach. Either she could not get home to him or he could not get home to her.

Only in the months before her capture had the dreams subsided, had she relaxed into her life. Now everything for which she has been grateful is gone. Her love, her daughter, her work, her home, her little Luloah. (For if Luloah was not hers, whose was she?) She still has her life, she supposes. If you can call this life. And relative health, all things considered. She is filthy, covered with insect bites, some of which have become infected sores, and her skin seems to be turning gray. But nothing serious. No, the only serious injury is the evisceration of her heart.

Before Finn, Miranda had contemplated having a child but never longed for one. Her biological clock had been faulty, ticking too quietly for her to hear. She and Vícenta had discussed the possibility of a baby from time to time, but neither of them had felt strongly enough to actively pursue it. They were so involved with their work, their friends, and each other. It had felt like enough.

At first it had felt like that with Finn. There was no intimation that their life together was lacking in any way. He was enough. They were enough. They traveled, they stayed in bed for entire afternoons, they read plays and poetry aloud, they took seven-hour treks in the mountains. It was he who had first broached the subject of a child, one weekend in Istanbul as they lay naked in bed demolishing the free fruit platter. "I'm happy with our life the way it is," he'd said. "And I could be happy with our life together forever. But I wonder if we wouldn't enjoy raising a little person together."

Miranda had paused mid-grape to look at him. He had been smiling, his tone free from anxiety or urgency.

"Finn," she'd said. "You're not a morning person."

"True. But if I can manage to get out of bed on time for work, surely I could rouse myself for something—someone—slightly more important?"

So they had pulled a sheaf of hotel stationery onto the bed and written up a list, Pros and Cons.

> Pros: Free entertainment. Unconditional love. The chance
> to observe human development up close. Opportunity to
> buy limitless stuffed animals and reread favorite children's
> books. *Harriet the Spy*; *A Wrinkle in Time*; and *The Lion, The*

Witch and the Wardrobe. Lego. Fulfillment of biological destiny. Contribute a new member to the Democratic Party (Miranda). Add voter to the Green Party (Finn). Someone to visit the nursing home and make sure we don't get bedsores in our dotage. A reason to sing in public without shame. People will stop asking us when we will have kids. Christmas.

Cons: Travel more difficult. Life more expensive (though not here). Diapers/Nappies. Environmentally unsound. Early mornings (not an issue for Miranda, who always wakes with the light). University tuition. Child would eventually be a teenager with access to Facebook. Bullying. Eating disorders. Public tantrums. Strangers glaring at us on airplanes. Constant guilt.

But they had failed to list the greatest con of all: the possibility of unabsorbable loss.

JANUARY 2, 2011
Imaan

Imaan sits in the dim hut across from her aunt, the question burning in her throat. She has been here two hours now, and there has been no sign of a child. No crying, no gurgles of joy. Nothing but an almost eerie silence. Why shouldn't she ask about the child? She chides herself. Isn't it natural to take an interest in a baby? It has been more than a month since her last visit to Aisha. To visit sooner, which has never been her habit, would have looked suspicious. She has handed over an invitation to another cousin's wedding—fortunately there is nearly always a cousin getting married, except during Ramadan. Fidgeting with the embroidered hem of her *abaya*, she misses her son. Without him she feels purposeless, doesn't know what to do with her hands. What did she do with her life before she was a mother? Kabir has focused her energies, lent them meaning. But she hadn't wanted distractions on this trip. Dry-mouthed, she picks up her tea-cup and finds it empty save for a sticky, sugary residue.

"I'll make some more," says Aisha, heaving herself to her feet.

"Please don't trouble yourself," says Imaan. "Sit. You must be tired, caring for those men all day."

Aisha only gives a curt nod and slumps back to the floor. "I have no complaints, praise Allah."

"Auntie," Imaan starts. There is no reason not to ask. There is *no reason* not to ask. "Where is the baby who was here last time? Is she here?"

Aisha lifts her head and stares at her for a moment. "That child," she says and then stops.

"She isn't dead?" Imaan's stomach tightens.

"She was very sick, Imaan. Very sick. She wouldn't eat."

Imaan thinks she might vomit from fearful anticipation.

"She would not take a bottle or drink the tea we gave her in a cup. But, Imaan, we could not allow that child to die. You don't know who that child is. Who her father was. Because of this, we could not allow her to die."

"But if she won't eat?"

"She will eat now. We have sent her to someone who can feed her."

Someone with milk, Imaan presumes. Could it be Miranda? Was she here, and if so, where has she gone? And who are the little girl's parents? Careful, she warns herself. You don't want to know too much. Aisha's men are dangerous men.

"When she can eat beans and bread, she will come back here."

"She will be okay?"

"*Insha'allah.* We must pray for her."

NADIA LISTENS TO her cousin's story with wide eyes. The two women have closeted themselves in Imaan's *diwan,* with the windows shut. "And you didn't ask who the father was? Even after she men-tioned it?"

Imaan shakes her head.

"Or where the girl was sent?"

"It didn't seem like she wanted to say." Somehow Nadia always makes her feel like an ignorant country girl. She envies her cousin's bravery.

"Imaan, think. Who important died recently?"

Imaan stares at her, eyes widening. "Can you really not remember?"

Nadia's hands fly to her mouth. "Forgive me. I wasn't thinking. I haven't forgotten. I will never forget. I promise you, Imaan."

They sit for a moment staring at the thin, filthy red carpet between them, the threadbare pillows, remembering the funeral procession through the streets, their keening mothers, the blanket-swaddled body lifted above the crowds, tilting over their heads. He had been their inspiration, their spiritual father, their protector from the president's men. From the president's planes.

Abruptly Nadia looks up. "You don't think—? Did he have—?"

Imaan slowly nods. "I think so, yes. With his last wife. I had forgotten."

"But she's a *girl*."

"A girl with a very important daddy. The most important daddy a girl could possibly have."

JANUARY 3, 2011
Finn

Kaia and Doortje sit next to each other on the pristine white sofa, their thighs and hands touching, seeking comfort. Fear hasn't loosened its grip; it is engraved on their faces. The women are thin, pale, blue veins showing through their wrists and temples, though they said their captors had fed them regularly and well. "Captivity doesn't improve appetite," Kaia says, smiling faintly. They are exhausted, having already endured their first debriefing.

Three days after the cash (sent via two separate couriers from Dubai) had been tossed, as instructed, over the fence of a small cement factory in a remote northern town, the women had been rolled out of the back of a van outside the InterContinental hotel. ("It's always the

InterContinental," the Dutch consultant had commented. "A perennial favorite with kidnappers across the region. I'm surprised they haven't launched a special hostage drop-off area.")

"I'm sorry to have to ask you questions now," says Finn softly. "I promise I'll be as brief as I can. I know you are anxious to get home to your families."

"It's all right," says Doortje. "But I am afraid we won't be much help. We haven't seen Miranda since the night we were first taken." The women take turns telling their story again, finishing each other's sentences. It is a story they have obviously been telling each other for months, looking for clues, looking for sense.

"Mukhtar was shot?" says Finn. "Is he dead?" He must be. Otherwise he would have returned to the Residence. And this means— Finn's heart lifts—this means that that shot he heard on the phone was not for his wife. There was also the drawing to prove that she had survived that first attack, though she may have been injured. Still, he was famished for proof, there could not be enough proof, until he could brush his fingertips against Miranda's flesh, warm and living.

The women shrug. "We didn't see him after that."

"So the men who originally took you, they still had Miranda when you were given to the second group of men? She wasn't given to anyone else?" If it was an opportunistic kidnapping, perhaps the original group of men was less lethal than any group to which she could be sold. AQ, to name one.

"We were all traded together the first time," says Kaia. Finn notices a slight tremor in the fingers resting on her thigh. "And then later we were given to the others."

"Did you ever overhear anyone mention Miranda?"

"They wouldn't have known her name," Kaia reminds him.

"Of course. But did you hear them mention, 'the other woman,' anything like that?"

Doortje leans forward. "Neither of us speaks much Arabic, so we didn't understand a lot of what went on. But we did manage to ask them why she was taken somewhere else. Because at that point they couldn't have known her nationality or her position. So why would they separate her?"

"I think I heard them say 'the other one isn't worth anything,' at some point," says Kaia. "Which only makes sense if they were aware that she was from a country that wouldn't pay a ransom." She flushes slightly with the guilt of surviving, returning. "And that we were from ransom-paying countries. We had said we were all French, so if they believed us, why would they have separated Miranda?"

Finn looks at them with renewed interest. "So . . . it is possible that they *did* know who she was." The women shrug again. "Which means . . ." He isn't sure he wants to know what this means. "This was planned," he concludes. "She was targeted. Or, you all were, but they had plans for her entirely unrelated to their finances."

DECEMBER 2010
Miranda

When Miranda opens her eyes, the darkness remains as pure as when she had them closed. What has woken her? The man next door? Another rat? A scorpion? Her pulse quickening, she sits, scooting toward the wall, scraping the back of her head on the plaster. Her body tenses, bracing for the inhuman—or all too human—howls from the adjoining room. Only then does she hear the knocking. It is soft yet insistent. What kind of guard knocks before entering a prison cell? thinks Miranda crossly.

"*Aiwa,*" she says without expression, without moving. It's a bit early for breakfast. Unless Ramadan has started. Didn't they just have Ramadan before she was captured? She cannot remember. Maybe it's her turn for a beating? The door creaks open and a man stands there, next to the guard. He is dressed like the guard, in desert camouflage and a puffy down parka. Mazrooqis run for their winter coats every time the temperature dips below seventy degrees Fahrenheit. Both men are shorter and slighter than she is. I could take them in a fair fight, she thinks. If there is such a thing. And then she remembers the guns. The great equalizers. And these are AK-47s; she has checked. In fact, she has studied them, trying to remember everything Tucker and Mukhtar taught her, just in case. She's so busy examining the guns again that it takes her a moment to realize that he is carrying something, a small bundle in a blanket. Not another one, she thinks. I cannot take another one. My heart can only break so many times. But when the man holds out the bundle to her, the child gives a familiar cry, reaching scrawny, grayish brown arms up to Miranda.

"Luloah!" she exclaims, taking the child. Then, wary of exposing her joy to hostile scrutiny, she falls silent, clutching Luloah to her chest. The little girl is frighteningly light again. Her face is pointed, elfin, not rounded like a baby's. Miranda wants to nurse her right away, but she must wait for the men to leave. They stand there, looking awkward. "I am to tell you that this child is not yours," says the man who had carried Luloah. "But she must not die."

"No," Miranda agrees. "She must not."

The men still stand there, staring at her with the child.

"Law samaht," she finally says. "This child needs to eat."

Looking slightly embarrassed, the men shuffle backward and reach for the door.

THERE IS A slight improvement in her food after Luloah's arrival. They bring her glasses of milk, of mango juice. She receives beans with her bread; she hasn't had much more than bread and rice for days. Sometimes there is even a banana or a couple of withered dates.

It hadn't been easy to get Luloah to nurse again. She had lost so much strength that it was once more difficult for her to suck. But Miranda was patient and determined. Soon, she thinks, she might be able to start giving Luloah a bit of her fruit. She instinctively knows to conceal this information from the guards. Because if Luloah can eat solid food, she might be able to survive without Miranda. But perhaps Luloah simply hadn't been willing to accept food from anyone else. Maybe that is why they gave her back.

Miranda is aware this is a temporary situation; the guards have made that clear. But she doesn't allow herself to dwell on this. Instead, she redoubles her efforts to survive, to stay strong. She eats every scrap of food, even when she has no appetite. In the mornings, when

Luloah naps, she does jumping jacks and presses her palms into the filthy floor to practice sun salutations. Something to keep her muscles from wasting entirely. Perhaps most important, she makes an effort with the guards. Swallowing her revulsion, she says good morning, good afternoon, and good evening. She asks them how they are. Surprised and wary, they are slow to respond, but finally, they do. They must be almost as bored as she has been. Every week or so a guard hands her a new bundle of clothing. She wonders where it comes from. Mazrooqi women in the cities never wear skirts like this; they wear skimpy dresses or tight jeans under their *abayas*. The customary covering keeps them from needing any other modest clothing.

She asks for a Quran and a few days later, for water and a bar of soap. "To wash myself for prayers." She doesn't know why she hasn't thought of this before. She uses the pitchers of water to bathe Luloah first, and then herself. Last, she rinses out the cloth diaper. When it is warm enough, she leaves Luloah naked on her sleeping mat and tries to rush her to the chamber pot in the corner when her face screws up and her body begins to strain. Every other minute of the day she spends feeding, entertaining, and rocking Luloah. When the cries of the man next door seep through the wall, she sings, loudly. Luloah must not absorb the toxins in those sounds. A few days after she first heard him, Miranda had listened to the man praying, in Arabic. He must be Mazrooqi. Why is he being tortured? Why torture one of their own and not her, citizen of a loathed enemy country? But these are questions she knows better than to ask the guards.

In the mornings, she lays Luloah in the tiny square of sunlight, hoping she will soak up enough UVB rays for her body to manufacture a few vital specks of vitamin D. When the girl has regained a little strength, Miranda props her up against a corner to practice sitting while she reads to her from the Quran. Luloah is, after all, a Muslim child. For at least half an hour every day she lays Luloah on her stomach so she can practice lifting her head, just as she had done with Cressida (who had hated "tummy time" and screamed until Miranda rolled her over). But most of all, she talks.

She begins with the memories she has been cataloging to keep from going mad, telling Luloah about her first drawings, the round figures with scribbles of hair and spindly arms and legs her mother had called her pod people. From there she moves on to school, paintings, boyfriends, girlfriends, art shows, college, travels, Vicenta, Finn. She tells her everything. When she has nothing more to say about her own life, she recounts every Islamic myth she can remember. Her women had told her dozens, though she can remember only a few. She remembers the *mi'raj*, the mythical predatory rabbit with a spiraling unicorn horn—not only because she has a fondness for bunnies but because the word *mi'raj* also means Mohammed's ascent into Heaven. She also tells Luloah about the *buraq*, the winged horse that carried the Prophet to Heaven during the *mi'raj*. She describes the *ababil* birds that allegedly protected Mecca from invading elephants by dropping bricks on the invaders. "Do you think Mazrooq ever had elephants?" Miranda asks her small charge. "And what ever became of the *ababil*, I wonder?"

As she talks, Luloah stares up at her with those huge, dark eyes and clings to her toes for dear life. She is a serious child, more solemn than Miranda remembers. Had this girl really ever laughed? Occasionally she ventures a few syllables out loud, for which Miranda congratulates her. She still speaks to her in a mix of Arabic and French, afraid to be overheard in English. Her dreams mingle these languages, only these, as if she has forgotten even how to think in her native tongue. It is too dangerous to think in English. Though they must know who she is by now. Finn wouldn't have been able to conceal her disappearance for long. *Where is he?* Cressie must be speaking in sentences by now. But this line of thinking leads only to bottomless despair. Better to focus on the child in front of her, the child who curls into her at night, pressing her snotty, drooling, filthy little face into Miranda's neck.

In an attempt to summon a smile from her grave charge, Miranda plays patty-cake with her, and Miss Mary Mac. She sings "Head and shoulders, knees and toes, knees and toes," lightly touching each body part as it is mentioned. It doesn't rhyme in French or in Arabic, but still. She attempts to translate "The Grand Old Duke of York," one of Finn's favorites. *"Al 'atheem duq al-York, qaada ashra alaaf rajul…"* It doesn't quite scan, but Luloah never complains. Miranda tells Luloah about the country in which she was born. "So many people here never leave their own neighborhood," she says to the child. "Some of my women have lived in Arnabiya their whole lives and have never been to the Old City. None of them have been to the deserts in the East or climbed the mountains in the West. You are not going to be like that. You live in an extraordinary country. You must see it all. I was lucky, *habibti,* I got to see it before the Brits locked me up in the Residence. Before I met your daddy—" Miranda stops, appalled by what she has just said. This is not her child, not Finn's. She pauses, takes a breath. Luloah simply looks at her, tiny eyebrows knitting together. "Before I met Finn, my husband, I traveled. Vicenta and I traveled together, and after she left I traveled alone. Especially when I knew I was about to lose my freedom."

Three weeks before she moved in with Finn, her Arabic teacher, Mahmoud, had driven her eight hours to the east, to the cities of mud-brick high-rises and fertile valleys where dates and honey were cultivated. This was what she had instead of a bachelorette party, a final taste of freedom.

"Shall I tell you the story, *habibti?* God knows we have time. And it's important that you know a little bit about your own country, no?" And she begins.

"We reached the first checkpoint outside of Arnabiya just before 9:00 a.m. There are checkpoints everywhere in your country, *habibti.* It makes getting around pretty tricky for a foreigner. But Mahmoud had brought a stack of about sixty copies of our permission-to-travel form, which he kept on the windshield and handed out at every stop. Fifteen minutes or so later, our police escort arrived, and we headed off to breakfast, the predictable *fool wa fasooleah* with stretchy white bread in a roadside *mat'am.* You've had a bit of that here, yes? When the guards aren't watching. Don't tell the French, but your people make better bread.

"Back on the road, we saw almost no other cars. We pulled over once, so I could photograph a mountain that looked like a camel's head. When I climbed out of the car, my camera swinging from my hand, a soldier by the side of the road forced a Kalashnikov into my arms. So Mahmoud took a picture of me, looking like every other adventure-seeking tourist here, holding the massive gun. I felt mildly ashamed, and of course the one thing running through my mind was that my father would *kill* me if he knew I was holding a gun. Funny that you can be in your late thirties and still worry what your father will think. I suppose that never goes away.

"We were about an hour outside Dibra, our first stop, when Finn texted me to say that a car bomb had just killed a van full of German tourists there, right on our route. Other friends also texted, saying, 'Turn around!' Mahmoud didn't seem remotely concerned, until all of *his* family members started calling to tell him he was insane to continue on our journey. They would not have worried were he alone, but he was with me, an ugly American, a walking, talking target. Mahmoud has about fifty or so immediate family members, meaning his phone rang pretty much nonstop. But we didn't turn around. Mahmoud had promised to show me his country's bounty, and damn it, he was going to show it to me.

"At every checkpoint, a police officer took a copy of our permission slip and asked my nationality. (This is something you will never have to worry about, my little Mazrooqi.) Every time, Mahmoud said I was French, while I kept my head scarf wrapped tightly around my head, my sunglasses obscuring my eyes, and stared demurely at my lap.

"We lost our police escort somewhere in the mountains before Dibra. 'I guess they think we're safe,' Mahmoud said, shrugging. He isn't much of a worrier, Mahmoud. But then in the city itself, we got *two* police cars, one to drive in front of us and one behind, which made us pretty conspicuous on the otherwise empty roads. Mahmoud conceded that it probably wouldn't be a good idea to spend the night there, but he thought we'd be pretty safe on a speed tour of the tourist attractions. After all, there had already been one bombing that day, what were the chances of another so soon? So we whipped past the massive dam, the temples, Dibra's Old City, so fast all of my photos are blurry. On the way back to town for lunch, we passed the remains of the car that had exploded earlier, behind pink police tape. It had shattered into such tiny pieces of confetti there was almost nothing left. Actually, you don't need that image in your brain. Forget I said that.

"Before lunch, we had to give our police escort money. When you get a police escort, you are responsible for the care and feeding of these men for the length of their time with you. Our first police escort demanded money before they turned us over to the second, whom we treated to lunch. It was the kind of restaurant you find everywhere here: a large, tiled room full of shouting men and abuzz with a thousand flies. Waiters spread newspapers over the long tables, banging down metal plates of rice and meat, tossing sheets of bread at diners like Frisbees. No menus in these places; they all serve the same thing. Mahmoud asked for lamb and rice, and *zabadi* and *khubz* for me. I was holding a pen and started doodling my name in Arabic on the newspaper. I wrote 'I am Miranda from France.' The men around us went into fits of excitement when they saw me forming Arabic letters. 'SHE WRITES ARABIC!' they shouted at each other. I felt like a child who had just learned to walk. You'll feel like that someday, *insha'allah*. Then the cook leaned out of the steaming kitchen window above us, and shouted to Mahmoud.

"'WHY IS SHE ONLY EATING YOGURT?'

"'SHE IS VERY POOR AND DOESN'T WANT TO SPEND MONEY.' This provoked laughter, as everyone knows that foreigners are rich!

"'HAHA! WHAT IS THE TRUTH? SHE IS TRAVELING AND SO ONLY WANTS TO EAT THE SMALL THINGS?'

"'THAT'S IT.'

"There were no other women in the restaurant, and the entire time we were there no one looked anywhere but at me.

"We left Dibra, with the car cooler packed with water and Pepsi. And thus began our journey through one of the vastest stretches of nothingness I have ever seen. Miles and miles of nothing. There was some relief in the swell of sand dunes, rising and subsiding like the sea. Families of camels strolled alongside our car, including many shaggy little babies. You would love the camels. I didn't know they came in so many colors; I liked the little black ones best because I'd never seen a black camel before.

"There were checkpoints every few minutes, an absurd, Kafkaesque number of checkpoints. About halfway to Qummash, we lost our police car escort, which was replaced with a police officer in our car. This police officer, who was also replaced at intervals, was laconic. He sat quietly, not even talking with Mahmoud. I found this odd, given that men in your country don't ever fall silent. I drifted off to sleep every few minutes, lulled by the incessant sameness of the landscape.

"The last police officer left us near Qummash, when the landscape began to change. Patches of date palms appeared, ornamenting the vast swaths of beige. The landscape had been just relentlessly khaki. And you know, I've never been a fan of neutral colors, *habibti*. I was so happy to see trees I wanted to get out and hug them.

"Then came a series of cute little villages, some with pink buildings! The sun began to slip in the sky. Things turned gold. I felt oddly tranquil. I'd been oddly tranquil ever since leaving the North. Maybe I was just happy to be alive, grateful that I had not been blown to smithereens in a car bomb?

"Twilight was descending as we arrived at the Hotel Noura. One of your country's most beautiful hotels, little one. With a pool! Streaked with dirt and sweat, I was desperate for a swim, so I changed and slipped into the water, and swam under a half-moon, in jasmine-scented air . . ." She is silent for a moment, remembering the bliss of that evening. How she misses this country.

"During my Arabic lesson Mahmoud gave me the verbs and nouns I would need to describe our day, and then I described it to him. *Dalā dalā.* Slowly, slowly. It's amazing how much better my Arabic has gotten since meeting you, *habibti*. Nothing educates like being kidnapped in a foreign land."

Miranda looks down at Luloah, who has gone limp and heavy in her arms. It was a wise choice to drift off before Miranda got to the part about the seven Japanese tourists who were blown up in the same exact spot where she and Mahmoud had stood to watch their first sunset in the East, on the cliffs overlooking the mud-brick city. She had almost forgotten how many near misses she had had. She wants to talk about the splendor of the land, the warmth of the people, but keeps tripping over guns and bombs. "I'm glad you're finding this all so riveting, *habibti*." Gently, she lays the child down beside her. "I just wanted you to know that all of your country is not like this. There is so much beauty out there, *habibti*, so much kindness. I won't let these assholes take that away from me, take this country away from me. The little mud cities in the East, the sunny beaches of the South, the jasmine of everywhere. Sleep, *ma petite puce*, and dream about these."

WITH LULOAH BACK at her side, Miranda thinks again of escape. She wants to get the child out before they come for her again. What kind of future could she have here? Like Miranda's students, like Tazkia, she would be taught to loathe her own body. She would be wrapped up in synthetic fibers, imprisoned by the wills of men, denied education. She could be married off to an old man at the age of twelve. Tazkia once told Miranda the story of a friend of her brother's who was forced to marry a girl who was raped and impregnated by her own father. Unmarried and pregnant, the girl could not accuse her own father. No one would believe her and her entire community would turn against her. So she accused Tazkia's brother's friend. He was imprisoned until he agreed to marry her, which he did. To his credit, he raised the boy as his own. He also had a second son with her. The girl, says Tazkia, is utterly submissive because she still feels guilt for having wrongly accused him, although her husband knows that she had no choice. He recently took a second wife, from the South, and the first wife said, "Well, of course he would want to do that, since he was forced to marry me." What is worse, the girl's mother knew that her husband was raping her daughter and did nothing about it. How can people be so inhuman? Miranda wonders. How could a *mother* continue to live and sleep with the rapist of her children? How could a *mother* not murder such a man? Miranda is a pacifist until she hears stories like these.

Clearly there are no plans for Miranda's release. If only she knew where she was, if only she knew what was outside. If only she knew if there were a reason they were holding her, other than her ability to feed Luloah. There must be. Unless the child is more important than she knows. She thinks about the guns and the size of the guards. She thinks about whether she could use a gun while holding a child. Does she remember how to sight, how to fire? She thinks about where she could hide. Surely if she could get out to a road, someone would pick her up. Ninety-nine percent of the people in this country are not terrorists. Ninety-nine out of one hundred drivers would stop to pick her up. What are the chances she would be kidnapped again?

This camp—or prison, or whatever it is—doesn't feel as isolated as her first. Outside she can hear cars rattling by, the muezzins of several mosques, the gasman banging his cans. These sounds suffuse her with equal parts hope and despair. There is only one door to her solid little room, and the only window is too tiny and high to be of any use. She considers throwing a note out the window before remembering she has no pen or paper. Here, she cannot even scratch an image in the dirt; the floor is smooth and hard.

"The guards are our only hope, *habibti*," she tells Luloah. "We've got to take down the guards."

DECEMBER 13, 2010
Finn

Finn had warned Celia he was coming. "I forgot something of Miranda's in the closet in the safe room," he said. "Some of her paintings." If Celia found this odd she didn't say. "I was wondering what was in there," she said over the phone from the embassy. "I haven't been able to find the key."

Finn apologized. He had only recently figured out where Miranda had kept it. He promised to leave it behind on the hall table, underneath the portrait of their monarch at her coronation. In turn, she had promised that no one would be in the Residence after 4:00 p.m., that he could have it to himself for two hours. That should be plenty of time for them to get all the paintings out.

Tazkia had arrived promptly on his doorstep in the Old City, an additional veil over her eyes. "There are times it is convenient to be a woman here," she says to him in Arabic. "Out of the house, we all look alike." In the taxi, she falls silent.

"What do you want to do with them?" he asks her.

"Burn them," she says without hesitation.

"You're sure? You don't want me to keep them somewhere safe for you?"

"Please, don't be upset, but that is too big a risk. I cannot relax until I know no one can use them to hurt me."

Finn nods. "I understand. You can burn them in our garden if you want."

"That is best, I think."

One of the guards unlocks the gate for them, his face impassive. He is supposed to know the name of everyone who enters the Residence, but Finn does not offer Tazkia's name. Together, Finn and Tazkia lug several large duffel bags through the garden and up the steps to the heavy wooden door. Celia has left it unlocked; there are guards, after all. In the front hallway, Tazkia stops to remove her shoes and Finn listens. Nothing. No clatter of pans from the kitchen, no swish of a broom. They proceed to the stairs, Tazkia finally flipping the *niqab* from her eyes. She takes the stairs two at a time and walks ahead of Finn, desperate purpose in her steps. When she arrives at the safe room, she stands waiting for him. The cramped hallway is dark, and he switches on the light.

"Please," says Tazkia, alarmed. "No light." Finn obliges before pulling the key to the cupboard from his pocket and sliding it into the lock. He twists it until he hears the bolt slide back and retreats into the bedroom without opening the door. "All yours." Tazkia pulls at the edge of the door with her fingertips until it swings open. A moment of silence, then a strangled cry.

"What is it?"

But Tazkia has sunk to her knees before the cabinet, her hands scrabbling at its floor, her fingertips searching the corners. "*Laa,*" she moans. *"Laa laa laa laa laa laa laa . . ."* Finn steps toward her and peers over her crouched form.

It is empty.

JANUARY 13, 2011
Miranda

Miranda is lying on her back playing airplane with Luloah, balancing the child on the soles of her upturned feet, when the guard knocks on the door with her lunch. Swiftly, Miranda lowers Luloah to the floor and yanks her skirt down to her ankles. *"Salaama aleikum,"* she says brightly, scrambling to her feet. Luloah remains in a sitting position, wobbling. Every day she manages to stay upright for a few moments longer.

The guard greets her and sets the tray down on the floor. Bread, beans, some sliced bananas. A tin cup of water. Luloah beams when she spots the banana. Stretching out her small hands, she lunges in its general direction, tipping herself over onto her stomach. Miranda grabs her, hoisting her up in her arms. "Not for you," she says pointedly. "You aren't ready yet." The child howls, uncomprehending. Miranda has been letting her have bananas for a couple of weeks now.

"Strong lungs," she says to the guard, who loiters in the doorway, studying the child with a fascination Miranda finds unnerving.

"Like her daddy," the guard murmurs softly.

"What?" Miranda's heart stutters. "Her daddy? Is he alive?"

The guard looks stricken. "You don't know?" he says. "Didn't someone tell you this child is special?"

"I know she is special," says Miranda, defensively, jiggling the girl in her arms to soothe her.

"Then you know why it is so important you keep her alive."

Miranda just stares at him.

"She is his only surviving child," he says. "So even though she is female we must keep her alive. When she is old enough to marry she will produce his heir."

Old enough to marry. The words send a shudder of fear through

Miranda. In this country girls are often married off as young as eight or nine. Over my dead body, she thinks. The word *heir* sticks in her brain. Heir to whom? To what? Then suddenly the pieces slip into place and the truth stands naked before her. She knows whose child this is. How could she not have suspected? When she heard he was dead, killed in the same government bombing that left Luloah an orphan? Her arms tighten around Luloah, who whimpers in protest. They are never going to let this child go. Not these people. And if Miranda were by some miracle to escape with her, she would be looking over her shoulder for the rest of her life. This tribe has resources, and an elite diaspora of its own. No, there can be no future for her with this child. And yet, thinks Miranda, looking down at the blue-black eyes, the soft, spiky hair, the fingers curled in tiny fists, there can be no future without her.

DECEMBER 13, 2010
Finn

At first Finn thought Miranda might have moved the paintings. Perhaps she wanted them to be somewhere completely secret, where not even he could find them. But even as he turns this possibility over in his mind, he knows what has happened. He knows with a profound dread that drags his heart down into his shoes.

He and Tazkia had searched the house as thoroughly as they could before Celia was due home, going through Miranda's old studio, her closets, the wine cellar, the *diwan* on the roof. Nothing. Tazkia was nearly hysterical with fear. "You don't know," she kept repeating. "You don't know what this means for me." Finn had an idea of what it meant for her, and it sickened him. But why would Norman want to hurt Tazkia? He might have understood Norman's motivation had the paintings been of Miranda, with whom Norman clearly had an unhealthy preoccupation. But he couldn't possibly have ever met Tazkia. Finn cannot make sense of the theft.

Still. At the same time some part of him has been waiting for this, waiting for Norman to make him pay. A rush of regrets nauseates him. He should not have overlooked Norman's weaknesses. He should not have pleaded his case with the FCO. He should have suffered the consequences of his dreadful error alone, before he had a wife. He should not have allowed the man near his family. He probably should never have had a family. Not when he knew how vulnerable they made him. Anyone in love is an easy target. But he had been good to Norman. Norman was supposed to be on his side.

"Tazkia," he says, struggling to sound confident. "I am going to take care of this. I will track down whoever took them, I will get them back for you." They are standing again in the front hallway, under the ever-vigilant eyes of Elizabeth II. There is nowhere else to search.

She looks up at him, her shoes half on, tears streaming down her face. "Someone has seen them," she says. "Someone has *seen* them!"

He wants to put his arms around her, to comfort her. But he knows this would be a serious mistake. He must be careful to do nothing that could be misinterpreted.

"What could anyone do with them here? It's not like anyone could *exhibit* them," he says, aware that he is babbling. "I mean, why would anyone want them?"

Tazkia looks at him as though he is a complete prat. "To ruin me. To murder me. My *family*," she says. "It only takes one person to tell one person and for that person or someone they tell to tell my family. If anyone knows, they will know. And if they know, I am not safe here."

Finn thinks of the countless stories he has heard of so-called honor killings, women slaughtered for daring to leave the house in high heels, marry someone they love, or get into a car with a man. What would they do to a woman who had modeled nude? He knows Tazkia's brother Hamid; he trusts him. Would he really do her harm?

"My family, they love me," Tazkia continues tearfully. "But this will kill them. They cannot let me live. Don't you see?"

"Tazkia, they may not ever know," says Finn, with a hope he does not feel. "Let me try to get the paintings back for you. I have some ideas of where they went. Do you feel safe going home tonight?"

She looks up at him and shrugs. "Where else can I go?"

"Look. If anyone in your family hears anything, get out of the house. Get out of the house and come to me. I will find somewhere for you, somewhere to keep you safe."

She nods miserably. "It's only . . . I don't want to lose my family. I don't want to lose my home. I don't want to lose . . . everything. *Everything.*" She looks up at him with the saddest eyes he has ever seen. "Finn. I was going to get married."

FEBRUARY 14, 2011
Miranda

She is dreaming. She is somewhere with Finn, not Mazrooq, but Seattle or New York, where they are meeting her parents and their oldest family friend. They get into a car with the friend. "Oh," Miranda says, realizing she hasn't introduced them, "This is . . ." And she suddenly blanks on Finn's name. Her own beloved, the man with whom she has pledged to spend her life, and she cannot remember his name. "My spouse . . ." Finally it comes to her, and she tries to pass it off as a joke. But later, alone in an unfamiliar bedroom, she turns around to find that Finn's head has shrunk to the size of an apricot, while his body has swollen up like that of Fat Albert. "SPOUSE?" he says. "YOU COULDN'T REMEMBER MY NAME?" Horrified, she tries to apologize and reassure him. But he is unrecognizable. His body keeps changing shapes, so that he becomes this big, fat schlump of a man who bears no resemblance to the real Finn. As he rants and rages, she hears a loud rumble and the ceiling splits in half, raining plaster and stones on their heads.

She wakes abruptly, suddenly aware that the stones are real. Real and rattling down around them like hail. Pulling Luloah underneath her, Miranda curls in fetal position, her hands protecting her head. What the fuck is going on? Luloah wakes and starts to cry, but her wails are drowned out by an explosion that sounds like it comes from directly overhead. There is a roar as an entire side of the room splits away, tilting outward and crumbling to the ground somewhere beneath them. Miranda is unaware of exactly what has happened until she feels the rush of cold air on her skin. In the silence following the collapse, she risks looking up to see—the world. There it is, just on the other side of where that wall had been. A nighttime world of tiny glowing windows and distant headlights. Just as she is craning her neck to see how far from the ground they are, the floor underneath them starts to tilt toward the opening. Holding the struggling Luloah tightly in her right arm, Miranda looks for something to hold on to as they start to slither across the floor. But there is nothing there but the rough cement, slipping from her fumbling fingers. She wraps both arms around the screaming child, tucks her chin to her chest, and lets her body slide into the cool, dark night.

For a moment, there is nothing around her, nothing touching her. They are falling away into the darkness, airborne, untethered. She stretches out an arm. A split second later the ground rises up beneath them, knocking the air from Miranda's lungs. She had turned so that her hip and not Luloah would absorb the impact, but her palm had struck the earth first. Not just the earth. When she tries to move her hand, a searing pain alerts her to the presence of the metal spike on which her hand is impaled. It's about a quarter inch thick, poking up between the bones of her thumb and forefinger. Before she has time to think, before the pain has time to immobilize her, she yanks her hand straight upward to free it. The thought flashes through her mind that perhaps it would have been better to leave the spike there, let a doctor remove it. But it was anchored to the earth. If she stayed there, surely her jailers would be first to find her. Blood pours from her palm. Setting the crying Luloah on the ground, she tears a strip of cloth from her skirt and wraps it around her hand. The blood, unabated, soaks the cloth in seconds. She ties the cloth more tightly and picks up the child. There is tearing pain in her left hip and right ankle. She has to move quickly. With her left elbow she pushes herself up into a squatting position and looks down at Luloah, whose wails are drowning out the sounds of the city around them. She has to quiet the child; they don't want to draw attention. Awkwardly she shifts Luloah underneath her shirt and presses her to her breast. She needs a moment to think.

Still crouching, she looks around her. The building where they had been held has collapsed into a mound of broken cement, stone, plaster, and fractured steel. This appears to be an empty lot, all cracked cement and ragged weeds. They are outside the center of the city, in what looks like a warehouse district. The remains of several other large cement buildings with roofs of corrugated metal strew the streets on either side. She can see figures moving in the darkness, finding their way out of the debris, shouting to each other. A car drives by, its lone headlight sweeping the lot, but Miranda and Luloah are crouched in the shadows. She listens for the sound of nearby voices. Nothing. Yet. Praying for Luloah's continued silence, Miranda searches around her for something she might use to defend herself, sweating with the agony of moving. Nothing. She needs to get away from here. Find someone to help them. Inching around the collapsed prison, she listens for footsteps. Nothing. Hadn't there been guards outside? Something catches her right foot, and she stumbles, nearly falling. When she looks down, it takes her a moment to make out what has tripped her. It is a hand. A human hand. A hand still attached to an arm that disappears under a pile of wreckage. A few inches from the curled fingers, she sees something of more immediate interest. A gun.

It's an AK-47, exactly like the one Tucker and Mukhtar taught her to shoot. She bends over it, her stomach attempting to turn itself inside out. The metal is cool under her fingers. "*Habibti,* I need you to be good for a minute," says Miranda. It is against every instinct in her body to pick up a gun while holding a child. Not to mention the fact that her left hand is more or less useless. Walking back a few steps, she tucks a calmer Luloah underneath a slab of cement slanted to the ground like a lean-to. "Don't move, *habibti,*" she says. "And no talking." Quickly, she returns to the gun and gingerly picks it up. She wonders if it is loaded. It's heavy. There is no way she could possibly carry both the gun and the child. Besides, if she has a gun, there is a possibility she could shoot someone. Which, despite her circumstances, is still not something with which she feels comfortable. And yet. She isn't in a hurry to be recaptured. She checks the safety, which, predictably, is not on. She slides it on and starts back to Luloah. As she nears the child, she hears the crunch of boots pivoting on gravel, sees a dark figure rise from a pile of rubble. Has he been watching them? Quickly, she sets the gun down just outside of the makeshift cave and rolls in next to Luloah. The man calls out something she cannot understand to someone she cannot see. But the voice is familiar. Cradling Luloah in her arms, she tilts her head to peer out from their shelter. His back is to her, but even in this dim light she can make out that he is missing an ear.

FEBRUARY 14, 2011
Tazkia

When her cell phone wakes her in the middle of the night, vibrating in the pocket of her nightgown, Tazkia bolts upright, her heart racing. She can't stop thinking of the paintings, can't stop waiting to be punished. She crawls over her two sleeping sisters and tiptoes to the hallway. Crouching on the stone floor in her long, pink polyester nightgown, she looks at the caller ID. Madina. Exhaling, she answers.

"I am sorry to be calling you so late," says Madina. "But did you hear the planes?"

"The planes?"

"Government bombers. Heading north."

"Madina, that happens all the time," she says, sighing. The sound of government planes heading north to bomb the heck out of the rebel tribes has become so familiar over the years that Tazkia doesn't even hear them anymore.

"No, no, but this is major, this is huge. They wiped out most of Qishriya city last night. Apparently one of the training camps is nearby."

"That's terrible. About the city, I mean, not the camp. But is there a reason I need to know this now?"

"Yes! Think, Tazkia. Make yourself a cup of tea or something. Wake up, I need you to listen." Obediently, Tazkia pads into their tiny kitchen and takes a glass jar of Nescafé down from a shelf, spoons the fortifying granules into a mug. "I'm listening," she says.

"Taz, isn't that where they might be holding her? If there is a camp there, maybe that's where they took her when they moved. It's the same tribe, no? The same people who were holding her in the other place?"

"Miranda?"

"*Yes*, Miranda! Add another tea bag to that cup. Who else do we know who is being held hostage up north?"

Tazkia's exhausted brain struggles to keep up. "Wait. So— Do you think she could have died in the bombing?"

"It's possible. But with all the chaos up there right now, this is the time to go."

"To go?"

"Yes, go! Up north. To look for her. I have a car. I only have it for forty-eight hours. We've got to move!"

"A car?" Tazkia's stomach, apparently comprehending more quickly than her mind, seizes with anxiety.

"Yes, a *car*." Madina is impatient. "Tazkia, we know what direction she was taken, do you want to go look for her? Now?"

"Now?" Tazkia seems capable only of repeating words.

"Because I don't have the car for long. I got it from this Syrian guy who—never mind about the Syrian guy. I have a car. And Nadia thinks she knows what direction we need to go."

"Wait. Wait. How do you know about the bombing, if it just happened? Is it on TV?"

"I know a guy at the government radio station. Who knows a guy in the army."

"And they told you?"

"My radio guy rang me. He knows about Miranda, and he's not a bad guy, took me to Suwaida Island once and was a total gentleman. Plus, he owes me a favor. But never mind about the radio guy. I trust his information. So, are you in?"

"You know a lot of guys."

"Yeah. You don't know what you're missing."

"I'm getting married this spring!" Though even as she says this, Tazkia wonders if it is still true.

"So, sadly for you, you'll never know more than one. But we can talk in the car, okay?"

Miranda. They can go look for Miranda. Among the many reasons they haven't gone to look for her before—none of the girls could leave their families without permission, they didn't know where to go, they had no escort—was the lack of a car. But now Madina has one. Still, while Madina has no parent or guardian in the country, the rest of the girls do. Madina never quite understands their restrictions; she is an odd hybrid, a Muslim woman with the freedoms of a Westerner.

"I can't," says Tazkia hopelessly. "My family."

"Tell them you're with me," says Madina. "And Mosi."

"Is Mosi coming?"

"He can't, he's in Kenya. But your parents still think we're married, right?"

Tazkia nods into the phone before realizing Madina cannot see her and says, "Yes." She had told her parents that Mosi was Madina's husband so that she would be allowed to go to their home, Miranda's former home. The other girls had done the same, and they had been able to meet there to share information from relatives in the North. These were less formal than their meetings with Finn, which they saved for when they had concrete information, like the drawing. Her mind whirls. Well, she couldn't really be in more trouble than she already is, could she? And if she were away when her parents heard about the paintings from someone, so much the better.

"Can you wait until after prayers? I can ask my parents then."

"Great. Nadia's doing the same. Tell them there's a women's overnight spiritual retreat in Tasreen. It's on our way anyway. Got it? We'll be spending forty-eight hours in prayer. Meet me at my house at five?"

"I'll see if I can get my brother to drive me."

"Never mind—I'll pick you up. Remind me where you are?"

Tazkia whispers her address into the phone, already looking around for things she needs to take with her. "Wait, Madina?"

"Yes?"

"The bombing, it has stopped?"

"For the moment. I think for the next forty-eight hours we should be okay. Say my sources. Look, do you want to find Miranda or what?"

"More than anything. How can you even ask? I will see you soon." After hanging up the phone Tazkia stuffs an extra *abaya* and *niqab*, bottles of water and Coke, her faux alligator-skin wallet, and packets of cookies into her largest purse. What else? Just before the muezzins announce morning prayers, she has one more idea. In stocking feet, she creeps into her parents' room and stops for a moment. No sound but their quiet breathing. Heart pounding, she opens her father's wardrobe and feels around the bottom until her fingers touch a slim metal box. Quickly, she tucks it into her sleeve and returns to the hallway. Funny, she thinks. While I am nervous about being blown to bits by a government bomb or accidentally shot by a rebel, I am far more nervous about getting into trouble with my parents.

When the muezzins wake them, Tazkia's parents, sleepy and cross, forbid her to leave.

"I'll be with Nadia," she pleads. "And Madina and Mosi are driving us."

Her mother frowns at her. "Well, I have heard of this retreat," she says. "But I thought it was for longer."

"This is just a special short one. Preparation for Ramadan." It's still many months away, but it's never too soon to spiritually prepare.

"Why is it so last minute?"

"Madina couldn't get a car until now." That much is true.

"We can trust Nadia's family," says her father finally. "And Tazkia is a happily engaged woman. It's not like she is running off with a man, is it?"

"No!" Tazkia smiles with relief.

"Go," says her mother. "Be careful, *habibti*. Come home soon to us." She kisses Tazkia, who kisses her father and flies to the door, the heavy metal box in her purse banging painfully against her thigh.

FEBRUARY 14, 2011
Finn

Finn lies awake, listening to the planes. He hadn't known there was another wave of government bombings, but he recognizes the noise of the engines. There had been a rash of bombings in his first couple of years, but they had stopped—or at least paused—during his most recent negotiations with the sheikhs, just before Miranda was taken. Now, he hears the sound of his years of work collapsing into nothing. Despite her best efforts, Celia had failed to convince the sheikhs to continue their talks—not with a woman at the head of the table. That roar overhead is the sound of failure. Heading north. Shit. *North.* Sitting up, he grabs his mobile from the floor next to the bed and dials Dax, who answers on the first ring.

"Sir?" he says brightly, accustomed to late-night calls.

"They're bombing the buggery out of the rebels again, Dax." Finn walks into the hall to avoid waking Cressida.

"Yes. We heard yesterday evening."

"We need to talk."

"Be there in ten."

Finn dresses quickly in jeans and a long-sleeved T-shirt. The nights are cold. By the time he gets downstairs, Dax is waiting at the gate, not a hair out of place. Does he ever sleep? "Care for a stroll?"

"I can't. Cressie."

"Right."

"Can we talk in the garden?"

Dax comes through the gate and looks around, as if expecting to find spies huddled in the corner of their scrubby patch of dirt. "Sure. Got a radio?"

Finn takes the stairs two at a time and returns with a portable. He switches it on to an Arabic music station, turns up the volume, and sets it on the ground in front of them. He and Dax sit down side by side against the stone wall dividing them from the neighbors. Leaning close to Dax so he doesn't have to raise his voice, Finn says, "Miranda is somewhere up there, no? Isn't that where we think she is?"

"It's likely. Though we don't have a hell of a lot to go on."

"We've got to get up there. What are they thinking, bombing somewhere she might be? What the *fuck*, Dax?"

"I'm sorry, we didn't have enough notice to warn them . . ."

"Don't they know? They must have at least as good an idea as we have."

"Oddly, I don't think they share our priorities."

"Do we have anyone who can go up?"

"I'll see what I can do."

"For god's sake, Dax, if no one else will go up I am going to walk right out of here and get a taxi."

"With all due respect, Finn, how far do you think you'll get without travel papers? Besides, you'll get killed. You're still right up there on the top ten list of preferred targets. Actually, top five. Any number of groups might take you on your way up."

"She could be dead, Dax. She could be injured. We've got to get up there. Is the pass open?"

"I'm not sure. I'll talk to Celia. We'll find a way."

"*Now*, Dax, please. Before the next attack. Before she . . . Just, *now*."

"I'm on it. Ring you in the morning." Dax stands, brushes off his trousers, and shakes Finn's hand before slipping out of the gate.

Finn cannot go back to bed. Instead, he paces his hallway, thinking. What else can he do? His passivity is killing him. He should be out there, he should be finding his own wife, not begging others to do it for him. If it weren't for Cressida, he would be up there by now. He would find a way.

FEBRUARY 14, 2011
Miranda

Miranda scrambles to her feet. "Mukhtar!" The relief she feels at seeing his familiar form is so strong she reacts without thinking. Mukhtar, her protector, is alive. Has he too been held prisoner? Was he the one tortured? They are saved, she thinks. Mukhtar can help them find their way home. "You're alive! Oh, I'm so glad—" But her voice staggers as he turns awkwardly around. She cannot quite make out the details of his features in the dark night, but something about his face is rigid, cold. He doesn't move toward her, doesn't call out. "Mukhtar?" she says.

Only then does she notice the AK-47. He holds it with both hands, low across his abdomen. Prisoners don't carry guns. He's dressed smartly in camouflage and heavy boots. Could he have picked up the gun after the bombings? But why won't he speak? Her mind races to make sense of his presence, coming at last to the only conclusion possible. Christ, *Mukhtar?* Their own Mukhtar? Mukhtar, who had taught her how to hold a gun, helped her into the car, helped her with her Arabic homework? Mukhtar, who lost an ear defending her?

"Turn around," he says. "Slowly. Get the child."

She stares at him, shock evolving into grief and rage. Blood beats faster through her punctured palm. The *motherfucker.* She had *loved* him. Behind her, the small girl, cold and confused, begins to wail—loud, agonized cries that carry in the relatively still night. Miranda takes a step backward, toward her.

"It was you," she says softly. Mukhtar stands absolutely still, staring at her with an inscrutable expression. "Why?" Miranda says. *"Why?"*

"You," he says, his voice trembling with emotion. "You are *haram.*" Miranda waits for him to say more. "You lie with *women.* You lie with the ambassador before marriage. He was a good man."

Miranda takes another few steps backward, feels with her left foot for the gun on the ground. How had he heard about Vicenta? Who in their right mind would have told him? True, much of the diplomatic community knew, but they would never share that kind of information with Mazrooqis. They knew the consequences.

"And this is how you treat him? You arrange to have his wife kidnapped?"

"You ruined him. You did some kind of magic on him. He let you be too free."

Too *free? Here?*

It is too dark for her to read the expression on Mukhtar's face.

"You took me to protect Finn?"

"We took you to send a message to your country."

She can feel her heartbeat shuddering in her neck. He hasn't yet lifted the gun. How long does she have? There's something odd about his posture; his left leg is bent almost balletically behind him. She squints in the darkness. His foot is caught on something. He cannot run.

"How many wives has your country killed, how many children? How else can we get their attention, how can we stop the drones?"

The drones. Those fucking drones. Her own country was killing her.

"Has it worked? Have you got their attention?" Her left foot nudges the gun, making sure of it.

"Of course not. They still think you are alive."

Miranda falls silent.

"The child is the only reason you have stayed alive this long. But I think now she no longer needs you."

Fear nearly paralyzes her. But she sees a sudden movement as his hands slide along the gun. There is no time for thought. There is no time for her to try to remember how to shoot a fucking AK-47. Crouching, she swiftly grabs the gun on the ground with both hands and sprints toward her former bodyguard. His arm is rising, metal glinting in the starlight, but his trapped foot throws him off balance. Miranda never shone at the range, but she was a pretty decent softball player. Raising the AK-47, she swings it like a bat, taking Mukhtar by surprise and knocking his gun to the ground. When Mukhtar reaches for it, she swings again, catching his rib cage. He lies on the dirt now, panting, making no effort to rise. "Why didn't you just shoot me?" he says.

"Mukhtar, you know I can't shoot straight." And she swings the gun once more, this time at his head.

FEBRUARY 14, 2011
Tazkia

In the car, Tazkia turns to Madina. "Did you call Finn?"

"No."

"Shouldn't we tell him?"

"I don't want to get his hopes up. Chances are, we won't find her. And if we do, we might not have good news."

Tazkia absorbs this. "You don't think he could help us? Not him, but the embassy?"

"What do you think the chances are that a foreigner would make it up there? Slim to none, kiddo. Slim to none. It has to be us. Two out of three of us are Mazrooqi, and I can pass for Mazrooqi. Besides, we're women. No one will take us seriously."

Tazkia can't argue with that. She and Nadia watch with admiration as Madina talks her way through checkpoint after checkpoint, explaining about the spiritual retreat and how they hadn't had time to apply for the travel permission slips. Whenever a man demonstrates any reluctance to let them pass, Madina pulls out a thousand-dinar note. "For cigarettes," she says, folding it and slipping it into his palm. And the men wave them through.

They haven't stopped since leaving the city, making do with the provisions each has stuffed into her handbag. Tazkia feels queasy after two bottles of Coke and her packet of cookies. Perhaps she should have brought a banana. Something healthy. Miranda was always going on about the amount of sugar in everything here.

At one of the last checkpoints before the northern territories, a policeman tells Madina the pass is partially blocked. They had forgotten about the pass. Madina hadn't known about it of course, being a foreigner. But the other women should have remembered. The floods of the rainy season often dislodge massive chunks of earth from the mountains on either side of the pass. It could be weeks before the heaps of sludge are cleared from the road.

But the word *partially* gives them hope. "Do you think we can get through?" asks Madina. The man looks skeptically at their rusted sedan. "It's not impossible," he finally says. "But you'll need help. If I were you I would wait."

Thanking him, Madina guns the car forward.

Tazkia closes her eyes. If they are meant to get to the North, they will get there. She thinks of Adan. It won't be long now. She imagines what it will feel like to run her hands over the smooth caramel of his skin. To wind her fingers in his thick, dark hair and inhale his scent. But there her heart stutters to a stop. Can she marry him now, with the paintings out there like a time bomb? Finn has promised to keep looking, but even if he finds them, there will always be someone else who has seen them. Has *seen* her. Has seen the part of her that only her husband should know. If she were honorable, she would break off with him now, before he is forced to leave her. But she cannot bear the thought of losing the kindest man she has ever known. The man who brings her tiny treasures each time he comes to see her: a miniature vase with a tiny violet, a painted porcelain thimble, a teddy bear the size of her thumb. Things she can carry with her. The man who wrote her poems, sheets and sheets and sheets of poems. If she cannot have him, whom can she have? Has she doomed herself to a lifetime of solitude? To a life without children? Sickened by this line of thought, she opens her eyes. She isn't the only one at risk, she reminds herself. Along with Miranda's paintings of Tazkia had been Tazkia's paintings of Miranda. She hadn't been able to bring herself to tell Finn. He had enough to worry about. And then, it might not even matter now.

Nadia, huddled against the back window, hasn't said a word the whole journey. Tazkia is surprised she could get away; her parents are strict, maybe even stricter than Tazkia's. But Nadia is the only one who knows the North, who knows this territory and these tribes. She and Madina had to have Nadia. Tazkia wonders how Nadia feels about Sheikh Zajnoon. Are her tribal loyalties to him stronger than her loyalty to Miranda? Maybe she and Madina should have talked about this, about what to do if Nadia turned on them, before they started out. Because surely Nadia should have remembered the pass?

The air cools as the car labors sluggishly up the several thousand feet of hairpin turns to the crossing. Falling silent, Madina focuses on coaxing the reluctant engine onward, over increasingly broken asphalt. Serrated peaks of blue rock rise on either side of them, obscuring their view of anything but the road ahead. It occurs to Tazkia that she has never been so far from home. Gripping the door handle with sweaty hands, she prays.

"Here we are," announces Madina. "Hang on tight." She presses her slippered foot to the floor. The car jumps forward, allowing Tazkia and Nadia a view of the wedge of mud and rock slumped across the two-lane road. The left side isn't too bad, buried in just a few inches, but the right is impassable, a wall of debris. On either side are vertical cliffs. "Good thing I learned to drive in Africa," yells Madina. "Time to pray!"

But the car lurches only about a third of the way through before its wheels begin to spin in the mire. Madina shuts off the engine and turns to her two friends. "So," she says. "Who brought extra shoes?" Only Tazkia is wearing sneakers; Madina and Nadia are wearing the slippers or heels they wear every day. "Everybody out," orders Madina. "If you don't want to lose your shoes take them off."

Uncertainly, Nadia tugs off her shoes while Tazkia laces her well-worn Reeboks more tightly. When they climb out of the car, their feet instantly disappear in the bone-chilling muck. "Quickly," says Madina. "Before we freeze." Yanking up the skirts of their *abayas* and tucking them into the waistbands of their jeans, then flipping back their veils, the women pick their way to the rear of the car. "Wait," says Madina. "We need something for the front wheels, for traction. Can you find small stones? Sticks? Anything not mud?"

Twenty minutes later the women have wedged a mosaic of rubble under the front wheels and gathered again at the back of the car. With Madina at the wheel, Tazkia and Nadia dig their numb toes into the ground and push. At first, the wheels flail in the mud, flinging up useless sprays of filth. "PUSH," calls Madina. "Harder!" adds Tazkia, her voice panicky. "Someone is coming!" Looking over their shoulders, the women can see a green truck a few turns below, making its steady way toward them. Terror of discovery in states of semi-undress has an invigorating effect, and seconds later the front wheels grip the stones. Stumbling as the car lurches from their shoulders, the women fight their way forward, heaving their whole weight into the car until finally it breaks free onto dry road. Madina pulls several meters forward as the women run to jump inside. Just as the truck commences its own struggle in the morass behind them, Madina presses her foot to the floor.

"I hate to say it," says Tazkia as the women untuck their *abayas* and use their socks to wipe their feet, "but with any luck we'll be coming back the same way."

"We'll make it," answers Madina, "if the rains hold off."

As they descend from the pass, the air thickens with heat. Tazkia sweats, wishing she could remove her *abaya* entirely. (She's almost grateful for her soaking feet, but not quite.) In between checkpoints she flips up her *niqab* and fans her face with a notebook. Madina rolls down the windows, but still the heat is oppressive. Suddenly, Nadia straightens from her slouch against the door. "Turn here," she says, pointing to a dirt road branching off to the left.

"Really? Here? But it's—"

"It's the best way," says Nadia firmly. "A back road to the city. We won't be so conspicuous."

As Madina steers off the tarmac and begins to bump the car along the dusty, serpentine road, Tazkia glances idly at her phone. Missed call. How could that be? She checks her ringer; it was switched off. The stupid ringer is always turning itself off in her purse. She picks it up to look at the number but doesn't recognize it. Good, then it wasn't her family or Adan. Probably a wrong number. She won't bother calling back, she has hardly any minutes left on her phone anyway. But she switches on the ringer and keeps the phone on her lap.

"How long now?" she asks Nadia, who is looking more confident as they near her hometown.

"Half an hour? Less? Depending."

Before they get too close to the city, Madina pulls the car over so that they can all pee behind the piles of rocks strewn across the flat countryside. It's easier than trying to find a bathroom in town. As she squats, Tazkia can see streams of people moving in the distance. Families, walking away from their bombed homes, she imagines. Could Miranda be among them? Or was her prison spared? Or have they gotten her location completely wrong?

"Taz! Phone!" Madina calls from the car. Tugging up her jeans, Tazkia sprints to the car and lunges for her phone.

"Tazzy, is it really you? Don't hang up." The voice cracks and begins to sob. Tazkia holds the phone away from her ear and looks at it in amazement. "Mira?" she finally says. *"Mira?"*

FEBRUARY 14, 2011
Miranda

Miranda stands looking down at Mukhtar's limp form, unsure whether he is dead or merely unconscious. She doesn't want to know. And she has no time to examine him. Quickly, avoiding looking at his chest or mouth for signs of breath, she goes through his pockets until she finds his phone. She takes this and a five-hundred-dinar bill and glances around her to make sure she is not observed. But everyone seems to be moving away, away from the blasted buildings, away from the city. She wonders if all of her other guards are dead. Luloah has grown quiet in her hiding place, having become fascinated with arranging pebbles in a straight line. Miranda limps back to her and scoops her up. Luloah protests, and Miranda retraces her steps to get her a handful of the pebbles before starting again toward the lights of the city. It is the dark places she fears, the emptiness with its invisible arms reaching to grab her. She and Luloah will be safer in town.

As they make their slow way down the mostly abandoned streets, they hug the walls, staying in the shadows. She has got to find something to make a sling for Luloah; the child is too heavy to carry for long, and Miranda's ankle yelps with every step. At each corner, she has to set the girl on the pavement for a few minutes before she can move on. It's already getting lighter, the desert sun burning away the shadows. People move past her, men on their way home from mosque, women carrying pink plastic bags of bread, parentless children chasing a cat. They stare at her curiously but say nothing. Miranda wonders what she looks like. It has been months since she has seen a mirror. Her hair is growing out, and stands out from her head in stunted, greasy ringlets. Her left hand is wrapped in a strip of cloth and soaked with blood. She wears a long black skirt and loose, ragged polyester blouse, both coated in dust. Of course many of the people she passes are also dusted with plaster, victims of the same attack. Wide-eyed and stunned, often bleeding, they pass without seeing her.

As soon as she feels far enough from her prison to stop for a few minutes, she dials Finn, heart skipping, amazed she remembers his number. Yet it doesn't even ring; a message in Arabic informs her that the line has been disconnected. Nausea threatens to overwhelm her. Could he also be in trouble? Perhaps he has left the country, taken Cressida to safety. Desperately, she tries to dial the embassy and the Residence but gets an error message both times. Damn it. Has she forgotten the numbers?

At a tiny storefront she stops to buy a bottle of water for her and a packet of crackers for Luloah, who turns them around in her hands marveling at them before running her tongue around an edge. The shopkeeper smiles at her and reaches over to pinch Luloah's cheeks with thick, grubby fingers. Squatting out of his sight, Miranda unwraps her hand and pours water over the wound. The pain is so acute she leans in to the wall and vomits onto the pavement. Luloah crawls toward her, pulls at her skirt. The blood is still coming from her palm, but slowly. She rewraps it in the bloody cloth, trying to keep the cleanest part over her wound.

What is she going to do? She crouches on the pavement for a moment and gives Luloah a taste of her water. She could ask a stranger for help, take a taxi all the way home to Arnabiya, or call someone else. The last is the only logical option. She isn't feeling particularly trusting of strangers at the moment, and she doesn't have the money for a taxi or the permission slips to get through the checkpoints. So whom should she call? Tucker? Dax? They are the logical choices. But she doesn't know their numbers. There are only two phone numbers she knows by heart, Finn's and Tazkia's. *Tazkia.* Miranda sits heavily down on the pavement. Luloah leans against her as she dials. She lets the phone ring a dozen times before giving up. No one in this fucking country ever answers the phone, and voice mail does not yet exist. Tazkia won't call her back; she never has minutes on her phone. Besides, she won't recognize the number.

Sighing, Miranda tucks the phone in the waistband of her skirt and hauls Luloah up again. When a small boy runs past her, trailing a Palestinian scarf like a kite, Miranda calls after him. He stops and stares at her. She pulls out her remaining dinars and holds them in her palm. "For the scarf?" she says. "Could I have the scarf?" Greedily, the boy scoops the coins from her hand, tossing the scarf on the ground before running off. Miranda picks up the scarf and uses it to tie Luloah to her waist. That's a bit better.

She walks on, passing mosques, bombed-out homes and businesses, shops, and half-built concrete houses with iron rods pointing skyward, awaiting a second floor that will never come. No one has to pay taxes on an unfinished house, so there is little motivation to complete any new construction. She squints, suddenly aware of how long it has been since there was sun on her skin. Tilting her face upward, she drinks it, gorges herself on it. Euphoria wafts through her: At this moment, she is free.

This feeling is quickly followed by vertigo and panic. She has no money. She cannot get food for herself or Luloah or take a taxi or pay for a room. At any moment she could be plucked off the streets again by men with malign intent. At any moment someone could take Luloah from her. The faster she gets off the street the better. Plucking the phone out of her waistband, she dials Tazkia again.

FEBRUARY 14, 2011
Finn

Finn is exhausted. He had finally fallen asleep after the morning prayers, only to be woken an hour later by Cressida's cries. She hasn't slept long enough either and is uncharacteristically clingy. Finn lurches downstairs to make her porridge and cut her up a mango, but she doesn't want to eat, throwing sticky pieces of fruit to the linoleum floor. "I know how you feel," he tells her, peeling up the pieces of fruit and rinsing them in bottled water. "But we have to somehow go on."

The empty day stretching before him is an affront. He needs work, he needs action. He rings Dax, who says to call him later. He is still working on finding someone to send up north. Maybe Finn *should* go back to London. Is he doing anyone any good here? All of his connections and friends have proved useless. He feels scooped out, impotent. And if he doesn't get out of this fucking house he will lose his mind.

Disregarding Bashir's warnings and refusing his company, he

takes Cressida out for a long walk through the Old City. He wants to lose himself. Cressie struggles to keep up, stumbling on the cobble-stones, and he lifts her to his shoulders. Despite his black mood, he is struck anew by the beauty of the city. It has no straight lines. Every building leans and curves. Narrow lanes lead past stalls selling hand-crafted daggers, carved wooden doors, multicolored scarves, intricate silver jewelry. As he passes one of the jewelry stalls, a man rushes out to greet him and shake his hand. It is the place Miranda had taken him that first day, where he had bought the coral necklace for his one surviving aunt. The man pulls him inside, disappears into the back, and reappears with a glass of sticky-sweet tea. "So happy to see you again," he says. Finn has been back several times since that first visit, every time he needs a gift for a visitor or friend back home. But this is the first time he has found his way here without his team.

He sets Cressie down on the floor and accepts the glass of tea. She wanders over to the wall display of necklaces and fingers the beads. "Your daughter?" says the man. Finn nods, sure that it is careless to admit such an attachment. But he is tired. Tired of caution, of fear, of being on constant alert. The man disappears again and returns with a glass of unnaturally orange juice for Cressie, who sucks it down hungrily. It must be getting close to lunchtime. Before they leave, Finn buys a strand of turquoise beads for Cressida, placing them around her neck, and a string of dark emerald beads, in the stubborn hope that he can someday give them to his wife. Cressida insists on wearing these too, and he lets her. Because he has to say no every time she asks for her mother, he says yes to almost everything else.

As they wind their way deeper into the city, Cressida makes him even more conspicuous than usual. A stream of women who want to touch her feet and cheeks slow their progress. "A doll!" they say. "Is she a doll?" He isn't sure whether the question is literal. Do they really think she might not be real? When they reach a pretty little square in front of a mosque, he sets Cressie down again, and they order *fasooleah* and sit in plastic chairs to scoop up the fried beans with their bread. Cressida is overjoyed to eat without silverware and treats the baguettes as paintbrushes, their table as her canvas.

Several men join them, asking the customary questions. Where is he from? Does he love Mazrooq? Is it not a beautiful country? How old is Cressida? She is very big for her age, is she not? How many other children? Why not? Finn answers them, asking them questions of his own about their lives and livelihoods. As he listens to them explain their family histories, their neighborhoods, their work, he thinks how often he would rather be talking with them than with the diplomats with whom he was forced into conversation at every national day. The men play peekaboo with Cressida, making her laugh with funny faces, and crouch down next to her to sing her songs. This is what he and his staff are missing in these high-security environments, where they are kept sealed away from most of the population. The everyday pleasures of everyday people. Finn finds himself suddenly very curious about all sorts of things. He asks the men their thoughts on the president, the chances of war, on the kidnappings in the North, and his ideas for new development projects. They are happy to rail against the government and condemn the kidnappings and offer critiques of his ideas. Only when Cressida's head starts to bob sleepily toward her remaining beans is he able to tear himself away.

At home, he is only about halfway through *A Pocket for Corduroy* when Cressida falls silent beside him. He curls around her on his bed, neither of them stirring until early evening prayers remind them of the world and its cares. Cressida wakes first and pats her father's face. "What's it all about, Daddy?" she says. "What's it all about?"

Groggily, Finn opens an eye. "I don't know, Cress. What's it all about?"

Cressie leans forward so her breath is hot on his face. "It's about *bears*," she says triumphantly. Isn't it, though? he thinks to himself. Cross to bear. Bear watching. Bear arms. Bear up. Bear in mind. Bear fruit. Bear witness. More than one can bear.

FINN IS IN the middle of cooking pasta for their dinner when his phone rings. Dax.

"We need you at the Residence."

"Why?"

"You know I can't answer that."

"I'm cooking dinner."

"Forget dinner. This can't wait."

Finn reaches to turn off the gas and put a cover on the pot. "Right," he says. "I'll get Gabra to come round and find a taxi."

"Don't you dare go anywhere near a taxi and never mind Gabra; you can bring Cressie. In fact, you must. We're sending a car."

FEBRUARY 14, 2011
Miranda

Miranda stares at the car as though it were a mirage. White, crusted in mud, four doors, battered and rusting, it is the most exquisite vehicle she has ever seen. It had taken several phone calls for the women to figure out where she was, how to find her. And now they are—improbably, impossibly—here. Standing together on a relatively unpopulated street corner in the outskirts of the city. For a brief moment, Miranda wonders if she can trust them, but she no longer has the energy for doubt. Besides, Tazkia is running toward her, tackling her in a sweaty, polyester embrace. "Careful!" she says, moving an arm protectively around Luloah. Her mind has suddenly gone numb.

"Who is she? Where have you been? How did you get out? Were you bombed? Oh, Miranda, I'm sorry—" She covers her mouth with a hand. "Never mind my questions. I'm just so happy to see you. Oh, you're hurt!"

"I'm okay." Miranda's eyes are dazed, uncomprehending.

"Come, into the car. We'll get you home." Gently, Tazkia touches her shoulder.

"I don't quite understand how you happened to be here." Miranda looks paralyzed, unable to move her legs.

"Quickly, help her, before anyone sees her," urges Madina.

She pushes Miranda and Tazkia toward the car doors, glancing around for any possible pursuers. Nadia moves to the front seat, and Tazkia climbs back in. "I'll take the baby. How old is she? Where did you find her? I'll give her back to you once you're settled. I can't believe you're alive!"

Miranda smiles weakly. "Me neither." Why is it suddenly so hard? Why can't she talk to these women she has known for years, women she knows as well as she knows anyone? But suddenly there is just too much to say. It all gets stuck somewhere around her sternum. Except for one question, the only one that matters: "Cressida and Finn?" She is still standing next to the car, unmoving.

"They are fine, *al-hamdulillah*. Do not worry. We'll explain in the car." Madina gets back out of the driver's seat. "Come on, *habibti*," she says, taking Miranda's arm. "It's not safe here."

As if to underscore her words, a bearded man is suddenly sprinting toward them. Shouting something undecipherable, he waves his arms. He is dressed in camouflage and black boots. It is possible that he is a soldier warning them to get out of town. Or that he wants a ride somewhere. Or that he is part of a particularly aggressive welcome party. But none of them is in the mood to take chances. Madina shoves Miranda into one side of the backseat as Tazkia emerges from the other. Stepping between the man and the car, she raises trembling arms, clutching her father's gun.

"NO," she says simply. "NO." The man stops in amazement, staring at the tiny robed creature before him.

Madina is back in the driver's seat. The car stutters to life. "Tazzy, *get in*," she yells. Keeping her gun pointed at the man, Tazkia backs toward the car and climbs in. Rolling down the window, she hangs the gun outside the car. It could have been the jolt of the car moving forward, or the press of Tazkia's excited fingers, but as they pull away, the gun fires, sending a bullet into the dust behind them.

"*Enough*, Tazzy," says Madina. "Don't give them a reason to come after us."

Reluctantly, Tazkia pulls the gun into the car. When she turns to her left, she finds Miranda backed against the door, her arms tight around the child.

"It's all right, Mira," she says, soothingly.

"Put it away," says Nadia. "You're scaring her."

Tazkia scrabbles around in her bag for the metal box.

"The safety," murmurs Miranda.

"What? I have a box."

"Fix the safety first." Miranda points to the gun without touching it, showing Tazkia how to slide the safety into position. Once the gun is secured, Tazkia returns it to the box and slips it into her purse.

Miranda realizes she has been holding her breath and exhales. They are moving. Moving! Her heart twitches with cautious joy. There are still so many miles between her and her daughter, her love, so many checkpoints, armed vehicles, so many *men*. Luloah has fallen into a stunned silence, staring around her with wide eyes.

"Her name is Luloah," Miranda eventually says softly to Tazkia. "Her parents are gone." That is all they need to know, for now. But Tazkia cannot be silent, not even for a moment. She has question after question after question. Miranda answers her as well as she can, but she has questions of her own. How did they happen to find her? How had they known where to go? Where were Finn and Cressie? The women interrupt each other, anxious to reassure her about her family and to tell the story of the drawing and Madina's helpful series of boys. Miranda struggles to take it all in. She doesn't want to talk anymore; she wants to close her eyes and let their voices wash over her, let them wash her into sleep.

"Your Arabic has got much better, by the way," says Tazkia, impressed. Miranda is startled. She hadn't realized she was still speaking it. Has she always spoken to her women in Arabic, or did she teach classes in English? Why can't she remember? She wants to ask them but doesn't want them to think she has lost her mind.

A few miles before they cross the first checkpoint, Madina pulls over. "I hate to do this, Miranda, after everything you've been through, but we can't risk them seeing you. We'll have to put you in the trunk until we're past."

"Wait," says Nadia, fumbling in her bag. "Wait, no, I have..." She pulls out a plain black *abaya*, *hijab*, and *niqab*. "She can wear these. They'll be too short, but they won't see that in the car." Miranda breathes a sigh of relief. She wasn't anxious to get into another confined space. Handing Luloah to Tazkia, she steps out of the car to change.

"Keep the veil down over your eyes," says Tazkia. "You have very American eyes."

Miranda almost laughs. "Don't worry, *habibti*," she says. "I'm not particularly in the mood to take any more risks."

They let Madina do the talking, and with each checkpoint Miranda's hopes rise. When they reach the pass, they find it slightly easier to cross, the mud having been tamped down by a succession of other vehicles. Still, they all must get out again to push, save for Miranda, who stands in the sludge looking bewildered, clutching Luloah in her arms. The baby sleeps for most of the journey, lying across her lap and Tazkia's. As they near the last checkpoint before Arnabiya, Tazkia leans close. Nadia and Madina are talking together in the front. "The paintings," Tazkia whispers. "They are gone."

It takes a moment for this to register with Miranda. "*No, Taz!*"

"Yes. I'm sorry to tell you now but I think you should know. Finn took me to get them and they were gone."

"But no one had the key but—"

"Finn found yours. But he says security also has one. Did you know this?"

Security? Mukhtar, she thinks. But no, Mukhtar was up north, near her. And then it occurs to her ... but no. Surely Norman would have had no reason to go into the Residence. But maybe there had been a drill? Her exhausted brain spins.

"Are you safe at home? Does anyone know?"

"Not yet. I don't think so. I can't leave home."

"I know." She squeezes Tazkia's hand. "We will help," she says.

Tazkia looks at her, a new solemnity in her eyes. "I don't think you can," she says.

MIRANDA WANTS TO go straight to Finn and Cressie in the Old City, but the girls want to take her to the Residence. "You'll be safer there," they say. "They can come to you there. There are guards."

Miranda thinks of Mukhtar and wonders how safe the Residence really is.

"You can't drive up to the door," she reminds them. "Just let me out near Baskin-Robbins. I'll walk from there."

The women are reluctant to drop her so far from the Residence, but they know they won't be able to get through the security gates at the entrance to the neighborhood. "We will wait here until you get inside and call us," they say. "Don't forget."

It is nearly sunset when they reach the outskirts of the city. Touched with rosy gold light, even the poorest boxy brown house radiates beauty. Miranda leans her forehead on the glass, hungry for the familiar sights of the president's mosque, the broken pavements, the bowling alley, the Huda grocery store, the spice and nut shop, and finally, Baskin-Robbins.

When she steps out of the car, her legs nearly give way. They are stiff and numb from the hours of travel. None of the women have eaten; they didn't want to lose time by stopping. Luloah has eaten a chocolate bar that Madina had in her purse but is doubtless hungry as well. Tazkia kisses Luloah's cheeks, hands her out to Miranda, and climbs out after her. "Will you leave?" she suddenly asks anxiously. "Will you go back to England?"

Back to England? Miranda has never lived there. Finn has a small studio apartment in Putney that they use on their infrequent visits. But they haven't gotten around to talking about another home, a permanent home where they will live in the distant future, after Mazrooq. They had each assumed that there would be plenty of time. Surely Finn would have other postings before they would have to pick a country to call home.

"I am not going anywhere," Miranda says. "Not anytime soon." The women kiss her quickly and get back in the car.

"We'll wait here," Madina reminds her. "But don't take forever, I have to pee."

Miranda walks slowly, Luloah perched on her right hip. It feels like they have been walking slowly together for a long, long time. Miranda has no idea what day it is; she forgot to ask the women.

There are so many things she has forgotten to ask. Few cars pass. She rounds the corner near the British Club, and suddenly she can see the Union Jack, raggedly waving from the top of the Residence.

Tears prick the backs of her eyes as she turns left and sees the gates up ahead. With the last of her strength, she shifts Luloah in her arms and knocks on the metal door in the gate. She has rarely had to knock. The guards always swung open the door before she even got there, having seen her approach on their CCTV screens. But the man who now opens the gate does not look familiar. He is young, slightly chubby, with his dark hair slicked back. He stands there in the doorway, wary. *"Aiwa?"*

"Salaama aleikum," she begins. *"Ana Miranda..."* She isn't sure what to say after that. I live here? But does she, anymore?

The young man stares at her, taking in her filthy clothing, her bandaged hand, the child, his face slowly opening. *"Antee Miranda?"* he says in disbelief. *"Miranda zawjat as-safir?"* Miranda, wife of the ambassador?

"Aiwa, zawjat as-safir." She is limp with relief.

"Hadda Miranda! Miranda zawjat as-safir!" the man cries, swinging open the gates. There is a shuffling in the adjacent guardhouse, and suddenly Miranda is surrounded by Finn's guys. They look for a moment as though they might actually hug her but stop themselves, rushing at her with extended hands instead. A barrage of questions assault her. Where has she been? How did she get here? Is she all right? Where is Mukhtar?

Then they notice the child. *"Meen at-tufl?"*

Luloah tightens the grip of her arms around Miranda's neck, looking fearfully at the men.

"Hiya Luloah," she says simply.

Finally one of the guards thinks to ring the house. A moment later a small blond woman flies down the steps and into the garden. "What on earth?" she says, stopping short and staring at Miranda. "You're alive!" Then, "You *are* Miranda? Finn's Miranda? You don't look much like your photo. But then of course one wouldn't expect—"

"I think so," Miranda answers. Celia frowns slightly, and Miranda realizes that she has spoken in Arabic. But the English words just won't come. They have rusted and gotten stuck somewhere. Fear of discovery has tamped them down deep.

"I'm Celia," says the woman, switching to Arabic herself and reaching out a hand. Miranda shifts the child to take it. "Let's get you inside. You must be exhausted. I'll ring Finn. Who is the child? Never mind, come, come . . ."

But Miranda cannot move. Her feet are fixed to the ground. "I'm," she starts. "I am . . ." The Residence wavers like the picture of a faulty television. She sees Celia's pink, open mouth as she reaches toward Luloah, and then she sees nothing at all.

FEBRUARY 14–15, 2011
Finn

Finn sits on the edge of the bed, looking down at his wife. There she is, curled on her side on the floor, close enough to touch. He could reach out and run his fingers across her rib cage. He could touch the short, springy curls of her hair—though he now knows better than to try. Still. She is here. Alive, relatively unharmed, his. She is home. Well, home? He is confused as to what will happen first. The Office wants her out, back to London, as soon as humanly possible. He can withdraw from post early, Wilkins had said on the phone when he rang to tell them. He and Miranda could come back to London so she can get whatever trauma counseling she needs and he can work on the Mazrooq desk until another posting comes up. "You won't be penalized for leaving early," Wilkins had said. "It's not as if you decided to allow your wife to be kidnapped."

Finn had hedged. He knew better than to make any promises before speaking with Miranda. And yesterday—today?—was not the time. There was so much else, too much else. He and Cressie had arrived at the Residence to find Miranda unconscious on the sofa in the front room. His heart had stopped before Celia quickly reassured him. "She just fainted, Finn. She's okay. She's fine. Looks a little banged up but essentially fine. I've rung Dr. Jay." Finn knelt down by Miranda's head. "I'll leave you," said Celia, retreating to the stairs.

He looked at his wife. Thin, filthy, shorn of her thicket of hair. He reached a hand toward her face, wanting to touch her, before thinking the better of it. He didn't want to startle her. Relief rippled through his body, releasing, finally, the tears.

"Is that Mummy?" For a moment, he had forgotten Cressida, so shocked had he been by the sight of his battered wife. She stood behind him, her fingers gripping his shirt.

"Yes, sweetie, it's your mummy. She's a little sick right now, but she is going to be just fine." Cressida looked doubtful. She stared at her mother, not moving.

"You can touch her if you want, give her a kiss. I think she'd like that." Cressie leaned past her father to get a better look. "She smells," she said, wrinkling her nose. "Why does she smell funny?"

"She's been lost, *habibti*. We will have to talk to her to find out what happened." His heart lurched. He was terrified of what she would have to tell him. She didn't look as though she had been tortured, but you couldn't always tell. How bad was the damage?

"WAKE UP, MUMMY!" bellowed Cressida, clapping her hands.

The sound of her voice and the tiny hands coming together near her ear snapped Miranda upright, her eyes wide and wild. With a cry, she pulled her knees to her chest, rocking back into the safety of the sofa. Staring at her, Cressida backed slowly away. "Not Mummy," she whispered.

Finn knelt next to his wife, careful not to touch her. "It's me, Mira, it's me."

A moment later Miranda's eyes cleared and registered his presence. "Finn?" she said, reaching out tentative fingers to touch the sleeve of his shirt.

"Yes." He sat there, grinning at her like a fool. She smiled back, as her body began to quake. The tremors started gently and then took hold until even her filthy skirt and blouse were shuddering—whether with relief or fear, he wasn't sure. "You're safe now," he said, laying a hand gently on her knee.

She just looked at him and shook her head, her eyes filling. "Not ever," she said. It was then she finally saw her daughter. "Cressie!" she said, reaching out a trembling hand.

But the girl continued backing away to the safety of her father.

"You got lost," she said accusingly. "And you smell." She turned to Finn. "Something wrong with smelly lady."

"You can *talk*! You're talking!" Miranda was crying and laughing, looking up at Finn, who took one of her hands between his. Only when he felt its rough texture did he notice the bloody bandage.

"I do smell," she said to him in Arabic, her teeth chattering.

"How could you possibly think I care?"

Miranda's forehead abruptly creased. "Where is Luloah?"

"Who?" He wondered why she was still speaking in Arabic.

Dr. Jay walked in then, just as Negasi appeared from the kitchen, a small, gray-skinned girl in her arms. *"Umi!"* the child cried, stretching her arms toward Miranda.

"Negasi!" Miranda smiled at their housekeeper through her tears. "That's Luloah."

"Madame," said Negasi, coming to hug her. Then Teru and Desta and the gardeners and Tucker and Dax were all there, reaching for her, crying and laughing and crowding near. Luloah began to wail in Negasi's arms.

"I fed her some banana and yogurt," she told Miranda. "Is that all right? She was hungry." Miranda reached up and took the child from Negasi, rocking it against her breast. As she hummed and murmured in Arabic, slowly her body stilled. Dax and Tucker retreated, promising to return later.

Finn knelt by his wife, euphoria and confusion fighting for dominance. Miranda looked suddenly alarmed. "Finn, can you call Tazkia? Tell her I am here and safe?"

"I'll call people later, sweetheart, when you're resting." He put a hand on her hair, gritty and oily under his fingers.

"No, no. It was the women who brought me. They're waiting. Please, just call?"

The women? Finn stood and pulled his mobile from his front pocket, searched for Tazkia's number. "She's here," he said simply when Tazkia answered. "You brought her back?"

"We thought the Residence would be safest. Is it okay? She is fine?"

"Is it *okay*? Tazkia, it is the most fantastic thing in the world."

Dr. Jay, the UK-trained Indian doctor who treated all embassy staff, waited quietly at the edge of the room, clutching a large black case. She didn't normally make house calls, but this was hardly a normal circumstance. It was Celia who finally dispersed everyone, reemerging from upstairs to shoo the staff back to the kitchen. "You can all talk with her later," she said. "But what Miranda needs right now is quiet. And a doctor." She led Finn and Miranda upstairs to their old room, where Dr. Jay could examine her. Miranda protested leaving the girls downstairs. "I need to see my daughter," she said. "And Luloah will be terrified."

"They can come up in a minute," Finn promised.

"You should examine Luloah too," Miranda said as Dr. Jay prodded her swollen ankle. "She's malnourished I'm sure and could have god knows what else."

"Actually," said Dr. Jay, who until then had hardly uttered a word, "before I bandage her hand and ankle, why don't we get her into the bath? The child too. They need to be cleaned."

After injecting Miranda with a painkiller, the doctor retreated downstairs for a cup of tea in the kitchen while Finn filled a bathtub with warm water and bath salts. Miranda lay still on the bed, looking up at him with exhausted eyes as he carefully undressed her. Had her shoulder bones always poked up in little triangles like that? It frightened him to see her so thin. The skin over her ribs was pale, bruised, and covered with tiny red bites. There were more on her legs and stomach and arms. Some were swollen and infected-looking. Dark hair covered her calves and armpits. One ankle had doubled in size, and what had happened to her hand? Only when he unwound the strip of bloody cloth from her palm did she stir, whimpering as he pulled the last bit from the gaping hole in her left hand. He fought back nausea and tried to smile reassuringly. Questions fought their way to his lips, but he was afraid to overwhelm her, to somehow accidentally aggravate her condition. If she had some kind of post-traumatic stress, and she probably did, he couldn't remember how he was supposed to act with her.

Squatting, he slid his arms under her naked body and carried her to the bath like a baby, like Cressie. She closed her eyes as her skin touched the warm water, turning it almost instantly gray and rusty. Finn lathered what was left of her hair, soaped her body, gently ran a flannel over her bites and sores. Afraid to touch her hand, he swished water past the wound. When he had rinsed her once, he let the water drain away and filled the tub again. Miranda lay still. As he shut off the taps, Negasi knocked, the strange child in her arms, Cressie holding on to her skirt. Miranda sat up with a jerk. "Give her here," she said.

Finn helped her to wash the baby, with Cressie leaning over the bath to watch, fascinated. "Cressie, this is Luloah," said Miranda. "She has had a hard time. Can you be especially nice to her?"

"Why she has hard time? Why?" It didn't strike Cressida as odd that her mother—or this woman purporting to be her mother—spoke to her in Arabic. Everyone except her father spoke to her in Arabic, or Amharic.

Miranda leaned out of the bath to kiss her daughter's cheek. "I missed you so much, *habibti*," she said. "I missed you more than anything in the whole world."

More than you missed me? Finn can't help but wonder. But he doesn't say it out loud.

Luloah was reaching up for Miranda, puckering her mouth like a guppy.

"Finn," said Miranda. "I need to nurse her. But I don't think Cressie . . . ?" Bewildered and yet understanding, Finn led his daughter out of the bathroom. Celia had left a stack of fluffy white towels on the bed, along with a terry-cloth robe and cotton sundress and panties. "We've sent the guys to the Old City for your things," she told Finn through the closed door. "They should be here in an hour or so."

When Miranda was dry and wrapped in a robe, she held out an arm to Cressida. "Sniff me now," she said. Her daughter cautiously sniffed near Miranda's arm but didn't move closer. "My mummy doesn't talk like you," she said. Finn saw a flicker of pain cross Miranda's face.

"She just needs time," he said.

Miranda nodded, blinking back tears.

Dr. Jay returned to examine both Luloah and Miranda, disinfecting and bandaging their various wounds, wrapping a splint around Miranda's ankle. "You will need to see a surgeon about your hand," she said. "As soon as possible and preferably not here. When you are back in London. There is damage to both muscle and ligaments, and possibly some of the smaller bones. You need a specialist if you want to regain the use of this hand. I'm also putting you on antibiotics."

Miranda shook her head emphatically. "I can't go to London. I have the children."

"And you'll need help with them, until we can get this fixed."

But Finn's mind had traveled elsewhere. "It's her painting hand," he said. "We have to fix it."

"I can't leave." Miranda looked at him pleadingly.

"Sweetheart, we'll talk about this later. We'll figure everything out, I promise."

"As for the child," the doctor continued, "she probably has a vitamin D deficiency. Which is easy enough to treat. We may need to take blood to see if there is anything further. I don't suppose you know if she has had any vaccinations?"

"I'm pretty sure she hasn't had any."

"We'll do that too, as soon as you both get a few days' rest and some warm meals."

Desta dragged a box of Cressida's outgrown clothing from her old room, and Miranda pulled a flannel sleep suit dotted with planets over Luloah's frail limbs. Once everyone was dressed, Negasi arrived with carrot-lentil soup and some bread on a tray. Halfway through her bowl, Miranda began to slide down the wooden headboard, like one of the spineless dolls Cressie rejected in favor of furry animals. Finn removed the bowl, helped Negasi finish feeding Luloah, and not knowing what else to do with her, tucked her in next to Miranda. He had expected Cressida to protest Luloah's claim to her mother, but his daughter was still cautious, unsure. Not in the least bit interested in climbing into bed with this stranger who was allegedly her missing mother, Cressie was happy for Finn to tuck her into her own familiar cot, which embassy staff had brought over along with the rest of their things. As she lay still, surrounded by a sleuth of bears, Finn read her the original Corduroy book, her favorite, read it over all three of them, like a benediction.

Hours later, he climbed in next to his wife, reaching out an arm to pull her into him. He wanted desperately to curl around her, to make her feel protected and secure. But the instant he touched her she had bolted upright, crying out, and it took him half an hour to talk her back into herself again. The child did not wake.

"I can't sleep," Miranda whispered to him around 2:00 a.m., when she woke for the second time. "The bed is too soft." And she slipped down, taking the top blanket with her. A moment later Luloah began to wail and was inconsolable until Finn set her down next to Miranda.

Now Luloah is stretched out on the floor beside her, the glowing Saturn on her stomach expanding and contracting with each breath. In a corner of the room, Cressida softly snores in her cot. Finn can't sleep either, but it isn't the softness of the bed keeping him from the arms of Morpheus. Why is Miranda nursing this child, and who are her parents? Where will they all go now? The Office will want to talk with her tomorrow, to convince her to get on a plane to London. It occurs to him that this is going to be harder than he thought. Much, much harder.

FEBRUARY 17, 2011
Miranda

She cannot sleep. On her back on the cool stone of their bedroom floor, she listens to the jazz symphony of her heartbeat as pain burns its way from her palm up through her forearm and triceps and the back of her shoulder. *Please, let there not be nerve damage. Let my hand emerge from this prison.* The ghost of that spike remains in her palm. Tentatively she flexes her fingers, sending sparks of agony up her arm. She rolls to her right side, propping her left arm up with a pillow, as Dr.

Jay had shown her, but it doesn't help. She should have taken the sedatives offered to her, but she hadn't wanted to dull her mind. Not now, when she needed more than ever to be present. Sitting up, she glances over at Finn, curled like a child on his side, mouth drifting open, breathing quietly.

There he is, so miraculously close. And yet, she is still trying to find her way back to him. For months she had dreamed of throwing herself into his arms and now she recoils from his touch. His unfamiliar scent. She doesn't understand it. Where is the physical ease they had always shared? Even talking feels difficult, sometimes impossible. So much seems to lie between them; the thought of trying to tell him everything that has happened, that she has thought and felt since she last kissed him good-bye, is overwhelming. She doesn't know how to begin. He is patient with her, undemanding, but she senses his loneliness. He wants his wife back—his real wife, lively and laughing, not the anesthetized ghost she has become. Luloah lies between them, close to rolling under the bed but unmoving for the moment. How can she explain Luloah?

A crush of thoughts crowds her brain. She had hardly arrived home, had hardly taken a long look at her husband and daughter, when the Brits began thrusting crisis counselors in her face and talking about getting her to England. Security staff want to debrief her, friends want to come see for themselves that she has survived, and Dr. Jay wants her hand treated in London. Decisions are being forced on her from every direction. If only she could pause everything until her mind has caught up with it all. For now, she wants nothing but Finn and Cressida, to sit with them relearning their faces and listening to their voices. She isn't ready to get on a plane. She isn't ready to be psychoanalyzed. She wants stillness and space. She wants to press her unfamiliar family against her skin until she relearns their shapes. Couldn't they just be left alone?

Shifting her weight onto her right palm, Miranda pushes herself to her feet and walks down the hallway to Cressida's room. Since Miranda's return, Cressida has not allowed her to pick her up or even touch her, backing away toward her father or a bear. Fearful of scaring her, Miranda resists doing the one thing she has dreamed of more than anything else for six months. Now, she stands over her alien daughter, still sleeping on her back, still surrendering in her sleep. Carefully, using her right arm and her left forearm, she hefts Cressida toward her. She is heavy, her weight unrecognizable. It takes the last dram of Miranda's strength to heave her up, but the reward is inestimable. Leaning on the end of the crib, sweating from the pain, she slides to the floor, cradling the still sleeping child. Miranda bends her head to inhale Cressie's scent, sunshine-baked earth with undertones of Finn's aftershave. She has hair now, most of her head covered with Finn's curls. Miranda kisses her eyebrows and her still-chubby cheeks and her nose and fingers and belly. She opens her mouth to sing to her, but nothing comes out. Her mouth is dry, empty. Still, she sits there soaking in her daughter, her greatest love, even while her arm burns.

She lacks the energy and motivation to rise. Only toward dawn, when Cressida awakes and cries to find herself in unfamiliar arms, does Miranda release her. A sleep-creased Finn appears in the doorway, cradling an equally distraught Luloah, and silently, they trade children.

MARCH 11, 2011
Miranda

The island air clings to their skin like damp silk, the relentless sun painting their bodies with sweat, but Miranda refuses to wear a hat. "I've missed out on a lot of UV poisoning," she said. "I have to catch up." She does, however, concede to wear sunblock, and slathered both girls with it so that they now resemble iced gingerbread people. They are playing at the edge of the water, Luloah sitting in a soggy diaper arranging pebbles in straight lines, Cressida in a long-sleeved UV-protecting suit, flinging gleeful arcs of sand into the sea.

Miranda sits on the sand a few yards away, watching them with her knees drawn up to her chest. She still isn't allowed in the water; her bandaged hand is recovering from surgery. "What I don't understand," she says, "is what they were hoping to accomplish. Even if they killed me, what would it accomplish? Did they really think that would stop the drones? Or have any effect whatsoever? I'm a completely unimportant person." They have already been over this, countless times, but she is still uncomprehending. Something is wrong with her memory; she hears things and they fail to stick, slipping away from the frictionless fingers of her mind when she tries to retrieve them.

"It's hard to know for sure." Finn sits several feet away from her, in a long-sleeved T-shirt, khaki shorts, and a panama hat. "We're thinking that it was a combination of things. Mukhtar was probably offered good money for delivering you. More than he would earn in a lifetime with the embassy. It's possible that the people who took you from him didn't initially realize they wouldn't get a ransom for you. Or they simply wanted to spread fear. If they can get an ambassador's wife with a bodyguard, they can get almost anyone. And then of course you were perfect—in their minds—for trying to make a statement. About the drones, US foreign policy in general. The usual. American civilians will be kidnapped and killed until the US withdraws from all Arab lands . . . That sort of thing."

"And it was just luck they got the other two women?"

"That was opportunistic, we think." Miranda can tell he is unsure how much to tell her. She is to be treated like a ticking time bomb with an elusive detonator, the therapists have probably instructed him. No telling what might explode her fragile equilibrium.

She is silent for a moment, thinking. Cressida scoops up two handfuls of Luloah's pebbles in her chubby fingers and tosses them into the sea. The little girl gazes in horror at the ragged disruption of her orderly line and begins to wail. Miranda scrapes up a handful of pebbles from the sand beside her and takes them to Luloah. "Here, *habibti*. Cressie, don't take things from the baby. She doesn't understand." Ignoring her, Cressida grabs another handful. "Sweetheart . . . No more, okay?" No answer. Her daughter no longer responds to her as an authority. Sighing, Miranda picks up Luloah, moves her a few feet farther down the beach, and turns back to Finn.

"And Tazzy's paintings? Who would take those?"

"I have an idea about that. I need to think it through."

"You mean you think you *know*? Finn, you realize there are paintings of me too, don't you? Did Tazzy tell you?"

Finn stares at her, the pupils of his hazel eyes shrinking to pinpoints in the sunlight. Apparently Tazkia had left that part out. "Finn, find those paintings. Please, as soon as we get back. I can't take on any new enemies right now. The last thing I need is the modesty police after me."

He nods slowly, still calculating what it all means. They aren't supposed to be back in Arnabiya for another two weeks. Miranda had, after a prolonged battle, miraculously convinced the Office to let them both stay in the country until the end of Finn's posting in June, on the condition that she accept trauma counseling and draconian security precautions. She and Finn haven't had very much time alone together since her escape. The Trauma Risk Management (TRiM) assessors showed up about seventy-two hours after her arrival, to debrief and assess her. Apparently they hadn't found her too irrevocably damaged, or they wouldn't be letting her stay. "Some people find revisiting the scene of traumatic events helps them recover," one counselor said to Finn. "It is possible she needs to be here for a little while, to somehow defuse or neutralize her memories of her experiences here."

Miranda had a simpler explanation. "I don't want to be afraid of Mazrooq, of my life here. This is not how I want to leave the place that has been my home for so many years. And won't the terrorists be impressed that I haven't run straight home to the cushy West?"

The counselor had patted her knee gently and said, "Let's not worry about impressing terrorists now, love."

One counselor has suggested that she try something called EMDR—eye movement desensitization and reprocessing—apparently the latest thing in treating trauma victims. This involves moving her eyes in a way that mimics the way they move in sleep, which is supposed to help store traumatic events in long-term memory, where they are less troublesome. Miranda is happy to try it—especially if she gets to stay in the country—but she feels pretty lucky on the trauma front. Really, what has happened to her? She was beaten only a few times, was never raped, and had eluded torture. She hadn't physically suffered as so many others had. As had the man in the cell next to hers. That is the memory that causes the strongest waves of nausea, the one she will use when she tries EMDR, she decides. But does overhearing someone else's trauma count as her own trauma? It doesn't seem right. And yet. She wonders where that man is now. Has he died in the bombing, or has he somehow also escaped?

Her greatest personal suffering had been living apart from her daughter and Finn. She still cannot believe she has both of them back. A dozen times every night she creeps out of her nest on the floor to press her cheek to Cressida's, to inhale her soapy scent, to listen to her quiet breathing.

Every day, she spends a couple hours sifting through the sediment of her memories with a therapist, complaining that the time would be better spent reconnecting with her daughter. Just one affectionate gesture from Cressida would improve her mental health far more than counseling ever could.

While the Office agreed to let them stay, it had insisted on a holiday of several weeks. But Miranda refused to leave the country because Luloah wouldn't be able to accompany them. The child has no passport, no birth certificate, nothing. Finn did not explain this to the Office. As far as they know, Luloah is one of Tazkia's nieces, who needs care while her mother is in the hospital. As a compromise, Finn and Miranda agreed to spend a couple of weeks on this island in the Red Sea, still technically part of the country though it feels a world away. Halim had joyfully welcomed them to his remote resort, tears in his warm brown eyes. "I never thought I would see this day," he says, every time he sees Miranda. For the duration of their stay he has allowed no other guests (not that tourists are clamoring to vacation here, given the events of the past year). At night they sleep in a round hut with a palm-frond roof, underneath layers of mosquito netting. Halim cooks for them himself, preparing salads, grilled fish and shrimp, hummus, bread. At night after the girls are asleep, Miranda and Finn walk down to the sea, holding hands as they stand staring out into the black night, so dark they cannot tell where the water ends and the sky begins.

The sound of grains of sand rubbing together under her feet

grates on Miranda's nerves, but the girls are euphoric here, which is all that matters to her at the moment. Finn too seems to enjoy designing improbable sand castles and catamarans, digging channels down to the sea. He never looks happier than when he is arranging a picnic for Cressie's bears or reading to her from *The Wind in the Willows*. He has also been kind to Luloah, singing to her at night and helping to bathe and change her. But his care is cautious, the kind of care one might take of a friend's child on a sleepover. There is always a slight remove, and a question in his eyes when he looks at Miranda.

Before they left for this island, Miranda flew to Dubai to see a hand specialist and undergo surgery. Finn wanted to accompany her, but she made him promise to stay with the girls. She trusts no one but Finn. Even when it meant possibly losing his job, he hadn't gone back to London to wait for them to be found. He had stayed here.

However, Finn agreed to stay in Mazrooq only when Miranda's father decided to face his terror of flying to meet his daughter in Dubai. "It must be love," said Miranda. "This is a man who has not been on an airplane since 1987." She didn't believe he would actually make it until he tapped on the door of her hotel room the night before her first appointment. He looked smaller than she remembered, pale and slight with just a fringe of white hair remaining, his eyes watery with emotion.

"That Xanax is wonderful stuff," he said, as she wrapped her arms around him.

They made themselves gin and tonics from the minibar and stayed up past midnight talking, Miranda sprawled on the bed and her father perched on the edge of the pink velvet armchair. While her father had initially been anxious to make sure she was really okay, mentally as well as physically, he eventually felt reassured enough to expound upon his latest research. Miranda didn't care if he sat there reading to her from a physics textbook; she just wanted to listen to the soporific rumble of his voice, as she had done as a child when he read to her of Ariadne and Athena. She must have drifted off while he was talking; when she woke just before dawn, he had gone back to his room.

The next morning he escorted her to the hospital. Miranda was grateful for his undemanding presence; he asked no difficult questions and read to her for hours while they waited for anesthesiologists and surgeons. He attended her appointments, asking her surgeon the questions Miranda lacked the energy or courage to pose. "It's her painting hand," he had repeatedly explained. "Please be extra careful." The operation had gone smoothly, though the post-surgical pain was acute when the drugs began wearing off. There was no reason she wouldn't be able to paint again, said the doctor, but it would take months to retrain the muscles.

"Sure you don't want to come back to Mazrooq with me?" Miranda asked when it was all over and they were on their way to the airport.

"Sure you don't want to come back to Seattle with me?"

"Dad, I've *been* to Seattle! You've never *seen* Mazrooq. Arnabiya is the most beautiful city in the world. More important, you could see Finn. He has always loved you."

"If you don't mind, could I visit you in Finn's next posting?"

"Wow, that Xanax must really be good. But I'm not entirely sure there will be a next posting."

Her father looked at her inquiringly.

"We have a lot to sort out still."

He nodded. "I imagine you do."

Her father had listened to what she had to say about Luloah, about her captivity, about Finn, and offered no judgments or advice. For Miranda, this was enough.

"No word from Mom?"

"Not yet."

Miranda stared out the window at the remote, glittering towers of Dubai. "I'm sorry."

"When she wants to be found, she'll be found, and not before. You know your mother."

"I do." She picked up her father's small, dry hand, and held it all the way to the airport.

WITH HER HAND bandaged, Miranda has to leave all of the diaper changing and bathing to Finn, who has taken over with grace.

She has told Finn everything she knows about Luloah. While it isn't much, it is enough to worry him. When she had confessed whom she believed the child's father to be, the vertical line between his brows deepened. "These are not people we want to piss off," he'd said.

"It's a little late for that. Do you think they'll be happy that I managed to slip out of their clutches? Surely you don't think I should have stuck around just to keep them placated?"

"Of course not. But she's not our child, Mira."

Miranda had only looked at him, doors slamming shut in her eyes. "Well, maybe not *yours*," she had said evenly. Finn had let the subject drop.

Finn

But here on the beach, as he watches little Luloah push her pebbles into the mouth of a plastic bottle that has washed up on the shore (the better to keep them away from Cressie), he feels compelled to revisit the issue.

"Mira, could we talk about the child?" he says.

She squints at him with sudden intransigence. "The *child*?"

"Luloah."

"Talk," she says.

"I can see how you feel about her," he says. "I only have the slightest idea of what you have been through, and I suspect that she helped to save you as much as you saved her. But we cannot keep her."

Miranda pulls her knees closer to her chest and stares at the sand, unwilling to look at him.

"First of all, adoption is illegal in this country—at least the kind of adoption that would allow us to take her home with us. No matter how much we might want her. You know that, don't you?"

Miranda remains mute, unmoving.

"And even if there were a way around the law, you know how I feel about adoption. I just couldn't feel the same way about her that I feel about Cressie. And is that fair?"

She looks up. "Could you *really* not?"

"We've had this conversation before."

"I know, but . . . Look at her, Finn. *Look* at her."

Finn looks. Luloah is already noticeably chubbier than when he first met her. Her hair is thick and spiky, and when she smiles as she shakes her bottle of pebbles at Cressida he can see two teeth in her lower jaw. "Mira, she is a lovely child. You don't need to convince me."

"Even if you don't love her like you love Cressie—and don't parents always love each of their children differently, biological or not?—wouldn't what you could offer her still be better than the alternatives?"

"She belongs to a tribe, Mira. She has her own people."

"So what are we supposed to do with her? Send her back to the terrorists to become a future suicide bomber? Or to be wrapped up in synthetic fibers, denied an education, and married at the age of twelve to a lecherous old man?"

"There are others in her tribe besides terrorists, maybe a family who could care for her—"

"You cannot be that naïve. Those men only kept me alive because of her. She is Zajnoon's only remaining child. Do you think she will be allowed to live a peaceful family life? Do you seriously think they won't be pressuring her to produce an heir by the time she turns thirteen?"

"There is the orphanage. You said the children were treated well there, that they looked happy."

"Only compared to my subterranean expectations! It's still an *orphanage*, where she won't have anyone's attention for more than a few minutes a day. Where she will come down with every Mazrooqi infection. She will have food and clothing, but what about love? What about when she is older? Where will she go? And actually, do you think Zajnoon's people won't find her there?"

Finn sighs. "So just what do you suggest we do?"

"We take her with us when we go."

"And how do you propose to get her a passport? I don't suppose you picked up her birth certificate up north?"

Miranda looks at him, tears in her eyes. "You don't understand," she says. "She doesn't remember any mother but me. What do you think it will do to her if I give her up now?"

"She's so young," says Finn as gently as he can. "She won't remember."

"Maybe not consciously, but her cells will know. All of her atoms will know that they were once loved and then thrown away."

"Oh, sweetheart," Finn says, a desperate sadness in his eyes. "I don't want to throw her away." He reaches a hand toward her and then withdraws it.

"Don't you?" The tears are coming fast now.

"Mira, Mira, stop. We can talk about it another time. Let's not let the children see you upset."

"I have been nursing that tiny girl for more than five months now. She is *made* from molecules of my milk. Do you see that fat on her cheeks? That is part me. Those toes? Little pieces of Miranda. If that doesn't make her part of my tribe, then I don't know what does."

Finn can think of nothing to say.

APRIL 3, 2011
Finn

Finn watches Miranda from across the sitting room as she leans in to listen to the Mazrooqi Minister of Islamic Affairs expounding from the chair next to hers. Her body is still, her eyes focused gently on his, her brow slightly furrowed. When the man on her other side interrupts to add his thoughts, she trains the same attention on him. It fascinates Finn to observe this evolution of his wife. Captivity has taught her silence, has taught her how to listen. When she does speak, it is to ask a thoughtful yet pointed question. She is naturally more anti-drones than ever, but she expresses her opinions tactfully and only after having drawn out those of her Mazrooqi companions. While he had personally enjoyed her combative stance at dinner parties, he realizes that what she has become is much more effective. Could she be—a startling thought—learning the art of diplomacy?

At the moment he is particularly grateful for her powers of distraction. Their most recent visitor from the UK, one of the country's few Muslim MPs, is nearly an hour late for the dinner they are hosting in his honor, and stomachs, including his own, are rumbling. Yet no one is glancing toward the dining room or checking his watch. A hand on his sleeve interrupts his reverie. "*Sa'adat as-safir?*" says the Minister of Water, to whom he is supposed to be listening. "I was asking what you thought about solar-powered desalinization plants." Reluctantly, Finn gives up trying to eavesdrop on Miranda's group and turns to the man at his side.

Finally, Fawzi Aswad and his entourage arrive. Finn tries not to show his annoyance at their tardiness as he escorts the MP to the table. No cocktail for him, not when he can't be bothered to show up on time for his own party. (They hadn't been sure he would drink anyway, but it turned out he was one of those westernized Muslims who were happy to accept a glass of wine if unobserved by other Muslims.) It hasn't been one of his better official visits. Earlier in the day Finn had taken Aswad to meet the president, and the MP had promised the president a whole host of things he could not possibly deliver. First, Aswad had assured him that the UK would entirely fund the renovation of a hospital in the South, where he was born. This would take millions of pounds. In fact, it would take the entire development budget for the country. Exacerbating matters, Aswad then promised the president that the UK would crack down on the pirate Mazrooqi TV station operating out of Britain, despite the fact that the station was breaking no British law. This promise sends unforgivable messages: that British laws are meaningless and that freedom of the press is unimportant. And because of these ridiculous messages, the president had dismissed them before they had time to address the situation with the North, which is disintegrating daily. The government has escalated its attacks, and the northerners have shut down all routes to their territories. Additionally, Aswad was late for nearly all of his meetings and had a habit of talking over other people. Why do we elect people like him? Finn wondered. Thank god Miranda is sitting next to him at dinner.

She does an admirable job of it too, smiling and nodding and asking him question after question about his political career and his thoughts on Britain's development priorities. It hadn't taken long for English to return to her, though she still prefers Arabic. Now, she pushes her coriander carrots and fish around on the plate but doesn't eat more than a few mouthfuls. "I don't know why I am never hungry," she once told Finn. "I was always starving up north." She doesn't drink that much either, though the TRiM assessors have warned him to watch out for increased alcohol use. A few bites of food and a few sips of wine are usually all she can manage. The variety and quantity of food in their kitchen seems to overwhelm her. One morning he found her standing paralyzed in front of an open cupboard. "We have *seven kinds* of cereal!" she cried, tears running down her cheeks. *"Seven!"* Unable to choose, she hadn't eaten anything.

She is happiest with the girls. With them, she loses her reserve, her frequent detachment, sitting on the floor of Cressie's room patiently building towers out of wooden blocks for them to knock over. Finn has tried every way he knows to persuade Miranda of the wisdom of finding Mazrooqi parents for Luloah, but she remains unmoving on the topic. Finn realizes his options are limited if he intends to keep his wife. He cannot exactly kidnap the child and drive her to the orphanage or up north without destroying Miranda's fragile peace of mind, and quite probably their marriage.

Now he wonders if he really wants to change Miranda's mind after all. While she was in Dubai, it was he and not any of the staff members who had given the child her bottles of frozen breast milk. At first she had resisted, just as Cressida had when Miranda disappeared, but in the end Finn had persuaded her. It is dangerous, this feeding of orphaned children, he thinks. Habit-forming.

Toward the end of the evening he can sense Miranda's exhaustion. She gets tired easily, often falling asleep with Luloah in the afternoon. At night she is restless, mostly sleeping on the floor. Finn is still careful never to touch her in sleep, afraid of startling her. It has been nearly two months now, and they still haven't made love. At night she lies in bed paging through books on her women Surrealists, lingering over images of solitary hooded figures. Why these artists?

he had asked. She so often had a reason. But she had just shrugged. "Nothing else makes sense right now."

He has promised himself to wait until she comes to him. Her therapists have told him to give her as much control over her life as possible, letting her make decisions about the structure of their days, their meals, their outings. He assumes this extends to sex. When the therapists advised him to be as predictable and reliable as possible, he had laughed. "I'm afraid I've never been anything but."

Fortunately tonight no one lingers over the tea and coffee, gulping it down and dashing for the door, in that uniquely Mazrooqi way. Aswad and his entourage quickly trail after them, and Finn and Miranda are left alone on their veranda, sipping coffee in the cooling night. "Thank you," he says. "I'm sure you were far more polite than I could have been."

She shrugs. "It's easy when nothing feels important."

"Nothing?"

"Not Aswad."

They are silent for a few moments. Finn can taste the honeysuckle in the air.

"Can I ask you something?" Miranda leans forward suddenly in her chair, the same chair he had been sitting in when he upended the table not so long ago while having tea with Celia. A lifetime ago.

"Of course."

"Did you ever find him? Mukhtar, that is?"

Finn debates how to answer this. He never lies to her, but he can no longer predict her response to anything and he wants to be careful.

"Yes."

"And?"

Finn runs just one finger across the back of her bony hand. "He was still alive, Mira. I don't know if this is good news or bad news . . ."

Miranda straightens in her chair, as if abruptly relieved of a weight. "He is alive?"

"You gave him a pretty bad concussion and a cracked skull, but he's alive and well and imprisoned in the Central Jail."

"Where he may not remain for long."

"Where he may not remain for long," Finn concedes. "Mazrooqi jails being Mazrooqi jails."

Miranda considers this. "Surely he wouldn't stay here? In this city?"

"I doubt it. If he gets out I think he'll head north. Though you never know."

"No," she says. "You don't."

She sits staring into her coffee for a moment and then looks up at him and smiles. "It's good news, sweetheart, don't you think? That I am not a murderer?"

"Yes," he says. "Good news indeed." And he takes her hand.

APRIL 29, 2011
Miranda

Miranda sits, staring at the blank canvas in front of her. Spread out on her worktable are colors and palette, brushes and Zest-it. The stink of oils and oranges wafts memories toward her: long afternoons of toil in her old city *diwan,* safe in the rocky womb of her house. Painting so seriously, as if the result mattered, as if it could end war or feed a child. Now, she hungers for these instruments of her craft not because she harbors the illusion that she will create something lasting, something important or praiseworthy. But rather because she believes if she can just empty her teeming head onto that blankness, spread out every theory, belief, and opinion before her, she will begin to understand them.

Yet she cannot touch the brushes. She is afraid. Too soon after her surgery, too soon after the bandages had been unraveled, she had tried to transfer an image to paper and her hand had moved as if a stranger to her. No longer an instrument of her will, of even her subconscious impulses, it had moved under the directive of some malign spirit. The result was a splotchy mess communicating nothing, revealing nothing. She remained locked in her own skull.

"Suddenly, I'm a fucking amateur Impressionist," she'd said tearfully, emptying an entire jar of gesso over her efforts. Later that night,

Finn had found her burning the canvas in their garden. Now, the matches have disappeared from the kitchen, along with the knives and any other sharp instruments. Finn isn't taking any chances on her mental state. She has promised him repeatedly that no matter how despairing she got, she would never harm herself, would never put him and Cressida and Luloah through that loss. So perhaps he is just trying to protect her work—though it no longer feels like her work. Nothing she creates has any relationship to her.

But she is stronger now. Twice a week she goes to the Saudi-German Hospital to see a stout Russian physical therapist who gives her exercises to improve her fine motor skills. She takes these seriously, spending an hour every morning slowly contorting fingers and thumb around a small red ball. Finn has been urging her to return to work. "So many times you have told me that your work is how you process the world," he said. "And when have you ever been more in need of processing the world?"

"Perhaps I don't always want to know what I am thinking," she responded. But she does. She does want to know. She is just too afraid to see how altered her mind—and her hand and her vision and her movement—has become. She is afraid that the voice she once had has been forever silenced.

Pushing herself up from her chair, Miranda picks up her phone from the desk and dials the only person she thinks might understand.

THE TWO WOMEN stand next to each other in the studio, staring at the empty canvas. It is the first time they have been alone together since Miranda's return. Tazkia has visited several times to play with the girls, but never to come to the studio. "I don't know how to begin again," says Miranda, wrapping her cardigan more tightly around her. "I don't know what to do if it doesn't work."

Tazkia, still clad in *abaya* and *hijab*, is silent. She looks at the easel, at the paints, and out the window at Semere cutting the grass. "After everything," she says. "This is what matters?"

Startled and dismayed, Miranda turns to her. "*Yes.* It matters. The mere act of doing it matters. I thought you might understand that.

Isn't that why you haven't been able to stop yourself for all of these years? Why you kept scribbling in those school notebooks, knowing the possible consequences? Of course it's not the only thing that matters, of course not. For me there is Finn and Cressie and Luloah. And you. And the thirteen million struggling women of this country. And safety and stopping the momentum toward war and hunger and pain and disease. But there is also *this*."

Tazkia looks down, examining her shoes. "I'm not sure I am the right person to help you."

Miranda turns to her. "Tazzy, I don't have anyone else. No one else here who knows what it means to speak with a paintbrush." Her voice is desperate, pleading. She hates the sound of it. What does she think Tazkia can do for her?

"I'm not sure I still know how. To speak with a paintbrush, I mean." Tazkia shifts uneasily from foot to foot.

Miranda looks at her in surprise. "Aren't you working?"

Tazkia shakes her head, her brown eyes lusterless. "Not since the paintings disappeared."

Taking Tazkia's hand, Miranda pulls her down on the studio sofa. "Tazzy," she says, stroking the short brown fingers. "We'll find them. I promise. We'll keep you safe."

Tazkia avoids her eyes, staring down at her lap so that the folds of her *hijab* fall across her plump cheeks. "I don't think that's possible."

"But we haven't heard anything at all yet. If someone had seen them, if someone wanted to expose you—expose us—wouldn't they already have done it?" Finn hasn't been able to track down the secret paintings. Late one night, fortified by a few gin and tonics, he had cornered Norman in the club. But the OSM had denied any knowledge of the paintings. "But you're the only one with a key," Finn had insisted. "Who else could have taken them?" Norman had shrugged. It is maddening, waiting for them to turn up. Terrifying for Tazkia. Thank god Norman is leaving in May; Miranda feels sick every time she sees his face.

Tazkia looks up then, but without hope. "What else would they do with them?"

Miranda sighs. "I don't know."

Tazkia looks away from her, toward the open door.

"What are the chances anyone would even know the paintings are of you? Maybe whoever took them doesn't know who you are."

Tazkia finally looks at her, with the first hint of hope in her eyes. "Maybe," she says. Only then does Miranda remember she had stupidly written Tazkia's name on the back of the canvas, in tiny, perhaps illegible letters. She does not say this.

"Why don't you paint with me a little? Add a little beauty to the world? Try to think of something else?"

"No." Her voice is firm. "Not me."

Miranda looks at her, leaden despair tugging at her gut. "Okay," she says, deciding not to press the issue. "I'm sorry, Tazzy. I'm sorry to bring you here if it upsets you."

"I wish I could help you, if this is what you really want." Tazkia looks again at the canvas, then down at Miranda's scarred left hand. "Do you remember the stick exercise?" she says abruptly, her tone lightening. "When we taped the sticks to our paintbrushes and you said we needed to let go of control?"

Miranda stares at her former student, disconcerted by the change in direction.

"This is what you need to do! Now your hand *is* the stick. It is keeping you from controlling your brushes in your usual way, no?"

Miranda turns her palm over in her lap, examining it as if expecting to find it sprouting leaves.

"Can't you let your hand talk in a new way, even though it doesn't feel right, doesn't feel like you? Because it *is* still you. A damaged you. An uncontrolled you."

Miranda looks up from her hand and stands. Without her customary control, perhaps her unconscious will finally take the lead. Perhaps there are wonders to discover, surreal juxtapositions she cannot purposefully invent. Slowly, like a sleepwalker, she steps toward her easel. Tazkia remains sitting as Miranda smears a paintbrush in a dish of black ink and holds it over the void. "Nothing is precious," Tazkia whispers, quoting her teacher. "What comes from your hand is not important." When Miranda touches down, begins moving the ink in shaky lines, Tazkia slips out the door. It is nearly an hour before Miranda notices she is gone.

MAY 5, 2011
Norman

Norman sweats his way to the check-in desk. He's wearing too many clothes for the afternoon heat, but his bags are stuffed to overflowing and he hadn't had room for everything. He is relieved to be heading home. It has unquestionably been an action-filled posting, and he is looking forward to a few months in the relative safety of his Clapham Common flat before heading off to Mali. His wife has gone on ahead to London, leaving him to organize the packers and their airfreight, and he relishes the prospect of a solo flight. He can already taste that first gin and tonic. A family of nine pushes ahead of him, dragging a tower of ragged suitcases and cartons. Damn these Mazrooqis. Why can't they learn how to queue properly? They all rush the ticket desk in a mob, and you have to fight your way through them to the front if you want a decent seat. Doesn't matter if you're flying business class; there's no business class until you're on the plane. Fucking third-world airports. These he won't miss when he retires. Heathrow has its drawbacks, but at least people there know how to queue.

At last at the front, he heaves his three suitcases one by one onto the scales, hanging on to the oversized paper-and-string-wrapped parcel of paintings. He hadn't known what else to do with them. He couldn't leave them behind, had been unable to think of anywhere to leave them that wouldn't give himself away. And he certainly couldn't have sent them ahead with the rest of his luggage for his wife to unpack back in London. He had to take them with him, and checking them seemed too risky. The airport people weren't supposed to check diplomats' bags, but the Mazrooqis were not renowned for doing the things they were supposed to do.

He is ashamed of his own weakness. He'd had no malign intent when he removed them from their hiding place. It was just—they were captivating. He had wanted to take them somewhere he could sit and look at them for a long, long time. It was the painting of Miranda that had first caught his eye, of course. But then he saw the other one. A woman, small, dark, clearly Mazrooqi. He'd never even seen an exposed female Mazrooqi face, let alone all that lay below. Not that she was anatomically different from any other woman; it was the knowledge of where she came from that made it so especially titillating. He wondered who she was. Obviously a friend of Miranda's. A *good* friend. And then it occurred to him—was she a friend? Or something more?

He had discovered the paintings while doing an inventory of the safe room just before Celia moved into the Residence. Finn must have forgotten them in his distraction over the kidnapping. Before Norman had time to properly examine his motives, he was stuffing them into bin liners and toting them to his car. Perhaps it had been merely erotic fascination that prompted him. But he'd be a liar if he didn't admit he'd briefly wondered if he could somehow use them against Finn. Then again, the kidnapping seemed punishment enough. Finally, Finn was suffering. It was a relief to Norman that he felt no need to make things worse.

While he has certainly enjoyed studying these works of art, if you could call them that, these works of primitive pornography, he almost regrets having taken them. What is he going to do with them in London except discreetly try to get rid of them somewhere? It isn't as though he could keep them in their flat. What's worse is that Finn knows he was the one to take them. No one else had keys. He was a fucking idiot sometimes.

"Sir, that parcel is too large for a carry-on," the pretty black-haired girl behind the counter tells him, nodding at the paintings. "You'll have to check it."

"Surely not," he says. "I'm flying business."

"Nevertheless," she says. "It must fit in this." She gestures to the wire display indicating the proper size for a carry-on. You have got to be joking, he thinks. Of all times to follow the fucking rules.

"Surely you can make an exception? I'm a diplomat, and this is an important package."

"You will have to check it." The woman picks up one end of the parcel, apparently with the intention of heaving it onto the conveyor belt behind her. Sweat soaking his armpits, Norman lunges at the package, catching just the edge. The thick paper tears. He watches in horror as a triangular strip of brown paper peels away to reveal, in all of its naked glory, a vagina. And not just an ordinary vagina, but a monstrously oversized vagina seemingly crafted from sweets, from the ribbons of red-and-white peppermint he had loved as child and a well-placed lemon drop.

For a moment, the airport is, for the first time in its existence, silent. Then a roar of outrage erupts. Two men grab Norman's arms, holding him still while someone shouts for security, for the police. His Arabic isn't good enough to understand all that swirls around him. The check-in counter girl has stepped away from the package in revulsion, as if afraid it will contaminate her. In front of him, several men tear open the rest of the package, exposing the sugar-sticky thighs, the dark hair, the sweetest and most sacred places of those two untouchable girls.

MAY 5, 2011
Finn

Finn is at the office when he gets the call from the airport. As soon as he has figured out what the angry man on the other end is shouting at him, he hangs up the receiver, waits for a dial tone, and rings Tazkia.

"Where are you?" he says. If it didn't involve gearing up an entire armored convoy, he'd be tempted to head out to get her.

"Home. We're in the middle of breakfast. What is it?" Her voice is anxious; she already knows the only reason he would ring her.

"Listen carefully. As quickly as you can, pack a few things, whatever is most important to you, and get to the Residence. You may not be able to go back. Do you understand me?" If only those paintings hadn't been titled and signed.

"I do." Her voice is small, terrified.

"Tazkia, do you have a passport?"

"I'm on my father's."

Finn winces. Damn these countries that don't allow women their own passports, where women are treated as perpetual children incapable of managing their own lives.

"All right. We'll think of something. If you have any identification papers at all, try to find them."

"I will try." She sounds doubtful.

"You are going to be all right, Tazkia, we will take care of you. Don't cry. Your parents mustn't suspect anything until you are safely here. Miranda will be at the Residence waiting for you."

"Yes. Thank you."

"As soon as you can, do you understand? I don't think you have very long."

"I understand."

Finn rings Miranda next to ask her to prepare a room for Tazkia before calling airport security back, bracing himself for a diplomatic shitstorm.

MAY 5, 2011
Miranda

Miranda sits watching Tazkia mangle one of Finn's blue silk handkerchiefs. Her tiny friend is curled in a ball in a corner of her blue studio sofa, as hysterical as Miranda has ever seen her. "I'm so sorry," she says. "I'm so sorry." What else is there to say? She has ruined the life of the one person she cares most about, outside of her family. If only she had said *no*, it wasn't a good idea for them to make the paintings. If only she had burned them as soon as they were finished. If she hadn't been stupid enough to go off hiking in the hills in the current security situation. If only one of Tazkia's many cousins didn't work at the airport.

"Tazzy. Tazzy, we have to talk about what to do." There is no response. Miranda gets up and makes her a cup of tea, with seven spoonfuls of sugar and lashings of milk. When she carries it back to the sofa, Tazkia accepts it with shaking hands.

"Where will I go?" she says finally. "Where is there for me? Nowhere. I have no family anywhere."

"You have us."

Tazkia looks at her skeptically. "I can't stay here."

"No. Not for too long. You can stay here for a few days, but I think we need to get you out of the country before your family figures out where you are."

"To where?"

"To wherever we can get you a visa. Do you have a passport?"

Tazkia's face crumples.

"Okay, okay. Look, Finn will help us. He will think of something." Miranda has no idea if this is true. "Taz. Would your family really hurt you?" She knows Tazkia's family, has eaten her mother's homemade flatbread, borrowed her sisters' sequined dresses for wedding parties, and discussed politics with her father. She cannot imagine any of them wanting to harm their youngest child.

"I don't know. I don't know. Nothing like this has ever happened. Probably not ever in this country. I don't see how they can ever forgive me." She blows her nose vigorously in the hankie.

"Maybe someday, maybe if you go away for a while, mightn't they someday forgive you? You can write to them, try to explain."

"They won't understand! And how could I explain to Adan?"

"The same way you explained to me why you wanted to do it?"

Tazkia just shakes her head. "He is the kindest, gentlest, most loving man I have ever met. But he is Mazrooqi. He is Muslim. There is no way for him to understand this. He lacks the—what is it you are always saying? The cultural subtext?"

"The cultural context. Oh, Taz. I have ruined everything for you."

Tazkia doesn't refute this, just sits twisting the mauled blue silk in her fingers. Maybe it was a bad idea to sit in the studio, where they are surrounded by paintings. Naked women, alone, entwined, embodying objects, confront them from every side. Miranda feels an impulse to turn them all toward the wall.

She struggles to come up with a scrap of hope for her protégée. "Most of my friends and family are in the US," she says, "but I don't think we can get you there. It will be too hard to get a visa. Same with the UK. Let me think . . . Do you have friends in any other Arab country? Jordan? Egypt?"

Tazkia shakes her head. "I have never had the opportunity to travel," she says. "My family has no money. People like us don't leave home. You know this." It is true; only women from the most elite families, with both money and political connections, are able to study abroad, develop careers.

"Is there anywhere you think you might like to go?" Miranda asks hopefully. "It's probably safest if we get you out of the Middle East altogether, actually."

"No." Tazkia is decisive. "This is my home. What I want is to be here. With Adan, with my family."

Her heart sinking, Miranda lists out loud the places she might have friends willing to help Tazkia. "I have a very good friend in Stockholm. But it's cold. Very cold. You get cold easily. And my friend is a man so that probably won't work. There's, let's see, there's Anna in Australia, but again, the visa issues. Saudi Arabia—no way. I don't know anyone there anyway. Okay, where is easiest to get a visa . . . The Dominican Republic? I have a friend who moved there. Or Panama? My friend Virginia from grad school moved there and she loves it. Or, what about—"

"Mira, I cannot go *anywhere* alone. I have never been anywhere alone in my life. I have never been in a car alone. I have never slept alone. I have never been in an airplane either alone or with someone. You cannot just *send* me somewhere, like a parcel."

Miranda studies her face, trying to think of a solution, any solution. "Okay," she says. "Okay. Well, we will just have to find a way to take you with us, wherever it is we end up going next. You are a sister to me, as much as anyone has been. Until we go you'll stay here."

Tazkia looks more miserable than ever. "You're not my family. This is not my home."

"No," says Miranda sadly. "We're not your family. But we are less likely to kill you."

MAY 5, 2011
Finn

Finn sits on the edge of the tub, watching the girls. Blissfully ignorant of the drama unfolding around them, threatening to uproot their lives once again, they are pressing colored foam letters against the tiles of the bath. Cressida sticks a purple *j* in place and turns to her father. "Look!" she says, pleased with herself. Her string of letters spells *efjkdssdvojewzapfjsvkdvj.*

"Clever girl," says Finn. "What word is that?"

Cressida frowns at him. "Not a *word*, it's a *story.*"

"Ah," he says. "Of course. Can you tell me the story?"

"Daddy," she says disapprovingly, "you can *read!*"

She turns her attention to the little wooden boats the staff have made for her, loading them up with tiny wooden people and laughing when they capsize. Luloah watches her, mesmerized. She can sit up on her own and has started to crawl. It amazes him how quickly Cressie has adapted to her presence, treating her a bit like a special pet. Cressida can, however, be a wee bit tyrannical, reveling in the fact that she has found someone smaller than she is, someone who knows less. She speaks to Luloah in a mix of primitive English and Arabic, explaining the world to her. *"Azraq, habibti,"* she says now, grabbing a bath crayon in her fist and smearing it on the wall. *"AzraqAzraqAzraq!"*

Cressie knows all of her colors now, in English and Arabic. She can count to five. And she has developed a close relationship with the elephant at the bottom of her porridge bowl. Sometimes when she is eating breakfast, she stops abruptly and says, "Elmer? ELMER?" with great anxiety in her voice. When that happens, he or Miranda scrapes a bit of the porridge aside to ease her mind that the elephant is still there. "Elmer!" she then shrieks with glee. "HELLO, ELMER!"

Luloah tries to imitate everything she does, though her little tongue cannot yet find its way around *l*'s. "Emma! Emma!" she yells with Cressie, banging a spoon. Luloah has great fun with spoons, though she cannot manage to get one anywhere near her mouth.

Sometimes Cressida tries to feed her, splattering Luloah's cheeks (and the table, chairs, clothing) with pureed sweet potato or lentils.

He can't deny it; Finn enjoys the chaos of an additional child in the house, this house that has always been too large for his small family. And it's difficult not to return Luloah's affection when she hands him a stuffed zebra or clings to his knee. The laughter of the two girls playing together takes the sharp edges off everything else, even off Miranda. Could he seriously consider returning Cressida to the quiet life of a solitary child? Not that she had been unhappy, but having grown accustomed to a sister, wouldn't she feel that loss were the girl taken away? He has stopped trying to convince Miranda to give up Luloah, and begun trying to figure out how they could possibly keep her. It will not be easy.

They cannot risk a fake passport. They cannot risk bribing Mazrooqi officials. And they certainly cannot risk sneaking across a border. He struggles to discover a legal way to do this. Finn has never broken a law in his life. He has never even parked on a double yellow line. Any way he can imagine getting Luloah out of the country with his family deeply contradicts his sense of self.

Miranda peeks into the bathroom and smiles at the girls. "She's asleep," she tells Finn.

He nods. "We'll talk once we get the girls down."

Now they have the additional problem of Tazkia. Where is she to go? How would they get her a passport? Miranda looks exhausted, grim, the lines etched across her forehead deepening. She blames herself, which probably doesn't help her psyche at the moment. Once again, Finn feels helpless.

"Come on, girls, time for books," he says, rising and grabbing two hooded teddy bear towels from the rack. Cressida protests with a howl, grabbing his wrist when he reaches to pull the plug. "Cressie sweetheart, I'll make a deal with you. If you'll be a good girl and climb out of the tub on your own, I'll sing you 'Teddy Bears' Picnic.'"

Works like a charm, every time. He dries his daughter while Miranda lifts Luloah out of the water and wraps her up. Finn sings as they carry the two girls to the bed and sit them beside each other.

Each girl gets three books before teeth brushing and songs. Just a week ago they started putting Luloah in bed with Cressida, to see what happened. At first Cressida protested, standing up in her cot to demand that Luloah be removed. But as soon as she was, Cressie changed her mind and wanted her back. "Sing songs to her," she says. "Need songs." And as her parents shut off the lights and backed out of the door, they heard her start. "I'm all across Tesas with two in my arms, a zoo in my arms . . ." The lyrics disintegrated even further after that, but the voice remained strong. It was the song Miranda had sung to her fretful daughter night after night that first year, as they danced around the darkened bedroom. When Miranda disappeared, Finn had found a recording on iTunes and played it to Cressie in their old stone house, in the hopes it would bring a tiny fraction of the solace she once got from her mother.

Tonight, as they shut the door to the girls' room, Miranda and Finn can hear giggling. It will be another half-hour or so before they quiet down, but this they can live with.

"Right," says Miranda, collapsing on her side of the bed. "Now back to our regularly scheduled crisis."

Crisis. Crisis. The word sparks something, the glimmer of an idea. He sits on the edge of the bed looking down at Miranda. It isn't really a choice between her and his career. He had already made that choice when he stayed in the country and risked losing his job. So how is this any different? Either he wants a life with her or he doesn't, and if he does, the path is suddenly clear.

MAY 5–6, 2011
Miranda

Miranda lies awake, watching her husband quietly breathe in the twilight of their bedroom. How can he sleep at a time like this? But she is grateful to be able to watch him, unobserved, uninterrupted. Since her return, she had been going through the motions of partnership, of marriage, numbly, automatically. While she was dimly aware that love for him still lived inside of her, it had become frozen, inaccessible like dinosaur DNA in amber. He was kind, patient, he listened, and she was grateful. But his lips on hers felt dry and foreign. She hadn't wanted to be touched. Until tonight. Tonight some shell around her heart had cracked, leaking a desire she had lost hope of rediscovering.

Perhaps it was the knowledge that Luloah would (*insha'allah, insha'allah*) soon and forever be hers—would be theirs. As Finn had outlined his plan, she had reached tentative fingers to his face, his eyes, his cheeks, unable to speak her gratitude, her hope. Then, pushing herself up to search his eyes for doubts and finding none, she had leaned down to kiss him. How long had it been since they had made love? But their bodies remembered, responded, retrieved what had once been so effortless. His skin was soft, scentless, his ribs more prominent than she remembered. She sank into him, became warm and human and hungry. Here he was again, her Finn, whom she had forgotten how to love. She was remembering now. She wanted to open all of his wounds and disinfect them with her tears.

When at last they lay still, their breath slowing, sweat evaporating in the desert air, Miranda twisted in his arms. "Sweetheart," she said, the fingers of her left hand fluttering over his right cheek. "Do you think that now you could tell me about Afghanistan?"

RELIEVED OF THE burden he has carried alone for so long, Finn sleeps deeply, unmoving. But slumber will not take Miranda, who lies watching her husband, piecing together this story with the rest of his history, with all that has happened since they met. What does she feel? A swirl, a muddle of compassion and regret, love and sorrow. Not anger, not blame. She thinks about the doomed Charlotte and her team of would-be rescuers. There is no getting around Finn's responsibility for those deaths. It's not a pain she can ever lift from her husband; it will live in him, like the tip of a poisoned arrow buried too deep to be removed.

Oddly, she dwells even longer on the girl, on the bewitching Afsoon, conjuring up her long legs and dark eyes. Had Finn not shared his plans with her, had she not told her brother, would Finn eventually have persuaded her to marry him? Is Finn sleeping beside Miranda now simply because he had trusted Afsoon and she had betrayed him? How different their lives might have been. What has become of Afsoon? Has Finn ever tried to find out? She needs to know. If Finn doesn't know, Miranda will do her own research. It feels important, to find out whether Afsoon has survived, whether she has found some kind of happiness. Well. It can wait. With any luck, there will be time.

MAY 6, 2011
Miranda

The two explosions are seven minutes apart. The first jolts them awake, sending Miranda halfway down the hall to Cressida's room before she realizes it hadn't been in the house. After quickly peeking at the girls, who astonishingly are still asleep, curled feet to heads in a lopsided ying-yang, she runs back to their bedroom. Finn is standing naked at the bedroom window, clutching his cell phone. "I think that was a plane."

"A plane?" She struggles to understand. "A crash?" They are just a few miles from the airport.

"Shot down. The sound was too familiar."

"What kind of plane?"

"I don't know. I don't know anything yet. It could have been—" The phone in his hand begins to vibrate. "Tucker," he says, answering it.

It *had* been a plane, a commercial passenger jet taking off from the Arnabiya airport. Tucker thought it was a domestic flight but wasn't sure. According to airport security, there may have been more than one hundred passengers onboard. It crashed just outside of the city, crushing an entire block of houses.

Finn is still on the phone when the shock waves of a second explosion rattle the shutters of their bedroom. "Christ, Tucker, what the hell was that?" He listens for a moment and sets down the phone on the windowsill.

"Start packing," he says abruptly, turning to Miranda. "If that was another plane, I'm going to have to order an evacuation. In fact, no matter what that was, we're evacuating." It's clear he has been waiting for this; it is not a surprise. They have spent several evenings discussing the possibility and mechanics of evacuation, but Miranda had never seriously believed it would happen before they were due to leave. They had so little time left.

For a moment, she cannot move, their newly formed plans crumbling at her feet. "This is war, you mean," she says. "That's what this means. That this is *it*."

He nods, already pulling on boxer shorts and a white undershirt. "I've got to get downstairs and make some calls. I want everyone locked down until we know things have settled a bit. If it's possible, if people can get here—local security is going to have roadblocks everywhere—there'll be a meeting here a little later, just critical staff. Pack a suitcase, just one. Passports, small valuables. I'll come up as soon as I know more. Just ... be ready. We have about forty-eight hours, I'd say. And I think this goes without saying, but no one leaves the house."

"We'll go together? All of us?"

"You know I can't go until everyone else is out." Seeing her face crumple, he drops his trousers to the floor and crosses to her. "I'm sorry, sweetheart." He wraps his arms around her and presses her cold, still-naked body tightly against him. "I wouldn't part with you for a second if I had a choice. We're going to have to be patient through this."

"But—" Pressing her palms against his chest, she tilts her head back to look at him. "But Luloah. Tazkia. Can we get them out?"

"We're going to try." There is no hesitation in his voice. He was built for situations like these. Nothing sharpens his mind like a crisis. Clearing a path through pandemonium, reassuring staff, generating exit strategies—these galvanize his energies like a drug. "Listen. We'll do what we had planned to do for Luloah and Tazkia. This is just a little sooner than we'd hoped. I'll get the ETDs issued this morning; Sally will help. Those will get them out of the country at least. I'll probably need a week to shut down the embassy, and then

I'll meet you in Djibouti or Dubai or Beirut or wherever you're evacuated to. We'll go to London together and sort things out from there."

Emergency travel documents would function as passports, allowing Luloah and Tazkia, who would pose as the child's mother, to travel through four countries, as long as the last one was the UK. Issuing them illegally, as would be the case with an orphaned Mazrooqi child and a Mazrooqi citizen, could cost Finn his job. The chances of discovery were high.

"Sweetheart. You're sure?" The question is for her as much as for Finn. Is she certain that she wants to accept the sacrifice? She will be stripping him of everything he has worked for, inviting a slow corrosion of their marriage. But getting Luloah out does not feel optional.

Finn's phone buzzes again, and he releases her from his arms to reach for it. Dax this time. Keeping his eyes on Miranda's, he listens. "Right. I suspected as much. How many inside? Have you talked to the Americans?" He listens awhile longer. "I'll get on the phone to the ambassador. We'll meet at the backup office as soon as it's safe." Whenever the embassy has to close for security reasons, the staff works from a backup office housed in the basement of the Residence. The warren of rooms—equipped with dusty desks and chairs, copy and fax machines, and several locked filing cabinets—is rudimentary but surprisingly vast. There is even a conference room and a small kitchen. Miranda has been down to the offices only twice; they don't exactly invite loitering.

"The airport's on fire," Finn says, snapping the phone shut. "Probably the result of several IEDs. Meaning there is no chance of evacuation by air, not that we could afford it anyway. But the Americans might have tried it; they've got fantastic helicopters. Listen, Mira. I've got to ring the Americans this morning, talk with their spooks, find out when they're going. If they evacuate before us, you're going with them."

"But—"

"We talked about this."

"They'll take Luloah and Tazkia? Even though the ETDs will say they're Brits?"

"We have an agreement with the US to take Brits if we don't have our own evacuation."

"But you will."

"We will. But the Americans will have extra room. They always do. If they don't let them go with you, they can come with us later."

"But the others at the embassy will wonder about Luloah, about the papers. No? Since they have seen them? Tazzy and Luloah can't travel with the UK staff or they'll be discovered."

Finn pauses, his forehead creasing. "Right. Okay. Of course. We'll just have to hope the Americans will take you all. Look, there will be a fair amount of chaos getting out of here, no matter how organized they are. They might not even thoroughly process immigration papers until you're out of the country. We are just going to have to risk this; there's no other way. Not now."

Miranda nods. There is no point in protesting. If there were another way, Finn would know it. The United States—the country she abandoned years ago—is their only hope.

MAY 6, 2011
Miranda

Miranda kneels on the floor of Cressie's room, pulling clothing and toys from her drawers. Her daughter stands watching her, curious. Tazkia, who has no need to repack her few possessions, is downstairs playing with Luloah in the dining room. It's difficult to know what to take. Very few clothes, Miranda thinks. Mostly photos, a few toys and books, diapers. Bears. She sorts through Cressida's clothing, setting aside the baby things she has outgrown—her first few onesies, covered with monkeys and lions; a tiny, strawberry-shaped woolen hat; a hand-knit Aran sweater. Will they ever see these things again?

"Look, Cressie," she says, pulling a woolly animal from the bottom drawer. "This is the sheep that used to help you sleep at night."

"How?" says Cressie. "How?" She's so tall now, it still catches Miranda by surprise. Every part of her is longer and thinner; her face has lost some of its roundness. Only her eyes are the same, wide and green, with her father's long lashes.

"It makes sounds, see, like this..." Miranda pushes the switch on the back until they can hear the sound of gentle rain. "Can you tell what that is?" Cressida reaches for the sheep and plays with the switch until the animal begins to shudder with a regular thudding sound.

"This sound?"

"That's a mummy's heartbeat. It was supposed to reassure you because it was the sound you heard when you lived inside me."

Cressida listens quietly for a few minutes, holding the sheep to her ear. "Where inside you?" she asks.

Miranda rests a hand on her belly. "Right here," she says. "You lived here. I'll show you..." On her hands and knees she crawls to the bookcase and pulls out a photo album from the bottom shelf. "Look, *habibti*, this is you." She has more than a dozen ultrasound photos—every time she saw the doctor here she got another one. These are definitely coming with them. Cressida looks at the photo in wonderment. "Is me?" she says, tracing her fingers across her profile at five months, her perfectly rounded head, tiny curled legs.

Miranda pulls out another album, with all of her pregnancy photos, and a third with their first photos of Cressida, her body still covered with its protective yellow wax, her eyes wide and bewildered. Cressida turns the pages, rapt.

"Mummy?" she says, pointing to a photo of Miranda, puffy-eyed and exhausted, holding the sleeping child. "My mummy?"

"Yes, sweetheart. That is your mummy. That's me. I'm your mummy."

Cressida frowns at the photo and then looks back at Miranda, as if comparing the two images. "Mummy," she says meditatively, inconclusively. But when Miranda touches her shoulders, she relaxes back into her arms.

MAY 8, 2011
Finn

The city is only just emerging from the shadow of night when Finn arrives at the embassy. He is the first to reach the walled fortress, glowing white in the sun's first rays, aside from the guards, who shuffle from foot to foot wrapped in down anoraks and earmuffs, rubbing their hands together to warm them. Once through security, Finn uses his keys to open various offices. Soon, his hastily pulled-together evacuation team will assemble to coordinate their departure. He wants to be prepared.

Miranda, Tazkia, and the girls had left the Residence just before him, in one of the armoreds and with two guards. They would drive to the American school on the fringe of town, the gathering point for the US evacuation. From there—after the chaos of queuing for hours and presenting their paperwork—they would join the convoy to the coast, some two and a half hours away. A military ship would await them. Getting the ETDs hadn't been as hard as he had imagined. He explained to Sally that Tazkia was in immediate and grave danger, a likely victim of a so-called honor killing, and that Luloah was her niece, whose mother had recently died after a long illness. Trusting him, Sally hadn't asked too many questions.

Now, anxious to join his family, he wants to ensure his own evacuation goes as smoothly as possible. In all likelihood—because of those fatal ETDs—this will be his final act as an ambassador.

As he passes the consular section, Finn sees a light from one of the offices. Could Sally have beat him here? It wouldn't surprise him; she is often here early, and today will likely be her busiest yet. But the light isn't from her office; one of the local staff has left a lamp aglow on her desk. Finn switches it off and walks next door to Sally's office. Dawn is creeping in the windows, bright fingers stealing across the butterscotch wood. In a neat row across the top are about a dozen recently issued passports, waiting to be claimed. Normally they'd be locked away in the safe, but Finn guesses Sally wants to get people on their way today as soon as possible. Any passports left here after the evacuation will likely be destroyed.

Taking the stairs two at a time, he returns to his office. Only a few more days now. Standing by the hulk of his mahogany desk, he glances around the room, memorizing its unremarkable interior. Fat black leather armchairs and matching sofas. The glass coffee table cluttered with Mazrooqi newspapers and magazines. Miniature UK and Mazrooqi flags flying from a wooden holder on his desk. He picks up his mug, the Seattle *Starry Night* one that Miranda had brought back for him once, with the Space Needle superimposed on Van Gogh's swirling masterpiece, and tucks it into his red lunch bag to take home. Well, his home for a little bit longer.

His heart trips as he thinks about leaving, about those ETDs. Finn loves being an ambassador. He loves the diversity of the work, the constant education, the chance to use all of his languages. Few things exhilarate him like mediating feuds and debating with presidents. He even secretly enjoys national days. Pick a country, any country, and he can hum you its anthem. In a perfect world, he would have loved another fifteen years of this. New countries, new colleagues, new foods, new friends, with Miranda at his side.

He is relieved to be rid of the lurking shadow of Norman, who had lost the Mali job and been reassigned to London after the pornography debacle. It's still possible that Norman will spill the Afghanistan story in his bitterness over losing his posting. But he can't blame Finn for the paintings. And at this point it hardly matters. After illegally issuing the ETDs, Finn won't be landing any plum postings in the future. Or any postings. That should appease Norman.

The paintings themselves have all been destroyed, though only after that cousin of Tazkia's who worked in customs had had plenty of time to see them. No one at the airport had recognized Miranda, and it hadn't been hard for Finn to talk the customs officials into burning such sacrilege. If only they knew what Tazkia's cousin had seen, what he would say. This evacuation could hardly be better timed; he just hopes Miranda can get Tazkia out.

He crosses behind his desk to duck into his private bathroom, making sure he has removed his razor and face cream. The room's sterility—the empty shelves and blank tile walls—triggers a surge of subterranean grief. In the stark fluorescent light, Finn stares at his face in the mirror. Lines that were faint when he moved here several years ago have sunk deep into his forehead, and the curls at his temples are flecked with white. Pain casts dark shadows in his eyes. *"Ma'a salaama, sa'adat assafir,"* he says. Farewell, ambassador. And he turns out the light.

MAY 8, 2011
Miranda

Miranda squats in a vacant lot across from the school, holding Cressida under the arms as the little girl urinates into the dust. Next to them, Tazkia jiggles Luloah on her hip, her face rigid with anxiety. "Good idea to go now," Miranda is telling her daughter. "It's going to be a long trip." She tugs up Cressie's pants and takes her hand. With her other hand she hefts the one suitcase she has packed for herself and the girls. Tazkia carries her own few possessions in a small backpack. "Ready?" Miranda says, turning to her friend. Tazkia nods stiffly, and they cross the street together. Sensing Tazkia's distress, Miranda wants to take her hand too, offer her some kind of reassurance. But there is no time, and she has no more hands.

Despite Finn's forewarning, Miranda is astonished by the number of Americans fighting their way to the front of the immigration lines. There are hundreds, maybe thousands, of women, men, and children streaming past them toward the rust-red doors of the flat-roofed, cinder-block school, lugging suitcases and jugs of water. Where on earth have they come from? Miranda almost never saw Americans in Mazrooq. Could they all be embassy employees, released at last from their gated community? Surely there are not so many.

"Okay." At the entrance to the school Miranda sets down the suitcase and releases Cressie's hand to rummage in her purse for the papers. There they are: US passports for her and Cressida (a dual citizen of the United States and UK), British emergency travel documents for Tazkia and the baby. Glancing up at Tazkia's stunned expression, Miranda is struck by sudden doubts. They haven't even given Tazzy's family or Adan a chance to react to what had happened. Still, she is here. Tazkia would not have come to Miranda in the first place had she not known herself to be in peril. Miranda thinks again of the unfortunate Aila, her scorched palms.

"Shall I take Luloah?" Miranda is wearing one of her new home-made slings, ready for the baby. But Tazkia simply stands there unspeaking, staring at Miranda. "Tazzy," says Miranda, gently lifting the child from her arms and tucking her against her breast. "Tazzy, we'll be all right. I'll be with you the whole way, I promise. Can you trust me?"

Slowly, Tazkia shakes her head, her eyes never leaving Miranda's. "I can't go," she says flatly. "I can't."

A bolt of panic spears Miranda's heart. "Tazzy, you must!" she cries. "You're in danger here. If not from your family then from this war; Tazzy, your country is about to fly apart."

The tiny woman does not move, her feet planted firmly in the earth. "Then I will fly apart with it." She lifts a hand, as if to reach for Miranda, then lets it fall. "You don't understand; there is no life for me without my family. There is no world without my family, no country, no home. We are not like you, we cannot transplant our-selves."

"But you've never left, you don't know—" There is desperation in Miranda's voice, desperation to save her friend, but also herself. Tazkia is the reason she has stayed, the one person who has given direction to her last several years. Could all of her work, her coaxing and cajoling, her careful cultivation—of all of them—have crumbled into insignificance? Has she done nothing but purposefully push her women toward a precipice they cannot navigate?

"Everything I know is here."

"But you can't create anything here! You cannot be an artist, you cannot be who you are!"

Tazkia looks at her curiously, as if seeing her for the first time. "If I cannot be who I am here, then who am I now? Who have I been for my entire life?" She pauses, the lines of her face softening, growing calm. "Mira," she says. "Painting is not life. Brushes and canvas and ink are not life. They are a pleasure, a luxury, but not life itself." She crouches down next to Cressida, who is sitting on the suitcase pretending to breast-feed a teddy bear.

"Cressie," she says, her small brown hand resting on the dark curls, "take care of your mama." She kisses the child's cheek and rises to face a bewildered Miranda. "I also need to say this. You should not take the baby."

Miranda stares at her, wordless.

"This is her home. Her people are here."

"She has no people left!" Miranda cries. "Tazzy, I thought you understood."

"She could have Nadia."

"Nadia?" Miranda's mind reels.

"Nadia comes from her tribe. Her family would take her."

"But, Tazkia . . ." Why has Nadia never said anything? She hasn't even come to visit the Residence since Miranda's rescue.

"You will do what you want, of course. I only had to say this. So that you will think, please, before you go."

For a moment Miranda cannot breathe. How could the person closest to her here fail to understand? Luloah knows no mother but Miranda. And Luloah would suffer here as Tazkia had, as all of her women did, her own life and all of its decisions handed over to men. If she survived at all. Miranda's windswept heart struggles to beat.

"*Ma'a salaama*, my friend." Once more, Tazkia kisses Cressida, Luloah, and Miranda before turning to walk away. She does not look back.

Not until she has watched—half-paralyzed with shock—her friend vanish among the throngs of refugees does Miranda realize she has a new problem. Without Tazkia to pose as Luloah's mother, she will not be able to get the child out of the country. The alarm this thought provokes temporarily overrides her heartbreak. Mourning and soul-searching will have to wait. "Mummy, biscuit, please?" Cressida is pulling at her skirt. Digging through her purse, Miranda comes up with a fruit and nut bar she hands to her daughter. Luloah whimpers, protesting her exclusion, and Miranda breaks her off a chunk. Having thus bought a moment's peace, she takes her phone from a pocket and dials.

THIRTY MINUTES AFTER she hangs up, Finn is there. Stepping out of the armored car, he presses a small brown envelope into her hand. "Use this," he says. "We'll cope with the fallout later. The important thing now is to get out." Cressie runs to throw her arms around her father's legs as Miranda slides open the flap, glimpsing the familiar burgundy of a UK passport.

"Whose is it?'

"It doesn't matter. Someone who hasn't come to claim it."

Miranda opens the cover to look at the photo. A dark-skinned baby, about a year old, stares solemnly at her. She doesn't look anything like Luloah. "You're sure."

"Stop asking me if I'm sure." His voice is exasperated. "I should think I've demonstrated my resolve by now."

"I'm sorry!" Miranda can feel the tears hovering close now. Is this how the end begins? "I'm so sorry." Only now does she suddenly feel the loss in all of its enormity: not only Finn's career, but their entire life together, everything they know. Everyone they know. She looks up at him, attempting a smile. "I was just starting to get the hang of this ambassador's wife thing."

"You were." He takes her hand. "I've got to get back." But he doesn't move. They stand for a moment looking at each other with naked eyes, the chaos around them sliding away. "Will we make it?" she finally asks. She doesn't mean to the ship or to a new country. She means something greater, something all-inclusive.

"I don't know," says Finn, resting a hand on the warm head of his daughter. "I hope so." She is not sure which question he is answering.

JULY 14, 2011, LONDON
Finn

Finn lies on the slender, unforgiving rectangle the guards euphe-
mistically refer to as a bed and gazes between the square, whitish
bars of his cell. The narrow bands feel momentarily a flimsy divider
between him and the criminal multitudes surrounding him. It is
mostly air that separates them, stale, anxious air. But he shouldn't
make such distinctions, not now. Isn't he here legitimately, as an
honest-to-god criminal himself? He is and he always will be. This is
the only thing that sends a shudder of terror down his spine, grabs
him like a recurring electric shock. Not the days and years he will
spend confined to this space, to its stink of disinfectant and male perspiration. He is used to bars by now; hasn't he lived behind bars for
the last several years of his life? These at least are honest bars, naked
in their intentions, unadorned by bougainvillea. No, it is the days of
freedom that lie beyond them that frighten him the most.

What would be waiting for him, beyond, in those future roofless,
wall-less days? No ambassadorship, no career, perhaps no employment at all. But Mira. If she were there, she and Cressie and yes, even
Luloah, if he found them standing at the gates five years from now, or
however long it would be, he could live. In fact, Luloah *must* be there;
her presence is essential for his life to retain any meaning at all. If he
has forsaken everything to get that child out of Mazrooq only to see
her slip back into the hungry chaos, the motherless abyss, awaiting
with murderous jaws to swallow her whole . . . Well. He can't dwell
on it. He won't.

They are still awaiting word on their asylum plea. Luloah was
an orphaned and abandoned child in a country where civil war now
raged. To send her back now would mean certain death. And if they
were to send her back, to whom would they send her? They knew of
no surviving relative. They had told the truth to the courts, the truth
as far as it served their purposes. Surely no judge could be heartless
enough to tear a parentless child from the breast of a woman who had
kept her alive with milk meant for her own daughter? If they were

fortunate enough to receive asylum for the child, they would begin adoption proceedings. He has agreed. He has wholeheartedly agreed. Not that he is in any position to parent at the moment.

They are not far from him, just a short expanse of rain-soaked pavement away, crowded into that bachelor apartment of his that he is now grateful never to have sold. Despite having been left alone with two young children in a city not her own, Miranda has not uttered a word of complaint. She had been furious with him for sacrificing himself without her explicit knowledge or consent but has moved on to loathing herself for not having guessed the result of their actions. "I couldn't have told you," he insisted. "I wasn't sure what my punishment would be, and if I hadn't done what I did, we'd have left Luloah behind." She would never have forgiven him for that. "We survived your captivity; with any luck we can survive mine." With the FCO wanting to minimize publicity, the cases against Miranda and Finn had been settled out of court. She had escaped with a fine for possession of false identity papers with improper intent, but Finn's crimes and punishments were greater.

He worries about her in London. One of the things he loves most is her American openness to the world, her need to launch herself into conversation with strangers, which here is consistently stymied. He once saw her attempt to talk with a woman on the Tube who was reading a biography of an artist she loved, only to be granted a chilling stare and subtle shift away. He cursed his insular, parochial people.

Yet he also has infinite faith in her ability to adapt, to gradually see beyond London's stony exteriors. The city keeps its colors close, secreted like packets of sticky boiled sweets in its many tweed pockets. But they are there. And Mira is an explorer. She will find them.

He doesn't worry excessively about Cressie; she is young, malleable. Her memories of him, of their time as a shrunken, compacted family, will fade into a dream past. Life with her mother—and sister—will come to seem enough. Yet the thought also destroys him, rakes his rib cage with pointy steel prongs. No less than Mira, Cressie is his love, irreplaceable and essential. He would not have survived Miranda's disappearance without her. That she will grow these next few years fatherless, because of him, because of something he did, is a saturating grief. How will they ever be what they were? It still spins his heart, to drag his eyelids open each morning to find himself here. He waited so long for Mira, so long, only to lose her again.

The guard, Albert (never Al unless you wanted to forfeit a meal or your exercise period), comes to unlock the door. "Your *Excellency*," he says, with oily emphasis and a faint bow. Finn can find no response to this daily insult and so, as usual, says nothing. It is exercise time. He has more time to exercise here than he has had in the past fifteen years. Mira was always trying to get him into the pool or onto the treadmill; she even once tried to show him how to do what she called sit-ups, but he couldn't manage even a few. It was an unnatural movement for his body, long accustomed to remaining upright unless knocked over by a ball. Finn rises from his cot and mutely follows his jailer.

Outside in the courtyard, he joins the slow parade of prisoners across the dusty stones. Never has he spent so much time in pure, undirected thought. This at least is a gift. He can think of it as a gift. All of the unsorted memories, the diplomatic knots untangled and still tangled, they are photographs not yet organized into albums. He spends his days pasting experiences onto mental pages, lining up their corners and pressing them flat.

Mira was always needing distractions, paintings to stare at and absorb, stories in which to soak, but for him the empty, unstructured mental space is a luxury. Free from the demands for "strategic thinking" and business plans and bilateral negotiations, he encounters his mind as if for the first time, like someone he has run into often at parties but to whom he has never spoken. In this new space he has room enough to dream up a possible future. He could teach English in Laos. He could translate for Congolese ministers. He could teach Guyanese children the alphabet. He has days to decide. He has months. He has years. Something will come to him.

AUGUST 11, 2011
Miranda

Culpable. The word curls around her as she sleeps. Defines her. It is her most constant companion, shaking her awake before dawn and pressing her eyelids open at night. It fills up her stomach, leaving her meals uneaten. She is so stuffed with guilt she has room for little else. How could she have failed to understand what would happen to Finn? How could she have allowed her vision to narrow so unforgivably? Her love for Finn, that love that once suffused every cell, has been found wanting. If she had loved him enough, she would have understood. She wants to fall to her knees and beg for some kind of absolution, some way to lessen the cloak of pain draped across her shoulders.

But falling to her knees to beg forgiveness from some kind of deity has never been a habit with her and is now impossible. After everything she has done, has been, she must not also become a hypocrite. So. She paints.

Finn's apartment—she still thinks of it as only his—has two small bedrooms, a living room–dining room, and a tiny kitchen. She has given the living room to the girls. The second bedroom is too small, too cramped, for the two of them. They should have room to sprawl on their bellies, spreading out their crayons and bears and toy cars around them. They need tables for drawing and overstuffed chairs for reading books. She tried giving Luloah a bed of her own, but the child would not think of it. She will sleep with Cressie or not at all.

Miranda sleeps in the smallest room—she has no need for space there—and has turned the slightly larger room into a studio. It has light, its one saving grace, from a recently installed skylight and two windows on opposite walls. This is where she stands now, windows thrown open, trying to find a way forward, a new way to live. She wants to press promises into her paint, promises and blood. Yet she also wants to untether herself from all of it, if only on canvas.

They have enough money to manage for a while, a year or two, but the precipitous decline of their bank accounts since moving here frightens her. She will find a job. The American school is looking for an art teacher for its primary grades. The work has a certain appeal; she feels weary of adults, fearful of their judgments and bored with their rigidity. If she worked there, the girls could have free schooling. There are also scores of universities across the city that might consider her. Art galleries that might consider taking her on, if she can create anything worthwhile. This time it is not ambition that propels her to the easel but a simple desire to survive—financially, physically, psychologically, emotionally.

Yet these challenges are oddly comforting, as are the daily routines of creating meals for her daughters, soaping dishes, and scrubbing a stain out of a small T-shirt. Something inside her loosens here, alone. This is more than she deserves. There is a relief in their downfall, in the revocation of their life of privilege. A serenity in subsiding into an ordinary life.

She never misses a visiting day at the prison and she always takes the children. The guards and some of the prisoners look at her with curiosity and condemnation. How could you take children into a place like this? their eyes say. How could you have locked your own husband away? But she wants Cressie and Luloah to have every scrap of time with Finn that they can. They are too young to know what a prison is, too young to understand its grimness in its entirety, though not too young to feel frightened, to wonder why their father cannot come home with them. When they arrive, Finn reads to them from *The Wind in the Willows*. Cressie always assigns everyone roles. "Lulu is Otter, I am Mole, Mummy is Badger, and Daddy is Rat," she says, making everyone change his or her voice to sound like the assigned animal. "Sweetheart," says Miranda, "I feel pretty certain that *I* am the Rat."

And Tazkia. This person she loved years before swinging a ripe fruit into Finn, years before Cressida and Luloah, years before her entire current life. This love that preceded everything, that made all the rest of it possible, she has betrayed. Every night lying alone in the cold double bed she catalogs the particulars of this betrayal, her failures of vision, as if consciously acknowledging them all will save her friend.

She has e-mailed Tazkia nearly every day since their departure, hoping that there are Internet cafés left standing in Arnabiya, hoping that Tazkia can find her way to one, hoping desperately that Tazkia herself endures. Her initial responses were terse yet kind. "I am well and at friends. Love your friend always even though how we parted. Tazkia." Miranda had asked with whom she was staying, but Tazkia had been afraid to tell her, afraid of hostile eyes monitoring the Internet. Not one of her classmates, she had said. It was easier to hide amid the chaos of war, though she was frightened all of the time. Nadia and her family have disappeared, she wrote. No one knows whether they went north to join the rebels or were dragged from their home and shot. Tazkia remains in contact with Aaqilah and Mariam, though they all have to be more careful than ever not to be found together.

Then, shockingly, one day she wrote that she had gone to Adan. "Because I waited my life for him, because I cannot see life without him, it seemed worth risk." Her friend had driven her to a coffee shop with quiet corners where he had promised to meet her. And she had told him everything, everything. After all, what did any of it matter, if a rebel bomb could split her apart any minute? What did she have to lose, having already lost family and reputation? Somehow, miraculously, he had not convulsed with rage. Perhaps Tazkia had been right, he was not like the others. She had carefully explained that she remained essentially pure, devout, virginal, and was willing to give up painting if it meant he could forgive her and restore her honor. After several days of prayer, he had returned to her, renewing his offer of marriage. Happiness spilled out of her subsequent e-mails. "I will write to you more soon in details because I feel i am a different person now . . . more deeper and more mature. Apparently, all hardships are there for a reason: to allow the real humans to pop up and to find the cause of our lives." In late July, she had written Miranda to say that she and Adan were preparing to go see her family, to beg their forgiveness. Several neighborhoods of Arnabiya had been obliterated by explosions, but Tazzy's family was still safe. "I need to make things right with them before I can move forward," she wrote.

That was the last Miranda ever heard. After sending a series of panicked e-mails and receiving no response, Miranda had called Tazkia and when there was no answer, had called her brother Hamid, whose number Finn still kept in his phone. Yet when she spoke her name, the line abruptly went dead.

Miranda tries to tell herself that the silence isn't necessarily sinister. That perhaps Tazkia simply can't get to a computer, or the phone lines have been blown up, or she and Adan had been caught up in a battle and are hunkered down in some primitive shelter. Perhaps Hamid had hung up on her because he didn't want her to further influence his sister. Yet she knows, dark in her bones, the truth.

MIRANDA SWEATS WITH the uncommon heat of the summer afternoon and the effort of forcing her fingers to move approximately where she wants them. "Let go," she murmurs to herself. Tazkia had been right about that. As soon as she had begun to think of her hand as that stick, as soon as she had given herself permission not to direct its every move, everything had changed. Those early efforts are not something she will show the world, not even Finn, but they are progress.

Tazzy wasn't right about everything; painting *is* life for her. Without it she was insensate, a somnambulist. This paintbrush, the one in her hand, is the only continuity, the one bit of her world that has traveled with her from her parents' home in Seattle to Mazrooq to this beautiful, melancholy way station of a city. She needs this one small thing.

Shifting her weight onto her left foot as she stands before the easel, she presses the brush into the canvas she has been working on for several days. In a corner are stacked a dozen or so of her previous efforts, none of them right. But she forges on, hopeful of illuminating some shred of her derelict soul.

In front of her now stands an enchantress, naked save for a head-dress of slender paintbrushes that fan out behind her corkscrew curls like a halo, each tip dripping a different color. She stands alone on an unmoored island, a dark sea bashing itself angrily against its shores. One hand is raised to the sky clutching a sturdy paintbrush; the other hovers at her waist, cradling a palette. Around her feet are gathered a circle of saffron-colored rabbits with ebony horns, the mythical, man-eating *mir'aj*. Chimerical sea creatures thrash the waters with teeth bared, while a line of *ababils* descend from the skies.

From every direction, black-robed women swim or fly toward the enchantress, answering some siren call. As they draw near, their robes slip from their bodies and transform into *ababils*. Defenseless, the women are seized by the beasts. Two exposed women already dangle from the beaks of the greedy birds. The enchantress sees none of this, her ecstatic eyes trained upward on the incandescent tip of her brush.

Only one woman has made it to shore, her discarded robe transformed into a bird behind her, her palm spiked by the horn of a *mir'aj*, and her feet seized by a leviathan. Slowly, she is being pulled apart.

Epilogue

SEPTEMBER 17, 2013
Miranda

Stretched on her back on the damp green grass of St. James's Park, Miranda props herself up on her elbows to watch her children spread out a picnic. Cressie reaches into their string grocery bag to pull out apples, grapes, and wedges of cheddar and Camembert, while Luloah arranges paper plates around the edges of a blanket. "Daddy likes ham," says Cressida, rummaging in the bag. "Did you get ham?"

"I did," says Miranda, smiling. They had bought as many of Finn's favorites as were practical: Dundee cake, saucisson, Cadbury's fruit and nut bars, Scrumpy Jack cider, and a fresh baguette. Luloah tires of table setting and pulls a stack of colored construction paper toward her, scribbling on it with her washable markers. Funny that she is turning out to be the artist; Cressida has more interest in animals and physical games, racing around the closest park every weekend with a neighborhood soccer team. At home, she spends her time with her pet rabbit and the new chemistry set her grandfather has sent from the United States, making potions to "cure throwing up and broken toes and chicken pox." Frowning, Luloah draws the stick figure of a man, arms stretched over his head, clutching a bouquet of uneven orbs. When Miranda asks what they are, she says, "Balloons for Daddy to ride."

Trembling with nerves, Miranda sits up and cracks open one of the ciders, welcoming the cool fizz down her dry throat. Done with setting out the food, Cressida is ripping up blades of grass and building tiny houses for her toy bears. Miranda hopes she has properly prepared her daughters, that they will welcome their father rather than resist his unfamiliar authority.

Slipping her feet from her sandals, she wonders how she and Finn will come together this time, how they will unearth their interred intimacy. Those charmed early years in Mazrooq, those gilded hours of ardor, leisurely debate, and indulgent painting, are a distant mirage.

They are free now, all of them, though freedom has its own terrors. So much remains to be decided. She and Finn have agreed to wait until they share a home once more before taking their next step. They could stay here, where Miranda has begun to make a modest name for herself and the girls have started school. They could travel to Oceania or Ghana or Bolivia or even somewhere as close as Norway, start again where no one knows their names. Or—or what? Does it ultimately matter? No matter how far they travel, a small, dark ghost will not be far behind.

During Finn's incarceration, he and Miranda fell into the habit of writing to each other several times a week, scraping their days and souls for more to slip between the bars dividing them. Miranda wrote him about her work, the girls, and the agonies of her conscience, while he unfurled musings on their future and tales of his fellow inmates and guards. On visiting days there was never enough time to talk, not with the girls there. But she had his letters. Charmed anew by his language, his funny turns of phrase, the clear pathways of his thoughts, she once more dares to hope.

"Don't come to the prison to collect me," he had said. "I don't want to meet you anywhere so grim." So they planned to gather by the duck pond, where the girls are now crumbling stale croissants in their fists to toss to the birds.

A book rests by Miranda's right hand, but she doesn't have the presence of mind to read. Glancing away from the girls for a moment, she spots a familiar gait on the winding pathway. A tall man in jeans and a blue button-down shirt strides toward them, swinging a small case in one hand. In the other, he carries a bouquet of balloons. Even before she can make out his features, she can see he is smiling.

"Girls," she calls. "Girls." Abruptly, they look up from the pond, pastries falling from their astonished hands. Cressida moves first, taking a few steps and then stopping, making sure it is him. Then she is running, her striped skirt flying up behind her. Eager to catch up with her sister, Luloah follows.

Rising, Miranda presses her toes into the cool grass, the ground becoming solid under her feet.

Acknowledgments

Infinite gratitude to the following people for their counsel and assistance:

My indefatigable agent Brettne Bloom, who encouraged me to write a novel and patiently edited several drafts

Kris Puopolo, my brilliant editor at Doubleday, whose thoughts vastly improved the story and writing

Assistant editor Daniel Meyer, for his perceptive comments

My copyeditors at Doubleday, unsung heros, for their meticulous reading

Author and Arabist Tim Mackintosh-Smith, for assistance with the Arabic and bits of mythology (any mistakes are my own)

Rosemary James and Joseph J. DeSalvo Jr., for their belief in this book from the first draft, their New Orleans–style hospitality, and their friendship

Dave Deacon and Lloyd Paterson, two reasons I lived long enough to write this

Mohammed, Yusuf, and the rest of the team, who saved me

The entire staff of the British embassy in Sana'a

Marina and Adria Merli, who catered to my every whim at Arte Studio Ginestrelle, the idyllic Italian residency where I finished the first draft

Nina Ball-Pesut, Bill Homewood, Dirk Lee, and Dana McCain, for their thoughts on the earliest and roughest of drafts

Rebecca Steil-Lambert, MSW, LICSW, MPH; Joanne Ahola, MD, PC; and Michelle May, MS, for their expertise in trauma

The Byrdcliffe Artist in Residence Program, for time and space

Crown Prosecution Service, for its guidance on identity fraud

Several nameless hostage negotiators whose stories proved invaluable

The dozens of British diplomats who helped me with technical details and questions of procedure (again, any mistakes are my own)

Irish artist Keith Wilson, who not only talked with me about painting and art, but took me to his studio and handed me a brush

Australian writer Anna Hedigan, for her encyclopedic brain

Roasters Boutique, for the best cappuccinos in Bolivia and a worktable

Ana Maria Yapu, without whom I would have no time to work

Maria Teresa Torres, for her friendship and support

Maria Cecilia Torres, for space and silence at a critical moment

BOSE noise-canceling headphones

My hiking companions Ingebjørg, Michele, Miruna, and Esmé, for bravery and serenity

Irene Colquehuanca and Hugo Márquez, for sustenance and good humor

The women of the A Room of Her Own Foundation, for their brains, artistry, and unflagging advocacy

Jill Conway Mehl and Marc Mehl, for their open door

Negesti, Alem, Emebet, Salaam, Yoseph, and Girma, who nearly ruined me for normal life

Sara Hijazi, for giving the first germ of this book time and space to grow

My parents, Cynthia and Gilbert Steil, the most enthusiastic publicists an author could wish for

Above all, I thank my husband, Tim Torlot, and daughter, Theadora Celeste Steil Torlot, for being constant sources of inspiration and joy, as well as the foundation of everything I do.

A Note About the Author

Jennifer Steil is the author of the memoir *The Woman Who Fell from the Sky*, about her experience as a journalist living in Yemen. Before moving to Yemen in 2006, she was a senior editor at *The Week*, which she helped to launch in 2001. Her work has appeared in the *World Policy Journal*, the *Washington Times*, *Time*, and *Life*. She currently lives in Bolivia with her husband and daughter. This is her first novel.